THE CRYSTAL BUTTERFLY

A RESISTANCE GIRL NOVEL

BOOK 6

HANNAH BYRON

DEDICATION

To all Dutch Jewish families, who lost loved ones in World War 2 due to deportation and murder by the Nazis.
To all descendants of Dutch citizens, who stood up against the Nazis to protect their (Jewish) countrymen and women.
To the descendants of the innocent hostages murdered by the Nazis.
To the descendants of all the Allied soldiers, who gave their lives for the liberation of The Netherlands.

May the brave spirits of your loved ones shine forever in my humble words.

Dance until you shatter yourself

— RUMI

ISBN eBook: 978-90-832156-7-9
ISBN Paperback: 978-90-830892-4-9
Book Cover Design by Ebooklaunch
Editor: Amber Fritz-Hewer
Website: Hannah Byron

1

THE STAGE IS SET

Amsterdam, December 1937

No one can touch the dancer.
No one can touch the dancer who may dance till the end.
If she may only dance till the end.

In the Royal Theater Carré on the River Amstel in Amsterdam, the stage smelled of floor polish, perfumed roses, and pine needles. The scents mingled with the hum of the Philharmonic Orchestra warming up their instruments. A piano scale, its highest tones fading towards the ceiling, a wailing violin stroke tugging at the heart, the brassy dominance of the trombone drowning in the hum of voices from the audience.

Sounds and smells filled the ringed theatre to the arched ceiling and yet, at intermission, there was a moment of silence, as if the building itself waited with bated breath. As if more were at stake than a ballet performance at the "Stone Circus of Carré" in the beating heart of Amsterdam. As if time itself wondered about the breadth of human capacity, both for good *and* bad. On either side of the closed curtains, all senses were heightened, waiting for the tale of The Nutcracker to unfold.

In the middle of the stage stood a towering Christmas tree decorated with lights and tinsels. Larry, the floor manager, was balanced atop a portable ladder to secure the red tree topper. It was his finishing touch. He'd been at it all afternoon, setting up the stage props for a dazzling Christmas Eve at the Stahlbaum house.

As Larry descended from the ladder to take a step back and admire his work, he was smiling to himself. Giving the magnificent tree a last glance, he turned to exit stage left, anticipating the joy his work would bring to the dancers and the audience.

Suddenly, he heard a loud crash, followed by a lull in the voices on the other side of the curtain. The tree had fallen over and was lying on its side. Rather pathetically. Larry rushed over to take stock of the damage and saw to his relief only the red tree topper had come loose. Tiny pieces of glass lay shattered over the stage floor like drops of luminous red blood. He quickly brushed up the pieces, pricking his fingers in his haste. With no time to waste, he worked the tree up to its full height again.

Sweating and cursing under his breath, he secured the floor-to-ceiling pine with rounds of sisal string. It looked amateurish and, without its red topper, unfinished, but time was up.

The falling tree had ruined Larry's premiere night. To him, it was a bad omen. Props didn't topple over when Larry De Jonge was in charge. A knock on the wooden doorpost on his way out begged for no further calamities that night, but the ease was gone from the floor manager's mind.

Backstage - in the corridors - dancers and personnel squeezed past him, everyone in a hurry to get the next task done, an eager expression on their faces.

Tonight was the night. The culmination of months of concentrated efforts to bring Tchaikovsky's Nutcracker to the Royal Carré stage. Rumour had it that even Queen Wilhelmina may attend the performance, accompanied by the young Princess Juliana. Everyone had to give it their very best. *Tout de suite!*

Premiere night. It was as much a triumph for the dancers and choreographers as it was for the floor manager, the ticket sellers, and the girls in the concession stands.

In one of the tiny dressing rooms, her dark hair lit up by a single lightbulb hanging over the oval mirror, Eddaline Van der Valk sat staring at her own reflection. Delicate, ringless fingers rested entwined in her lap. Her posture, straight as Cupid's arrow, was graceful and motionless. Not even the long lashes around the smoky black eyes batted once.

Edda was in her head, repeating the first tones of the Miniature Overture over and over, as she rehearsed her stage entrance as Clara. Prepping herself to portray the excitement about the Christmas party, the festive gathering of presents and guests.

All responsibility to set the exact right tone for the opening scene lay on Edda's slender shoulders. The stress sent tumultuous thoughts through her head while not a muscle in her body twitched. How to throw a party when one was riddled with nerves?

How?

By being still.

The dark-brown hair, usually curly and unruly, was bound tightly on top of her well-proportioned head, drawing people's attention to her pronounced cheekbones even more. Tight as tight can be. In contrast, her makeup was soft and dreamy. Just a light touch of rouge and a dash of eyeshadow to portray a young girl named Clara.

Edda's bosom, as flat as that of a thirteen-year-old, heaved slightly above the white satin top, exposing the powdered skin of her chest, the elegant collarbones, the swan-like, slender neck.

Perfect polish and poise revealed nothing of Edda's inner state. Only a trained eye would have spotted the slight clench of the jaw, the tensing of fingers into fists. Edda was eaten by nerves, but years of practice had trained her to hide all inner turmoil from onlookers. She could control the display of feelings as well as she could control the precise turn of her ankle or the graceful arc of her arm.

Control.

Tonight was *her* night. All she'd dreamed of since the age of five. Tonight she would shine. Despite the nerves. Tonight she would shine.

She took in a deep breath and then slowly puffed out, releasing the air first from her belly, then from her chest. She who controls the breath, controls the body. That was the drill.

After two more full breaths, she closed her eyes. It was time to let the music in her head go. Time for the moment of emptiness as Miss Sterling had taught her.

"It's not *your* music, it's not *your* dance. If you hold on too tight, the magic will escape you."

Mysterious words Edda wasn't sure she fully grasped. The ballet mistress was a repository of proverbs, like the Delphi oracle, deep and wise, and infinitely puzzling. *Empty yourself of yourself*, was another saying now flitting through Edda's mind. How on earth did one empty oneself from oneself?

Edda couldn't. With her eyes closed, softly breathing, her body was still dancing in her head. The music wrapped around her like a gossamer veil. She was floating, first *en pointe*, then on full feet, with seamless grace and ease. As she closed her solo in a whirl of pirouettes and petticoats, her arms like slender branches reaching for the sky, the crowd erupted in applause. It was done. Her dream fulfilled, flawless and phenomenal. Nerves were now but a distant memory. *Ahhhhh!*

A brief rap on the door shook Edda from her dream. Quickly opening her eyes, she saw in the mirror how the ballet mistress, Marlene Sterling, leaned her elegant frame against the doorpost, a pink cashmere cardigan draped loosely over her shoulders. She was tapping her Cartier tank watch.

"I'm coming." Edda said, leaping from the stool with an apologetic expression on her face. She brushed quickly past her teacher into the chilly hall. The sudden cold after sitting close to the electric heater in the dressing room stirred the goosebumps on her bare arms. Clenching jaws to prevent her teeth from clattering and with a stomach that made uncontrollable somersaults, Edda stumbled forward in the direction of the stage, far less graceful than expected from a prima ballerina. Until the British voice of the ballet mistress called her to an abrupt halt.

"No need to rush, Edda. Always look where you place your feet. We can't have you injuring yourself now. Come, let's have a little chat before the show begins. In my office."

"Oh?"

Edda turned on her ballet flats, the gauze skirt swirling around her muscled upper legs, the dark eyes filled with confusion. "I'm sorry, I misunderstood you, Miss Sterling."

"We're having a sudden attack of the screaming meemies, aren't we?"

Miss Sterling, a recently retired but dyed-in-the-wool ballerina in her forties, seemed to read her pupil like a book. Edda stood gazing at her mentor, fidgeting fingers knitted together in front of her rebellious belly. Face-to-face with Miss Sterling, it was impossible to hide what really went on inside her.

"I guess so. I thought I'd forgotten the time."

Miss Sterling smiled. She always smiled, benign, beguiling, rather byzantine. Edda thought there wasn't a creature more graceful and sophisticated than Miss Marlene Sterling. But also no one as unfathomable. A showgirl exterior with the soul of a mystic.

A mass of lush blonde curls invariably held under control by a colorful bandana, eyes the color of molten honey and clothes that breathed Coco Chanel or Madame Isobel, the famous British designer. Just one of Miss Sterling's many society friends.

She whipped up fear and fascination in Edda, beyond that perpetual smile. Yet Miss Sterling had, without fail, been patient and encouraging towards 'her star pupil'.

Edda followed the ballet mistress's elegant back towards her office near the entrance to the stage. The office was another enigmatic thing about Miss Sterling. The 3 by 3 metres square space was hardly bigger than the dancers' dressing room and filled to the brim with theatrical props and a clothes rack. As if Miss Sterling's life could not be contained by a life in an office.

With difficulty it held a tiny desk and three stools crammed in a corner, also laden with attributes for the show. Miss Sterling's expensive mink coat and Chanel handbag hung, almost forlorn, among the theatrical props but still shone a light of their own. Like their owner.

"My life's on stage, not crammed in this office," was what Edda had heard the ballet mistress retort to Monsieur Grimond. The Carré director had clearly been appalled that the famous Marlene Sterling would be sharing a minuscule dressing room with her dancers when she could have had a spacious office on the ground floor.

"Come in, Edda." Miss Sterling pushed the door open and cleared a stool for her pupil. "Sit."

She remained standing as Edda perched on the edge of the wooden stool. The honey eyes took her in with unusual sternness, though the red lips held their invariable smile.

"Are you ready?"

"Are you doubting me, Miss Sterling?"

"Always, my dear. The day I don't have doubts anymore will be the day I die. But that's not it."

Not hearing that last sentence, Edda bit her lip.

"But we went through all the moves, over and over. I know all my steps by heart." If her mentor was having doubts now, Edda was in serious trouble. Panic set in, real panic. The ballet mistress waved a ring-covered hand.

"It's not that. I have no doubts about your preparation, Edda. I don't have any doubt you'll portray a decent Clara, a very decent Clara. Your dance is your forte, my dear."

"Then what is it, Miss Sterling?"

"It's not you. It's her!" Tapered red nails pointed to the door. Edda was surprised to see Maria Petrova saunter into Miss Sterling's office.

2

ALL LIFE'S A STAGE

"*Vous m'avez appelée*, Mademoiselle Sterling?"

Maria hardly spoke English and no Dutch, so usually fell back on the French both she and Miss Sterling spoke fluently.

"Yes, I called for you, Mademoiselle Maria. Come in for a moment. I'll be quick." The voice was terse.

"*Mais...*"

"No buts. Not this time." Miss Sterling's voice had an unusually sharp ring. Edda wondered what was going on. Maria's presence further unsettled her already tense nerves.

Whenever she could, Edda avoided the tall, willowy Russian dancer with her heavily accented French. She was overbearing and loud, though a sensational dancer. Petrova was said to have fled the Soviet Union because she got into some sort of trouble with the Kremlin. Edda didn't know what that was. It was all rather hush-hush.

What was certain was that Maria Petrova had been one of the Bolshoi Theater's top ballerinas before arriving in Amsterdam through Monsieur Sergevey, Miss Sterling's partner. But *La* Petrova made it no secret Amsterdam was just a stopover for a career with The London Ballet.

The Russian moved as if a flower in full bloom, swaying softly in the light breeze, gazelle-like, graceful legs in soft-pink tights. *Pura eleganza. Magnifica!* That's how Miss Sterling typified Maria Petrova's gait, reverting to Italian when she found the English language lacking in superlatives.

So why were they both called to Miss Sterling's office when the ballet mistress clearly thought highly of both her star dancers? There was an uncomfortable moment in the fit-to-burst office in which no one spoke. As if the ballet mistress held them both on a string to see them squirm. But surely, Miss Sterling was anything but a limb of Satan.

"It's something you said to me yesterday, Mademoiselle Petrova." Miss Sterling's upper-class voice had a hesitance that made Edda even more on edge. The ballet mistress didn't do diffidence. Maria looked unperturbed. She just slightly inclined her finely pencilled face with the bronze cropped hair, widening her light-gray eyes just a tad to feign surprise. She said nothing, but the concealed smile on her painted lips showed she knew what was to come and that it was to her satisfaction. Miss Sterling turned to Edda.

"I had no time to discuss this with you girls earlier–as I should have. Mademoiselle Petrova deemed it necessary to stay out late in Hotel Americain, and only returned after breakfast, which forces me to give her a warning now, so very close before the show. Sorry, Edda, but you need to hear this."

Edda straightened her back, alarmed. 'Mademoiselling' Maria meant Miss Sterling was upset or angry. Which she seldom was. Dancers were called by their first names, or 'my dear.' Flitting dark eyes from her mentor to the Russian, Edda tried to understand why she acted so strange. Maria's attitude was more on guard now, her nostrils flaring as a horse sensing danger.

Miss Sterling's voice dropped low, little more than a whisper. Everyone in the ballet ensemble knew what this meant. *Better listen up. This will only be said once.* Maria shifted her weight from one slender foot to the other. Edda sat perched on her stool.

Miss Sterling pointed the painted nail first to Edda and then to Maria, saying sotto voce, "*You* are Clara, and *you* are Sugar Plum."

Edda frowned. No news there, unless...

"I only told Monsieur Sergeyev that I *could* dance Clara, Madame. I've danced her many times in St. Petersburg and Moscow. With outstanding success." Maria waved apologetic hands with long fingers in the air.

Edda held her breath. So, this was what it was all about. Maria wanted her part, she wasn't satisfied playing second fiddle. Miss Sterling rose to her full height, which was almost as tall as Maria. The red-tipped finger went up towards the ceiling and then started wagging left to right, like a metronome.

"You are warned, Mademoiselle Petrova. No games. Dance Sugar Plum as if it is your last dance on earth. Now out, as I talk to Edda."

"Don't bite my head off. I meant nothing by it." Maria gave Edda a dirty look, as if she was a pile of unwashed dishes blocking her worktop. Then turned her back on them.

An instinctual reader of bodies – it came with being a dancer - Edda saw how the Russian's shoulders on her proud back just sagged a fragment. Not defeated but spoken to in a way Mademoiselle Petrova didn't approve of. She mumbled an angry "à tantôt" and Miss Sterling replied with a breezy, "yes prepare yourself, Maria. You'll do fine. Please, close the door behind you."

The ballet mistress blew out a long breath through her teeth.

"I think that will do it, Edda. We all know how headstrong, and - let's say - bad-tempered Maria can be, but she's the best of the best for dancing the Nutcracker. I understand she preferred to dance Clara to Sugarplum but..." Miss Sterling paused. Edda thought there was that hesitation again in her mentor's eyes and her breath stuck in her throat. *She wasn't the first choice for Clara?*

"I wanted this for you." There it was. Not said in so many words, but implied. All feathers had been ruffled since Maria Petrova's arrival two months earlier. She was a league above them all.

"Oh, I see." Tears started pricking behind Edda's eyes. Her shoulders slumped more than a fragment.

"No. I'm not explaining myself well." Miss Sterling tapped her fingers together for a moment, mincing her words, then continued in a rapid voice, "Let me be crystal clear with you, Edda, so you get the full picture. You were to dance Clara from the beginning. We trained you for that and Monsieur Sergeyev and I were in complete agreement about it. You were ready. You *are* ready."

"But Maria's arrival made you reconsider?"

Miss Sterling shook her head. "Not me, Pyo... Monsieur Sergeyev put the suggestion in my head, but I said a firm 'no' right from the start. We'd never expected Maria to stop over in Amsterdam. Apparently, she has a boyfriend of some sort here, some German count, don't ask me about it. She would dance a lot better and more focused if she wasn't in love."

Edda felt her heart sink further. Monsieur Sergeyev, himself one of the star dancers in his role as Drosselmeyer, had been her other prop-and-stay within the company. And now he doubted her performance?

Miss Sterling continued as if reading her thoughts. "It's not what you think, my dear, Monsieur Sergeyev has complete confidence in you as Clara. He was just worried about our position in the international dance world. That we were giving one of the world's leading ballerinas a secondary role. I told him straight up it is my goal to give new talent a chance, and he agreed wholeheartedly. But Maria must somehow have gotten wind of our conversation, or she just tried her luck, Monsieur Sergeyev being a fellow Russian and having invited her here. That's all there is to it."

"Oh." Edda didn't know whether to be relieved.

"I called Maria in here to make sure she understood where she stands. I think she does so now. Let's leave it at that and continue to our pep talk. I can see in your eyes that you need a little boost after this drama."

∾

A LITTLE LATER Edda left Miss Sterling's office with much more confidence. Ten minutes left before curtains up. She had to hurry.

"Hey!" A hand grabbed her wrist from behind. Edda spun on her heels quicker than lightning to look into the eyes of Maria Petrova. The Russian's fingers held her tightly, but Edda wrung herself free.

"Let me go. I need to prepare."

"I mean you no harm, Edda. You'll do fine as Clara. Truly. At least, I hope so." It sounded snooty, not very reassuring, the husky Russian-accented voice betraying a heavy smoker. Edda stood still as a brooding dove.

"What do you want from me, Maria?"

Maria took a step towards her, giving her less space, but Edda stood her ground. She had Miss Sterling's backing now and wouldn't be intimidated by the more experienced dancer.

"You must be over the moon being allowed to dance Clara, instead of Sugar Plum." Again, that condescending tone! Edda turned her back on Maria, unwilling to get into another argument about the role division the ballet mistress had decided on.

"Wait!" Maria caught up with her, "I know you dislike me, like all the others, but can't we bury the hatchet over such an insignificant issue as who dances Clara? Besides..." Maria fluffed a hand over her shoulder as if dismissing an irritant fly. "I've had *my* moment as Clara. Three encores in St Petersburg for *me*! So good luck with that, Edda."

"I don't dislike you. I don't know you, so how can I dislike you? Now please, let me go to my dressing room to prepare."

Edda stood firmly on both legs, the feet turned slightly outward as in position one, a deepening frown of chagrin on her powdered forehead. The intrusion was the last thing she wanted but fighting with Maria didn't seem the right course.

"I'm glad your Clara was so well accepted, Maria. I wouldn't have expected otherwise. You're a brilliant ballerina. See you later."

"One more minute. What age are you, Edda, seventeen, eighteen?"

"I am twenty, as a matter of fact, and have danced since I was five,"

Edda snapped. Oh, the woman was impossible. Determined to get under her skin.

"Alright, point taken."

A slim hand waved in front of Edda's face.

"So, what is it then?" Maria demanded.

"Nothing. I didn't ask you anything. And I wish you'd stop talking me down." Edda bit back. A sudden pang of strange churning in Edda's stomach made her almost double-over, but her training kept her straight as a lance.

"I'm not talking you down." Maria looked her up and down. "I'm trying to help."

"By implying I'm not ready seconds before I have to go on? Is that your idea of helping?" There was exasperation in Edda's voice.

"I'm talking about your *nerves*, *chérie*, as Marlene told me to."

None of the dancers or staff addressed Miss Sterling by her first name. The nerve the girl had. And she was sure Miss Sterling had done nothing of the sort.

"Well, what can you tell me about my nerves?" Edda said defiantly, but secretly hoping the Russian could give her a tip that would settle her revolting stomach. For a moment Maria seemed taken aback, stared past her, then sighed rather dramatically.

"I'm not sure I can be of much help. I still am terribly nervous, every time I go through the side curtains onto the stage. I think it's just part of our job. Not being nervous wouldn't work for a dancer, I suppose."

Surprised at the sudden honesty, Edda checked Maria's expression to see if she could trust this new version. It might be another trap. There had been so much hostility in the air until now that this mellower Maria sent Edda on even higher alert.

"That's not much help either, is it?"

Maria looked stung, the light-gray eyes taking in Edda with a nonplussed expression.

"Oh, but it is. You just have to live with it, *chérie*. That's what I'm trying to tell you. You'll be alright, it's part of the game."

Edda shrugged. "Oh, well, thanks then." If this was Maria's way of helping, to say it couldn't be helped. There was some comfort in it, knowing the steely ballerina with her haughty habits suffered from nerves as well.

"I wish you luck, *chérie*. You'll do fine."

"You too, Maria."

Mumbling a half-meant 'thank you', Edda rushed through the narrow hallway to her dressing room. In front of her door, she almost bumped into Vincent, who was dancing Fritz, her stage brother. Relieved to encounter a likeable team member, she took Vincent's hand by instinct. As they danced hand in hand during most of the first act, it felt natural to hold his hand now and the reassurance it gave her.

"What's up, Vince? I've got to rush."

"I was looking for you." Vincent van Rijn was a dark-blonde Amsterdam hulk of a man with exquisite jade-green eyes and the body of a demi-god. Not your typical male ballet dancer. He could as easily have been a wrestler or a gymnast. At least a decade older than Edda, he was tried and tested on the stage and Edda's strong right arm on her opening night.

"What for?" She demanded, the recent encounter with Miss Sterling and Maria still fresh on her mind. Vincent only mouthed 'come' with a finger to his lips and pulled her with him. With hands clasped, they sneaked along the corridor, through the back curtains onto the stage.

"Oh!" Edda's eyes twinkled as she saw the tall Christmas tree in full adorn.

"Yeah, the tree is great. Larry did a superb job, but that's not what I wanted to show you." Vincent propelled her towards the closed curtains.

During their stage rehearsals the curtains had always been wide open. Miss Sterling would sit in the front row, so she could hop on the stage for instructions. Sometimes there were one or two other people in the theatre hall, sitting in the dark, but for the rest it was empty, rows and rows of connected red plush seats in semi circles.

Now the burgundy drapes were tightly shut, like a dark wall of vertical waves, protecting the dancers from the prying eyes of the audience, and from all that was the other world, the subdued murmur of voices, coughing throats, and the orchestra playing an intro waltz.

"This will make it real for you," Vincent whispered. "Take it in, Edda. They're all here for you!" He opened the mid-section of the curtains just a fraction and Edda peered through the slit he held open for her. She couldn't see left or right, just straight ahead, the tops of freshly coiffed heads and shining bald scalps bobbing in a sea of a thousand festoon lamps. The heads went right up to the frescoed ceiling.

She scanned what she could see of the first row, hoping to get a glimpse of her mother and father. They must be right there, but she didn't see them.

Suddenly the sea of heads made her slightly sick, as if giddy with too much light and noise, she backed away from the curtain.

"Now you've seen there are people out there, forget all about them, Edda. It's just you and me and the other dancers."

Edda nodded, clasping Vincent's hand again as they passed the Christmas tree on their way backstage. She wasn't sure she'd wanted a glimpse of the real world, but she knew Vincent meant well and it probably served its purpose.

Edda was tired, as if a shadow had fallen over her in the past hour and for the first time she doubted whether she could portray a decent Clara. Her thoughts were muddled, her body revolted. She felt like a tiny vessel bouncing up and down on the wild ocean.

Concentrate, Edda Van der Valk, and go, go, go!

Edda would never back down from a challenge, and she didn't do now. Sick, tired, dead-scared–whatever - Edda would dance.

3

BATTLE ROYALE

The Philharmonic orchestra released the first notes of the Overture. *Wait, wait, wait in the wings.* Edda was counting her heartbeats, holding on firmly to Vincent's hand. Hers was slippery with sweat, so she had to tighten her grip. He gave her a reassuring squeeze, but their eyes didn't meet. She stared straight ahead through the back curtains, fixing her eyes on the floor just in front of the Christmas tree. *Go there and dance! Dance like you've never danced before.*

The *Allegro Guisto* was over before she was fully done counting the 182 bars. Scène 1 was here, *L'ornement et l'illumination de l'arbre de Noël.* Still hanging onto Vincent's comforting paw, 'Clara' darted onto the stage with 'Fritz' at her side as if she didn't have a care in the world, up to the magnificent Christmas tree that filled the middle back of the stage.

Thrusted into the heady lights in her fairy-tale costume with the gush of sweeping awe from the audience below, Edda mentally transformed into Clara. In that transformation all anxiety died, as if Edda herself no longer existed, and she felt serenely safe. As Clara, she was untouchable. She could float above it all, the pettiness, the problems, the pretensions, encapsulated as she was in movement and music and magnificence. Being the masterpiece.

Her body curved in graceful, lyrical moves, each step intuitive and instinctual, though anchored in all the rehearsed steps. Her arms swayed like a willow in the wind, her feet danced in dazzling patterns, while her eyes sparkled with the joy of her own performance.

Becoming one with the music Edda felt a tremendous power in her heart, as if through her own being she could transport the audience below to a different realm. Her every cell vibrated in perfect harmony with the instruments, with 'Fritz', with the other dancers at the Stahlbaum's party, even with the Christmas tree.

Some part of Edda's conscious mind registered the dissipation of nerves. And what Maria had said. That nerves were part of performing. But nobody had told her they would evaporate like the ocean foam on the beach when you were in your role. It was exhilarating, dangerously intoxicating. *May this never end* was all Edda could think as she spun and pirouetted, basking in the stardom that finally kept all eyes on her. On her alone.

Sensitive and receptive, she was now fully attuned to the arrival of her mysterious stage godfather, Drosselmeyer. The moment he would bolt in from the wings, his black coat fishtailing behind him like a dark sail. Then the splendor of the Nutcracker ballet would truly take off. 'Fritz' was her introduction as the young Clara, 'Drosselmeyer' helped her grow up and finally 'the Prince' would turn her into a woman.

Of all Miss Sterling's dancers, it was her Russian-born lover, Pyotr Sergeyev as Drosselmeyer who knew how to mesmerize the audience, make everyone feel as if they were part of what was happening on stage instead of being merely a spectator. Monsieur Sergeyev simply swept every person in the theatre into the shimmering world of the Sugarplum Fairy. He leapt like a phantom, movements so effortless and light he seemed almost as if floating on weightless air. When he waved his golden staff, the audience were enthralled, even the dancers were all under his spell.

Pyotr Sergeyev, the sensation of London and New York, was and had been the essence of The Nutcracker story for as long as Edda could remember. Both on and off stage, he was the Magician, the Dreamweaver, everybody's friend. But his most special connection was with Edda as 'Clara'. They shared a vibrational energy that was uniquely theirs. Monsieur Sergeyev was Edda's lover *too*, though only in a platonic sense. She danced feeding off his energy and skill and expertise.

The wink he gave her as they passed each other in galop gave her butterfly wings. She could sense his approval so strongly. Marveling in her achievement, he was spurring her on to even higher heights. And so Edda gave all she had, balancing precariously on her slippered toes, while Fritz whirled her around, her left leg stretched behind her in the most alluring arch.

It was almost hard to concentrate on the Nutcracker himself, who was to be her male lead in the next scene. Edda couldn't help seeking her stage godfather's nearness, feeling their chemistry, that special bond, being the source of his dance storytelling. It was exactly how Miss Sterling had told her to dance. Share the limelight with Monsieur Sergeyev and all will be right.

When it was time, Edda let go of Vincent's hand and navigated towards the Nutcracker, performed by the Belgian René Deschamps. Rene made for an adorable-wooden-nutcracker-turned-dashing-prince and Edda had no problem portraying Clara totally in love with her Prince.

Edda's exhilaration was such she'd fall in love with the entire cast for the duration of the show, even with her stage parents and uncles and aunts, including the Christmas dolls and the Christmas tree itself. Surely her heart would burst out of her dancing body in its tight, embroidered top, giddy with happiness and triumph.

The mood changed both on the stage and in the audience when the lights dimmed to signal the darkness of the Mouse King, as his retinue swarmed the stage. The battle between good and evil was about to begin. Edda, spooked and fearful, despite the many dress rehearsals, danced as if it was the first time she was in the dark, ultimately throwing Clara's slipper at the Mouse King as if he really was evil. When she heard him utter a surprised *ouch,* she realized she might have used a little too much force. A visible breath of relief escaped her heaving chest on seeing she'd rescued Clara's beloved Nutcracker from the evil Mouse King, who was actually none other than the rather charming British dancer, Tony Revel. It was all so real to Edda, as real as the evil in the real world.

The audience collectively shared in Edda's relief. The mood in the theater shifted from fear and trepidation, to joy and excitement. The audience erupted in cheers and applause, celebrating the victory of good over evil. The story told on the stage felt real to everyone. Even if the world was trembling on the edge of war, this girl's righteous actions kept the fire of hope burning. If the good prevailed, the darkest of times could be borne and survived.

As soon as the curtains closed after the first act, the other dancers came to stand in a circle around Edda to congratulate her. She stood wiping the sweat from her brow, panting, and grinning from ear to ear. She knew she'd never danced like this before. The audience was still a palpable wave of awe, while the cast was whispering *Bravo! Outstanding performance! The best one yet, Edda!* Edda couldn't stop beaming, tears in her eyes from all the emotions. The feeling of accomplishment was almost too big for her slender frame.

As the dancers hugged her and then each other to celebrate the success of the first act, the applause and the cheers echoed through the theatre, filling the air. Edda couldn't help but feel proud of everyone. They'd worked so hard to make it all come together, and it had paid off.

"*Bravissimo!*" Miss Sterling was clapping her hands. "Well done, Edda, well done, crew! *Magico, fenomenale!* Didn't I tell you to trust yourself? You're what I call a 'fighter dancer.' It may not come to you easily, but your grit and warrior spirit will take you places."

Monsieur Sergeyev was patting her shoulder jovially. "*Ma petite prima ballerina!* Soft on the outside, steel on the inside."

"Thank you. Am I really?"

Steel on the inside? Edda didn't feel that way, more the other way around, but if Monsieur Sergeyev said so, she'd better believe it. Coming back down to earth after the first high, Edda needed the approval from her mentors, especially as she felt the sourpuss expression of one dancer resting on her.

In the first moments of exuberance, she hadn't paid attention, but now she saw that Maria Petrova in her sugary pink outfit wasn't cheering with the rest. There was a glint in her eye that made it clear she'd throw Edda into the shade with her own performance as Sugar Plum in the second act.

Miss Sterling's voice reassured her as she led the animated ballerina backstage.

"Absolutely first class, Edda. You've surpassed yourself! Now quickly refresh before you have to do the heavy lifting in the second act. Just make sure you smile a little more like being in love with René, that's all. Your chemistry is fine. Just beware of the facial expressions."

"Yes, Miss Sterling. I won't forget."

With Maria's preying stares on her back, Edda skipped to her tiny dressing room and sat down panting on her stool. The reflection of her black eyes sprang back at her, vivid and ecstatic. Larry came in with a cup of tea and a slice of cake.

"You did fine, Edda. We're so proud of you."

Edda felt like kissing the wiry floor manager's cheeks. If they were all that happy with her Clara, she must have been as good as she imagined.

Briefly wondering how her loving but authoritative father and always-finding-fault mother would have rated her performance, she dismissed worrying about their views as she blew on the hot tea. If the professionals thought she'd done well, her parents would now perhaps see that the time and effort and money poured into their daughter's dance career had not been wasted.

Edda sipped the tea, savoring its warmth and sweetness, and feeling a new bubble of pride and accomplishment for her family spread through her chest and stomach. For them, she'd wanted to outshine herself. Though her parents' support had been grudging, to say the least, certainly when Edda had called it 'her career', they wanted her to succeed and had bolstered her dream to become the prima ballerina of the Amsterdam Ballet Theater.

Edda smiled as she thought of her father's extensive, blue-blooded Van der Valk relatives. They'd never stopped raising eyebrows over the dancing daughter of a high-ranking politician and verbalizing 'it simply wasn't done'. Her mother's family in Prussia were certainly not amused either, but as they were miles away, their judgment didn't weigh as heavy as that of the Van der Valk clan.

Tonight Edda was proving those who'd doubted her and her parents' support wrong - even the daughter of a marquess could have an artistic career without ending up in the Circus. Edda felt she would no longer be seen by her uncles and aunties as the little Van der Valk girl whose parents let her indulge in frippery. She was a hardworking dancer who'd fought for her success every step of the way. Papa and Mama could sleep better tonight.

EDDA WAS DANCING *the magical forest scene with 'Hans', the nutcracker-turned-handsome-prince. Her tightly fitting ballerina costume in lily-white suited her fair complexion and dark hair, covering her arms and body and smoothing down over her thighs. She had become the enchanted princess, totally in love with 'Hans' and forgetting he had been a toy nutcracker at first.*

All Edda's senses were on high alert in the fairytale woods surrounding her and her stage lover. It smelled of pines, twinkling stars guided them, and a soft breeze enveloped their glowing bodies. As she twirled into the forest clearing in René's arms, they moved as one, fluid and love-struck, the perfect couple, their steps in effortless synchrony.

Morning came and the sun, portrayed by a chandelier that poured rays of light from the ceiling, broke through the artificial trees and bathed them in a warm, fluorescent radiance. The playful light further melted the couple into one though they still operated in separate bodies.

Edda could almost believe she was truly in love with her stage partner. The orchestra increased the tempo, and they spun and leapt as if they had been dancing together through the ages. Far below them, Edda instinctively knew, the audience only had eyes for Clara and Hans, captivated and enthralled as they were. The beauty of the moment was filling the air and every heart.

When the music, after the stage-filling crescendo, died out in soft melodious tones, 'Clara' and 'Hans' let go of each other and bowed while the audience applauded as one. Edda took René's hand one more time, one more bow, accepted all the praise before exiting the stage. Still enchanted by the magic of their forest scene, they had hardly reached the back curtains when they were called back for an encore...

"TIME FOR ACT 2, EDDA." Miss Sterling rapped on the dressing room door.

With a jolt Edda snapped out of her enchantment, realizing she'd only visualized the complete scene. It was still to come. With body and mind primed, she rose from her stool, ready to take up the challenge. The real challenge would be 'Sugar Plum' vs 'Clara' in this round. Not 'Hans and Clara'. They would be fine, as she'd seen in her mind's eye. More than fine.

"Let Maria do her thing in this scene," Edda mumbled to herself, "I've had my moment in Act I and will have it again in the final scene." That would be all Clara, waking up in her own bed, a dream within a dream. The last dancer the audience would admire was Clara. Not Sugar Plum.

Edda danced Act 2 even better than the first. Carried by the audience that had loosened up after the tight atmosphere at the end of Act I, clapping and cheering rose from the hall when she tiptoed onto the stage in wonder. It didn't bother Edda in the least. It further electrified the energy on stage. The dancers, too, loosened up as they performed the forest scene. The chorus moved in perfect sync with the lyrical pas de deux in Andante Maestoso. It was the sweeping magical scene, just as she had envisaged.

Rapturously 'Clara' gazed up into 'Hans's' eyes, just as Miss Sterling had told her to. She let him swing her around and around on the stage, feather-light and always smiling. Every pirouette, every tour en l'air, every pas de deux, every grande jeté was perfection. The audience was again bewitched by her... by her... by her alone! Edda couldn't help herself. She couldn't not shine. Even if she'd wished to. Which she didn't.

A knife-like pain in her left ankle made Edda stumble, almost lose her balance, grasp wildly around her, until she felt a hand help her steady herself. It was Monsieur Sergeyev as Drosselmeyer! *En-pointe* was impossible on that foot. She had to come down. Sheer willpower forced Edda to continue dancing, smiling sweetly despite the unbearable pain. Her ankle was swelling with every turn, her foot hardly fitting in her pointe shoe, the ribbons around her ankle pressing ever more in her flesh.

Do not think of the pain. Just concentrate on the music. Don't let the others down. The seconds crept like hours. The smile on her face was frozen, her heart sunk. And that constant throbbing pain with sharp, sudden jolts. What on earth was it?

Finally, finally, the curtain fell and only a few encores were needed. The long row of dancers bowed and bowed, and nobody seem to pay attention to Edda. She'd pulled it off, but the pain was too much to be proud of her accomplishment. With tears in her eyes, she limped to her dressing room, suddenly almost unable to walk. Too afraid to look down her left leg to see the damage, her head confused by what had taken place.

"Edda, my dear, let me have a look at that left leg. I saw you stumble for a moment." Miss Sterling rushed in, looking stern but mostly worried. Edda cringed. She'd made a mistake. How could she have thought Miss Sterling wouldn't notice? Behind the ballet mistress was her Monsieur Sergeyev. And behind him, René peeked his head around the door, but Miss Sterling brushed him off.

"I'll be in here with Edda for a while, René. Would you be so kind as to look after the other dancers?"

"Of course, Miss Sterling, right on it."

The ballet mistress had already sunk on her knees in front of Edda, easing off her left pointe shoe. Edda bit her lip. The pain made her want to scream, but she kept quiet. Her lower lip started bleeding as she bit it too hard. Drops of blood trickled on the white fabric of her costume. Monsieur Sergeyev handed her a handkerchief that smelled of gentleman's cologne. She dabbed her lip, longing to bite on the scented linen cloth to ease the pain.

Edda's thoughts raced as Miss Sterling inspected her ankle. Having been lavished with praise for her performance in Act 1, how could she have let her mentor down in Act 2? Though it felt like she could never stand on her legs again. Still, she would dance tomorrow night and the night after, and the night after. Demonstrate the strength and discipline drilled into her over the years.

More tears, more blood on the handkerchief. Monsieur Sergeyev's hand on her shoulder. Miss Sterling looked up into Edda's face. Despite her lamentable state of affairs, Edda was able to spot the admiration in the liquid, honey eyes, but she also didn't miss the deep line of concern in between the eyes.

"You're a big-time brave one, Edda Van der Valk. You have the backbone of a grand ballerina but..."

Edda smiled through her pain. This was exactly what she needed to hear. She would not let Miss Sterling or the other dancers down. Every professional dancer knew what pain was. They were trained in pain, danced till their toes and heels bled, but their hearts soared. It was part and parcel of the ballerina's life.

"... but that ankle is broken."

"What? No!"

Fresh tears welled in Edda's eyes, both from pain and disbelief. "No, no, no! I need to dance Clara tomorrow night. My ankle can't be broken. It can't be!"

"But it is, my dear. Alas."

Miss Sterling shared a glance with her partner, while Edda

started sobbing with no holds barred. Monsieur Sergeyev gave her trembling shoulder a gentle squeeze as he did so often.

"Miss Sterling is right, *ma pauvre*, your ankle is broken. No dancing for you for a while, I'm afraid. I'll phone the hospital. And shall I inform your parents? Will they still be in the theater?"

Edda wasn't able to respond intelligibly. Loud sobs were all that came out of her. She also didn't grasp the meaning of what her mentors were saying. Broken. Unable to dance again. Her parents.

"It was an accident, Edda. Accidents happen." Miss Sterling's golden eyes met the dark, troubled eyes of her pupil. "It wasn't Maria's doing if you thought so."

"M...maria?" Edda was still nonplussed, only the uttering of her name shook her from her stupor. Maria's breath was on her neck, then seconds later, something had landed on her instep. It had been dark the one moment the lights were dimmed. Had she really felt it? It was all a blur now, but could it have been Maria?

With red-rimmed eyes Edda gazed from Miss Sterling to Monsieur Sergeyev, the tears still flowing.

"It *was* Maria," she whispered in utter horror.

Miss Sterling took her hand and said in that low-pitched voice that meant *this will only be said once,* "It wasn't Maria, Edda. I kept a close watch on her all the time. It was an accident, that's all it was. I know the girl is trouble with a capital T and has a mouth that's too big for her own good, but she wouldn't injure another dancer. It would be the end of her own career."

"But... but... I didn't misstep, Miss St... Sterling, I really didn't."

"Accidents happen on stage, my dear. I, myself, twisted my knee in Gisele in New York and Monsieur Sergeyev here was out of the running for months because of a shoulder injury. I know how upset you are, sweet girl, but we'd better get you sorted at the hospital as fast as we can." Miss Sterling's eyes swept from Edda to her partner again. "Would you, Pyotr?"

Monsieur Sergeyev nodded, handed Edda a glass of water and left the dressing room. After he was gone, Miss Sterling rose to her feet and listened at the door for a moment. His footsteps retreated.

"I believe you, Edda, when you say you didn't misstep. You're an honest girl. And I know ankles don't break of their own accord. I didn't want to say this with Monsieur Sergeyev present as he'd put his hand in the fire for that Petrova girl, but I promise you I will interrogate her. It won't be pleasant."

An enigmatic smile curled the ballet mistress's lips. The smile evaporated into a sigh. "I also still find it hard to believe she would do such a thing. It was dark. It could have been any of the chorus girls swaying back and coming to stand around you. Maybe one will come forward and say she stumbled. So don't worry about others now. Let's focus on getting you to the hospital first. In the meantime, take one of my powerful painkillers. I've had them ever since my own twisted knee."

She handed Edda a small white pill, which she swallowed with a large mouthful of the water. It seemed to work wonders within seconds. No need to question what that strong pill was. She was just glad she could think straight again. Miss Sterling was right. She had no proof Maria was in any way involved in her broken ankle. The thought—no matter how devastating the result—made Edda feel better. She knew deep inside herself she hadn't made a mistake herself; it had come from outside. The culprit would step forward. She could leave that to the ballet mistress.

"Who's going to dance my part... Clara tomorrow, Miss Sterling?"

She thought Miss Sterling looked ashen; her lips pressed into a thin line.

"I don't think I have a choice, Edda. Maria will dance your part for the coming weeks. There's no one else ready for the role except Mademoiselle Petrova. I'm sorry, my dear, really sorry."

Edda felt tears well up again. *See*, she wanted to shout, *that's been Petrova's plan all along and now she's getting what she wants.* But she said nothing, swallowed her tears. Monsieur Sergeyev came back in and caught on Miss Sterling's last words.

"It's business, Marlene, don't take it personally," he said soothingly and to Edda he added, "the ambulance is on its way. Your parents will meet you at the Wilhelmina Gasthuis. They were about to leave but said they'd tell the chauffeur to stop at the hospital for as long as needed."

It was a comforting thought she would see her parents. She needed them in her hour of despair, and she felt grateful to her father. The family celebration had been planned for after the second performance as tonight her father had had to be back in Leiden for some important meeting. The idea had been she would celebrate tonight with the dance ensemble and tomorrow with the family. |Her father, the Marquess, had already reserved a table at Grand Hotel Krasnapolsky on Dam Square.

"Thank you, Monsieur Sergeyev."

"Oh, and your father said you shouldn't worry about his appointment tonight." She smiled a weak smile and accepted Monsieur Sergeyev's help getting into her winter coat. Groggy from the pain, coming down from the adrenaline of the performance, and the realization about her injury, Edda was unable to walk.

"I'd better wait inside for the ambulance. Will you tell the other dancers what happened and excuse me?" She asked.

"I'm coming with you." Miss Sterling suddenly announced, slinging her own fur coat around her shoulders and grabbing her Chanel handbag. "Pyotr, dear, please deal with the group for me. I need a breather." She let him kiss her cheek as she applied a fresh layer of bright-red lipstick.

"Take your time, Marlene. I'll give them the wrap-up speech and close up here. I hope it won't be a long convalescence, Edda, though ankles are tricky devils. Give it time!"

Befuddled and in a blue funk, Edda let Miss Sterling push a miraculously present wheelchair out of the stage door. A white ambulance with a red cross was already waiting for them with the engine running.

This was poles apart from how Edda had imagined the end of her first important stage performance. Crippled as a result of being an easy target for a bully ballerina. The thought didn't leave her.

The EMTs were kind, propping her up in the back of the ambulance and tucking a blanket around her. Miss Sterling, too, was gentle, her face soft with concern.

"We'll get you home and taken care of, Edda," she said, pressing her hand on hers. Edda nodded, her breath hitching as she tried to keep her composure. But it was too late. She'd been made a fool of on the stage, and there was no way to undo the damage. A single, silent tear rolled down her cheek, and she knew her dream of becoming a professional ballerina was over. At least for a long time.

4

LIFE IN THE OTHER WORLD

For Edda the ride in the ambulance from Theatre Carré in central Amsterdam to the Wilhelmina Gasthuis at the Eerste Helmersstraat in Amsterdam-West passed by in a haze. As Miss Sterling's magical pill was already wearing off, the pain intensified again and the bumpy ride over cobblestone roads wasn't much help. With each bump, she gasped, squeezing Miss Sterling's hand for support.

The only sensation that penetrated through the pain in her foot and the fog in her head was the screeching sound of the ambulance siren. It went off every time the vehicle took a bend, which seemed a rather excessive maneuver for a broken ankle. It wasn't as if she was having a heart attack.

"Busy outside," Miss Sterling observed. "Everyone must have left their homes to admire the Christmas decorations. Such a fine night for wandering about."

The ballet mistress's small talk was clearly aimed at distracting Edda, but she kept her head down, staring down at the hand covered in rings with the fine, blue veins that held hers instead of looking up out of the window. She was aware that her own fingers reflected white, almost deathly so, in the small light attached to the van's roof.

As the car hit another bump, a wave of nausea spread from her stomach up into her gullet. Suddenly, a bright light shone right into the car from outside, lighting up the whole interior and, like a searchlight, disappeared again. Panic gripped Edda about the hellish blue shaft of light. *What was it?* Shivering over her whole body, she fought to keep the bile down. The light flashed once more, sideways, and was gone.

Was it a déjà vu or something still awaiting her?

Gripping Miss Sterling's hand even tighter, she mumbled *sorry* at squeezing her hand like it was her only lifeline. In her singsong voice Miss Sterling said, "that's the trouble with us ballerinas. We're like thoroughbred horses trained for the race course. Strong and lenient, but as we're so high strung, we're also prone to serious and painful injuries. Alas, our overtrained bodies snap when the pressure becomes too much. As I told you, I injured my knee dancing Giselle in New York..."

Despite her effort to take in Miss Sterling's story, Edda's befuddled brain latched on to the horse analogy. A racehorse, that was exactly what she was, always had been. From the moment her tiny four-year-old feet hit the parquet floor of Madame Tissé's Ballet School in Leeuwarden, Edda knew she was a dancer. Racing and racing around the dance floor as if a horse in a courtyard with a whip to her flank. Higher, better, smoother. She just was her own jockey, her own slave master. No one else was to blame for her insane will for perfection.

"Are you alright, dear?" Miss Sterling wrung her sore hand free and put it on Edda's muscular thigh. Edda nodded, even trying a mismatched half-smile.

"I hope my p... parents will be able to stay with me at the h... hospital." It came out through clattering teeth. Miss Sterling would soon have to return to the group. She was only here for the ambulance ride. Edda dreaded the moment of her mentor's departure. After the deliverance into her parents' care, Miss Sterling as go-between would vanish in the wings, maybe for good. New tears welled. It was over. Just too hard to grasp the truth yet.

"I can stay for a while, dear. Don't stress yourself. And I'm sure your parents will take excellent care of you. That's what parents are for."

If only you knew, Edda despaired, but kept quiet. As the ambulance swept past the brick entrance of the Wilhelmina Gasthuis and the barricade closed behind them, it felt like she was sentenced to a life in prison. Her life's work snapped in two like a matchstick. Like her ankle.

She'd never felt this miserable. Not during the years of toil in the chorus line, not when she'd been unable to attend friends' parties or celebrate birthdays with her family. *Edda has to dance, Edda has a practice, Edda must rest.* There had been so much missing out on ordinary life, but it had all been worthwhile, and Edda had taken it in stride.

Despite the rules arranged around Edda's routines, dance had been a balancing act for her. She'd had to fight for her passion every step of the way. Artistic, childless Miss Sterling would never fully understand that, nor the turmoil her pupil was in now. Coming from a long line of dancers, the ballet mistress was oblivious to the harshness of what life was outside the stage, the spotlights, the star dancers.

But Edda knew how thin the veil of acceptance her strict parents had for what they called *her craze*. All the while she worked so hard, they'd prepared their remedy. The suitable suitor. A broken ankle would be ample reason to get *dear Eddaline* out of that bohemian rabble and get her settled with Van Limburg Stirum something.

Edda couldn't even bring herself to pronounce his Christian name. It was so utterly ridiculous. Ludovicus. Almost twice her age and an attorney like her father. Balding, boring, brooding. God forbid they force her to hobble down the aisle to become his wife before she can even dance again.

Angry, desperate thoughts interlaced with pain and foreboding filled Edda's head. The cramped space of the ambulance was suffocating. She was about to scream when the elongated, white van finally came to a screeching halt in front of the emergency unit.

In an emotional haze, Edda peered out of the small window to get a glimpse of her parents. Miss Sterling spotted her mother first.

"That must be her."

Following the long, lacquered nail, Edda spotted her stout mama underneath a glaring lantern. She was huddled in her habitual ankle-length rabbit-fur coat, the stylish felt hat with the ostrich feather topping her dyed-blonde head. The black patent shoes with small heels showing puffed-up ankles above them. Small flecks of snow whirled down from the yellow light above her and spattered her hat and coat with tiny, white dots.

The sourpuss expression on her mother's perfectly symmetrical face gave vent to the Marchioness's discontent with this late-night upheaval. Though exuding a different, prouder personality on the exterior, Olga Van der Valk-Scherzinger was, without doubt, the older version of her ballet-dancing daughter.

Next to her mother towered her father, the Marquis Johannes Van der Valk, clad in all-black, including hat and gloves, now also decked with white flecks. A frown of irritation and unfulfilled cravings on his broad forehead. A cigar smoldering clumsily between black leather fingers.

But Papa was there, as he had promised. There was no sight of Duifje, Edda's half-sister, from her father's earlier marriage. She'd probably gone home to her husband and baby son.

Seeing her middle-aged parents stand there in the cold further aggravated Edda's conflicting emotions. She longed for her parents, and yet... how would they comment on her present state? For a moment she wondered if she should ask the driver to turn around. Take her to a different hospital. Away from the foreshadowing that closed around her heart like a clamp. But she knew it was impossible. Too late.

She'd have to face it, whatever the future would bring. A world away from her elated performance only an hour ago. Too late.

Fie Edda! a stern inner voice reprimanded her. *These people love you. They want the best for you. They're on your side.*

Then why this sickening feeling of doom? The answer came of

itself: because everything had been a struggle in her life from the moment she was born. Maybe even before that. A difficult birth, a sickly baby, then a wilful child, though not in a loud, demanding way. Just stubborn and determined. Edda had always known it. Life was a struggle, and here she was.

In the seconds left to her, she turned her gaze away from her parents to the familiar sights of Amsterdam at night. The tall Canadian poplars in the Vondelpark stretched their barren branches to the sky as if they had a prayer of their own. Accepting the snowflakes with much more gratitude than humans ever would. The inky-blue water reflected the street lamps and the illuminated houses along the canal. Two cyclists passed by, their slightly intoxicated voices falling to pieces as they disappeared into the night.

This city had become her home in the past two years—the days and nights of toil and laughter, the times of uncertainty, all the joys and sorrows that had made her who she was now. And what she'd lost in the snap of a second.

A matronly nurse in a stiff, white uniform swung open the ambulance door and without further ado grabbed Edda by the armpits and half lifted, half pushed her into a waiting wheelchair. The breath of her chirpy voice made a white plume in the cold air as she announced.

"Ah, there's the young Marchioness! We've been expecting you. What a misfortune. But we'll fix you up in no time. Mark my words."

Thrown out in the cold, Edda shivered from fatigue, pain, and weariness while her stately, Prussian mother strutted towards the wheelchair to put a protective hand on her daughter's shoulder. Her lips brushed the top of Edda's head while she addressed the nurse in her German-accented, nasal voice.

"Any idea how long *this* is going to take, Nurse? My husband needs to..."

"Let it be, Olga," her father grunted, "I can stay. Eddaline's health is more important than serving the country." Her father took his position on the other side of the wheelchair as if a general in the army. Edda sighed a breath of relief. Did Papa actually say that she was more important? Her heart swelled. For a moment the pain in her ankle lessened.

"We have to ascertain the young Marchioness's injury first," the nurse replied. "Doctor Geuze is prepared to put on a cast. I guarantee you Doctor Geuze is the very best orthopaedic physician we have in the Wilhelmina Gasthuis. We will give the young Marchioness the very best treatment."

Edda wished she would stop addressing her as 'the young Marchioness.' Though the nurse clearly bent over backwards for blue blood. Edda cared little about being a descendant of one of Holland's oldest families. She was a dancer, that was her identity, all the rest was just a lot of fuss she would rather do without.

The nurse was already wheeling her inside as if she was made of crystal instead of firm flesh and bones.

"I'll go now, Edda. I'll try to phone you tomorrow. Alright?" The ballet mistress's posh British voice sounded like a clear bell through the frosty air.

"Wait," Edda instructed the nurse, "wheel me around." If the medic wanted aristocratic authority, she could get it. Her command was instantly followed, and Edda faced her mentor with a pleading face.

"How will you get home, Miss Sterling? Can't you come in and phone Monsieur Sergeyev from here?" Hope laced Edda's voice. If Miss Sterling disappeared out of sight, the last bond with her dream would disappear with her. Edda wasn't sure she was ready for that. She needed easing into life in the other world.

"Don't worry, my dear. I'll get a taxi. Talk to you tomorrow."

Papa shook Miss Sterling's hand warmly. "Thank you for all you've done for our Eddaline. Your teachings turned her into an amazing 'Clara' tonight." Mama followed suit, smiling her radiant smile and showing her perfect teeth. "I wish we'd met under different circumstances, but we'll take care of Eddaline from here."

Eddaline. Eddaline. Only her parents called her that. She was Edda. Just Edda.

A last wave. A goodbye to what she'd hoped would have been a row of spectacular performances, but Miss Sterling's nimble footsteps danced away, out of Edda's vision. The tie was broken, the spell gone. Would she ever be that amazing Clara again?

As the small ensemble made their way inside the brightly lit hospital corridor and the flapping doors closed behind her, Edda, who would now be Eddaline, knew she had no other choice but to surrender to the other world.

Don't cry!

Duifje had always teased her when she was younger. *Cry baby, you're just a cry-baby!*

The wheelchair took a turn and, in the doorway, stood an elderly doctor with snow white hair that peaked at his ears and a friendly, wrinkled face. Blue eyes, the color of a cloudless sky at noon, took in the young patient with the tearful face. The doctor in his knee-length white coat looked like a soothing wizard to Edda's befuddled mind.

"Occupational hazard, I presume? Wrong landing?" He beamed as if she'd been successful instead of a failure. "Come in, yes, all of you." He included the parents with a swish of his long, thin arm. "Let's have a look at that ankle."

The beaming evaporated when he manipulated the ankle that looked like it had engulfed a football. Now the doctor was all focused professionalism, but his kindness still seeped through as he mumbled a heartfelt *sorry* to Edda's yelp. The pain wasn't just physical. The misunderstanding hurt as much. How could she tell this cheerful doctor it wasn't a bad landing, but most likely a brush with a bad colleague?

"We'll need to take an x-ray," Doctor Geuze stated. He let go of Edda's ankle and focused the clear-blue eyes on her. Then more to the parents than to the patient, he explained, "it is a lateral malleolus fracture but I'm cautiously optimistic the broken bone isn't displaced. If that's the case, we can avoid surgery and there is a good prognosis for complete recovery. But we must ascertain my diagnosis of non-displacement first."

Doctor Geuze offered Edda another of his generous smiles. Despite the late hour, nothing seemed to erode his upbeat mood, though it had little effect on the Van der Valks. Silently, but with bad grace, they took in the news of Edda's broken bone.

"Nurse, x-ray! Now!"

The stout, white-clad matron, who had escorted them to the first-aid room, wheeled in the portable x-ray machine. Edda glanced at her mother. Everything in Edda wanted to feel her support, her compassion. The Marchioness, who'd been staring vacantly at the drawings of skeletal bones on the wall, shook herself from her stupor. Releasing one calf-skin glove from the pocket of her rabbit coat, she strutted over to her daughter and placed the gloved hand on Edda's shoulder where it rested like a dead bird.

"You'll be alright, Eddaline. You'll see." The words were probably more to console herself than Edda, who started sobbing.

"Stop crying, Eddaline. Doctor Geuze said you'll be alright. Johannes, tell her..." Olga turned her coal-dark eyes to her husband pleading in her feminine way.

"You'll be alright, Eddaline. Just listen to the doctor. Follow the orders." Her father wiped a weary hand over his broad forehead, thereby tipping the rim of his Homburg hat back and revealing the silver-threaded hair. Edda tried to stop crying, nodding weakly. All she wanted was to cry her heart out, but it was no use. The doctor handed her a paper napkin to wipe her nose and face.

"I'm so sorry to have upset your schedule, Papa," she sniffled.

"Well, never mind," he boomed, "your mother and I said to each other on the way here, it's probably all for the good. We'll take you back to Leiden and... uh... your Amsterdam life is off the charts for a while. Time to plan your future with a little more common sense and a little less artistry."

Edda cringed while her lower leg was put in the contraption and it zoomed around her ankle with an eery sound, clicking and flashing blue lights. The tears dried temporarily, but the message was clear. Just as she had foreseen. From now on, she would be imprisoned in the mansion in Leiden with no escape. Dogged gravity surrounding her on all sides. All the foreseeable future would bring her was a fight to continue her own life and not be cornered by that middle-aged lawyer.

Regardless of Duifje's remarks in her memory, the tears soon flowed again. Her mother wiped them away with her scented handkerchief, muttering an exasperated, "now, now, my child."

The chirpy doctor stepped in.

"It's indeed a non-displacement, lateral malleolus fracture. Just as I suspected. The most common type of ankle fracture, dear girl." And in a more professorial tone he added, "the lateral malleolus is the knobby bump on the outside of the ankle, here, in the lower portion of the fibula."

His words were intended to comfort and reassure Edda, but they made her only tear up more. Her brain understood she could physically dance again one day, but her heart saw her future in a blur. A life without dance, even for a short time, was no life at all.

"Get a hold on yourself, Eddaline. It is not the end of the world." Her mother squeezed her heaving shoulder, and retrieving a clean dry handkerchief, dabbed Edda's face. As she was still wearing her 'Clara' makeup, the new handkerchief was also smeared in no time.

"Why on earth do they doll up ballerinas as if they're harlots?" her mother grumbled. "It's not like you don't have distinct features of your own. Bah." She disposed of the soiled linen in the sink.

"I'm sorry," Edda apologized again, unable to explain that makeup was part of getting into the role.

"We'll also have to get you into something more decent after that cast has been placed."

It was only then that Edda realized she was still in her ballet costume. The warm blanket Miss Sterling had thrown around her shoulders after they'd helped her into her winter coat had made her forget there had been no time to change. Of course, her parents wanted her out of her last tie to the stage as quickly as possible.

She didn't miss the glance of relief her mother shared with her father. Despite all her pride and sourpuss German-ness, Olga Van der Valk-Scherzinger's first loyalty lay with her husband. What he wanted counted. She did love her daughter, even did her best to show affection to her husband's daughter from an earlier marriage, but her primary focus was her marital bond.

So, it was her father's face Edda studied. He could be such a dark horse. One moment accept her passion for dance, and later declare it an unwise folly.

Her father seemed content. "Well, that's excellent news, Doctor. Now, when can we take our coryphée home?" His skewed smile under his full brown moustache didn't solve Edda's enigma. He would not give his verdict now. Probably tomorrow.

The doctor, clearly a wise man and sensing the strange family dynamics, looked up from pasting the last layer of cast on Edda's left leg.

"What would you like, Edda? I could keep you for observation here for a night, or I could send you home and expect you to be back tomorrow for a check-up?" The blue eyes under the bushy white eyebrows communicated understanding. Edda hesitated, suspended between her two worlds, but her father made immediate mincemeat of any plan of keeping her in the hospital.

"No need, doctor. We're not talking of a serious injury here. We'll be careful and take Eddaline home. My chauffeur will drive her back for the check-up tomorrow. We can easily manage all that. But thank you for the offer."

And with that, the decision was made. Being utterly tired and shaken, Edda now only wanted to sleep. Even a strange longing, a flicker of hope that she would be coddled and pampered at home made her cave in. Say adieu to hard work and discipline. Tomorrow morning, she would have a full breakfast and sleep in.

THE CAR RIDE in the black Mercedes from Amsterdam to the stately mayor's house on the Rapenburg in Leiden was shrouded in darkness and complete silence. Edda was sitting upfront to give her leg extra space, next to Klaas Bollema, her father's chauffeur and schoolfriend from their Frisian days. Her parents were invisible in the back. Only the sound of her father sucking on his cigar and puffing out smoke, which curled over Edda's shoulder and into her nostrils, were signs they were still back there.

IT WAS LATE; it was cold. Edda wondered how it was possible that her life could have changed from sheer delight to utter misery in the space of a split second.

But for now, she just wanted to sleep. Not to think of tomorrow.

5

MOTHER AND DAUGHTER

Leiden, December 1937

There were red roses and white lilies with sprigs of delicate fern leaves on her dresser when Edda awoke the next morning. The lavish bouquet seemed out of season on the frosty December morning. Outside, the windows were covered by flowers of their own, in icy white patterns. A nipping wind rattled the wooden shutters.

Instead of leaping out of her narrow bed in her tiny Vondelstraat flat in Amsterdam to bury her nose in the scented lilies and tear open the perfumed card to see who had admired her performance, Edda frowned at the fancy bouquet. Then turned her weary self to the wall. The bouquet spilled Count Ludovicus Van Limburg Stirum's extravagant style all over. Neither now, nor ever, would her heart be interested in his middle-aged advances.

Groggy from the pain and fitful sleep, Edda squeezed her eyes shut again, hoping slumber would welcome her back into its forgetful, white arms. But sleep eluded her. Turning on her back, she took to staring at the stuccoed ceiling above her, decorated with fat-bellied cherubs with trumpets surrounded by bulging grapes on winding stems.

"You're a hideous bunch." Edda grimaced, closing her eyes so as not to stare up at their stone bodies. Her left leg throbbed and her heart ached, but a new thought took root. If she had one other interest next to dance, it was interior decoration. Though her taste was the opposite of the Venetian Renaissance that pervaded the house in Leiden. Edda loved Art déco, and sometimes a touch of the earlier Art nouveau, but nothing futuristic or bold like Dadaism or Bauhaus.

"Give me pretty," she'd say. "Colors and flowing shapes, just like in dance."

But Edda's taste wasn't that of her parents. The Van der Valk spouses were both brought up with the belief a house needed to be furnished in a solid, classical style - oak, mahogany, leather, and long drapes in dull mauve or ochre.

"I could ask Mama if she'll let me redecorate my own room," Edda pondered aloud. The last thing her mother had said before she went to sleep was, "now think of something that might take your mind off dancing and let you focus on healing, Eddy." *Eddy* was only used in the rare moments her mother was close to emotional.

Poor Mama, Edda thought, *would greatly benefit from learning to show her emotions as Miss Sterling taught her ballerinas - facial expressions, opening one's heart, breathing deeply and freely. Poor Mama!*

But her mother's suggestion to take her mind off dancing had sown a seed. Looking around the old-fashioned room with its bulky brown furniture and drab window dressings, Edda's spirit revived with the thought of bringing light and grace to the space.

She'd never really occupied this large square room before. Situated on the second floor with light filtering in from the bay windows, it had been assigned to Edda when her father was appointed Mayor of Leiden two years earlier. As it had been a personal desire of the Führer to have his Frisian friend stationed in the important Dutch town, the Van der Valks had left their family estate near Leeuwarden in a bit of a haste.

The move had coincided with the start of Edda's training with Miss Sterling in Amsterdam and her desire to live closer to the ballet school. Hence the flat in the Vondelstraat through the week, and the house on the Rapenburg in Leiden being more of a weekend place than Edda's real home.

"I'll help Mama redecorate the house, starting with this room," Edda announced to the hideous cherubs as she swung back the bedclothes. Grimacing with pain, she let her plastered foot land on the parquet floor. Though strapped tightly, the ankle was as weak as a baby's. It felt as if it would take ages to heal.

The house was silent as a tomb. During weekdays, her father left early for the town hall and her mother was still asleep or taking her breakfast in her boudoir. The servants stalled until the mistress of the house made her appearance and started handing out commands.

Edda hobbled to the window and pushed open one curtain. The chestnut tree outside her window sported barren branches with a solitary robin eyeing the sudden movement suspiciously. Though the view of the tree-lined canal with its patrician houses and regular arched bridges was attractive, it wasn't a view that made Edda's heart sing.

She already missed Mevrouw Meulenbelt, her next-door neighbor in the Vondelstraat who had a habit of cleaning the doormat every morning, but really was only looking for a chat. Life, though filled with hard work, had an easy rhythm to it in Amsterdam. A daily routine, rituals, regimen, and then the much-needed recuperation. Just the life Edda needed to calm her sensitive and overactive brain. Here she had none of that, squashed between two formidable parents who meant well but had no clue what she really needed.

A sudden flash of hope. There was a check-up in the Wilhelmina Gasthuis today. She could phone Miss Sterling and ask if Bernadette, one of the chorus dancers, could stay with her to look after her. Then start training the day the cast came off. Edda shook a weary head. It wouldn't work.

Or she could stay with Duifje and Teppo? That option was cast aside immediately. Her half-sister was alright when not in the claws of brooding hysteria or dramatic outbursts. But not the most stable person to be around during rehabilitation. And Teppo Van Leeuwen, her brother-in-law, was an odd fish. He'd once pinched her behind when his wife wasn't watching. No thank you.

Edda sighed. The most obvious option was to stay at Huis van Leyden for a week or so and opt for redecoration. It wasn't like her mother had turned the sprawling, 17th-century canal-side mansion, which had been the former city palace, into a warm and homely place yet. It was simply too big and too drafty. Confiscated by the Dutch Fascist party, the NSB, from the Roman Catholic Parish Boys schools to house their newly-elected NSB mayor, it was basically still a school building with a dorm.

Ordinary Leidenaren didn't generally share the Johannes Van der Valk's adoration for the charming, blue-eyed Führer of neighboring Germany, nor his Dutch counterpart Anton Mussert. However the residents of Leiden had had no say in the matter of who their new mayor would become, and were taken by surprise when the ungracious eviction of the Roman Catholic monks was already a fact.

Edda felt the eyes prying on her back whenever she left the stately front door. And that was only what happened outside the house. Inside Huis van Leyden, the atmosphere was even more terse. Leidenaren hadn't exactly lined up to serve the new mayor after the popular Mr Adriaan Van de Sande Bakhuyzen had been replaced by the NSB. Their new 'first citizen' and his even stauncher Nazi wife may be vocal in their support for Hitler's Germany, but the "Sleutelstad", city of the key, was as old and dignified as its first Count of Holland in 1100.

The butler, the maids, the footmen, and the garden boys were all compelled to work for Leiden's first citizen, paid a low salary, and were dismissed as soon as they showed signs of recalcitrance.

Nobody trusted the person next to him, especially because Klaas Bollema, who was as Frisian as his boss, was the one who had the whip hand and would report the slightest mishap to the Van der Valk husband-and-wife team.

The few times Edda had been home, she'd eavesdropped on the agitated whispers in the corridors - *Nazi lovers and Hitler's pet* - being the worst connotations attached to her family.

Oh, her heart yearned for her own cozy flat, away from nasty politics and conniving staff. The full scope of her imprisonment was now clear. A hostile place, her dance career on hold. Staring at the unyielding chestnut tree, her slender fingers gripping the windowsill, she felt herself slipping back to being the shy girl of her teens, her trained dance body slumped like the stem of a yielding flower in the wind, the graceful limbs drawn in like a startled beetle.

Just concentrate on redecoration. Just that.

A loud rap on the door rattled Edda's tense nerves and made her jump. Pain shot up her ankle from the sudden jerk her body made. It must be the maid.

"Come in. The door is open."

Leaping back to her bed as quickly as her injured leg would let her, she sat up and pushed some cushions behind her back. Employing what hopefully was an adequate smile on her lips, she was ready for the grumpy maid with the breakfast tray.

The dark eyebrows raised to her hairline when the Marchioness sailed in, still in her silk morning coat, looking like an oversized, Japanese geisha.

"Mother?" The smile on Edda's lips became genuine. Somehow, her mother in informal attire made her look more approachable.

"Eddaline, how are you this morning?"

There was something in the chirpiness of her mother's voice, half a scale above normal, that alarmed the daughter. After Edda had kissed the smooth forehead, her mother sat down on the eiderdown and took her daughter's fingers between her own chubby hands, which made her rings flash in the light.

"I'm fine, Mama."

"That's good to hear. But, my girl, you look so thin. Have you been skipping meals again?"

Her weight. She should have known.

"I have *not,* Mother." She replied with indignation and authority, hoping her mother would not harp on it. Edda's weight was a sensitive topic between mother and daughter. If this went on, they'd start off on the wrong foot.

The Marchioness' shoulders heaved as a sign she'd cave in for now, but only until breakfast.

"Did you get any sleep with that sore ankle?"

Letting go of Edda's hand and heaving her stout body up from the eiderdown, Olga waddled to the window. "I need to see you better, my dear. My poor eyesight is troubling me again."

What happened next made Edda chuckle inside and warm to her clumsy mother. She started making a fuss of opening the draped curtains further. A domestic task the mayor's wife clearly was not accustomed to as she pulled on the heavy cloth until they got stuck in their rails instead of using the gliders. After some impatient, unsuccessful jerks, she gave up her effort with a triumphant *voilà*!

Leaving the curtains in disarray, the Marchioness turned her dark eyes back on her daughter, studying her attentively. Edda took in her mother too, the smooth skin, high cheekbones and finely placed eyes and mouth. Bracing herself for the judgment that would surely follow, she felt again like the fifteen-year-old who'd failed her arithmetic exam at the Secondary Girls School in Leeuwarden.

Her mother's verdict over her dance mishap would be the next topic. That's how Olga Van der Valk operated. She touched the subject of her discontent lightly, then let it rest for a bit to return to it later with more force.

Edda tried to breathe into the heavy feeling that knotted her stomach, but it stuck like a ball of clay. How she hated this confusing tension that always hung between them. Love and judgment were her mother's pillars of strength. Had she not been so powerfully present in both, there would simply not have existed the Marchioness Van der Valk. Love and judgment, all meant for the best but a difficult mix, nonetheless.

"You've always had a touch of the stumbler about you, Eddaline. That clumsiness was the reason I insisted on getting you ballet lessons in the first place. Very much against your father's wish. As you know." A deep sigh followed, not without drama. Her mother sat her behind in one of the chintz chairs opposite the bed and folded her fleshy hands with the big rings in her lap. "If nothing comes of your dance career after this, dear, you can at least praise yourself that you tried. That's more than little Moni and Annabelle from the Leeuwarden ballet school can pride themselv..."

"Mama, please. Don't compare me to my friends from kindergarten. Moni and Annabelle never sought a career in dance. My life is so..." This time her mother interrupted *her*. Edda's cheeks turned red with indignation. The Marchioness shook her head.

"A career, my dear? Is that what you call it? It must be that Miss Sterling who got those ideas in your head."

"No, it wasn't her, Mother, and you know it." Edda sat straighter in her bed, her eyes ablaze. "It's not like we haven't had this discussion before. I'm fine with the fact Papa and you don't understand me, but please..." Edda fell silent at the expression on her mother's face. The lethal mixture. It turned all Edda's words into wax, seeped the life out of her.

"Eddaline, my dear. We love to see you dance. It's not that, and you know it. After all the battles I went through over your dancing with your Papa, he was so intensely proud of you last night. We don't want to take dance away from you. Ever. You can do your dancing all your life if you want, just don't call it a career. A woman's career is in the house."

Edda let her head hang. For a moment she felt like a clumsy duckling ready to be dragged to the altar, just as her mother wanted to see her. Maybe she was right. Maybe her life had been but a dream. Like Clara's dream of the Nutcracker. Clumsy, shy Edda, pretending to be a brilliant ballerina.

But no! She wouldn't cave in, not after dedicating all her sweat and tears to ballet. Edda gazed straight into her mother's eyes, knowing the next tool in her toolbox as if she was a carpenter of the soul.

"My dear, I really don't understand why you are so *stubborn*, deciding on your so-called *career* in dance with *your* type of locomo-tive. Now, let this tripping over your own feet be a lesson not to hanker after the unattainable..."

There it was... stubborn. Stubborn stuck as an ugly signboard to Edda's personality. Stubborn was her mother's most done-out-of-love attack on that *horrible* trait in both her husband and her daughter. The blemish of their Frisian roots.

"I am not *stubborn,* and I am not clumsy! I didn't trip over my own foot; it was Maria Petrova who stepped on my foot out of spite."

"Eddaline, watch your tone!" Her mother's brows knitted as a sign she was about to match her daughter's fury, but Edda couldn't help herself anymore. She needed her mother's respect. Desperately. And she needed to defend herself, rid herself of her mother's labels. She'd accepted these unfair, untrue labels for too long. It was as if Miss Sterling's voice whispered in her ear.

You're gracefulness embodied, Edda Van der Valk. Now show yourself. Less docility, more pride.

Edda's eyes still glared with indignation at her mother. The Marchioness exercised her distinctive huffing sound. Raising from her chair, the hands dramatically in the air, she proclaimed.

"Well, if you know better, my dear, I rest my case. I just want the best for you. I simply hope this dream of yours will not fall apart, as you seem to be so set on it. Now, breakfast." The affectionate kiss placed on Edda's forehead was still riddled with contradiction. Break-fast would be their next fight, but for now, the kiss sealed a temporary truce.

"Yes, Mama. And sorry for raising my voice to you. I shouldn't have."

"There, there," her mother patted the dark curls as if Edda was still three years old and had just had a tantrum. "You've always been a bit of a fire-and-ice girl. My side of the family." The smug smile revealed the Marchioness' approval of a bit of a fiery personality, of which she seemed to think herself a good example.

Edda watched her mother walk to the door, the silk Japanese kimono with the large cranes swishing around her voluminous hips.

"I love you, Mama."

"I'll meet you for breakfast." It wasn't exactly a threat. "And I love you, too."

6

THE SISTER

"Alas, no dance for at least six weeks, Miss Van der Valk." Doctor Geuze studied the new x-ray the nurse handed him. He raised his celestial blue eyes to her in sympathy. "I'm so sorry you'll have to interrupt all your performances with the Amsterdam Ballet Theater for a couple of months, but I suppose you expected so much after last night?"

Edda nodded. She was sitting on the examination table in the white room with a small window overlooking the hospital's winter courtyard. Her dark eyes sought those of the compassionate physician.

"And after the couple of months?" she asked hopeful.

"Eddaline, focus on your healing first. The future will come soon enough." That was her mother, practical and interfering.

"I'd say six months with little exertion after the cast comes off. Ankle fractures are tricky and - if not given the time to heal properly - could cause problems for the rest of your career." The white-haired doctor remained unperturbed under the Marchioness's huffing and puffing on his use of the word *career*. His gentle gaze rested on his patient as his hands examined her other ankle and the muscular lower leg.

"You'll dance again, Miss Van der Valk. You were made to dance. I've never seen a pair of legs so well-muscled and healthy. With such a fine constitution and passion for your profession, I'd say there's no doubt you'll be able to shine on the stage again. Provided you follow *my advice* to recuperate well from this fracture." There was renewed huffing from Mrs Van der Valk at the doctor stressing the words *my advice*. She no doubt thought that was *her* job.

"So, it's rather good news, then?" Edda did her best to replicate Doctor Geuze's optimism and disregard her mother's huffing. Her mind feverishly sought for a way to shoulder the bleak couple of months ahead. No dance. Such a long stretch without the bar, without *plier, étendre, glisser, relever, sauter, tourner, élancer.* That hadn't been on the cards for over fifteen years. How she would miss it all and long for Miss Sterling's royal French when it came to ballet.

"Consider it good news, Miss," the doctor affirmed, "I'm convinced you still have a dazzling career ahead of you. You're still young. Best accept injuries as part of the world of physical professions. It happens to the best, and the best athletes always come back stronger afterwards."

Then, turning to her mother, he wisely included her in the plans. "I'd like to see your daughter back in four weeks, Marchioness Van der Valk. Please make sure Miss Edda doesn't become a wilting flower. Keep her mind occupied, now her body must rest. She needs an outlet for her burgeoning vitality. Go on a trip together, find her a new hobby."

"My husband and I will do everything to get Eddaline back to fine form," Mrs Van der Valk beamed, happy to be tasked with responsibility for Edda's wellbeing by the kindly doctor. "We'll also make sure she can socialize more. With her strict dance routine, Eddaline has greatly neglected her social life."

Edda cringed. *Oh no.* That meant being dragged to her mother's tea parties and soirées where no doubt Van Limburg Stirum would make a so-called surprise appearance.

"I'd rather travel with you, Mama. Maybe we can go to Switzerland? Visit that place in Lausanne you always talk about? That special school you went to as a debutante and liked so much?"

"We could." The Marchioness tilted her coiffed head with pursed lips, a sign she didn't want to contradict her daughter in front of the doctor.

Edda hopped off the examination table on her good foot and leaned on her crutches as Doctor Geuze scribbled something on his prescription notepad. She assumed it was a recipe for painkillers, but as he tore off the tiny sheet, he folded it in four and pressed it into her palm.

"Here. Read this when you feel you've reached your lowest ebb. It's my favorite quote. See you in four weeks, Miss Van der Valk."

Stuffing the paper in the pocket of her duffel coat, Edda hobbled out of the doctor's office room into the hospital corridor filled with busy nurses and bewildered patients. Her mother was silent as a tomb at her side.

What now?

Hopping on one leg among these rushed strangers, Edda felt as if it were her last moments in freedom. There was no way she could ask Mama to let her stay in her flat by herself. No, they would only pass by the flat to pick up clothes and toiletry items.

Klaas Bollema, their chauffeur, stood waiting for them next to the two-toned gray Mercedes. Six feet tall with a wide-legged stance, and stolid, his sand-blonde quiff as an almost boyish attribute on his broad, middle-aged head. The man never failed to send a shiver up Edda's spine.

Invariably clad in a calf-length black leather coat and black boots, while proudly sporting the NSB insignia - the red and black upturned triangle with the golden lion - the Frisian son of a grocer, made no secret of his political stance. A stance passionately shared by his employers, but unnerving to Edda.

Her mother seemed to notice Edda's hesitation about getting into the car.

"Come on, dear. I have a plan that will cheer you up. We'll go shopping for new clothes together with Duifje. No need to pass by your flat and make you miserable again. How about that?"

Edda was of two minds. She longed to see her flat, but this time her mother could be right. Not visiting her own little place may make her pine for it less. And she'd enjoyed the clothes' shopping sprees with her fashionable and generous Mama in the past. However, go with Duifje? There was always drama there and Edda's two older female relatives never seemed able to execute a solid plan together. It invariably ended in chaos and commotion.

"But I can't walk without crutches, and not very well with them. How on earth can we go shopping?" A fresh problem arose.

"Duifje can push your wheelchair. I'll push Benny in his stroller." Her mother had it all worked out.

"What wheelchair?" Edda looked doubtful.

"It's all arranged, Miss. The wheelchair is in the boot. Picked it up from the hospital," Klaas's booming voice sounded from the front seat. They all seemed to share in the conspiracy around her now. It was puzzling. Where did her mother's sudden urge to drag her step-daughter into her plans stem from? They hadn't the warmest of bonds, though Edda liked Duifje on her good days.

"Take us to The Hague, Klaas. We want to visit Duifje."

Klaas turned his broad head to give the Marchioness a grin. It wasn't exactly impolite, but it certainly wasn't the kind of smile an employee gave to his employer, and Edda wondered again what was going on.

"Rightio, Ma'am." And the gray Mercedes drove off, the engine roaring like a minor flying machine. Edda and her mother settled in the leather upholstery on the back seat. She closed her eyes, weary and bewildered, and was asleep within seconds.

She woke when the car came to a halt with a sudden jolt and her left leg twitched.

"Ouch!"

"Careful, Klaas." Her mother said sharply. Edda rubbed the skin above the cast. Klaas always boasted he was an excellent driver, but he was far from it. Why her father put up with this chauffeuring style, she didn't understand. The man's driving was as boorish as his personality.

Edda gazed out of the car window. Duifje and Teppo's residence was a semi-detached, thatched-roofed house on the leafy side of The Hague's middle-class neighborhood of Bezuidenhout, close to the Haagse Bos. A much more modest abode than the *Valkena Estate* on the outskirts of Leeuwarden, where the half-sisters had spent their childhood. Duifje had given up most of her high-class status on marrying hardware son Teppo Van Leeuwen, whose family owned three stores in The Hague.

In late December, the stately oak trees on the Laan van Nieuw-Oost Indië were barren, their branches sticking to the sky like thin ballerina arms. A mother, or nanny, scurried past on the sidewalk, pushing a black pram that danced on its springs against the chilly wind. For the rest, the street was deserted. Some modest family cars stood parked under the trees, older Ford models, the occasional Peugeot or Fiat.

Klaas braked one more time and brought the luxurious Mercedes 230 to a hiccupy stop in front of number 10. Edda noticed with relief that the Van Leeuwen's 1934 Renault Monaquatre wasn't in front of their house. Her brother-in-law must be at the shop.

"Maybe they're not home?" she observed.

"Of course, Duifje's home. Why wouldn't she be? She was already suffering from one of those mysterious migraines when she came to your performance last night. Teppo had to come and fetch her in the break. She'll be in bed today. It always takes her three days to recover from those attacks."

From the cutting way the words came out of her mother's mouth, Edda knew she didn't believe one iota of Duifje's ailments. And that's why they were here. To make short work of her step-daughter's phantom illness.

"Well, let's ring that bell and find out the current state of affairs." The Marchioness waited for Klaas to open the car door for her. Then he stood as if standing to attention, awaiting further instructions.

"Unload the wheelchair and leave it at the door. And, pick us up here at six, Klaas. We'll take a taxi to get to the center from here."

"Very well, Ma'am."

Edda had to open her own door and hobbled behind her mother, who was pushing against the rickety front garden fence with a dismayed look. The shutters were down, which gave the house a forlorn look, but her mother wasn't disconcerted. She rang the bell firmly. The repetition of its clinging down the hallway sounded like the echo in an empty cave. They waited, Edda hopping on her one good foot while leaning on her crutches. Nothing moved or stirred inside.

"Let's go."

Edda wanted to rest, not being dragged around town with an unwilling sister.

"Hush… I hear something." Her mother put her ear to the door.

There was a shuffling of approaching footsteps. The latch was unbolted. The veneered mahogany door swung open. Duifje's only servant, a rather worn-out looking girl called Corrie stuck one bluish-grey eye around the corner of the door. On seeing the visitors were her mistress's next of kin, she opened the door wider. The young maid looked exhausted. Juggling the roles of housekeeper, nurse-maid, and confidante to the demanding Mrs Van Leeuwen was clearly too much for the eighteen-year-old girl.

"Yes?" She tried a wan smile.

"For heaven's sake, Corrie, let us in. We've been standing here in the freezing cold like a pair of beggars. Eddaline has a broken foot, and she needs to sit down *tout de suite*." Without further ado, the Marchioness pushed the frazzled maid aside and pulled Edda with her into the cold, tiled hallway.

"Is Mrs Van Leeuwen at home?"

"She is, Ma'am, but the missus is resting after a bad bout of migraine yesterday. And Benny's asleep."

"Well, we need to come in anyway and direly need a hot cup of tea. We've just come from the hospital in Amsterdam. Some lunch would be great as well. Thank you."

Edda felt positively embarrassed as her mother marched unannounced through the hallway towards the Van Leeuwen's front sitting room. Her rabbit-fur coat sailed behind her like a Viking ready to raid Britannia.

Corrie still stood in the doorway, clearly torn between the orders of two captains. Edda was sure Duifje had instructed the poor thing not to let anyone in. With pursed lips, Corrie said in a low voice. "I will do as you ask, Ma'am, but please be as quiet as possible. Benny wakes at the slightest sound and then he's grumpy and refuses to eat his lunch."

The Marchioness made her particular huffing sound before disappearing into the sitting room. Flinging the coat over a chair, she installed herself on the sagging beige sofa that protested under her weight. It was an odd sight, the great madam on a sofa she clearly despised, still wearing her hat and gloves as if expecting germs to crawl over her anytime.

Edda had followed her mother inside. *What else could she do?* She sat down on a straight-backed chair at the table that was missing one cross-leg support. Her leg throbbed. Her mouth was dry. Her head pounded with a hammering headache.

When physically unwell or gripped by nerves, deep breathe into your belly. It will still the system.

Miss Sterling's instructions. Edda tried to force her breath down, but it remained shallow and refused to pass her midriff. She looked around the room, her ears finding the silence in the house eerie.

Pale northern light filtered through the gauze curtains in the floor-to-ceiling bay windows and bathed the room in a soft mauve, even on this gray winter day. What the room needed was a sprawling sea-blue sofa with matching chairs, a warm Persian carpet on the parquet floor, a couple of colorful art déco lamps, and a bookcase with rows of brown leather volumes. Edda visualized the space around her as if she'd already redecorated it.

Instead, it held a mismatch of furniture, some stained, all chipped. The fireplace looked as if it hadn't had a good cleaning for a while. In the middle stood the most monstrous eyesore of it all; a chubby-looking table littered with magazines and unemptied ashtrays.

The silence didn't hold. Benny's wailing voice sounded from the upstairs landing. The walls of the Bezuidenhout semi-detached were paper-thin. Seconds later, Duifje's throaty voice called from the upstairs bedroom, "Corrie, where are you? See to Benny."

Her mother got up from the sofa with difficulty and went over to the sideboard. After filling two glasses with water from the crystal carafe, she handed one to Edda.

"Doesn't look like we're going to be fed any time soon." With a grimace that showed her discontent, she rummaged in her pocket coat and retrieved a minuscule tin that held two coconut macaroons.

"Always be prepared for the worst," the Marchioness instructed her daughter. "It may not seem ladylike, but a good pair of pockets in your coat or dress go a long way."

Mother and daughter nibbled on the sweet treat in silence, and Edda was grateful for her mother's foresight. Though she was seldom hungry because of her strict regime, she was weak with emptiness now. Her diet could be loosened a little now she couldn't dance. Whether that was a good or a bad thing, she had no time to consider as the sitting-room door flung open.

Duifje, dressed in an old-fashioned dressing gown around her sylphlike frame, a cigarette in one hand and a wet sponge in the other, came hurrying into the room. Corrie's footsteps could be heard speeding upstairs towards the loudly lamenting Benny.

"Mother? Edda? What are you doing here?" Duifje seemed more surprised than sick, the blue eyes and wavy blonde hair so very much like their father.

Having never met Duifje's biological mother, who'd deserted her first husband to elope with an American steel magnate and presumably lived in New York, Edda had no clue if Duifje looked anything like her own mother. No photographs or memories were shared about the estranged, first Mrs Van der Valk and Duifje never mentioned her. She'd been only three at the time and Olga

Scherzinger had come into Johannes Van der Valk's life when Duifje was five.

Only in appearance was Duifje totally her father's daughter. The mood swings were attributed to that other woman. Duifje's stern blue eyes took in the two women in her sitting room. The Marchioness rose to the occasion.

"Fie Duifje, do we have to give a reason for visiting you? We're your next of kin."

"But I saw you only yesterday at Edda's performance, Mother. Remember, I came despite being ill?"

Duifje never called her stepmother Mama like Edda did. The battle of affection for the stepparent clouded her sister's face, that robust face with the distinctive Van der Valk features. Caught in the middle of the wrangling between the two forceful women, Edda needed to intervene. Which wasn't the first time. Rising unsteadily, she went over to her tall sister and hugged her, ashes spraying all over her dress. Duifje reacted as Edda had hoped.

"Lientje, I'm so sorry."

Her older sister using her pet name for her broke Edda's last reserve and while still being hugged against the bony body in its silk wrappings, she burst out in tears. Duifje patted her back affectionately.

"You'll dance again, Cry Baby. Mark my words."

"Don't give her ideas, Duifje." Their mother's voice said behind them, but Edda clung to the warm body of her sister and to hope. Duifje smelled of tobacco and bedclothes and baby soap. Not unpleasant, just not how she had smelled when they were young.

A flash of them close together in the toy wigwam at the back of the Valkena Estate, eating the fruit drops Duifje had stolen from the kitchen. Back then, Duifje had smelled of fresh air and washed hair and a smell so unique to her that Edda had no words for it, so she'd called it love. She clung to that vague love now.

"Get dressed, Duifje, and ask Corrie to prepare us a bite of lunch. Get Benny ready as well. We're going shopping." That was the Marchioness's form of love and one that would work like a spell on

Duifje. Edda cared little for clothes, used to always wearing her ballet outfits. She sometimes even forgot to change into regular clothes after a long day of practice.

"Shopping, Mother? Really?" Duifje let Edda slip from her embrace but kept an arm around her sister's shoulder. Duifje was taller, more outspoken, the leader. All signs of migraine seemed to have evaporated from her on the word 'shopping', just as strong sunlight burns away a morning fog.

The Marchioness looked annoyed. "Yes, but only if you get going. That child is screaming his head off and our stomachs are rumbling."

Duifje let go of Edda, who dried her tears on her sleeve.

"Shall I help Corrie in the kitchen, while you see to Benny?" She asked, grateful to her sister for her inconsistent affection.

"You'll do no such thing," their mother quipped, "Corrie is perfectly capable of making us some sandwiches and Duifje can mother her son."

"Don't bite my head off," Duifje remarked as she hastened from the room to get dressed and comfort her little son.

"Auntie Edda!" Benny ran into the room in an adorable mini sailor suit, all chubby legs and gurgling smiles. Edda sank on her hunches, ignoring the pain in her foot. Benny flung himself straight into her open-stretched arms.

The Marchioness immediately started making her particular huffing sound as a sign the young lad lacked the manners to greet his grandmother first. But Edda didn't care who was first or why. She clasped the small boy in her muscular arms, kissing the wisp of blonde hair that had been combed into one curl on top of his head. Her three-year-old nephew snuggled against her like a puppy, the sweet, open face with the protruding elf ears firmly against her chest.

"Auntie Edda read story."

Duifje had not wasted a second slipping into a comfortable merino dress, her blonde hair in a simple high ponytail. She rushed back into the room, skipping on one foot to attach the leather strap of her other high-heeled pump.

"No time for a story, hun. We're going to have lunch and then go in the stroller with grandmama." Duifje plucked Benny from Edda's lap. After letting him brush his lips against his grandmother's cheek, she placed him in his highchair at the cluttered dining table, a burning cigarette balancing between her pale lips. A practiced "Corrieeeee" was yelled through pursed lips.

Benny gazed with marble-sized eyes from his mother to the visitors and cooed, "stoller." Duifje took the cigarette long enough from her mouth to pop two aspirins on her tongue, which she gulped down with some water. The Marchioness made a neat stack of the ladies' magazines on the table and sat down next to Benny. Edda took the other seat, pushing aside an ashtray and a disarray of toy cars.

A car rumbled into the driveway. The front gate creaked.

"Papa!" Benny was the first to react.

The women at the table each reacted differently to the unexpected interruption. The Marchioness looked annoyed, Duifje looked pleased, and Edda stiffened. She knew her mother's discontent was prompted more by the hold-up of her plans, than a dislike of her son-in-law. Teppo van Leeuwen would dominate, and hold spellbound, the household for at least an hour and a half during his lunchtime.

Duifje sat up straighter, straightened her ponytail, and lit another cigarette.

Teppo van Leeuwen sauntered into the disorderly sitting room as if entering a Broadway stage. Benny cheered; his wife gazed at him adoringly. Edda understood but didn't share her sister's infatuation with the dashing Teppo. He *was* handsome; he was jovial; he was big fun to be around. But it was always and everywhere all about Teppo.

Benny stretched out his arms and against dinner rules, Teppo swung his son out of his highchair and around in the air. Still with his son dancing in his arms, he bent down to kiss his wife full on the mouth. The Marchioness huffed.

"Mother," he greeted his mother-in-law with smiling eyes, but didn't shake her hand or kiss her. Edda got a brotherly nudge with his elbow. "Ah! All my favorite family are together at my house. What a lucky man I am. I was on my way to the store on the Grote Markt when I thought: 'turn around Teppo, and surprise Mama and the boy.' I'm just dropping by for lunch."

"How delightful," Duifje crooned. "Put Benny down in his chair, darling. Corrie will bring the lunch in soon. I'm afraid it's simple sandwiches. We didn't expect you to...,".

"Sandwiches? And here's me craving lamb chops in gravy all morning."

Teppo slouched his long frame in the last empty chair at the table to pout like a child. Benny immediately followed his father's example and, smashing his spoon on his highchair, cried, "lam tops, lam tops!"

Duifje looked stricken. "Maybe Corrie's got some leftovers from yesterday," she said hesitantly and howled like before, "Corrieeeee!"

"We were supposed to go shopping," the Marchioness stated in a clipped voice. "A simple lunch will be so much easier."

Teppo waved his long arm through the air, as if dismissing a staff of ten. His mercurial expressions changed again and, looking through a lock of his raven black hair, he let the sherry-brown eyes dance from his wife to his mother-in-law.

"I won't be the one holding you up, dear Mutterchen. I can dash out the door and have a lonely lunch at Hotel De Zwaan."

"Don't be silly, dear," Duifje and the Marchioness said in one voice but with a different intonation. Edda was annoyed. Exactly as she'd expected, happened. Vague plans leading to nothing. Why was everything always chaos with her family? The long years of discipline and action–one, two, three and dance!–had instilled a dislike of looseness in Edda. She'd almost forgotten how every Van der Valk plan seemed to dissipate before it could materialize. Her father, more a do-er like Edda, withdrew into his work to prevent being delayed by up-in-the-air initiatives and floating proposals.

Corrie, flustered and long-faced, ran into the room with a plate of jumbled-together sandwiches.

"What's the matter, Ma'am? I've only got two hands."

"Mr Van Leeuwen wants lamb chops, Corrie," Duifje said unperturbed. "That's why he came home for lunch."

The audacity, Edda thought, but she'd underestimated Corrie.

"I haven't had time for grocery shopping yet, Mr Van Leeuwen. I'm sorry. I can warm some of yesterday's stew for you?" The maid's black eyes held a mixture of disdain and fear. She clearly needed the job but was at the end of her tethers.

"Never mind, Corrie, I'll grab lunch on my way to the shop. Just bring me a cup of coffee. Strong and black." Teppo lit one of his wife's cigarettes and flung the golden lighter on the table with a bang. He put his other arm around the back of Duifje's chair and caressed her hair.

"Alright, Sir."

The plate with unappetizing sandwiches landed on a cleared spot in the middle of the table. Serviettes were handed out instead of plates. Much huffing went on from the Marchioness's side. Edda had lost her appetite entirely and longed to be out of the stuffy house, away from this unrestrained lot.

Her mother was visibly fuming, possibly also angry at herself for making the detour to the Van Leeuwens'. *But you're part and parcel of this inoperable excursion*, Edda wanted to tell her. Hadn't her mother decided on a whim she wanted to go shopping in The Hague? She knew, too, there was always some sort of drama brewing at Duifje's. It was the same-old-same-old.

And we're not done yet. She was sure of it. So she braced herself for what was yet to come. The disappointment of missing out on his yearned-for homemade lunch was spreading over Teppo's handsome features.

Through the smoke, she felt his intense eyes on her, and she shifted uneasily in her chair. Here we go again. The young gazelle and the hungry tiger who kept caressing his wife's back in a sensual manner. Duifje stretched against his hand like a cat in ecstasy. Corrie exited the room. The Marchioness stared at the pile of sandwiches in disgust. There was a weird tension in the room, as if the planets wanted to break free from their orbits. Benny broke into a piteous wail.

"I'm hungry!"

Duifje broke the uncomfortable spell with her usual blow-hot-blow-cold.

"Let's pack it all up and have lunch at Het Verre Oosten on the Laan van Meerdervoort. I've been wanting to try Chinese food since it opened. Must be so exotic!"

Teppo looked sour. He wasn't ready to let go of hope for the taste of tender lamb chops on his palate yet. The Marchioness waved an impatient hand. "What about our plans to go shopping? Edda needs new things."

"Never mind me," Edda retorted quickly. Getting out of the house and to a restaurant, where they would be surrounded by other people–she didn't dare to think 'normal' people - felt like an excellent alternative. At least a lot better than sitting in a wheelchair and being pushed around from shop to shop with two indecisive women and a toddler.

"Will they have anything for Benny? We can't possibly feed the boy spicy rice?" Teppo observed.

"Spicy wice," Benny echoed.

Teppo's reservations were waved aside. Nothing could stop Duifje now. Forgotten were the withering sandwiches and all of Corrie's work. Duifje was all movement and excitement now, raising from her migraine and chagrin like a phoenix from the ashes.

Throwing her arms in the air, she chirped, "the Chinese for sure will have some sort of sherbet for Benny. Don't worry, honey. You're always so sweet to think of these things. Makes me feel like an awful mother! Are you coming, Mother, Lientje?"

This time, Edda answered for her mother. "Sure, we're coming." Though she didn't share her sister's enthusiasm for putting foreign food to the test, her dancer's body needed nourishment, and she knew her mother needed to be helped out of her rut as well.

They all crammed into the Van Leeuwen's old Renault. The Marchioness in the front with the plume of her hat cracking against the car roof. Duifje and Edda were wedged in the back with Benny on his mother's lap and Edda's crutches at their feet, the wheelchair abandoned on the front steps because it wouldn't fit in the trunk.

It was a wild ride. Like most events in her sister's life, it was swivel-eyed and screw-loose. Klaas may be a bad driver, but Teppo was a good driver who took risks he shouldn't. According to Teppo van Leeuwen's laws, he always had the right of way and if not given it, he would take it. He was the kind of man that took when he shouldn't.

The Marchioness's huffing turned into soft moaning. Duifje and Benny enjoyed the ride as if they were seated on a merry-go-round. Edda just prayed she wouldn't break her other leg as well. Drawing in a deep breath, she vowed to herself.

I'm going to Switzerland on my own. I need to sort out my life away from dancing and away from this family. And I refuse to be trapped in a complicated marriage like Mama or Duifje.

The decision was made. Edda's head was crystal clear, while her leg throbbed with every corner that Teppo took, and the trees on the Laan van Meerdervoort whooshed past. It would simply be a matter of getting Doctor Geuze's mandate for treatment in Lausanne and her parents' blessing.

You're always a bit of a loner in your dance, Edda, in the group but not of the group. The role suits you. Explore it until you meet your match.

Why did she suddenly remember one of the first things Miss Sterling had said to her when she started practising with her at age eighteen? She'd shrugged it off. She wanted to be a team player, not a loner. It had sounded like an ugly word, but now, exiled from her daily routine, she saw what Miss Sterling had meant. Even as a little girl, she'd felt the observer of her family and longed for a way out of their labyrinth of love and lather.

Edda sighed as the Renault came to a screeching halt in front of a huge, red building with golden ornaments and Chinese lettering. The motor purred, then hiccupped to a stop. Elation and dissatisfaction struggled for prominence with the car passengers.

With a family like this, nothing would ever be easy in Edda's life. But without them? She had no clue.

7

SWITZERLAND IT IS

A couple weeks later - Leiden, January 1938

Christmas came and went. Then, 1938 started with a bitter cold and uninviting January. None of Edda's plans to help her mother redecorate Huis van Leyden unfolded. Life had become way too slow for the cooped-up dancer, uninspiring and dull, though there was plenty of activity at the mayor's mansion.

High-ranking German officials came and went, the heels of their black boots clicking on the tiled entrance floor. Coarse, guttural voices bellowed *Frohe Weihnachten* and a slim week later, *Glückliches neues Jahr.*

The German tongue was nothing new to Edda. She spoke the language fluently thanks to her summer holidays at her grandparents' Schloss in East-Prussia, but she didn't share her parents' ardour for the Germanic languages like German and Dutch.

The escape into English with Miss Sterling and French with Mr Sergeyev had freed not just Edda's tongue but also her emotions in the past two years. She doted on Miss Sterling's posh English and Monsieur Sergeyev's romantic French.

Sitting in the windowsill of the canal mansion, her eyes followed the Dutch citizens with their collars up and shoulders bent as they went about their chores. Most of them increased their pace as they passed Huis van Leyden and no one's eyes glanced up at the Germans bustling around their Mercedes and Volkswagens.

Only a handful of passers-by stopped to take a longer look at the gleaming automobiles and uniforms. Some even accepted the Sturm Zigaretten that the Germans handed around. Edda knew, because she already knew too much about German politics, that those cigarettes were intended to fund the Nazi Party's Sturmabteilung. The more the Dutch enjoyed these cigarettes, the more money the SA would gather for their political messages. And they seemed all too keen to get in touch with the Leiden citizens and invite them for a chat.

Edda shivered in her woolen cardigan, while her long slender arms lay wrapped around bare pointed knees, with both her good leg and injured ankle tucked into leg warmers instead of her normal ballet tights. To her, it felt like her family were pariahs instead of Leiden's first family. To distract herself from that gruesome train of thought, she returned to reveries around her love for the sound of languages.

"I love French best of all," she told the people below who couldn't and wouldn't hear her. The window steamed up as she continued her monologue, but she cleared the view with her elbow. They may not want to see her, she wanted to see them. "French is so soft and has rhythm, like a poem or a song or a dance. German sounds like dry words on paper. Ugly words. And Dutch? It sounds harsh and grating, like people are always raising their voice."

Her unwilling audience seemed unimpressed, so she added, "you should really listen to the sound of French, the way they say their vowels. It's perfection incorporated. But you have to pronounce those vowels without fail, or French isn't French. *Je vais demander au Docteur Geuze de me donner permission d'aller en Suisse.*" Mimicking Monsieur Sergevey's perfect French, who—though a Russian—had lived many years in Paris and had musical ears and thus a knack for sound. Edda sighed. She hadn't managed 'perfection incorporated.' She needed to practice and for a moment doubted whether she shouldn't go to Paris instead of Switzerland, where the French wouldn't be as perfect as she desired.

But she shrugged off that idea. Her mother had talked with ardor about that fine finishing school in Switzerland and Edda craved the Alps, fresh air and nature. For once, being away from trauma and hard work. No, Switzerland would be perfect, whether their French was perfect or not.

"Eddaline!"

A firm rap landed on her bedroom door. Edda checked her wristwatch. She'd only come up to collect her shawl and thirty minutes had passed. Time to get ready for the dreaded car ride with Klaas to the Wilhelmina Gasthuis. Without enthusiasm, Edda slipped from the windowsill and accidentally landed on her left foot. She checked again. No pain. She balanced on her injured leg, stood shakily, but stood nonetheless, dividing her weight equally over both legs. *Halleluiah.*

"Eddaline!" The door handle rattled. Then she remembered bolting it in case one of the German visitors—most of whom stayed in the other bedrooms on her floor—would blunder into her room.

"Coming!" she called and walked to the door. No dance steps yet, but she could walk on two legs to the door with only a slight help of her crutches.

"What's taking you so long? The Mercedes has been waiting for ten minutes. Your father needs the car this afternoon." Her mother, dressed to the nines because of her important countrymen around her, her dark hair styled, a cameo brooch pinned on her voluminous breast - even a dash of coral lipstick—gazed at her daughter with a puzzled look. Edda never idled; she wasn't like Duifje.

"Nothing important, Mother. I think I simply dread going to the hospital. But look, I can stand on my foot." Her mother's eyes softened, then took on an air of dissolution, slight bewilderment.

"I wish I could come with you, dear, but..."

"... the wives of the Nazi officials are coming to lunch. I know, Mama, don't worry. I can handle Doctor Geuze on my own."

"Can you, dear? I could ask Papa...?"

"No need, Mama. Really. It's alright. I'm healing well, so I'm ready for Doctor Geuze's verdict."

She kissed her mother's cheek as she passed her in the door, while pulling her warm shawl around her shoulders.

"You're so accomplished, Eddaline. I'm proud of you. Don't forget you're supposed to give *acte de presence* this afternoon as well." The presence of her countrymen around her clearly made her mother in a good mood, softer and more approving.

"I'll try to be on time, Mother. But don't count on me."

"But Eddaline...," her mother called after her as she descended the stairs. She was still holding onto the banister but already testing the strength of her left leg and foot. Her mother didn't continue, so she turned around and looked up at her.

"Pray tell, Mother."

"No, nothing, or you won't come at all."

"Now you have me thinking you're expecting someone I don't want to see?" Edda's mood couldn't be squashed anymore now she felt her old self returning.

"Maybe. Take care, my dear. I can't wait to hear what the doctor has to say."

"I know what he'll say, Mama. It will be Switzerland for me. Mark my words."

"Switzerland?" The bewilderment was back in the Marchioness's dark eyes, and she repeated with hesitance, "Switzerland wasn't on the cards, was it?"

"It is. First and foremost, dear Mama. Now, go take care of your guests."

Edda zipped out of the door and felt better than she'd done in weeks. Even passing by all these menacing, black-clad Nazis was a breeze. And she wouldn't let Klaas bring down her mood, either. As she hopped in the backseat of the Mercedes, she ignored his growl "been waiting for fifteen minutes" and greeted him with a chirpy, "*Bonjour Klaas, comment-allez vous aujourd'hui?*" Deciding she would practice speaking French *tout de suite*.

The blonde Frisian looked at her as if she'd lost her marbles.

Closing the door for her and stuffing his heavy-set body behind the steering wheel, muttered a "I don't understand that sissy language."

"*Ach so.*" Edda replied in German, letting the irony roll off her tongue. After that, they continued the forty-minute ride to Amsterdam in silence, but it wasn't a silence that worked on her nerves. Soon there would be action, and forward action was all Edda craved. *Sauté, battement, demi-detourné echappé.* She closed her eyes, and in her mind, made all the movements. How she craved them, but above all echappé. To escape. Literally.

"WELL, well, have I never! I don't know what I'm seeing. The new bone structure seems to have grown faster than lightning. I don't think I've seen anything like this in the decades I've been studying fractures of the lower limbs. You're a miracle, Miss Van der Valk. Such capacity for rapid healing. Well done!" Doctor Geuze raised his eyes from studying the new X-Ray and let the azure-blue gaze rest on Edda, a warm smile spreading over his aging face.

Edda smiled too, then giggled.

"I'm not aware I've done anything, doctor."

"Oh, but you have, dear girl! You've dedicated many years of your life to building the body of an athlete. That pays off in your healing now. I suggest we take off this heavy cast right now and continue with a much lighter one. You may also cautiously–I stress *cautiously*–start putting a tiny bit of weight on your left leg." The wrinkles in the outer corners of the penetrating gaze deepened.

It was as if Atlas' weight was lifted from Edda's shoulders, and her ankle felt as if the new cast was already in place. She was healing. She would dance again. One day soon.

"Would I be able to go to Switzerland with the new cast?"

"Switzerland? That's the first I'm hearing of Switzerland." The doctor raised bewildered white eyebrows. "I don't think we're heading for war that fast, my dear. It's all just big talk by stupid politicians. No need to flee to a neutral country like Switzerland. And who knows, we might ride out our own neutral state here this time too, should it come to war."

"Oh no, it's not that Doctor Geuze!"

But before she could explain her vision of the Alps and healing time, he waved his white-coated arms.

"Apologies, Miss Van der Valk. I spoke without thinking. This is my predicament. I have so many Jewish friends and colleagues who currently feel unsure about their future in Holland, as we border Germany." The old physician sighed, and Edda could sense the length of his worries. "I just heard this morning I'm going to lose my right-hand man here at the hospital. Doctor Samuels is emigrating to New York with his family. He has been my co-worker at the Wilhelmina Gasthuis for thirty-seven years. Thirty-seven years! And a capital doctor. Impossible to replace."

"I'm sorry." It came out no more than a mumble.

The blue gaze rested on Edda, and she shrank under it. Did Doctor Geuze accuse *her* of losing his colleague? Was he referring to people like her parents who enabled Hitler's anti-Semitism in the Netherlands? For sure, he knew her father got his position as mayor of Leiden because he was a prominent member of the NSB. Anton Mussert's close, personal friend. She cleared her throat.

"I hold no political views, Doctor Geuze. And I'm not fleeing the country." A stolid block of resentment rose in her throat, making speaking up hard. Why did her parents have to be so outspoken about politics when they could just as easily live a contented life without upsetting any apple carts?

"I don't do politics either, dear girl. I wouldn't know a duck from a politician. My apologies again. I shouldn't have shared this personal information with you. Pray tell, what's in Switzerland for you?"

Edda hesitated. Suddenly she wasn't so sure anymore that she wanted to go. Everything was so complicated, but then she sat straighter. *You can do anything you put your mind to, Edda.* Her mentor was whispering in her ear. She could do it. She could do anything.

"I intend to go to a finishing school for a few months, doctor. Before I can spend my days at the barre again. It's a place called Le

Manoir. My mother very much enjoyed her education there in 1918. I thought I'd try it, though I might not enjoy table-setting and painting aquarelles as much as my very accomplished Mama. Anyway, I need a change of environment from their house in Leiden, and I love being in the mountains. A totally different place will hopefully take my mind off my lack of dancing." She smiled and added quickly, "and I love French. I want to improve my proficiency in that superb language."

"Aha, *maintenant je comprends*. Now I understand. It sounds like a perfect plan. I see no reason you couldn't go if you treat that leg with calm and caution. Where about is it? I have a dear friend who works at the Lausanne University Hospital. I could refer you to her for check-ups?"

It seemed like a benign sun was pouring its warm rays down on Edda. She nodded eagerly. "That must be meant to be. The school is near Lausanne. Thank you, Doctor."

"Then good luck, Edda Van der Valk. Don't forget to send me an invitation next time you shine as Gisele or Odette on the stage."

"I will, Doctor. I promise."

"Good. Now, don't forget to give my warmest greetings to Doctor Michele Keller. I'll phone her today to let her know she can expect a visit from you in the coming weeks. You first settle in that finishing school of yours and then you pay her a visit when you're ready. No need to worry about a specific date to take off the new cast."

Edda hesitated as she shook the doctor's hand. He felt like a friend to her, so she blurted out before she could regret it.

"I truly hope you won't lose any more colleagues, Doctor. I abhor how people think and talk about Jews. Half of my dance company are Jewish. Some talk of leaving, but others are just arriving here. Poles and Russians, mainly."

"Thank you, dear girl. Let's hope this absurd inequality blows over soon. I pray for world peace every day, but I fear my prayer is like a solo voice crying in the wilderness. I'm glad I found a like-minded soul in you. Now take care *et bon voyage*."

"*Bon voyage*, Doctor Geuze."

THE JANUARY SUN, watery and uncertain, broke through the clouds as Klaas took the Leimuiderdijk back from Amsterdam to Leiden. As they drove along the dike, Edda stared at the play of sun and clouds, the stretched-out meadows interlaced with ditches filled to the brim with icy water, the windmills dotted in the landscape, turning their mills as slow as if they were listening to a solemn adagio sonata. Above the flat lands, a flock of geese traced the sky in a perfect V and disappeared eastward.

This was Holland, the land she knew and loved so well, horizons so wide, it felt like you could see the entire country spread out to its outer corners. And yet she was ready, more than ready, to replace the Dutch meadows and canals for the mountains and lakes of Switzerland, at least until she returned in the spring.

Even Klaas seemed in a good mood on the return drive as he was whistling the popular Bob Scholte song, *Ik heb een huis met een tuintje gehuurd*. Edda wondered if the rigid Frisian ever dreamed of renting his own house with garden, which was the theme of the song. As she was feeling so good about the lighter cast and her upcoming travel, she was more forgiving towards the bulk of a man she usually disliked.

As long as she'd known her father's bachelor chauffeur - and that was as long as she could remember–Klaas had lived in the coach house at the Valkena Estate. After the move from Leeuwarden to Leiden, he'd established himself in one of the former dormitories from the house's time as a boys' school, devoted as he was to her father and to the cause they stood for.

Klaas, possibly sensing the thaw in his passenger, struck up a conversation after he had let the last line of the song roll off his tongue. Even turning his solid neck in her direction, he asked from the front seat.

"So, when is it you need to be taken to the hospital again, Miss? Your parents are invited to meet with Herr Hitler on the rally in

Munich next week, so it can't be next week. Just thought you needed to know."

Edda tensed. She should have known. The man simply needed to upset her. The only Van der Valk without the NSB pin on her breast. He was a mean creature. And by mentioning Hitler's name and her parents' visit, he'd successfully cornered her. Gone was the good mood, replaced with worries instead. And the sly chauffeur knew all this.

"I won't be needing the car next week, Klaas. I'll be leaving the country for a while myself."

She wouldn't give him the satisfaction of telling him her plans. She was pleased to hear him embark on another silly song. She tried to relax her back against the soft leather of the back seat.

The Führer's face appeared in her mind's eye and with her thorough mind -a trait she'd inherited from her Prussian Mama - Edda pondered why he and all he stood for unnerved her so much. The one time she'd met him in his Berlin house in 1935, the Austrian had been polite and entertaining. He'd even asked her about her dance career and confided in her he wasn't a ballet connoisseur, but that his *Reichskulturkammer* had spared no time or energy to translate all these hideous French ballet terms into German.

Edda had been too baffled to answer him, and the dark-haired man with the small mustache had turned the back of his light summer suit to her to engage with a more interesting discussion partner.

"That's it," Edda thought from the back seat of the Mercedes. "The man abhorred French." That was what she'd disliked about him. But she knew that wasn't the real reason. Held so much in awe in her household as if the German chancellor was some sort of demi-god, Edda had found him to be fake under the lacquer of self-contained polish and sociability. As if he could explode any minute and turn into a hefty hellhound. There was definitely something uncontrolled under the surface there, on which Edda couldn't put her finger but she definitely sensed it. And Edda was all about inner control.

Suddenly it was all quite enough for her. "Drop me off at the nearest train station, Klaas. I need to get my suitcase and clothes from my Vondelstraat flat."

"But Miss..."

"Don't argue with me. Just do as I tell you." Her voice was sharp. She'd never get out of this rigmarole if she didn't take control. Had she not just been thinking of control?

"I wanted to say I can turn the car around and drive you back to Amsterdam?" Her sharp tone had affected the Frisian bully. Edda thought quickly. It would save her a lot of time if she made the detour by car, but she desperately wanted to get out of this entanglement with the Germans. Then her common-sense side won. She'd have to deal with Klaas.

"Alright. But make it fast. I've got a lot of planning to do."

EDDA SWALLOWED hard as they drove into her street with the crow-stepped, gabled houses, all with low stone steps in front. How she'd missed her flat, away from the drama and unfinished business. Her other life.

"I'll be back as quickly as I can." The light cast made walking so much easier, and Edda left her crutches in the car. But her left leg still felt alien, and she limped and hobbled up the steps to her front door. Her flat was on the ground floor and had its own entrance. Above her lived one of the Philharmonic violists and the second and third floors had elderly couples.

On opening the front door, it stuck, and she pushed hard. Peering around the door, she saw a mass of cards and envelopes that had landed on the mat. Her heart sprung up. Her friends from the other life had not forgotten her.

She would have to pile all the mail in her suitcase so she could read it in her leisure at her parents' house, but her eye fell on one thick envelope. She bent to pick it up. Her name and address were written in Miss Sterling's firm, curly typescript, as elegant as the ballerina herself.

Edda tore it open. She was sure the envelope held the photographs of the dress rehearsal of their Nutcracker performance. Staring at the contents, she gasped. There she was, the star of the show. This was who she really was.

Still and poised, on pointe, in her divine Clara outfit with the embroidered top and tutu, the flesh-coloured tights that hugged her legs, her bare arm elegantly stretched with her hand just touching the tip of that of the Prince, her face sweet, smiling, serene.

Her stage godfather, Drosselmeyer, flapping his black coat in the background, all motion and whirlwind. She studied her stage love's face, the Belgian René Deschamps, and saw his love for that evening, the dance, life. Oh, life had been so good then, so kind and full and... real.

Her legs were whole, her body and spirit were whole, her life had been whole. Edda stared at her enchanted self for a little longer in the chilly entrance to her small flat, the January wind sweeping dead leaves and dust into the hallway. Her ankle hurt. Life was not good. The girl in the picture was a creature from another planet. A creature so unattainable right now.

As she studied the other pictures, she noticed Maria looming in the background with a menacing look on her pretty face. Maria was focused on her. Edda quickly stuffed the photos back in the vaguely perfumed envelope and went to collect her suitcase.

"I'll be back," she comforted herself. "I'll be that girl again, but for now it's Switzerland for me."

8

THE TRAVEL COMPANION

A couple weeks later – Leiden, January 1938

"I'm coming with you to Le Manoir."

Edda looked up from packing her suitcase. With a pair of ballet tights rolled in a ball between her hands, she turned to face her mother who stood in the doorway.

"Aren't you supposed to go to Germany with Papa?"

Edda didn't know whether to feel pleased or put on edge by her mother's surprise announcement, but she was certainly perplexed. The expression on her mother's face was unreadable, but she thought there was a tinge of uncertainty, rather unlike the proud Prussian aristocrat who'd tell her daughter what to do and where to go. Stepping into her daughter's room, dressed as usual in one of her soft-toned but expensive deux-pieces, the Marchioness added almost nonchalantly.

"I told you I'd love to see Madame Paul again. And Papa also thinks that letting you make the long trip on your own with your leg still in a cast would be irresponsible. Klaas can drive us as far as Paris and then we can take the sleeper train to Lausanne."

Edda felt a flutter in her chest. Hadn't Papa said at the hospital that she was more important than politics? That her mother would prefer her over a meeting with the Führer. She walked over to her mother and planted a kiss on the powdered cheek. Mama smelled of rouge and lavender.

"Thank you. I'd love to travel with you. I already went to the station to check the international trains. I've set my hopes on taking the train to Paris the day after tomorrow, but if we depend on Klaas, we might have to reschedule. There's a sleeper to Lyon, and then to Switzerland, every evening except Sundays."

"I know. I ordered your father to look into trains so it wouldn't conflict with Germany. We can stick to your plan, Eddaline, and depart on Wednesday. We'll just have to inform Madame Paul I'm traveling with you, though I don't expect to be put up at Le Manoir itself. It's not a hotel."

Her mother sailed out with no delay, leaving the door open, and Edda wondered what was going on. She'd heard her parents argue the other day when she unexpectedly returned to the dining room because she had forgotten her shawl. Her mother had looked pink and flustered, which she never did, and her father had sucked on his cigar as if it was the enemy himself.

Edda sighed. Of course, every couple was supposed to quarrel from time to time, but her parents' marriage was solid. She'd never caught her parents ruffling each other's feathers. They always seemed so placid together, like two solid bricks in a wall, never visibly romantic or moved in each other's presence but certainly not capable of being at each other's throat.

Unlike the unstable, ostentatious relationship Duifje and Teppo had, or the passionate artistic love between Miss Sterling and Monsieur Sergevey. The latter being Edda's absolute sublime interpretation of a grand love affair.

The most worrisome part of it all was her mother not accompanying her father on one of his most important missions, visiting Herr Hitler, who was their mutual idea of what a real leader embodied.

Edda shivered. It made little sense, but to erase the unanswered questions from her mind, she continued packing, meanwhile thinking how her travel would change with her mother at her side.

"It might actually be fun," she told herself aloud. "We're usually at our closest when uninterrupted by the rest of them."

With a bit of luck, her mother would also confide in her daughter what was really going on so Edda could put worries about looming marital issues between her parents to rest.

MOTHER AND DAUGHTER Van der Valk arrived at Lausanne Central Station on a cool and breezy afternoon in late January. The travel had been long but uneventful and they had enjoyed a reasonable night's sleep at *Le Train Bleu*, as the night train between France and Switzerland with final destination Bern was called.

Edda had studied her mother most of the way. She seemed to become strangely mellower by the day, sweet even, which, in the Marchioness's case, was more worrisome than welcome. There were new dark shadows under her eyes, and despite her good mood and attentiveness towards Edda, she seemed to have lost her appetite.

This was the most worrisome change, considering the stout aristocrat prided herself on three full healthy meals a day and would have none of that 'salad picking' her society friends did to keep a slim figure. And Edda, of course, with her dance diet consisting of plenty of proteins and vegs and only one high dose of carbs right before a performance, had been a thorn in the Marchioness's flesh.

The moment they disembarked from the train, her mother seemed to revive miraculously from what it was that had been bothering her, exclaiming, "Oh, how I look forward to being in the Alps again. And, I definitely crave a Swiss roll. There's no jam dessert in the world that can compare to it. You simply must try it, Eddaline, not once but preferably every day. You'll be right as rain in no time again."

"Right as rain, Mama? I think I'm fine." Edda joked, happy to see her mother's good spirits return.

The look her mother gave her as she scanned her tall, slim daughter huddled in her duffel coat spoke volumes. Slices of that infamous Swiss roll were certainly her mother's way of saying she'd regained her appetite. She was shedding the tired, semi-ill skin like an old coat on Lausanne station, making Edda sigh a breath of relief. Her mother's odd behavior had given rise to all sorts of panicky thoughts in the devoted daughter.

"I'm curious if Madame Paul still remembers me," the Marchioness chirped on, as she looked around her for a porter. After having been cooped up in the dark compartment for hours, Edda blinked in the light filtering through the station's arched glass ceiling. She suddenly realized her own body, her leg in the cast, her own adventure that was about to evolve.

"Garçon! Garçon!"

She heard her mother call as she waved one of her lace handkerchiefs as if bidding someone goodbye instead of calling a porter to her. Nobody seemed to pay attention to the two ladies on the busy platform, one on crutches, amidst an array of suitcases. The gallant Swiss gentleman who'd brought their suitcases down from the train for them seemed to have been the last helpful soul on the planet. All porters were occupied and stone-deaf to cries for help.

"Sit down with our luggage, Eddaline, while I get one of these sluggish porters to show some manners." Edda did as she was told, glad to sit down on her suitcase. Her mother's broad back zigzagged through the throngs of people, shouting, "S'il vous plaît, garçon! Garçon!"

"Mademoiselle Van der Valk?" A deep male voice asked behind her. She turned to see a short, stocky man in a black uniform with a huge cap on his dark brown hair. Brown eyes, with a glint of curiosity, stared at her from a bronzed, middle-aged face.

"Yes?" She got up from the suitcase.

"I'm Monsieur Maltese, Le Manoir's chauffeur, and I'm here to pick up you and your mother. I'm sorry for the delay." Though he spoke French, his accent was strong, and Edda guessed he was Italian by birth. Uncertain if she should shake the chauffeur's hand–she would never shake Klaas Bollema's hand–while scanning the crowds for her mother, she said hesitantly, "thank you, Monsieur Maltese. We did not know we would be collected from the station. My mother is looking around for a porter. Could you...?"

"Who's that, Eddaline?" Her mother, a little out of breath, hurried towards them. Edda saw the chauffeur tap his cap, his dark eyes going from the daughter to the mother, and back again. A slim smile played around his lips.

"At your service, Madame. I would have picked you from the crowd as Mademoiselle's Madre without a single doubt."

"Now would you, Sir?" Edda saw the return of some of her mother's usual iciness towards servants. To Edda he was like a character from a ballet. She was fascinated. He dressed like a chauffeur, and he was as polite as expected, but there was something about Monsieur Maltese. She couldn't put her finger on it, but she was sure he wasn't meant to be a school chauffeur. There was more to the man than met the eye.

The liberal-minded Italian remained unperturbed under Edda's unveiled scrutiny, told them to call him Filippo, and snapped his fingers while turning on his heels. Within seconds, a porter in white jacket and black trousers was by his side rolling an empty trolley towards them.

"The car's in front of the station, Richard," the chauffeur instructed as he pressed some Swiss francs into the young man's hands. And to Edda and her mother, he said, "follow me please. Madame Paul is waiting for you." Edda thought he gave her a conspiratorial wink but dismissed it instantly as something she'd imagined. She wasn't in a ballet, where facial expressions mattered every second.

Still, there was a freedom around Filippo Maltese's being - the way he composed himself with natural confidence - that warmed

Edda to the chauffeur, rather unlike her mother, who resorted to her huffing as she marched behind their escort.

As soon as they were comfortably installed on the back seat of the black Renault with *Le Manoir* in golden lettering on the front doors, a woolen blanket tucked around their legs and their luggage safely in the trunk, the marchioness's good spirits returned.

"Oh, how I remember that charming view of Lake Geneva. Isn't it a picture postcard right now? All decked in pristine snow. Like a fairy tale. When I arrived here in 1918, it was springtime. I saw such lovely greens and blues, a truly merry arrival. A tremendous relief, after almost four years of war in Prussia. Not that I saw anything of the war. That was mainly taking place in Russia and France, but people weren't merry and peaceful like here in Switzerland."

The Marchioness prattled on, while Edda in her turn enjoyed the sights from the car window. It *was* like a postcard and a very welcome change to her as well.

"My Mutter, bless her soul, was very much against my traveling through a war zone to get to neutral Switzerland, but it had to be done. It simply had to be done. Vater agreed."

"Why was that, Mother?" Edda was happy her mother finally seemed to perk up. Keep her talking, keep that bond of intimacy. She knew so little about her mother's youth, and now that they'd returned to a place where she'd been happy, it was best to just let her talk. But it was clearly the wrong question, though. Her mother's face darkened.

"Ach, Eddaline. I was twenty like you and engaged to be married. We'd postponed my finishing school education for three years because of the war, but my Wolfgang wanted us to get married. He kept saying to me when he was on leave, 'life's so short. I can be killed any day.' He was under the arms, of course, a major in the German Empire. Stationed in Northern France most of the time."

There was pride in her mother's voice when she talked of her fiancé. Edda held her breath. She never knew her mother had been engaged to someone else before her father. The sadness in her mother's face was foreboding, however.

"Wolfgang died in the third battle of the Somme. We never knew exactly where he fell or how. His entire regiment perished on the same day. He's buried in French soil on the Fricourt German War Cemetery near Albert." The Marchioness stopped talking for a moment, gazed sadly out of the window that seconds earlier had sent her into raptures.

"How my dear Wolfgang would have hated the idea of being buried in foreign soil. But what can one do? I knew nothing of this, of course. I was still happily preparing myself to become Frau Altenbach. My parents didn't want me upset so far from home, so they waited until the war was over and I could return to Schloss Scherzinger in December 1918. Only then was I told my fiancé was dead."

Edda grabbed her mother's hand, dismissing the sights of the Alps and the vast twinkling Lake Geneva.

"I'm so sorry, Mama. I never knew. Why did you not tell me before?"

"What was there to tell, my dear? I found happiness with your father, so that restored my heart."

Making use of the intimacy they now shared in the backseat of Filippo Maltese's Renault, Edda asked, "Are you afraid we're heading to war again, Mama? Is that why you wanted to come with me?" Her mother's dark eyes rested on her daughter. She seemed to think, weighing her words, but then kept silent. Just shook her head.

"We're almost there," the chauffeur informed them from the front seat. He pointed to a tall square building in between pines with a sloping white lawn towards a small strip of beach and the rippling waves of the lake. Mother and daughter stared at the impressive building with its rows of windows and snow-topped awnings. The Marchioness slapped her hand in front of her mouth. Edda thought she saw a glistening tear in the corner of her mother's eye. Her mother emotional? This school must have meant an awful lot to her.

Filippo parked the Renault on the gravel right in front of the stone steps that led to two big red doors. Before they were out of the car, one of the school doors swung open and, in the entrance, stood a woman, or rather a lady, that Edda immediately took to be Madame Paul.

She wasn't especially tall, but she carried herself very erect and composed, giving the impression of significant height. Edda guessed she was in her early forties, but preserved with great care, both her figure and her countenance. Dressed in a dark-blue merino dress with a rabbit fur stole around her shoulders, the light-brown hair done up in a fashionable roll at the side of her neck, glasses hanging on two pearl strings on her bosom. Slim, prim, and trim.

But what made Madame Paul truly unique were her eyes. Byzantium blue, Edda dubbed them, a color she'd chosen for her sofa in the Vondelpark flat. Other people may simply call it blue, but its crystalline quality made for a special celestial shine, a diamond-like quality, intriguing, unforgettable. Edda had never seen eyes like that, as if reflecting their own light, thus beautiful and at the same time giving away nothing. At least not at first sight.

"Marchioness Van der Valk, *enchanté*. What a pleasure!" With two hands stretched out and a fine smile on her pink-pearl lips, the school mistress descended the steps in her high heels and walked across the gravel as if it was smooth marble.

"That's the way it's done," Edda thought, and she instantly admired Madame Paul's grace while the two older women greeted each other as if they were old, school friends.

"Weren't you here the first year I was in charge of Le Manoir, Marchioness?"

"I was indeed, Madame Paul. In 1918. It seems ages ago. I was here while there was that half British-half French girl who ran away. Such a stir she caused. What was her name again?"

"Oh, you must be talking about Countess Madeleine de Dragoncourt?" Madame Paul rolled dramatic eyes. "Nightmares that girl gave me."

They were still holding hands. Her mother's calfskin gloves were in the pale hands of Madame Paul. Edda seemed forgotten but couldn't care less. Everything was fascinating here, and the chemistry between these two women gave a new dimension to her mother, who generally was quite aloof with other women, inclined as she was to be the hostess of her husband's mainly male, political friends.

"Meet my daughter, Eddaline." Her mother finally let go of the schoolmistress's hands to signal Edda to come forth. She felt the Byzantium blue eyes rest on her, and was scanned from head to toe in a way not even Miss Sterling used to do. It happened in the blink of an eye, very professionally, and the verdict was as fast as well.

"Eddaline, what a pleasure to meet you. Your mother told me you are a dancer. I absolutely adore ballet. And look at that posture! You will be able to teach those slumping students of mine something about bearing. Welcome to Le Manoir."

A cool, perfumed hand shook hers. Firm, like they were sealing a deal.

"*Enchanté*," Edda murmured, impressed and curious in equal measure. She'd met no one like Madame Paul, though in her twenty years she'd come across a wide variety of folk, from barons to politicians to dancers.

"Do come in. You must be travel-weary." Madame Paul didn't wait but glided over the gravel back to the stairs.

"I'd better go and find a hotel," the Marchioness observed. Madame Paul pivoted on her heels, the pencilled eyebrows slightly raised. She lifted a long index finger with the same pearl pink as her lips and wagged it.

"Nonsense, Marchioness. You're staying at Le Manoir. The maids made the guest room in my private quarters ready for you. I can't wait for all the catching up with you! All those years!" The fine smile she gave Edda's mother was genuine enough, and yet it was studied.

Edda was grateful for her mother's presence. Without her mother there, Edda was sure she'd be getting the brunt of Madame Paul's educational arrows first thing in the morning.

Out of nowhere, the first tunes of the Nutcracker jumped into Edda's head and in her mind her feet were already dancing to the tune. The jolt back into her dance life, that real life, struck Edda as strange. That, in spite of the surroundings and the appeal of Le Manoir, she was unable to deny the tug at her heart to get back to dance. As if this melody was a reminder Le Manoir was temporary until she could dance again.

What silliness to think pearl-pink lips and matching nails would be enough in her life.

I want to dance!

9

LE MANOIR

One week later – Switzerland, February 1938

W hen a week later, her mother departed for the Netherlands, Edda was relieved and sad at the same time. Though her mother had been challenging at times, instructing Madame Paul in front of other students to turn Edda into a marriageable young woman, and comparing the deft household skills of some of the–mostly blonde--German girls to Edda's 'clumsiness', Edda had cherished the special time together.

So, she clung to her Mama rather girlishly, as she was about to step into Filippo's Renault.

"Mammy, I'll miss you."

"Hush, Eddaline, behave yourself. You'll do fine. Now don't forget to call that hospital, as Doctor Geuze instructed you. And just have a great time. You'll enjoy it as much as I did." And she was gone . The last Edda saw of her was the hat with the ostrich feather bobbing up and down as the car rumbled down the cobbled street.

"Mammy."

Cry-baby, sneered Duifje's voice in her head. Edda straightened her back, pushing down her strange premonition that this may be the last time she'd be close to her mother. That darn intuition.

Resolutely Edda turned around and faced the school. She saw Madame's Paul's curtain move. The Sphinx, as the other students called Madame Paul behind her back, had even studied how Edda coped with saying goodbye. She'd probably get a sermon on not showing ostentatious emotion in public, not even with one's close family! Wag, wag, pearl-pink fingernail.

Minutes later Edda sank back on her single bed in the room she shared with an enigmatic girl called Anna Adams. Anna spoke English with a German accent and French with an English accent. Edda stared at her roommate's immaculately made bed, nothing personal but a copy of a novel titled *Rebecca*.

Though the two girls had shared the room for a week now, they had hardly exchanged anything beyond the 'good morning' on waking and 'sleep well' when they both turned off their identical side table lamps at exactly 10 pm.

Being an ardent people-reader, Edda wondered who the dark-haired, multi-lingual girl with the pale complexion and large-framed glasses really was. Her face was so narrow and pinched it made the glasses look even bigger. But it wasn't Anna's exterior that piqued Edda's interest. It was her solemness, her solitude, the abstention from giggling and gossiping with the other girls. There was a secret there.

At that moment, the latest object of Edda's interest opened the door and walked in, carrying a large-sized portfolio under her arm. She started on seeing Edda sitting on the bed, made a movement as if turning around again, but then stopped, pushed the glasses up her nose and gave Edda a narrow smile.

"I didn't know there was anyone in the room. I just came to bring in my herbarium." More words than had been exchanged thus far.

"My mother just left." It came out before Edda could check herself.

"Oh, I see." Anna just stood there, the herbarium with the green leopard cover with leather bindings between lean fingers. "I'll leave you alone then."

"Can you stay for a moment?"

Anna checked her wristwatch. "I told Monsieur Georges I would practice the pianoforte but... but I may have five minutes."

She sank onto her own bed, the portfolio clenched to her chest. Edda met the somber, gray eyes.

"How long have you been here, Anna? You're from London, right?"

"Which question do you want answered first?" Edda saw a tiny laugh wrinkle next to the eyes.

"Oh, sorry. Both, I guess. Hope you don't find my questions too intrusive? I'm just trying to find a connection to people here."

"Alright, Edda. Let's do one question each, back and forth. I've been here since November. My turn. Is it true you are a professional ballerina? That's what the rumors are." Anna placed the herbarium next to her and with swift movements tucked her legs under her as if she was a Buddha. *Some nimble limbs there*, Edda thought and followed suit, though the plastered leg didn't make the position very comfortable.

"Yes, I am a dancer, but I broke my ankle during a stage performance, so I needed a change of scenery while I heal."

There was a glint of empathy in the gray eyes.

"I'm sorry. That must have been rotten. So yes, I live in London. I'm British." Anna spoke the words with sufficient stress and no smile, which communicated *don't probe further*. Not about the foreign accent, or the secret, whatever it was. But then Anna added in a friendlier voice, "last round. What do you make of Le Manoir so far?"

"I don't know yet. It's all rather foreign to me." Edda struggled for the right words – she didn't want to say 'absurd.' "I've been doing dance, combined with schooling, since I was five, so I'm not accustomed to sitting in classrooms doing things I consider pastimes, like flower arranging, music lessons, and etiquette. To be honest, I had no idea schools like this even existed. It's like we are constantly prepared to become our very best for somebody else. I'm trained to become the best for me and a team, not for something or someone in the future."

Anna nodded. "I understand. Sounds like we're both just hiding out here." She hopped off the bed without further explanation. "Got to go now. See you later."

"See you later."

There was a hint of friendship, and Edda was grateful for it. As for the rumors...maybe Anna listened to gossip after all.

AN HOUR later Edda walked into Monsieur Petrov's etiquette class and was greeted by a row of surprised looking students.

"Am I in the wrong class?"

"Not at all, Marchioness Van der Valk. Do come in."

"I'm just Edda, Sir, or Mademoiselle Edda. Please, no titles." Edda was not her mother; she'd nip all references to blue blood in the bud.

"We were just talking about you." The Russian etiquette teacher seemed unperturbed by her remark. Monsieur Petrov was nothing like her own Monsieur Sergeyev. Though outwardly, a studious, serious professor in an immaculate three-piece suit, complete with stiff upturned collar, bowtie and lace pocket square, Monsieur Petrov was actually a jovial man who wore his heart on his sleeve.

"Anything I should know?" Edda asked, making a slight bow for the teacher. She didn't know why, but he was just the kind of man one bowed to as a greeting.

Monsieur Petrov smiled amiably behind his enormous mustache, making his side whiskers dance.

"Delicious girl, I wanted to use you as a guinea pig but then *les autres étudiants* told me you were saying goodbye to your dear Mama." Bulging blue eyes behind a pince-nez looked at her with glee.

"A guinea pig?" Edda smiled back. Somehow this cute teacher with his heavily accented Russian French and his busily flapping petite hands brought out the clown in her. "I've been a milkmaid, a polar bear and even a tree in my career, Sir, but never a guinea pig."

"Ha, ha, ha!" He clapped his hands enthusiastically and Edda felt all eyes on her. It was nothing like being on stage, but it was pleasant, nonetheless. Something of her former shine returned. *A limelight girl*, Miss Sterling had called her.

"Demoiselles Esther and Océane, come forward please and you, *Mademoiselle* Edda stay right where you are."

Edda saw the two girls, who'd presumably also arrived recently and were roommates, step forward. One was tall and blond, the other tiny and dark. They looked like they had become immediate friends and seemed nice. Certainly, different from the Scottish girl called Sable, who snorted at everything Monsieur Petrov said and snickered behind her hand with a group of French girls. That group seemed unpleasant, which was a pity as it would've been nice to have some French friends to practice her language skills with.

"Alright, Mademoiselle Edda, you know the routine. Show how it's done to the girls."

"Sure, Monsieur Petrov, with pleasure." The silly books-on-head ceremony had been her introduction a week earlier and had created a lot of *ohs* and *ahs* because she apparently could do the routine with no prior exercise and still a cast on her leg.

Edda made another slight bow towards the Russian teacher. With a straight back and employing her natural ballerina movements, Edda went over to a stack of books that lay on the table while Monsieur Petrov put Bach's Adagios on the record player.

She moved to one side of the room, then balanced the five heavy volumes on top of her head, waited for the music to start and slowly, steadily walked across the room, straight as a lily on its stem and with a grace that let all the girls in the room hold their breath.

Arriving on the other side, she took the books from her head, made another bow for Monsieur Petrov, and handed the books to Esther. Monsieur Petrov clapped his hands again.

"Bravo, bravo! That's how it's done. Remember, dear girls, grace *can* be learned and is a lady's greatest asset, especially..." he wagged his finger at them while his signet ring flashed in the electric light, "especially in the face of danger! And that also holds good for men, but I'm not teaching men here. However, it was grace and good manners that helped me out of Russia when the Bolsheviks took over in 1918. Nothing else. I may have lost my estate, had all my belongings in one small suitcase, but I walked to the Moscow Kiyevskaya railway station to get on the train to Warsaw with my head held high and my manners intact. So, this is lesson one, new demoiselles. Walk straight, even when we increase the weight on your head. Your turn, Mademoiselle Esther."

Edda felt the blond girl's hesitation. Sea-green eyes sought her help.

"You'll do fine!" Edda mouthed.

She saw Esther take her position at the end of the room and how she tried to place the books on her head, but they slipped to the floor immediately with a loud thud.

She murmured a distressed "sorry", while Sable and her friends snickered. There had been an unpleasant encounter between Sable and Esther the evening before in the music room. Edda had heard whispers about it, but she'd been practicing as much of her old ballet routines as the cast would allow her in the gymnastics room and had missed the drama. Anna hadn't been involved either.

It seemed Sable was picking on Esther most, so it was good the American girl, Océane, had her back. That tiny firecracker didn't look like she'd let the Scot tamper with her friend. Was Sable another Maria Petrova? Probably. Esther was meanwhile grappling with the books and picking up the routine in no time.

"That's right," Monsieur Petrov was encouraging her, "hold on to them for the first time. You'll get the hang of it. Don't worry."

Edda saw there was musicality and grace in Esther. And a lovely, lovely soul.

"A natural! Just practice, practice, practice!" Monsieur Petrov exclaimed in his peculiar French with the trilled R's and soft consonants, remnants of his Slavic background. Esther was beaming, while

Océane doggedly struggled through the assignment, unperturbed by the snickers or the praise.

"I've never experienced a more nonsensical exercise in my life." She muttered, which vexed Monsieur Petrov, who exclaimed a hurt, "*Ah mais non*, Mademoiselle Océane. This exercise makes all the sense in the world."

"Not in a hospital," Océane barked, and Edda remembered the gossip about the American girl being a medical student. Edda took her in with more interest. What was a medical student doing at a finishing school? She probably also had an obscure reason to take a break from her professional training.

Océane seemed to feel Edda's eyes on her and looked her way. Hazel eyes, Miss Sterling's intelligence and confidence, but with a more scientific outlook on life. Though there certainly was a streak of artistry there, as well.

Ah well, we come from all walks of life and perhaps only a handful of us are really here to train for managing our marital households, Edda thought. Sable didn't look like she was ready for a marriage with mansion and man, either.

The lesson continued with how to shake hands properly, how to hold a wineglass, how to open your napkin when at a formal dinner. Edda's and Océane's eyes crossed many times. They raised their eyebrows. Esther lapped it all up. She was the one ready for the marriage with mansion and man. Anna was nowhere to be seen, which was peculiar, as Monsieur Petrov's lessons were mandatory.

I'm going to phone Doctor Michele Keller at the Lausanne University Hospital, Edda promised herself. Her body yearned to get back into dancing. Le Manoir was only going to get a fleeting visit from her.

10

STAYING OR GOING?

Six weeks later – Switzerland, March 1938

As Filippo drove her through the center of Lausanne to the hospital, he chatted with Edda, "so, Mademoiselle Van der Valk, what will you do if the cast comes off today? Stay at Le Manoir, or go home?"

Edda shifted uneasily in the backseat. Why did this stranger have to ask the exact question she had no answer to? Papa had paid the school tuition fees for an entire year, though she'd told him she wasn't sure she would stay that long.

"I don't know, Monsieur Maltese. That decision has kept me awake most of the night."

"Well, it shouldn't have, Mademoiselle." He lifted his cap, which had slipped down over his forehead, and their eyes met in the rear mirror. Edda didn't answer. It was as if he could look right into her soul. Not in a bothersome way, but nonetheless unsettling. He *was* so very different from Klaas, not least because the Italian was a first-class driver.

"I don't know what you mean, Monsieur Maltese." Her confused mind wanted his input, strange as it sounded. Squandering her father's money – and a considerable sum it had been -- was not Edda's style.

"It's Filippo for you, Mademoiselle." He said no more as they arrived at the hospital. I guess *I'll decide for myself. After all, what does this chauffeur know about my life?* Edda scolded herself. But as he opened the backdoor for her, he fixed his dark eyes on her and before letting her out, he said, "I know what it should be, but you're right, Mademoiselle. Decide for yourself. I'll be waiting for you here. Take your time." He tapped his ridiculously oversized cap and, taking a polishing cloth from his pocket, started to rub the dust of the golden letters on the driver's door.

Puzzled but somehow relieved, Edda made her way into what looked like a late nineteenth-century, sprawling hospital in red brick with white window frames. It was tall -- at least five storeys -- and right next to what looked like a similar university building. Medical students and staff alike populated the square in front and thronged through the sliding doors in and out of the building.

"Doctor Keller's office, please. I have an appointment." Edda handed the receptionist her carte d'identité.

"Mademoiselle Van der Valk? Oh, yes, the doctor is waiting for you. That corridor. Room 6." The fair-haired receptionist handed back her passport and pointed to the left wing.

Doctor Michele Keller was a tall, bony woman with gray hair and eyebrows but remarkably smooth skin. She possessed observant and practical bluish eyes, with an attitude that stated she didn't intend spending more time on a patient than was strictly necessary. Edda wondered how a woman like Doctor Keller could be talked about so warmly by her Amsterdam colleague, but she had no time to ponder this question further.

"Miss Van der Valk, take off your pantaloon and on the table, please." No handshake, no welcome.

Edda struggled out of her duffel coat and then her one shoe and slacks. The authoritative doctor made her self-conscious in her briefs.

"Let me see." The doctor retrieved a half-rimmed pair of glasses from her coat pocket and took the x-ray herself. It was a much smaller, hand-held apparatus. Edda just hoped it would do the job.

"All done. You can dress and wait outside until I call you in again."

"Yes, doctor." These were the first words Edda spoke in the exam room, and she scurried out as fast as she could. What an unpleasant person. She truly hoped Doctor Keller was as good as Doctor Geuze had said she was and that her ankle would be fully healed -- Edda wanted no other encounter with this frigid physician.

"Come in, Miss Van der Valk."

That was quick, Edda thought. She could have just stayed in the examining room. A male doctor was standing next to the curt Doctor Keller, who was sitting in her office chair speaking into the mouthpiece of a black telephone. To Edda's surprise she was smiling, speaking Dutch. She must be talking to Doctor Geuze. Edda's heart sprang up. He'd have given her a much warmer welcome, put her at ease.

"*Dat is goed. Zal ik doen.*" Doctor Keller put down the phone while Edda wondered what Doctor Geuze had said. The brief chat with her Dutch colleague seemed to have defrosted the female doctor, who managed a small smile.

"Please, sit down, Miss Van der Valk. I have good news for you. My assistant, Doctor Göpfel, will take the cast off and you're free to dance again. But with moderation. And you need to have a check-up again in two months, either here or in Holland. Understood?" The smile had already evaporated from her clinical lips. She excused herself and left the room. Edda didn't even have time to thank her.

"Doctor Keller is very busy," Doctor Göpfel said apologetically. "Now let us free this leg." He took an enormous pair of scissors and started making an indent at Edda's shin. Snip, snip and it was gone. She gasped. A thin, sickly-looking ankle appeared from underneath its cover. Tears sprang into her eyes. That ankle would need months to be strong enough again.

"What's wrong, Mademoiselle? The ankle looks fine to me." The junior assistant deftly prodded the thin joint.

"Nothing," Edda sniffed, not sure showing emotion in this strange hospital would be her best course of action.

"Clearly, something is the matter. Here, take my hand and carefully try to stand on that leg." Edda eyed the young man with suspicion. Somehow, she didn't expect friendliness in Lausanne University Hospital, but he looked at her from under black curls and smiled. "It's okay, I won't bite. Easy now."

She stood, first grasping his hand and then alone.

"Now I want to see a proper first position. Remember, it comes from the hip joint and there's nothing wrong there," the young physician ordered.

Automatically Edda pointed her toes out, feet together, heel to heel. The ankle didn't protest, just felt stiff.

"Second!" he encouraged her.

"What do you know about ballet?"

He shrugged, "two little sisters."

Edda obeyed, putting her feet apart, heels opposed.

"How does it feel?" The doctor hunched on his heels to feel the ankle. "Strained?"

"A little, but it's fun. As if it is my very first ballet lesson."

Doctor Göpfel rose to his own feet again. "It won't be your last, I assume, but now we're coming to the tricky part."

"Third?"

He nodded. "Do it very, very carefully and immediately come out of it when it aches only a tiny bit." Edda took a deep breath. She knew that if she passed this test, she'd be going home... to Amsterdam.

She eased into third, feet together, right foot behind the thinner left foot, overlapping by exactly a half foot length. *I can do it*, a voice in her exulted. *I can dance again.*

As if she'd spoken aloud, the doctor said, "Yes, you can dance again. Goodbye, Mademoiselle Van der Valk. I can't wait to see your name in neon letters on theatre boards all around the world. It's been an honor to meet you."

And thus, Edda left Lausanne University Hospital in high spirits and with a plan. Filippo was leaning against the Renault, grinning widely.

"I should be sad because I like you and you're leaving so soon, but a passion is a blessing to live for. So, live your passion."

"Yes, I'm going to tell Madame Paul that I'm going home, Filippo. You seem to know a lot. Do you have a passion yourself?"

He was behind the steering wheel again, manoeuvring the big black car through Lausanne's busy city center.

"I do, Mademoiselle, but not one I can tell you." His voice was solemn, and Edda sensed a secret.

"Then I won't probe further, but I'm convinced it's not chauffeuring well-to-do demoiselles around southern Switzerland," Edda said light-heartedly.

"Correct. It's not that."

And Edda knew she would never know Filippo's passion, but she wished in silence he could execute it soon. Like she could now.

EDDA REVIVED like a dim winking lamp. Without the cast and with regained confidence in her ankle, she immediately adopted her former ballet-way gait, feet slightly turned outwards, spine erect, smooth and easy. She even yearned for her ballet tights and sweaters instead of blouses and slacks.

This was who she was. This was what she was made for. Not for compiling herbariums, or setting opulent tables, not even for redecoration. On closer inspection, she wasn't even sure she had a steady eye for colors and shapes. It was all a pastime for her and even if Ludovicus Van Limburg Stirum thought she was waiting for his ring, he was wrong. Wrong, wrong! Edda was free. Edda danced through life.

She tapped on Madame Paul's door and waited. Nothing. When she was about to turn around, thinking the schoolmistress was otherwise occupied, the door opened.

"Yes?" Madame Paul fixed her with those unique blue eyes. In the two months Edda had been at Le Manoir, she'd learned to read that unreadable face. Edda was good at cracking enigmatic faces. Just a slight raise of the left eyebrow, the eyes a tight too narrow. Madame Paul was not pleased, despite the affable smile.

"I'm sorry. Are you busy, Madame Paul? I wanted to request an appointment." Better to bring it formally, but the face didn't crack yet. Edda knew Madame Paul didn't like students to leave halfway during the course, although she was paid for the full year. Le Manoir was Madame Paul's passion, and it vexed her when students either didn't do well, or–like Edda–weren't motivated. It was like a personal assault on the mistress herself.

So, she kept Edda waiting, neither sending her away nor inviting her in. Edda would not announce her departure on the doorstep. Le Manoir was a cesspool for eavesdroppers, and she wanted to tell Anna herself that she was leaving, even perhaps Océane and Esther. Not be outflanked by that Sable clan.

"Can I come in, Madame Paul, or should I come back another time?" Edda was done waiting.

The door was pushed open further and Madame Paul, almost huffing like Edda's mother, walked straight-backed around her immense desk and sat down in her leather chair. A manicured hand pointed to the chair on the other side of the mahogany monster.

Edda nipped down on the seat, bracing herself for the iciness that was to come her way. That's why she was surprised when Madame Paul's features softened and she said in an almost maternal voice.

"How like your mother you are, Mademoiselle Eddaline. So much potential. I sincerely hope you will follow in your mother's footsteps and not squander your talents."

And what would these talents be? Edda thought but aloud she said, "Thank you, Madame Paul. I hold my mother in high esteem as well."

"As you should, child, as you should." A pain slid across the usually unclouded, blue gaze and Edda tensed. Madame Paul wasn't one to use 'child' for one of her students. The odd fear about her mother returned. Had she confided to Madame Paul about her marital state? The row between her parents Edda had walked in on?

"I wanted to tell you I'm leaving Le Manoir, Madame. It's not that I don't enjoy the courses here, but I've worked so hard for my dance career, and I fear that if I don't return to it now that my cast is off, recuperation will take even longer."

"I knew as much, Mademoiselle Eddaline. I must confess, I may have interrogated Monsieur Maltese on your return from the hospital."

Edda looked at the schoolmistress in surprise. Madame Paul waved the manicured hand. "Don't assume one minute that I don't know Filippo is excellent at extracting information from my students. He's a clever man, Mademoiselle Edda, and I usually let him be, truly. But...," the smile she gave Edda was genuine. How beautiful Madame Paul must have been as a young woman, so radiant and happy.

"Yes?" she asked when the schoolmistress faltered.

"But in your case... Well, anyway, I would have loved to keep you here a little longer. It is seldom we get a girl this accomplished and so independent. You would have been a terrific example for my other students, but I know that's selfish. The stage needs you and you need the stage."

"Thank you, Madame Paul." Edda was confused, moved. She saw the formidable woman opposite her was moved too. In a soft voice Madame Paul added, "It was so wonderful to talk with your mother about the old days. You know, when we were young ourselves and full of glorious dreams. I wish that for you. Truly I do."

There was none of the Sphinx left opposite Edda and she could think of nothing appropriate to say, so simply repeated, "Thank you, Madame Paul."

"I wish you well, dear girl. May God keep and protect you." Madame Paul made a sign as if blessing her and Edda rose befuddled and touched.

Still murmuring, "thank you," she exited the room, a timetable for the departure times of trains pushed in her hand.

"I'll ring your parents." Was the last she heard from the schoolmistress's office.

∼

EDDA WAS PACKING her suitcase when Anna came in, looking slightly ruffled.

"Is it true you're leaving?"

"So, the gossip stole my thunder?" Edda said bitterly.

"What do you mean?" The glasses were pushed up the bridge of Anna's narrow nose.

"I'd wanted to tell you myself, but the news must somehow have slid through the cracks. Who told you?"

"It came through Filippo."

"Filippo?" Edda looked furious. "He shouldn't have."

"Please don't be angry with Filippo, Edda. It wasn't his fault."

"What are you talking about?" Edda's hands stopped in mid-air from folding her bathrobe.

"I usually hate eavesdropping," Anna explained, "but after that prank Sable and her lot played on Esther last week, telling her it was okay to play the piano after dinner when it wasn't, I've been on my *qui vive*."

"We all have," Edda replied, "that was a low blow, but what does it have to do with Filippo?"

Anna shrugged, "I don't know the ins and outs, but apparently Filippo had to flee Italy because of Mussolini. I think Sable found out something incriminating about him and so she uses it to her advantage. She keeps telling people she'd be a perfect secret agent, as she can blackmail the heck out of anyone."

"So, you actually knew through Sable?" Edda shook a weary head, glad to leave the cesspool of connivances. The dance world could be a bit like that, but Miss Sterling kept a firm grip on gossip and backstabbing. Well, had she? Maria Petrova came to Edda's mind. Maybe it was impossible. Where groups gathered, people talked. She just hoped she would never become one of them.

"I heard her tell her clan that you were leaving. Yes, that Filippo told her."

"Honestly, I wanted to tell you myself, Anna. But you'll be okay.

Just hook up with Océane and Esther if you need friends. They seem cut out of a different material."

"I don't need friends, Edda. I'm fine by myself."

Edda glanced at the pinched face, once more wondering about the secret Anna hid and then put it to rest.

"Bye, Anna. I hope you will be well."

"You too, Edda. I'll be scanning the papers for a photograph of you as Clara."

"Clara?" Edda's cheeks reddened.

"Yes, the lead in the Nutcracker. You must know who Clara is?" It was Anna's turn to be surprised.

"Yes, of course. I know who Clara is. Inside and out," Edda mumbled.

11

AN UNWELCOME SURPRISE

A few days later – Switzerland, March 1938

As Edda got ready to depart for Lausanne's train station, she saw Océane and Esther come her way. Edda waved. Océane called, "Wait a moment!"

"Mademoiselle, we must catch that train." Filippo was busy putting her luggage in the boot but now tapped his watch.

"I know, Filippo. Give me one second. The girls were constantly busy with classes, so I had no opportunity to say goodbye to them."

"They're the most decent two, indeed," Filippo observed.

"We'll miss you," Océane said.

"We never had a chance to become friends," Esther added.

"I know. I didn't expect to leave so soon myself, but I want to get back into my dance routine as soon as I can."

"Can we hug?" That was Océane.

"Of course." Her candid request made Edda smile. And also, a little sad that they had no more time together.

As they stood embracing, Esther said," My fiancé's best friend, Asher Hoffman, is a ballet dancer as well, but he's still in Austria.

Maybe you will dance together on a stage in London or New York. How cool would that be, and Carl and I could come and see you?"

"When I'm in New York, I'll be part of that party," Océane giggled and the comradery all three felt was special.

"I'll keep an eye out for a dancer called Asher Hoffman," Edda promised, "and if we ever cross paths, I'll tell him about you, Esther Weiss."

"Time to go, demoiselles," the chauffeur interrupted, "or Mademoiselle Edda will miss her train and I'll be vilified by Madame Paul." The girls disentangled from their embrace.

"One more second." Edda got a pen and paper from her duffel coat, the notebook in which she made sketches for a choreography that was in her head. She ripped out a page and wrote down her Vondelstraat address and handed it to Esther.

"Will you look out for yourself, Esther? I'm glad you and Océane are friends. Give these bullies a a taste of their own medicine, will you?"

"I will," Esther smiled and Océane slung a slender arm around Esther's waist.

"In case either of you ever makes it to Holland, you've got my address. Or you can write me." She called as she got into the back of the Renault.

"We will."

They stood arm-in-arm on the gravel, as Edda saw the last glimpse of them, and of Le Manoir.

Focus on the future, Edda. That's all you've got. But her heart was temporarily heavy for what could have been. Socializing was again going to be something not for the likes of Edda.

"Don't worry about the future, Mademoiselle Edda, you'll be alright. Like the girls said, I too will scan the papers to see your star rise. We're so proud of you."

And with that high praise, Edda left Switzerland. She hadn't even visited the Alps.

∼

EDDA ARRIVED at Leiden Station at the end of a Friday afternoon in the middle of March. On the way, she'd seen the first crocuses and daffodils waving their colorful stems at her and she'd been glad to be back in her native country.

I'll visit the Alps another time, she promised herself as they first passed through Rotterdam, then The Hague and finally Leiden Station came into view. The train would eventually go on to Amsterdam as the final destination, but Edda thought it appropriate to pay a visit to her parents first. Now she felt she had a lifetime of dancing ahead of her again, she wanted to share that happiness with her parents. And hopefully they *would* share in it.

The train came to a screeching halt and Edda scanned the waiting crowds for the towering blonde Bollema, but she didn't see him. He'd been notified of her arrival, including train number and arrival time, so she assumed he was a moment late.

Scrambling to get her own luggage into the hallway of the train, she looked in vain around her for a porter to help her. The train would leave in two minutes. Depending on her former strength, Edda started hauling the two heavy suitcases – just in case she'd stayed the full year at Le Manoir -- towards the train's narrow exit.

She started sweating, debating whether to head for Amsterdam after all if she didn't make it, when she heard an upper-class male voice call for her from outside. She blinked, looked twice. Ludovicus Van Limburg Stirum. What the heck! Was this some sort of trap?

Edda now seriously turned around to head for her own home, but he called again, "Wait, Eddaline, I'm here to fetch you. It's rather urgent. I'll explain in a minute." Edda felt the hairs stand up on the skin of her arms. What on earth could be so urgent to send the boring suitor her way?

Helpful, though not very muscular, the middle-aged attorney with the balding spot on his distinguished scalp hauled first one and then the other suitcase onto the platform. Edda followed with her hat box and handbag, still suspicious at this unasked-for welcome committee.

The train sighed and heaved and started moving only seconds

after Edda stood on the platform, firmly on two legs, with a questioning look on her face. Van Limburg Stirum stretched out his hand – still without a wedding ring, she noted with frustration -- and she shook it. What else could she do? The grip was firmer than expected, more sympathetic as well.

"What's going on? Where's Klaas Bollema?"

He hesitated with his answer, the slate-colored eyes blinking a tad too much. Edda became impatient, and ugly thoughts about her parents setting her up after all buzzed around her mind. Was this their way of showing discontent with her unfinished finishing school?

"I'm here to take you to the hospital, Eddaline. Your mother... hm... has been operated on." The nervous blinking intensified. Edda felt like turning into a pillar of salt. "Mama!" she yelped. "What's wrong with Mama and where is my father?"

"Please, Eddaline, let me explain. One thing at a time. Your mother had an operation on her breast, but she's recuperating. Mr Bollema had to drive your father to an important meeting with ministers in The Hague, so they asked if I could pick you up and take you to the Academic Hospital."

"Oh. I see. I'm sorry," Edda stammered, as a porter loaded her luggage onto a trolley and she followed Van Limburg Stirum to his Traction Avant. The small trunk didn't look like it could hold the bulky suitcases, but under the circumstances, Edda couldn't be worried about the lid being tied with a piece of rope if need be. They were silent as they got into the car. Edda didn't know what to think or feel. She was numb, travel-weary, shocked. Her mother's breast. What was wrong with her breast? Had her worries about her mother been justified after all?

"How is she?"

Van Limburg Stirum was steering the clunky automobile awkwardly through Leiden towards the hospital. As if he was driving a car for the first time, rather in fits and starts. He remained silent, as if he hadn't heard her question. She studied his profile, the prominent forehead – a sign of intelligence? – the slated eyes focused as if he was studying an important court case, the angular nose, pressed white lips. It was hard to read what was going on inside that head of his.

Edda had never been in a car with Ludovicus before and she was aware he was quite ill at ease with her next to him, but she had no time for his feelings or the lack thereof. If he needed all of his attention on just managing the vehicle, fine, but she wanted, nay needed, an answer. He was currently the only one with knowledge of what was going on in her family before she had to face her sick mother in a hospital bed. He'd been sent to pick her up. He must have more information. Perhaps a brilliant attorney, Ludovicus Van Limburg Stirum certainly wasn't a socially-equipped conversationalist. Edda repeated her question, chewing on her lower lip.

"How is she, Lu... Ludovicus?" Using his Christian name – after all, they'd formally established on one of her mother's dull soirees they'd be on a first-name basis – she hoped he would snap out of his ill-at-ease self.

"Sorry, that darn traffic. What was that, Eddaline?"

For the third time Edda asked after her mother's health. *Impossible man*, she thought, but her exasperation with his behavior was perhaps a welcome distraction from her worries.

"I don't know the ins and outs, Eddaline. Sorry. But your parents told me to tell you not to worry."

"More easily said than done," Edda snapped. "Just drop me off and I'll find my way."

"I was asked to wait for you so I can give you a lift to Huis van Leyden."

"No need, I'll get a taxi."

"Sorry," he said again. "I understand this isn't the nicest way to come home from abroad."

"Thank you. I shouldn't take it out on you. You've been very kind to me," Edda sighed as she got out of his car and raced to the hospital entrance as fast as her weak left leg would carry her.

"What about your luggage, Eddaline?" He shouted after her.

"Drop it off at my parents' house. Thank you!"

The first person she encountered, as she rushed through the hospital doors, was Duifje, who was smoking a cigarette and hugging an oversized woolen cardigan around her willowy body.

"Lientje," she cried. "Oh, Lientje!"

Edda fled into the arms, being sprinkled with ashes as usual. How good it was to feel her sister's embrace. It made everything easier to bear.

"How is she, Duif? What happened? She seemed fine when we went to Switzerland."

"I know, darling. Mother said nothing, but apparently, she's been under supervision for a year. It's breast cancer, but the operation was successful."

"Why did nobody phone me?" Edda sobbed against Duifje's chest.

"They didn't want to worry you, doll. That's all."

Edda suddenly remembered how her mother told her about not knowing her first fiancé had been killed in the Great War while she was at Le Manoir. Had it been her mother's way of saying she might do the same to Edda? Had she known then that she would be operated upon? Was that what Madame Paul had alluded to when she said former days would never return? Was Mama dying? *Noooo!*

"Come, dry your tears. I'll buy you a coffee and a bun, and then we'll go and see Mother." Duifje slung her long arm around her sister and directed her towards the hospital restaurant. Edda obeyed like an automaton.

"Will she live, Duif?"

"Of course, doll. Don't be daft. Mother's as strong as an ox. Good Prussian blood, that sort of thing. Women have these operations every day and live to grand old age."

Slightly comforted, also by the perspective of something to drink and eat after her long journey, Edda sat down on the hard Formica chair and didn't let go of her sister's hand. Duifje snapped the fingers of her other hand irritably in the air to get the waiter's attention.

"I've been here since morning, as Father was away and we knew you were coming. I have no more patience with these loitering lackeys."

"They're not lackeys, Duif." Edda burst into laughter, which relieved some of the horrible tension.

"Whatever they are, they're slow as molasses." Duifje's blue eyes darkened as she lit another cigarette. "Well, sis, how have you been, doing your own type of lackeying? Wonder why Mother and Father never sent me to that school. Would have done me tons of good in managing my household." Duifje grinned, showing slightly yellowed teeth from all her smoking.

Edda laughed again. Oh, it was so good to see Duifje, who, despite her chagrin about the serving staff at the hospital, seemed in an excellent mood.

THE LIGHT in her mother's room was dimmed, but there was a lamp lit next to the bed. Her mother was reading a German novel, her reading glasses half-way down her nose. She looked up, her face pale and visibly slimmed, but she was smiling when she saw her daughter. Edda thought there was also a guilty glint in her mother's dark eyes.

"Mammy!" she ran to the bed like a little girl and flung herself at her, only then realizing her mother had had an operation.

"Ouch!"

"Oh, I'm so sorry, Mama." Edda sprang to her legs and took a meter's distance.

"It's alright, Eddaline, I'm all padded up." Her mother tapped her chest that indeed looked like an in-season cock-pigeon. "Come closer again, my dear, and let me have a look at you."

"Mama, why?" Edda sank down on the chair next to the bed, taking her mother's limp hand. "Why didn't you tell me?"

"Would you have gone, my child?"

Edda shook her head. Duifje called from the door.

"I'll be back in a sec. Just need a fag."

"How are you now, Mama? Will you be okay?"

"Of course, Eddaline." Her mother regained some of her former Prussian pride. "It'll take more than this to get me six feet under."

"But how long have you been ill? How long have you known?"

"To the first question, I have no answer. To the second question, six months. The doctors thought it was minor and told me not to worry, but before we left for Switzerland, I had another check-up and they told me the thing had grown." She pointed to her left breast, circling her finger around. "I had to be operated upon. That's why..." The Marchioness hesitated, "that was the reason I wanted to go to Switzerland with you and not accompany Papa to Germany. He wasn't pleased about that, but as I didn't know how the operation would go, I wanted to be with you. Also, because you were going through a tough spot yourself."

"Ah, Mama." Edda kissed the limp hand, tears welling in her eyes. "You shouldn't have. It was dangerous. What if something would have happened to you on the way?"

"Oh no, silly child, the doctors said I could easily make the trip. It helped me greatly to take my mind off myself. Something those war-mongering men wouldn't have managed."

Edda looked at her mother sharply. Was this the same Mama that had proudly boasted about being a personal friend of Hitler? Who doffed herself up every time one of her father's high-ranking Nazi friends came to stay at Huis van Leyden? But she said nothing, though she felt relieved. As if Mama was in *her* camp now, not that Edda had a camp.

"Now tell me, dear, did Ludovicus keep his promise and pick you up from the station? It was such a rigmarole with Teppo having some sort of hardware conference in Arnhem and Papa needing to have a consultation with Prime-Minister Colijn. As if we haven't got enough cars to go around." Again, that guilty glint in her mother's eye.

"He did, Mama, and he was most kind, though awfully quiet."

"He's not the gossipy type, Eddaline, if that's what you mean, but he could win a debate with the likes of Abraham Lincoln, had they been contemporaries."

"Mother," Edda giggled. "You seem much taken by our friend Van Limburg Stirum."

The Marchioness smiled as well. "Especially after I found out he's actually your father's cousin, once removed. There's been a branch of the Van der Valk family that fell out with the Van Limburg Stirums, but he's family, dear. And yes, I like him. I like men that have a brilliant brain and are a little inept. Your father can be that way, too."

"How is Papa?"

"Oh, you know. He doesn't show his inside, but he brought me flowers. That says enough. He hasn't done that since he started courting me." She pointed to a vase with yellow chrysanthemums. The look in her mother's eyes told Edda the flowers meant a lot to her.

"When are you coming home, Mama?"

"I think I will be released tomorrow. So, all's well that ends well. Now you go home and rest and next time we meet, I'll be home. Give my regards to Ludo."

Edda didn't have the heart to tell her mother he wasn't waiting for her anymore.

She kissed the damp forehead, swallowed her tears. "See you tomorrow, Mama."

"Yes, child, and don't fret. You're walking like a gazelle again, so you can return to Amsterdam soon."

Edda shook her head. "I'm staying with you, Mama. You are more important than my dance career."

The Marchioness sat upright, adjusting her purple bed jacket, looking sternly at her daughter.

"No!" she said firmly. "If this illness has taught me one thing, then it is not to stand in the way of anyone's passions, yours or mine. You dance, Edda, as you were born to do."

"Oh, oh, oh my cry-baby," Duifje said as Edda left the room sobbing wildly. "My little sis, the cry-baby."

But Edda didn't care about the label this time. She cried all the tears she'd wanted to cry ever since someone stepped on her foot and it went 'snap'.

12

THE FATHER

Three weeks later, Amsterdam, April 1938

Edda arrived back in Amsterdam when the magnolia blossomed, and the winter coats were packed away. Her mother's recovery had been swift and satisfactory, and both parents had agreed Edda could return to Amsterdam. But before she left, her father had called her into his study.

"Sit, Eddaline." He pointed to the chair opposite his desk, and she slunk into it, feeling more like one of his clerks or a passing dignitary than his daughter. She'd not been in this austere office before, and felt uncomfortable with the portraits of Adolf Hitler and Anton Mussert side by side on the wall behind him. Both fascist dictators staring down at her over her father's shoulders seemed like a bad omen.

"What is it, Father?"

He kept himself busy, putting his signature on documents and seemed absorbed in the action. But finally, he clicked his fountain pen shut and looked up at her, with tired blue eyes.

"Yes, I wanted to have a word with you, Eddaline," he began, lighting a cigar in very much the same way Duifje lit her cigarettes.

"What about, Father?"

The formal setting gave rise to using Father instead of Papa. Speaking in this setting with her didn't come easily to him, and Edda recalled how her mother had said that her father could be inept as well. He certainly was now, and it made her uncomfortable. As if there wasn't just an enormous desk between them but also an ocean in feeling. He had such a hard time speaking about personal things while he could rattle on at any dinner table about politics and the ways of justice.

"Are you not happy I'm going back to dancing, Papa?" She decided to try a direct route to his heart.

"What? No! It's not that. Your mother wants it for you and that's what counts. I know nothing of the whole thing, though I can enjoy a Wagner Opera. Your mother has assured me you won't be falling for one of these men in tights that snip their legs in the air as if they're scissors. As long as you take your dancing seriously and don't compromise yourself, I have no problem with it."

"I have no intention of falling in love, Papa. I do take my dance career seriously. And by the way, that jump is called an *entrechat*."

It was the first time a vague smile curled under her father's mustache.

"What does the cat have to do with it? Bah, all those French words. They sound so feminine."

But when he saw the vexed look on Edda's face, he apologized. "Sorry, I keep forgetting you love it all. It's just not my world, Edda-line, but I want my women to be happy. So, as I said before, as long as you don't run away with the circus, I'll condone your dance mania."

"But you enjoyed the Nutcracker? You said so yourself."

"It wasn't bad because *you* were in it. Let's leave it at that."

"Thank you, Papa. So can I go now?"

"No, there's something else. Um... your mother's illness has... uh... made me reconsider my will. As she's so much younger than me, it had never occurred to me she could... uh, pass before me."

Edda looked at her father in astonishment. Then suddenly realized he was a man in his late fifties, but he looked healthy as a May morning, and had never been ill.

"Is something the matter with you, too, Papa?" Her eyes grew big with fear.

"No, silly goose, I'm fine. It's just that I have no son and Teppo, kind and nice as the boy is, isn't really the type of fellow to carry the Van der Valk flag, so to say. Benny's a toddler and Duifje's a scatter-brain. That leaves you." He stopped, fixing his tired blue gaze on her.

"But Papa," she began, suddenly feeling as if an heavy lorry was heading her way and she would have no time to jump aside. "I don't have a head for business or politics, either. I wouldn't know where to start."

"Well, you don't have to, Eddaline. I just want you to know that should anything happen to both your mother and me, you're in charge of the estate and all that belongs to it. My solicitor, Jan Sipkema, will assist you with all the knowledge and experience he has."

Edda gasped. She had no clue who Jan Sipkema was, but if he was anything like Klaas Bollema, she would run like the wind.

"But Papa..." she began again and felt like crying.

"Don't worry about it now, Eddaline, go and dance to your heart's content. Just know that maybe in twenty or thirty years –if nothing happens in the meantime to make me change my will again –it will be yours to handle." He got up and did something he seldom did. He planted a kiss on her forehead. To Edda it felt like the seal of doom, and she shivered.

"Just stay alive forever. Please, Papa," she whispered, and he laughed. Really laughed this time.

"I can't, my dear, but what I *can* promise you is that we're heading to a glorious future. Strong men like Adolf Hitler and Anton Mussert will turn our two countries into economic paradises. I intend to benefit from that personally, so one day you'll be a very rich girl. Better choose your husband carefully as he, too, will have a lot to handle."

"I'll never marry, Papa.' She mumbled, but she saw she didn't have his attention anymore. He'd said what he had to say, and it was time for her to leave. Edda rose from the chair, stared down on her father's thick crop of gray-blond hair as he bent over his papers again.

Stop that horrible intuition, she told her gut, but it was there, as glaring as the faces of her father's two heroes on his wall. It wouldn't be twenty years. It wouldn't even be ten years. And it would be a catastrophe. *Please no!*

"Bye, Papa."

"Be a good girl, Eddy."

He never called her that these days. The eighteen-wheeler was still rolling Edda's way, but she decided to jump aside. She had no time for more family drama.

13

ASHER HOFFMANN

Three weeks later – April 1938

It was a beautiful spring morning when Edda hoisted her stuffed ballet bag onto the back of her bicycle and cycled through the Vondelpark to the Stadsschouwburg on the Museumplein where the Amsterdam Ballet Theater was practising for Giselle. How she loved being back in the game, though she'd agreed with Miss Sterling that for the time being she'd dance one of the chorus girls as she was still not back on top. Of course, the enviable Maria Petrova was to dance Giselle.

Edda parked her bike and, taking two steps at the time, skipped up the stairs to the dressing rooms. Looking forward to a day on the stage boards, she was also looking forward to seeing more of the ballet mistress's latest acquisition in the form of a new dancer. Every female dancer had been swooning about a certain Asher Hoffmann, whose only interest to Edda was that he was acquainted with Esther Weiss from Le Manoir.

Asher, or rather Ash - as he'd announced he preferred to be called - was Austrian, of medium height with a shock of dark blonde hair that was way too long for a male dancer, and explosive Slavic eyes, a face as if carved out of marble and a nose slightly out of joint.

She'd met him the day before as he sat cross legged on a hard chair with his neck wrapped in a hand-knit shawl, his torso in a black sleeveless top and his legs, in black tights, swaddled to the knees in black leg warmers. His ballet shoes were worn and crinkled.

Edda had instantly recalled her father's warning, 'no boys in tights'. Well, Edda wasn't going for any boy, tights or not.

Yet there had been something about this Asher Hoffmann as everybody flocked to his side, as if wanting to get into his good books. The fuss had made Edda give him a second glance. True, he was no ordinary 'boy in tights.' He was a boss in tights, and he seemed to know it. The way he'd brushed her over and smiled at her, the way his muscled arm lay over the back of the sofa, relaxed and graceful like a bark-less branch in the forest. The way he'd wrapped *tout le monde* –including Miss Sterling - around his elegant pinkie, on which glittered a huge topaz ring.

Edda, too, was intrigued, and she hated it. She had no time for this nonsense. It meddled with her longing to give every last fiber of her being to her rehabilitation, but she also hated it because Ash made the whole group shine. It was as if he'd stolen Drosselmeyer's magic wand and had enchanted them all. Especially Maria Petrova, who was to be in Ash's arms most of the time, shone in his presence like God's most precious diamond. Because Ash, without apparently doing anything but being his magnificent self, had pushed all the other male dancers down the ladder.

Though only in Holland for a couple of weeks and the new kid on the block in the Amsterdam Ballet Theater, Asher Hoffmann would dance Albrecht, Count of Silesia, betrothed to Bathilde, and the beloved of Giselle. And Edda wasn't even going to be Bathilde. Not that she cared. Or so she told herself.

"Silly goose," she reprimanded herself. Staring for a moment at the bouquet of roses on her dressing table. They were starting to wither. It had been a welcome gift from the team. Such a sweet gesture. Without further ado she got into her dance costume, a simple pink bodysuit and matching tights. They weren't at the stage of dress rehearsals with full costumes yet.

There *had* been other dazzling, male dancers who'd kept her interest for a while, but it had always been because of their technique. Sometimes she'd been intrigued by how they bent their personality to their technique. Those aspects she'd studied and learned from, not whether a dancer was of any personal interest to her.

Edda studied herself in the mirror as she bound the wriggly, dark curls into a tight bun. And then the flutter was there again, but it had nothing, or at least very little, to do with Asher Hoffmann. They were so close to dress rehearsals. Suddenly, the idea of being a part of a new ballet performance made her shudder. Would her ankle hold? What if it broke again or in another place? She was to be a chorus girl, so constantly near other dancers. What if one stepped on her toes? She'd experienced the devastating effects of such a split second and could not face it again.

This was nothing compared to what Miss Sterling had called the "screamy meemies" before her big entrée as Clara. That had been stage fright for the audience. This was fear for those on stage with her.

There was a rap on the door and Edda quickly put in the last hairpins, expecting to see Miss Sterling in the door opening. But the door didn't open.

"Come in," she called, surprised as Miss Sterling wouldn't wait.

Edda frowned. It was Maria.

"What are you doing here?" Edda didn't turn to face her, but looked straight at her in the mirror. The familiar mistrust, a kind of rumble in her abdomen, made Edda tense.

"Can I come in for a moment?"

Edda thought fast. Whatever Maria's exquisite moves on the stage, she disliked the girl and didn't want her meddling with her already wobbly state.

"I don't know. What do you want? I have to be warming up at the barre in five minutes."

"This will only take two. I just wanted to say, I missed you. And Miss Sterling and Monsieur Sergeyev weren't the same after you left."

Swiveling around on her stool, she faced the Russian head-on, who was towering above her but averted the cat-like light eyes. Edda shrugged. There would not be an apology, at least not yet, but why this hogwash about missing her?

Well, Edda could do haughty, too. Lifting the dark eyebrows, she scoffed. "Anything else, Maria? Otherwise, I'd like to get on with my preparations." She would not give *La* Petrova the satisfaction of seeing her nervousness.

"No, that's all. I just wanted you to know we missed you." Maria fingered the card attached to the bouquet of roses and Edda now understood it was Maria's handwriting. "Welcome back, Edda-Clara, we missed you!"

"Thank you, Maria. Good luck with dancing Giselle." The look the other dancer gave her made Edda wonder what on earth was going on inside her? There was pain, or was it regret? Miss Sterling must have given her a firm dressing down. Well, she'd deserved it. But Edda frowned after Maria closed the door behind her. Either she'd been sent there by the ballet mistress to apologize and couldn't munch up the words, or something else was going on with her.

"Well, it's none of my business," Edda told her mirror image. "Let her enjoy being swirled around in splendid formation across the stage by that new phenom and let me just get one foot in front of the other decently."

"GIVE IT TIME, EDDA!" Miss Sterling's voice sounded behind her as tears streamed down Edda's cheeks. Even the simple positions at the barre seemed like her body had decided to be of firm oak instead of elasticity and agility. She quickly smeared her sleeve over her wet cheeks. Keeping her eyes down, away from her mentor, who could see her face anyway in the mirror behind the barre, she felt five years old again, angry with herself and angry with the world that first position should be anything like an effort to her human physique.

"Turn around. Look at me," Miss Sterling demanded.

She had no choice. Slowly she spun, her eyes fixed on her ballet shoes, suppressing a sniffle.

"What did you expect, my dear?" the ballet mistress's voice was soft, soothing.

"Oh, Miss Sterling," Edda yammered, "I've lost so much. Will I ever be..."

"With your drive, I'd say two weeks, Edda. So, listen carefully. Maria is leaving for London soon. I want you to dance Giselle."

Without explaining further, the ballet mistress turned her back on Edda and strode away in her typical elegant gait, a mint cardigan draped around her shoulders.

"Wait," Edda called. "I can't, you know I can't, Miss Sterling. Not yet. Please don't ask that of me."

The blonde head with the colorful scarf turned abruptly. There was a mocking smile on the perfectly painted lips. "Why not? Are you worried about your own physique or is Asher Hoffman in some way off-putting to you?"

"It's got nothing to do with Asher Hoffman...," Edda retorted, then bit her tongue, realizing he *was* part of her refusal. Hadn't he been absolutely picture perfect with Maria? How would he feel dancing with someone who wasn't sure of her own body yet? But then, she understood. Her mentor was putting her to the test. It was Edda's job to pass that test.

"Cry as much as you need, my dear, when your body protests. It will release the tension. Then dance Giselle. For me. For yourself." And with that, Miss Sterling disappeared into her office, but left the door open.

Edda returned to the barre. Let her eyes go travel down the length of her body. It was slim. It was strong. It was set to go. Ash or no Ash. For now, Edda didn't need that open door, but it was good to know it was there.

For the next five hours there was nothing in the world but Edda, the barre, and her body, bending and stretching, bending and stretching. It was heaven. She was back. Every muscle hurt, every joint protested, but her mind was as clear as if the angels had washed it and her spirit soared. Even Giselle in two weeks seemed viable. But for now, it was noodle soup and bed. In her own cozy apartment. Life smiled at her again. Breathing deeply and freely, Edda made her way to the dressing room and started packing her shoes.

I'm too tired to change now. I'll do it at home. She thought and grabbed her coat.

"Impressive!"

Edda looked up from stuffing her shoes in her bag. Asher Hoffmann stood resting his shoulder against the doorpost of her dressing room, looking around the room more than at her. Confusion and irritation gurgled up in her.

"Do you mean my dressing room? They're all the same," she shrugged. Okay, hers might be a little neater than most, as she liked it that way. But impressive?

"You know I'm not talking about your dressing room."

Edda rose to her full height. She didn't like his tone. It was too intrusive. What was he doing here anyway, entering without knocking? Was that the way people acted in Austria? But Esther had been very courteous and polite. And she liked this man. He was her fiancé's best friend. Edda shrugged again. Maybe this Asher Hoffmann still felt out of place and as a result exaggerated his confidence.

"If not my dressing room, what *are* you talking about Mr. Hoffmann?"

He burst into laughter. "Mr. Hoffmann is my father! Nobody has called *me* Mr. Hoffmann before."

"Well, there is a first time for everything," Edda said laconically, and brushed past him to get to her bike and cycle home. That was what she craved.

"I meant your dancing, *Mrs.* Van der Valk," he joked.

Turning on her heels, Edda glared at him.

"Have you been spying on me when I was practicing at the barre? That's rude."

For a moment he looked shocked; she saw the dark-gray eyes squint.

"No, honestly. I wasn't. I mean, I passed by and caught a glimpse of you in the mirror. I simply had to look. I've never seen a technique like yours and Miss Sterling told me you had just had a serious injury, so I was even more impressed."

Edda wasn't sure if she could trust him. She was not ready to be the plaything of some Austrian star who thought every girl got knocky-knees on coming into his orbit. But he seemed overly cocky now, so she hesitated. Still uneasy, though, in the knowledge he'd been watching her when she'd struggled so much with her inner demons.

Ash was the first to speak.

"It wasn't just curiosity, Edda. I suppose Miss Sterling told you you're going to be my Giselle?"

"I'm not *your* Giselle,' Edda snapped. "Go try your charms on the other girls and leave me alone." She raced out of the door. He was horrid!

"Ouch, you're hurting my ego."

"Good!" she shouted over her shoulder. "I'm sure you'll soon find someone to bandage your ego for you."

"You're an *impressive* dancer!" was the last thing she heard as she flung the door shut. She grabbed the handle again in flaring anger, ready to go back in and demand he'd never ever spy on her while she was practising, but then let go.

"He's not worth it," she murmured as she unlocked her bike, wondering deeply how such a sweet girl like Esther could have spoken so favorably of a guy like Asher Hoffmann.

Still full of rage, Edda pedaled through the streets of Amsterdam until she was stopped by a parade of rows of men dressed in black, waving National Socialist banners and shouting their slogan, "Houzee!" while they stretched their right arms halfway into the air. Edda pumped her brakes or would have ridden right into the first row.

Upfront was Klaas Bollema, his booming voice overpowering the others. Her father's chauffeur and Edda recognized each other at the same time. Edda stood gaping at him, wondering what he was doing in a parade in Amsterdam. If her father even knew. Klaas waved his red-black flag with the NSB triangle demonstratively at her and chanted even louder. "Holland boven alles" and "Weg met de Joden."

Before Edda could recover from her shock, they'd turned the corner of the Stadhouderskade on their way to the Leidseplein. She could still hear their slogans "Holland above all" and "Away with the Jews" in the distance.

"Stelletje collaborateurs!" An old man shouted after the NSB men, but his wife hushed him, "don't call them collaborators, Jan, or they'll come after you." But the old man grumbled, "let them come, they don't frighten me."

But they did frighten Edda. Was Klaas in that parade at the request of her father? Was this what her parents wanted? To spread fear and hate? These black-clad men had looked menacing and the way they were marching towards the city center didn't bode well.

Edda shuddered as she cycled on, much slower now, confused, her tiredness temporarily forgotten. Monsieur Sergeyev was Jewish, her brother-in-law was half Jewish, the floor master Larry de Jonge was Jewish and, of course, the man she'd just had a confrontation with...Ash Hoffmann.

He'd fled Austria because of how his people were treated after the Anschluss on the 13th of March. Esther had told her the Hoffmann's hadn't wanted to wait any longer, whereas her family still stuck it out in Vienna.

Would Vienna come to Amsterdam now? But no. This wasn't Hitler or the SA. These were Dutchmen gone astray. She should draw strength from that old man and not worry unnecessarily. It was all just a bluff. Bluff and idiocy. Nothing would come of it.

Miss Sterling's trust in Edda's physical recovery had been sound. With every day, Edda gained more strength, more suppleness, more self-assurance. She blossomed like a rare flower, giggled and joked with the team, and felt ready for the first rehearsal as Giselle. Maria Petrova had mysteriously disappeared, not even said goodbye, but Edda shed no tears over that. Good riddance and good luck.

But the day she was to start dancing with Asher was not exactly the one Edda looked forward to. Their first confrontation had had the right effect, and he hadn't tried his advances on her anymore, but she was constantly irritated by his overbearing presence and the zealotry of the other ballerinas.

When the aloof Maria had been his dance partner, no jealous eyes had been on Edda, but now it was announced that she was cast as Albrecht's big love, the dynamics in the group changed. Even Miss Sterling had asked Ash to dim his light a little and not to be so openly zippy with the girls. Edda hadn't exactly been eavesdropping, but she'd overheard the conversation while walking past the ballet mistress's door. And the door had been open as usual.

"Am I?" she'd heard Ash ask. There had been genuine surprise in his voice. He wasn't acting. "I promise I'll do my best to be less 'zippy,' Miss Sterling, though I'm not sure I know what it means."

"I think that's the whole problem, Ash. You're not aware of how you come across. I'm just telling you that Edda is a serious girl, so treat her with respect. She may not appreciate that carefree, easy-going spirit of yours."

"Oh," Ash had replied. "Thank you for telling me that. I have been wracking my mind over how to approach Edda Van der Valk. She's... she's different from the other ballerinas. There's something gritty about her, strong and serious yet gritty."

Edda's cheeks had reddened at these last words. She'd quickly moved away from the door, feeling she oughtn't have listened in to that conversation.

Gritty? Was she gritty? And what did that mean? One thing was clear to Edda, though. The Ash who'd been talking with Miss Sterling was not the showstopper he gave the impression to be. And Miss Sterling had done her a serious favor to warn Ash to treat her right.

They were to dance a tragic love story together and in order to bring that across as sincere and heartfelt, they needed to have a personal connection, they needed to establish a form of trust. And trust was lacking. They had no connection at all. She'd avoided him and he had left her in peace after that first clumsy attempt.

Knowing she had to die from heartbreak as Giselle made it a hard ballet for Edda to dance. Giselle lacked the lighter parts the Nutcracker had. Giselle was a tragedy, people trapped in a love they could never have. And the unconvincing 'happy ending'- Giselle lying at peace in her grave - wasn't anything like the revelation in the Nutcracker that Clara had 'only' had a fantastic dream.

Maybe she didn't want to dance Giselle. Maybe she should ask Miss Sterling to let her be Berthe, Giselle's mother, or even the wicked Martha. Edda distinctly felt she wasn't ready for Giselle. But she also knew Miss Sterling wouldn't budge.

A good ballerina dances the lead role in one or two ballets before getting married and giving up the stage. A great ballerina dances Clara, and Giselle, and Julia, and Odette, and Cinderella, and La Sylphide and Nikiya.

To the question if Miss Sterling herself had danced them all, she'd replied with an indignant, "of course!"

Edda sighed, sipping her cup of strong, hot tea before going to the rehearsal room and having to face Ash. Her long fingers wrapped around the warm cup, she sat with an arched back, hunched on the stool with her arms around her knees, making herself as small as possible. Feeling her breath fight for space in her belly, revolting against her backbone to find room there. She loved that feeling. It was vibrant, alive.

A rap. Not Miss Sterling but Asher Hoffman. A diffident "may I come in?" She noticed the lingering German accent, reminiscent of Esther, and nodded, not answering him. He kept standing, looking down on her saying nothing. The gaze was intense, but she withstood it. Huddled within herself, just breathing, she could withstand anything. And he'd come to her, so he clearly had something to say to her.

"Are you ready?" It sounded kind of shy. In the mirror she could see he was standing like a schoolboy waiting for a dressing down.

"Sit, please." Edda unwrapped herself. "And, thank you for coming."

"Really?" A mock smile slid over the handsomely carved face, but he quickly corrected himself. "I doubted whether I should, but I'm getting the feeling you don't really want to dance with me. I thought it would be a bad thing to start off on the wrong foot, so to say."

"Tea?"

"Do you think we have time for that? Miss Ster..."

"Yes or no?" The roles were reversed now. Edda took control. "Miss Sterling knows like no other that the chemistry between her dancers makes or breaks the performance. So, I think we need to have this talk."

"I agree."

He let out a breath of relief and in that instant she knew for sure there was more to Asher Hoffmann than met the eye. He wasn't as he wanted to come across. He was hiding his sensitivity under a polished, Don Juan layer.

Later, she could pinpoint with certainty that had been the moment she fell in love with him, when she handed him that cup of tea and their eyes met on a soul-to-soul level. The other certainty was she knew he'd fallen for her, too. Her sixth sense told her while her brain shouted, 'no way!'

They drank the tea in silence, but the negative charge between them was gone. That tension had evaporated in the exchange of gazes. Now a new tension made the silence pregnant with curiosity, contemplation, and cognizance.

Edda's eyes took in the almost otherworldly beauty of his presence with great gulps. The completely black attire over a body made by the grace of God and Ash's own hard work. The long wavy hair, the same color as the light, blond wood of the ash tree, held back with a headband so it wouldn't fall into his eyes. The eyes themselves, now cast down, focused on his teacup with the dark lashes blinking now and then.

Edda could never determine the color of Ash's eyes. They changed from pale blue to deep gray-black depending on the emotions he felt, and Asher Hoffmann clearly felt deeply. He felt everything.

She followed her lingering gaze over the jawline, as if hewn out of basalt, the cheeks with their powerful lines, and the nose slightly out of joint. So Ash, so much more Ash. Her senses were getting intimately connected to his physique, his heartbeat, his scent --woodsy, earthly musk -- the grace with which every move originated from something deep within him.

And nothing of Asher Hoffmann frightened Edda Van der Valk anymore. It stilled all the fright in her. For she now knew she could pull it off. Dance with him, be with him, bring to life Giselle and let her die. For the first time in her life, Edda felt real power, and it was intoxicating.

"I think I'm ready," she whispered. "More words would just kill the feeling."

He raised his eyes to hers. They were deep and troubled, almost black, and Edda started. Had she imagined it all? Had she been led astray by her intuition? He looked dangerous, and dangerously troubled. But then the eyes changed color, first to a somber dark gray, then lighter to soft blue, as of a robin's egg. Thin-skinned, vulnerable.

"Let's try, Edda, but by God you knock the props out of me."

"Wait till we dance, Ash. I know it will become crystal clear."

14

DANCE UNTIL YOU SHATTER
YOURSELF

On their first movement together, Edda knew. She'd been here before, she didn't know how or when, but she'd been there before, and it was exactly what Heaven looked like. There was no her, no him; there was one graceful movement, and then the next, and the next.

She didn't even have to think of the steps, Ash drew them out of her as if her feet were on elastic bands attached to his heart. All she needed to do was follow his movements, which were really hers, or perhaps the Divine's. Left, right, up, down, straight ahead, back, turn, wait. No thinking, no calculating, just space and energy and her wide-open heart.

The osmosis was like a one-body sensation Edda's whole being craved. When Ash twirled her across the dance floor, she was wrapped tight in his heart. The elastic band uncoiled but held as she pirouetted away from him. But her heart was merely waiting to be back in his arms, feel his strength, his breath on her, brown eyes drowning in blue eyes.

Everything in between was no time, gritty. There was that word again, where had it come from? But now she knew what he'd meant. She'd been gritty, granular, unless she was in his arms. And yet her own *jetés* and *pirouettes* were perfect as well, only meant for him, to make him more in love with her, his arms stretching out to her, so she'd race back to him.

They became 'Giselle' and 'Albrecht' to their cores. Their on-stage love affair, though exuberant and overtly, was still strictly platonic.

Enwrapped with every fiber in Ash's dance, as they portrayed the forbidden romance in Act I, Edda sensed she was watched from the first row by Miss Sterling and Monsieur Sergeyev. She was sure they saw what was happening. *Wait till you find your match.* That's what her mentor had said. Marlene Sterling found *her* match in the Russian Pyotr Sergeyev, and now Edda had found hers in Austrian Ash.

The ballet mistress clapped her hands. "That will do for today, dancers, go and change. Edda, Ash, when you're ready, please come to my office."

Edda woke from her dream. Had she overdone it? Was there too much love, where there usually hadn't been enough? Like with the Belgian Rene Deschamps, when Edda had to dive deep into herself to present artificial love.

She gazed over at Ash who stood panting on the other side of the stage, as they had been on opposite sides after Giselle had found out who Albrecht really was -that he was already engaged to Bathilde and that he had betrayed their love. She saw the same doubt reflected in his eyes. Love in classical ballet was sublimated, sophisticated. Dancers weren't supposed to expose the kind of raw love she and Ash had brought to Giselle.

"We'll be okay. We'll tone it down next time," Edda mouthed to him. He nodded, seeming to get her message as he rubbed his dripping face and shoulders with the towel.

Before facing her mentor's verdict, Edda briefly returned to her dressing room to hydrate and put on an extra layer of wool to keep her muscles warm. Still panting, her chest heaving with every intake of breath, she studied herself in the mirror.

Almost surprised to see she was still the same girl, one string of unruly hair having escaped its stern style, how appropriately. Her eyes had a new shine, though, and her heart hammered a new rhythm in her chest. In novels, couples found love at first sight, but that was not the making of reality. At least, not Edda's reality. Love wasn't on the cards, not now, not ever. She'd fight it tooth and nail because Asher Hoffmann was creeping under her skin. Edda knew stage love. Real-life love was something else.

So, she told herself her exultation was just the result of dancing a passionate choreography together with a star dancer. Happy with her conclusion, she rose to meet her mentor with a confident, calm heart. On her way through the corridor, she was only ballerina Edda Van der Valk, already cutting out both the tenderness and the power of her partner's embrace. Strictly professional.

Head high and defiant. She knew what she had to do. Dance until she shattered herself, not until her heart broke. Because with a guy like Asher Hoffmann, who'd have a girl hanging onto his every finger, especially the pinkie with the topaz ring, her heart would be shattered, sooner or later. It was not worth it. It was not worth her career.

"Edda, I'm glad you're here first, as I wanted to have a word with you separately," the ballet mistress started. "Is it alright that Pyo... Monsieur Sergeyev is present?"

Edda looked at the ballet mistress's partner, whom she liked dearly. "Of course, there are no secrets. But Miss Sterling, I wanted to tell you it will not happen again. I won't let myself go like this next rehearsal. I promise."

"Let yourself go? Heavens, girl, I wanted to compliment you on this rehearsal - this type of dancing - and I'm sure Pyotr agrees." The honey eyes flashed to her partner in love. She didn't even make a fuss of the Monsieur part anymore. Sparkling more brightly than Edda had ever seen her mentor, she snap-snap-snapped her fingers. "This is what I've been trying to get out of you in the past two-and-a-half years, my dear. This!" And she snapped the agile fingers again.

"I agree," her partner chimed in, "this is it, Edda. If it means love, it means love."

"But...," Edda began, wanting to protest. She'd just come to another conclusion. Restraint. Sophistication. Staying the technical ballerina, the proud Van der Valk.

As if guessing her thoughts, her mentor finished the sentence for her "...'but it's unprofessional, it's raw, it's too much.' I know, my dear, but it's exactly what art needs, that passion. Pyotr and I are here to help Ash and you channel this new surge of emotions, so you don't have to worry about your *pas de deux* still looking professional from the outside."

As if he'd heard his name, Ash came in, rather red in the face, apologetic.

Miss Sterling immediately put him at ease. "No worries, Ash. I was just complimenting Edda on your mutual performance today. We'll just need to smooth it a little around the edges, don't we?"

"Did I give Edda enough respect, Miss Sterling?"

The ballet mistress laughed. A myriad of small wrinkles popped at the edges of her slanted eyes.

"Did she feel gritty, Ash?"

He gave a small chuckle. "She didn't. She was smooth."

"Then there's your answer." And turning to her partner, the ballet mistress prompted, "Pyotr, was there anything from the choreography perspective you wanted these kids to take away."

"Kids, Marlene?" Monsieur Sergeyev said in mock dismay. "I think these kids have just become adults."

"So, it wasn't too intense?" Ash asked. "I actually thought I made that fish dive in the first forest scene a little too wild."

Monsieur Sergeyev held his head slightly tilted. "You may have, Ash, but overall, I think what your *pas de deux* needs most is *more* unrestrained passion. Wouldn't you agree, Marlene?"

"Absolutely. For now, more, more, more!"

Edda and Ash stared across at each other. Even more passion? A shudder went through Edda. This was such unchartered territory and, after having been away from dancing, it made her doubly unsure. Then Miss Sterling made it even worse by saying in that low voice that meant *only once*.

"I'm going to sentence you to as much time together in the coming weeks as your schedules can bear. It's the shortest route to a virtuoso performance on premier night. *Innamorati, miei favoriti!*"

Fall in love, my favorites!

The newly crowned 'adults' exchanged another look. Ash's expression was unreadable, but Edda could see him tense.

"What do you mean, Miss Sterling? I told you..."

"Yes, you told me, Ash. You need to help your father set up his business on the Damrak. Then take Edda with you when you have to work."

Edda gazed from one to the other in surprise. How could an accomplished performing ballet dancer like Asher Hoffmann have a second career? Where did he find the time?

There was a silence in the room, then Miss Sterling continued, "I don't want to throw you two together for a whim of mine. I feel that the more you know about each other, and not only dance together, the better you'll make our Giselle. You have a natural chemistry that could develop into one of the greatest lyrical ballet couples of all time, but you need to bridge the knowledge gap about each other. You both come from exceptional families but with very different backgrounds, different cultures, different religions. Melt it all into one and the world will see something they've never seen before.

"A new Giselle, in which the ballet's usually heavy theme is transformed. The world needs a transformation right now, as of a caterpillar into a butterfly. That's what we want to see, don't we, Pyotr?" snapping her fingers one final time on 'that.'

"Agreed."

Somehow, Edda understood what she meant. She could invite Ash to her flat, of course, make him a meal, show him the Vondelpark, her favorite spots in Amsterdam, but what if he needed to work for his father? He would have no time for freewheeling.

The prospect of spending time with Asher Hoffmann made her feel giddy in a most unprofessional way. But, whether Ash felt the same remained to be seen. He was unfathomable at the moment, as if struggling with an inner demon, of which she had no knowledge. That was what Miss Sterling wanted her to lay bare. Was he a demon or was he a diamond? Go to the bottom of Ash's soul. Well, she had a couple of dark spots of her own. Her family dynamics to begin with, and the menacing parade of black men incited by politicians like her father. Darkness all around.

But more than anything, Edda wanted to dance with Ash. Dance until they shattered.

"So, what is it you have to help your father with?" Edda asked as they left the Stadsschouwburg together. Ash hesitated, and she wondered if the question was too upfront, but then he said, "my father had a jeweler's shop and workshop in Vienna, and he's trying to set up his business here in Amsterdam. But the Amsterdam jewelers don't seem to be keen on having another Jewish goldsmith in their midst. They say the market is saturated. So, my father has temporarily set up shop in our backroom with the tools and materials we brought with us. He's trying to sell his pieces to colleagues, but he has his eye on a tiny property on the Damrak. Just a few square metres. He wants me to negotiate a price with the landlord. It's just that."

"Oh, I see. Maybe I can help since I speak Dutch?"

The smile he gave her was as if the sun breaking through the clouds and radiating all its splendid warmth.

"Would you? That's very kind of you. I am trained as a goldsmith myself," Ash continued. "As the eldest and only son, it is my duty to take over the family business after my father passes. Ballet thwarted both my father's and my plans. So, we've agreed on a compromise. I can dance, as long as I stay up to date with the jewelry business and do the accounting."

He sounded offhand, neutral, as if it was just a side job, but Edda had seen glimpses of a deep and troubled Ash in the past hours and sensed both his frustration with and his loyalty to his family.

"I had heard of you before. I knew you were from a Viennese jeweler's family."

"How so?"

Edda told him about Esther and her own jeweler-fiancé, Carl.

"Esther, Carl?!" Ash exclaimed, and he even grabbed her hands in excitement. "What a coincidence! How was dear Esther doing? She had such a hard time leaving Vienna after Hitler marched in and she had to leave Carl behind. Carl wasn't himself either. His parents are much older than mine, and his father is quite sickly, so Carl runs the jewelry business for his parents. He's also an only child. I, at least, have a sister."

"Esther was fine, after an initial bumpy start," Edda replied. "but I only stayed at Le Manoir for a brief time, so I didn't really get to know her. She talked about you, though, and told me your parents didn't want to wait to see what would happen to their country. Her parents intend to stay in Vienna, I understood, just like Carl's, so I assume she will return to Vienna after she's done with finishing school."

Ash looked doubtful, the eyes clouding over again. "Once upon a time, the Bernsteins, the Weisses and the Hoffmanns were the primary goldsmiths and jewelers of all Vienna. Together we've created the wedding bands for about ninety percent of Vienna, and maybe even of all Austria. Our three families were competitors, but mostly friends. Together, we've run the gold and precious stone business for generations."

"So, why did your parents decide to leave?"

Ash looked at her and she saw the color of his eyes darken even further.

"Do you really want to know?"

"Of course, or I wouldn't have asked."

"Because of me. A male, Jewish ballet dancer under the Nazi regime will not last long. I was beginning to make a bit of a name, got an offer to go to Paris, but my father, though not in favor of my dancing, said, 'no we're going to Amsterdam. Holland has always been a liberal and neutral country and there's not going to be war there.' My father fought on the German side in the trenches in the Great War and he didn't want me having to fight for the Nazis. He also has friends here in the diamond business. So, we decided on Amsterdam until Hitler leaves our country. We have every intention of returning. Father left much of his gold and precious stones behind. Even many finished items with his friend Franz Weiss, Esther's father, who's keeping them in his vault."

"Oh," Edda uttered, pushing away thoughts of that nasty black parade and what it stood for.

"And what about you, Edda?"

They'd meanwhile arrived at her bicycle. It was past five o'clock, but still sunny and bright in the late afternoon in April. Two pigeons, wildly in love, were cooing in the tall chestnut tree on the Museumplein and people were strolling past, chatting and laughing. Amsterdam felt light and breezy.

"There's nothing to tell about me. I've just always danced. That's all I do. All I can do."

"I doubt it." He looked at his watch, "as Miss Sterling has condemned us to each other, would you care to go for a coffee or tea with me?"

"Do you have time? I thought you'd have to go home?"

"I have time, Edda." It sounded curt.

"Why not go to the park?" she suggested, ignoring the curtness. "It's nice there. I'm not really looking forward to being cooped inside right now after having been indoors all day."

"Sounds like a plan, but only if you tell me about you. Here, let me push your bike."

And before she knew it, she'd told him about her life, every little detail but one. Her parents' political views. She omitted those. With reason.

It was after nine when Ash parked her bike for her against the façade of her house. Darkness had fallen, and the street lamps flitted on, one after the other. They had dined on sandwiches with sardines and drunken the last cold coffee from Ash's thermos. He'd wiped the crumbs from her mouth and the topaz ring had glittered with the color of Ash's eyes in love.

"Here we are," she said, suddenly shy and uncertain, as if all the talking and even the dancing had been a mirage.

"Come here." His eyes were demanding, yet gentle. She lingered, as if having to cross a path of crystal ice between them. When his arms were around her and his mouth on hers, a sob escaped her chest. It was so much, so marvellous, so miraculous. Edda was home, in her body and in his, and she knew she'd never leave their house again.

"My crystal butterfly," he murmured in her hair as he finally let her go, and somehow she understood what he meant.

"Just never break, my darling. Promise me you'll never break."

"I promise."

15

THE END OF FREEDOM

Two years later – Amsterdam, 10 May 1940

The menacing rumble of Nazi bombers filled the air as they flew over Amsterdam. The docks, canals, and streets below were alive with the sound of cannon fire as German tanks rolled through, leaving destruction in their wake. Shock and terror spread like wildfire among the citizens of Amsterdam, who could do nothing but watch in horror as their beloved city was taken by a relentless enemy force.

In spite of fierce resistance, the Royal Netherlands Army was eventually overwhelmed and had no choice but to surrender, battalion after battalion. With that, Nazi occupation began in Holland and World War II, although a 'Phoney War' since the invasion of Poland on 3 September 1939, had officially began.

Operation Fall Gelb, the occupation of Holland, was a fact, warned about in vain by the Dutch military attaché Major Sas from Berlin, based on information he received from German officers that an invasion of the Low countries was about to take place.

Fear seeped into every corner of every Dutch city, town, and village, filling the hearts and minds of the proud Dutch with a monstrous uncertainty about what would come next.

. . .

T HE WAR *of the low Countries may have started on 10 May. All wasn't lost yet.*

Until 14 May.

Until the bombardment of Rotterdam.

BEFORE THE OCCUPATION, *life in Rotterdam had been peaceful and serene. But on that fateful day of May, the citizens of the Maas port city felt an impending sense of doom as they heard the distant rumble of ninety Heinkels approaching their city at 11.45 a.m. The sound of bombers coming closer and closer made the citizens break out in a cold sweat and fervent prayer. It couldn't be true. But it was. That friendly, brotherly nation had turned into one big, roaring beast.*

As the sky over Rotterdam filled with Hermann Göring's Luftwaffe, the Radikallösung, the 'radical solution,' was an irreversible fact. Mistake or not, the bombers came in waves and carried out their carpet bombing, a terrifying new phenomenon in warfare.

Then came the devastating explosions, as buildings and homes were reduced to rubble. The smell of smoke and dust permeated the air as people ran for their lives, seeking shelter from the relentless bombardments.

The Heinkels eventually dropped their loads -- a total of 1308 bombs -- destroying the entire inner city and killing 814 civilians. The fires that broke out as a result of the bombardments destroyed more than 24,000 houses and made some 80,000 inhabitants homeless. This happened in the course of one sunny May afternoon.

The unwinnable war had come to Holland. The once vibrant city of Rotterdam lay in ruins, its buildings and homes no more. What remained were streets buried in rubble, and the air thick with the smell of black smoke and death. Rotterdam would never be the same again. Realizing his city was ruined and his people weeping and wailing, the Dutch commander of Rotterdam, Colonel Scharroo, capitulated to his German counterpart Schmidt.

The Dutch had lost their country; their queen and their government had fled.

EDDA HEARD about the bombardment of Rotterdam on the radio. Meanwhile, she and the other Amsterdamers had their own troubles to grapple with. Though in shock, her mind was clear, and she knew with absolute certainty that she would remember where she was, what she'd done, and how she had felt on that day of doom for the rest of her life.

Edda had always been a sixth-sense type of girl, though over time her butterfly-feelers had become idle and neglected. In her strictly Calvinist upbringing, she'd been warned from an early age: *we don't allow that sort of witchcraft in our family.* So, she'd stifled all inner knowing, berating herself for her keen intuition. The 'knowing of bad things in advance' had been fully stifled by the time she reached puberty. She still knew things, but she didn't allow herself to pay attention to them. Still, her observations had been nothing but innocent and had never failed to surprise Edda herself.

Duifje was going to fall off her bike and her knee would bleed. Papa would come down with the flu. Her pony, Michelangelo, was going to limp for a week. Innocent injuries or maladies but not welcome in the Van der Valk's household.

Without any military, or even political insights, Edda had known war was coming with a certainty that had at times made it difficult to breathe. But most times she'd ignored her feelers, as she'd been trained to. Training came naturally to the bred-in-the-bone ballerina.

Despite the general denial around her, despite the broadcaster assuring them the German bombers were on their way to England, and Holland would never be at war with Germany, Edda knew it was a misdirect and that the bombers would turn around above the North Sea and head for The Hague, the seat of the Dutch government and the Queen's palace. So, she stood still as the planes rumbled over, her buttered knife in mid-air, and prayed the Lord's Prayer.

Onze Vader die in de hemel zijt
Uw Naam worde geheiligd
Uw Koninkrijk kome
Uw Wil geschiede, op aarde zoals in de hemel.
Geef ons heden ons dagelijks brood,
En vergeef ons onze schulden
zoals ook wij onze schuldenaars vergeven,
En leid ons niet in verzoeking
maar verlos ons van de boze.
Amen.

Over and over, she prayed and prayed, as the planes came in waves before turning their noses around. She knew Göring's pilots already had their hands on the switches to release their deadly bombs on their innocent Brüdervolk. She knew her prayers were to no avail. God couldn't stop Hitler, only his own insanity would.

As a painter who sees the broad canvas in front of him, Edda understood what 10 May 1940 meant to Holland, and what it would mean to the world. She understood what Holland's near future would look like. None of it was clear, conscious thought; it was a deeper, inner knowing, and it was grim, ghastly, and godforsaken.

She shuddered once over her whole body, as if her system screamed a mute, drawn-out wail to the universe, like the last vibration of a huge machine just turned off. Then she became calm. The loner in her took root, transformed her into a warrior. She would face it head on, whatever the Germans would throw at her. After all, she was half-German herself, a descendent of an old Prussian family on her mother's side. They couldn't subjugate her. She would not flee or give up dancing. She would stay put and live through it, every which way it came.

Without a doubt, Edda could move to London or New York and dance there. She had enough experience under her belt and made enough of a name for herself. But she would only leave Amsterdam if Ash wanted to leave. Only then.

On that early sunny spring day, with a blackbird singing in her tiny back garden, the window open and her lunch sandwiches half prepared, Edda sank onto the kitchen stool. Her first reaction was to phone Ash, but she postponed it. No need to worry anyone with her worries.

It might be a normal day at the barre for them. Still in the early preparations of Romeo and Juliet, it was supposed to be a day of practice. She and Ash had danced Giselle for over a year on almost every stage in Europe.

Though a huge success with many encores, it had been great to be back in Amsterdam in May. No more traveling from city to city, no more photograph sessions, no more the terribly strict regime of bread-bed-ballerina for a while. Edda needed to recuperate, and though she'd rather be with Ash all the time like they'd been together on the road, she'd actually been grateful to withdraw into her own tiny flat and sleep in her own bed. Her body, her mind, and her heart needed a little respite.

And Ash was busy. His father's jewelry business was finally finding its footing on the Damrak, so Ash helped out his father as much as he could.

The telephone rang, a luxury her father had deemed necessary for the safety of his young, unmarried daughter alone in the big city. The penetrating ringing startled Edda. Barefoot she ran to the phone in the corridor.

"Edda, is that you?" Miss Sterling's voice.

"Yes."

"Don't come to the studio. They say there's going to be war. Stay indoors."

"But..."

"No buts. I've got to call everyone, but I'll check in with you later." *Tuut-tuut-tuut.* The ballet mistress was gone. The entire phone call had not lasted thirty seconds. Edda would later wonder whether it had happened at all.

Slowly she made her way back to the kitchen and sank down at the table. There it was. The radio voice got all agitated as if he was reporting on a sports match instead of announcing the beginning of a world war.

The Heinkels are no longer above the North Sea, they're heading back towards us, dropping bombs on Dutch territory. The Germans are attacking us... us! We're at war with Germany, who would have thought? Who would have thought?

Edda turned the switch off and listened to the distant drone in the air. Would she have to go to the cellar? Should she phone her parents? Phone Ash? But she just sat there, hands folded in her lap, listening, gauging where the Germans were, where the bombs would fall.

They wouldn't fall on *her* head, but they would fall on other people's heads. Her father might be in The Hague as he was often. Edda rushed to the phone to call Huis van Leyden, hear her mother's comforting voice while war unfolded around her as out of control fireworks. It was real, but the phone was dead.

Panic seeped in. What was she to do? Miss Sterling had said *stay home* and now she couldn't reach her parents. Edda was all alone in the world, so she did what she had planned to do for a long time, but had been putting off. She opened the drawer of her bedside table and took out a black leather-bound diary with a golden lock, a present from Duifje for her twenty-first birthday.

"You seem just the girl who travels with a diary and talks to it as if it is her best friend," Duifje had said in that offhand manner of hers. "I'd never have the patience nor the coherence to put two words together, but you will, dear sis."

Duifje, pregnant with her second child, as erratic and in love with demanding Teppo as ever. Duifje was in The Hague and the bombers were heading there. Edda's breath stuck in her throat and tears welled up. *Cry-baby!*

When she opened the journal, she saw a folded paper and remembered Doctor Geuze had written down a quote for her that he'd told her to only read when she was deep down in the dumps. Well, she needed his words now, so she opened the prescription sheet with Wilhelmina Gasthuis on it.

The two most powerful Warriors are Patience and Time – Leo Tolstoy.

Edda read it twice, didn't understand it, but smiled at the memory of the nice Doctor Geuze. How devastated he would be that their country was pulled into this useless war after all. She folded the paper and put it back in the sheet between the cover and the first page.

Then she unscrewed her fountain pen and wrote.

Amsterdam, 10 May 1940

I don't know who will win this war, the Dutch, or the Germans, but I do not believe in the right of one country to attack another. It's not that I'm against Germany, I have German blood myself, but I believe Holland should stay a sovereign country.

As I write this, I'm surprised at myself. I never take sides, not in a political sense, so why do I strongly feel sending bombers and dropping bombs on civilians is the worst way to create stability? Well, the answer is obvious from the question. A child could answer it.

So, Herr Hitler, you are terribly wrong, but I fear it will take a long time before either the world or you will reach a full understanding of your blunder.

Patience.

Time.

Doctor Geuze's quote begins to make sense to me after all. As does this diary. I will hide it carefully because I'm going to give Herr Hitler a piece of my mind every day. Not that he will ever listen to me, but maybe the world will one day.

Marchioness Edda Van Der Valk.

SHE CROSSED OUT HER TITLE, then put it back in. Looked at it and decided to leave it. This wasn't the message of the ballerina. This was the message of a member of the Van der Valk dynasty. But Edda, not Eddaline.

Closing the diary, she locked it and stuffed it deep under her mattress, the key went in her dress pocket. Hadn't her mother taught her to always have dresses with pockets?

The doorbell rang and Edda jolted into the air from fright.

"Edda! Eddaaaaa!"

Someone was banging her front door. Ash!

Edda raced to the door and flung herself in his arms. He caught her as ever, off stage and on stage, and held her as she sobbed against his chest. Still with her in his arms, as if she weighed nothing, he swung around and closed the door with his shoe. "Edda!" he said again, and she could hear his voice breaking too.

They were sitting hand in hand on her Byzantium blue sofa, too fazed for words. Edda had switched on the radio again. Queen Wilhelmina and the government were planning to leave the country, no one knew where. Chaos, confusion, the first casualties reported.

"They will pay for this!" Ash said through clenched teeth. "One way or another, they will pay for this."

Edda plucked up the courage to ask the question that had bothered her all morning.

"Will you and your family be leaving again, Ash?" Her voice was tiny. She held her fist against her mouth, terrified to hear 'yes' for an answer.

"Leaving?" He looked at her in utter surprise, the dark-gray eyes softening to blue at seeing her anguish. "Why on earth would we leave now Father's business is finally off the ground?"

Edda squeezed his hand. "Oh, I'm so relieved. I was making all sorts of plans of coming with you."

"No need for that, my butterfly. This lunacy won't last. Hitler has overplayed his hand this time. He's also attacking Belgium. The man's mad as a rat in a trap! The rest of the world won't accept his pranks any further. Great Britain and the United States will certainly come to our rescue."

"But they didn't when Poland was attacked, nor when he marched into Denmark and Norway. Why would they do anything now? And it's not like the Dutch army is able to withstand the Wehrmacht. They're far too powerful."

Ash was silent for a while as the broadcaster spewed more atrocities into Edda's sitting room. He let out a deep sigh then drew her to him.

"Look at me, Edda Van der Valk." His eyes bored into hers with a viridian blue she hadn't seen before. The intensity of his stare was almost too much, as was his bodily power and his passion. Ash could tether on the edge of too much and he was close to that state now. Still, she withstood his fierceness. "We are going to forget all about this silly war, you and I. We will never mention it. We will dance and dance and dance until they forbid us to dance, and still we will dance. Dance to our graves, if it must be."

"Ash," Edda gasped. "Don't say that and don't look at me this way. You scare me."

For a moment the gaze softened as he said, "you'll never need to be scared as long as you dance with me, Edda. You will never be scared dancing. I promise."

Then he kissed her and when she didn't answer him, he said with a half grin, "I'll kiss you until you promise to dance with me to the end."

It felt like a solemn moment, almost as if he was asking her to marry him. It wasn't a light promise, Edda knew. And in her heart of hearts, she wasn't sure she would be able to dance with him till the end. If Hitler would let her. But she wanted to promise him more than anything in the world, so she said "yes."

16

THINGS GET REAL

Six months later - Amsterdam, November 1940

Almost everyone agreed, the German occupation wasn't as bad as what it initially had looked like. Sure, the Dutch now had a German government under the leadership of the enigmatic Arthur Seys-Inquart. And the slow but certain Germanification of their country was a fact, but the Germans mainly seemed to want to do business with the Dutch and doing business, well that's what 'Hollanders' were excellent at. Making money had been their bread and butter for the centuries.

For most of the Dutch, the new situation was therefore one of acceptance and profit. Men even lined up to work voluntarily in Germany for what they thought would be better wages. With the effects of the horrendous 1929 stock market collapse still fresh on their minds and big brother's economy next door a booming business under Herr Hitler's rule, why not dream of a status quo that would be beneficial for the small country bordering the North Sea?

So, it wasn't just Dutch NSB members welcoming the Nazi occupation. Initially most of the Dutch population blindly believed all would be well if they kept their heads down, scrubbed their front steps clean, and did as they *were told.*

Even in the port of Rotterdam. Though the heart of the city was ravaged and ruined beyond recognition, the port itself was—once again— a beehive of business and industry.

The two main groups for whom the German presence was a thorn in the flesh were the Communist party in Amsterdam and the Geuzen in the Rotterdam area. Right from the early days of the war, they committed acts of resistance and brought out pamphlets and circulars in an attempt to open the eyes of the slumbering Dutch and make them aware of how the Wehrmacht had crushed their sovereignty and what Nazidom really was.

These small groups were shouting in the wind. Most of them, still not underground but loudly protesting, were quickly arrested, and locked up in Hotel Oranje in Scheveningen with petty thieves and random burglars. Some were tortured, most were manhandled, and the first resistance fighter fell to his death, quite literally thrown off the balcony of Hotel Oranje by the Sicherheitspolizei. The first executions after the phoney 'Geuzen process' were carried out in early 1941.

Did Holland wake up, or was it too late?

EDDA KEPT her promise to Ash, and they successfully danced Romeo and Juliet for a wide array of visitors—from Dutch housewives and dignitaries, to SS officers and their wives. Edda danced and danced, and loved Ash as never before, but she also kept her secret diary in which she wrote about her admiration for the early resisters who kept warning about what she only sensed was going to happen.

But she had nobody to talk to. If she'd said anything about reading illegal pamphlets, her family would have been aghast and probably handed her over to the SA themselves. And Ash, well they did not talk about the war. Ever.

Miss Sterling, too, had made it a policy that no political ideas were spread against or in favor of the new situation.

"We as the Amsterdam Ballet Theater bring art into the world," she'd said rather enigmatically in one short gathering following the invasion in May. "And art holds an exceptional position in society. We transcend Conservative, Liberal, Communist and Social-Nationalistic movements *and* encompass them at the same time. Look at us, we're a motley group from various political, cultural, and racial backgrounds. That's what we want to be, that's what we're proud of. We want to cherish that liberty above all. So, should any one particular movement force us into their doctrine, then, yes, then our answer will be to rebel. But if we can continue to do what we're doing now, I want to hear no word on politics in this company."

Edda had written in her dairy that night after her mentor's sermon.

15 May 1940

Miss Sterling is right, of course, to forbid us to squabble about being for or against the Nazi occupation, but I fear she's overlooked the fact that one particular movement has already forced us into its doctrine. All political parties are forbidden now, except Anton Mussert's party, the Nationaal-Socialistische Beweging, which is an exact copy of Hitler's NSDAP.

It won't be long before they want French ballet terms translated into German here, just like Hitler prided himself on in Germany as far back as 1935. Oh! I'm just so confused, because I want to concentrate on dancing and not have these horrid thoughts, but I would have loved to tell Miss Sterling we're already forced into a tight box. Only we don't feel it yet. But we will.

I didn't say anything of course, because she made it very clear she wanted no one to reply. I don't know what we could do about it. Miss Sterling in her eternal wisdom is probably right.

I will concentrate on my art. Just leave us alone, Herr Hitler. We do no harm. We just dance.

EDDA OFTEN RUMINATED on why she couldn't stop herself listening to Radio Oranje, though it was strictly illegal, and putting herself in danger by picking up anti-German pamphlets. She tried to be what Miss Sterling told her and what had kept her so happy and fulfilled before the war: her art form, dance. But it wasn't enough. It didn't stop her from feeling wronged. She came to the conclusion that the seed of her dissatisfaction had been sown long ago when she'd seen through Hitler's polished veneer and understood its danger, but it had been his invasion of her peaceful country that had sent her over the edge.

She'd written in her diary.

If I have any political color, I think I would call myself a pacifist. I simply don't believe in violence, of one person against another, or of one nation against another. But I cannot forget 10 May of this year, try as I may.

As a Van der Valk, Edda had been spoon-fed politics from an early age. Her forefathers, both the Van der Valks in Friesland and the Scherzingers in Prussia, had always been ministers or government advisors. It had simply never occurred to her that matters of state could hold her interest, because she'd never felt any connection to the very Conservative—now National-Socialist— beliefs of her parents.

Her interest in how people found ways to resist the new political climate was a new, almost shocking, experience to Edda. Handicapped by limited free time and no one to talk about the ideas germinating in the back of her mind, she felt extremely lonely and somewhat cut off from the world, as if those illegal thoughts and diary confessions didn't really exist.

It soothed her troubled mind to listen to Radio Oranje, to read the resistance pamphlets, to know that there were people out there who openly rebelled against the status quo. It meant not all was lost yet. She may not be able to take part in it, but she sent them her blessings.

There was one resister in particular who fascinated her above all others. His name was Hendrik IJzerdraat. This Rotterdam tapestry-restorer, originally from the east of Holland, had been warning against *both* Fascism and Communism since 1936 in the *Eenheid door Democratie* - Unity through Democracy - movement. It was IJzerdraat's thinking that appealed to Edda, who also disliked every form of extremism, whether left or right.

Mr IJzerdraat, whose last name meant Iron Wire, had organized the first Dutch resistance group, *De Geuzen,* immediately after the bombing of Rotterdam. The name originated from the nickname *Geuzen,* meaning beggars, that the Dutch used in the 16th century during the Eighty Years' War opposing Spanish rule in the Netherlands.

IJzerdraat had published the first resistance pamphlet, called *Geuzenbericht,* on 15 May, just one day after the bombing of Rotterdam and now had a group around him who fiercely resisted the Nazis.

Edda had found out about the *Geuzenbericht,* which was mostly distributed locally, through her kind, elderly neighbor. How Mevrouw Meulenbelt got hold of these pamphlets Edda didn't know —maybe through a son or a friend in the movement.

For equally mysterious reasons, she put the pamphlets in Edda's letterbox. At least Edda assumed they came from her neighbor, but she never caught her in the act.

Every time Mevrouw Meulenbelt came out to bat her doormat in the morning and remarked on the day's weather, Edda was tempted to ask her about the Geuzenbericht but she never did. It was like an unspoken agreement between them. Only the weather and the price of milk or the cat's health were the silently-agreed topics. But the elderly wrinkled face, with the white crown of hair and eyes the color of summer violets, spoke of a deep knowing that Edda understood.

IT WAS 8'o clock on a Friday night when the phone rang. Edda quickly switched off the radio and picked up the receiver.

"Eddaline?"

"Mother, is everything alright?"

"Of course, it is. What a silly question. I wanted to invite you and that boy to a small party."

"Which boy, Mama?"

Her mother huffed. "The one Duifje says you've got your eyes on. I haven't told your father he's a ballet dancer, as you know what he thinks of that. I'd like to meet him."

"He's called Asher Hoffmann and he's not a boy, Mama."

"Whatever, child. It will just be a small gathering for our silver anniversary. On the fifth of November. Klaas will pick you up at five in the afternoon."

"Oh." Edda grimaced. Why couldn't her mother first ask *if the date suited her? If Ash actually wanted to come?* They were just given orders from above. Her mother was certainly in good health again.

"What does 'oh' mean, Eddaline? I thought you would like to show off your beau to your family."

Not particularly, Edda thought, but didn't say.

"Will Duifje be there?"

"Hopefully. But little Elly isn't sleeping well, so Duifje is having her headaches. I've invited them, though."

"Who else will be there?"

Duifje there would be a relief. The Van Leeuwens had already met Ash twice and Teppo, despite being big-ego Teppo, had gotten on well with the Austrian dancer.

"Got Jewish blood myself, brother. Nothing to be ashamed of," he'd cried throughout the restaurant in his blundering way. Duifje had swooned over Ash's physique and pinched her sister under the table then rolled her eyes and mouthed "oh-la-la".

So, it would be great support if the young Van Leeuwen family made acte-de presence as well.

"We will try, Mother. I'll phone you back after I've spoken with Ash. He's very busy helping his father, so I have no idea whether he's free on a Friday night."

"Then tell him to take the evening off, Eddaline. If he's serious about you, he'll do that for you."

"I'll let you know, Mama."

Edda hung up with a tangled feeling of unrest in her stomach. What a strange phone call. At times her mother could be curt and uninterested in her daughter's affairs, but this was different. As if it was more her father than her mother who ordered Edda's and Ash's 'audience' at Huis Van Leyden.

Edda was already making all sorts of plausible excuses in her head on behalf of Ash and seriously considered not even mentioning the invitation to him.

She picked up the receiver again and phoned her sister, pleading with the Bakelite apparatus to make her sister home and approachable.

It was Teppo, who before she could even start asking her question, began complaining about his newborn daughter who wouldn't stop crying.

"Night and day the child wails," he sputtered. "Who could think a tiny body like that could put up such an ear-splitting racket? Benny never did anything of the sort but he's starting to imitate his little sister. Duifje is in bed all the time and that leaves me to cope with this mess. Corrie ran out and I have three shops to run, do you hear me...?"

Edda did hear him but had no time for her brother-in-law's complaints right now.

"Teppo, can you put Duifje on the phone. It's rather urgent." Edda intervened but he wouldn't listen.

"What can be more urgent than getting some order in this household? Your sister is in bed and blocked the door. There's no way I can get to her."

"Can you please shout at the door it's me?" Edda was beginning to get desperate as well.

"I can try to break the door down if that's what you're asking me?" he snarled.

"No, don't do that, but do me a favor and ask anyway? You've got an extension in your bedroom, so she needn't get out of bed. Oh Teppo, put an advert in the paper for a new housekeeper."

"Me?!" he shrieked. "That's my wife's job, isn't it? Can't a man be a man these days anymore?" But she heard him ascend the stairs and shout, "Edda's on the phone."

"Lientje?" Her sister's voice sounded broken and frail, and Edda regretted having been curt with Teppo. The family had clearly seen happier times.

"Are you alright, Duifje?"

"Am I ever, sis?" She sounded very low-spirited.

"Yes, you are, you have great moments of fun and two adorable children and a husband who dotes on you." Edda replied as chirpy as she could muster.

"Not at the moment, Lientje. Ever since Elly's birth, I'm a wreck and Teppo has lost patience with me, and Corrie left in a fury."

"Yes, I heard. Will she not come back if you raise her salary?" Edda wanted to add "and treat her better" but swallowed the words.

"What a good idea, sis! I'll tell Teppo to drive by her house with a sack of coins *tout de suite.*" Duifje clearly latched on the salary increase and Edda could hear her strike a match to light her cigarette.

"I hope you'll feel better soon."

"I will be right as rain if Corrie changes her mind. She's not the easiest of housekeepers, but she's the only one who can put up with me. Except for Teppo," Duifje added in a rare moment of self-insight. "So what did my little sis want from me?"

There it was— how Duifje switched moods like a light switch. It was something Edda would never understand but knew inside out.

She had to ask her question in that short window of opportunity her sister had for other people's pains.

"Mother invited me and Ash to their silver anniversary party."

"Heavens, how revolutionary to want a Jewish ballet dancer at their NSB dinner table," her sister said sarcastically.

"Stop it, Duifje, it's not funny."

"I didn't mean to be funny. Did mother say why they wanted to be introduced to your beautiful lover?"

"He's not my lover, Duifje, he's my dance partner and my *beloved*. And no, she didn't with so many words. She just said she'd heard from you that we were seeing each other."

"Not your lover but your beloved?" Duifje ignored all else to probe this interesting titbit. "Are you saying you didn't have sex yet? Are you mad?!"

"Stop it, Duifje," Edda warned for the second time. "We'll get to that when we're ready, okay?"

"Just let me know if you need some help there?" Duifje offered in her characteristically careless manner.

"We don't. Thank you." Edda's cheeks were red with indignation and shame. The assumptions her sister made and the freedom with which she uttered them! She, Edda, would need to change the topic before this went completely out of hand.

"So please tell me you are also coming to Mother's and Father's wedding anniversary celebration?"

"I will, sis, if only to support you and *ton ami ravissant.*" There was the generous Duifje again, meaning what she said, amidst all else that left her unchecked mouth.

"Thank you, Duifje. I hope you get better soon, and that Elly starts sleeping better."

"I hope so too, Lientje. You take care."

AND SO IT happened that Edda, dressed in a silver lamé dress that hugged her beautiful, dancer's body, her dark hair for once not tightly tucked on top of her head but in loose curls down her back, and a fur cape around her shoulders, with Ash, dressed in an evening suit, settled in the back seat of the grey Mercedes that now openly sported the NSB triangular flags upfront.

Klaas was stolid and silent as a grave, as Edda had expected. She didn't feel very welcoming to her father's chauffeur either. His chanting "Weg met de Joden"—"Away with the Jews"—even before the war was still fresh in her ears, though she didn't know whether the NSB man knew Ash was Jewish.

They rode in silence. Edda grabbed Ash's hand in the dark and he squeezed it. There was a heavy feeling in her body and several times she wanted to say to that broad, blond head upfront, "Turn around, Klaas, and take us back to Amsterdam!" but she didn't and knew she should have. All her intuition screamed 'don't go!'.

Duifje, for once, was trying to be an angel. She stood waiting for them on the steps to Huis van Leyden, looking sickly and shivering, smoking a cigarette and wrapped in a shawl too thin for the November gale that had picked up. But she was smiling broadly.

From the corners of her eyes, Edda spotted several German cars parked in the driveway and next to the NSB flag, the mansion sported the Nazi flag with its swastika. Black-red-black-red. The storm pulled the cloth of the flags so tight it made Edda think of the tightness with which these men kept their arms in a salute. *Go home*, an urgent voice whispered inside her, but Duifje had tottered down the steps and pulled open the door before Klaas even switched off the engine.

"Darlings," she cooed, "come in quickly. We have punch and presents for all. Teppo and I want to celebrate with you!"

17

THE PARTY

Unfamiliar staff—maids in black dresses and stiff white aprons—scurried through the entrance hall and up the stairs, as Edda and Ash entered Huis van Leyden. With Duifje in between them, who'd hooked her arms in both of theirs, they stopped in their tracks like bloodhounds sensing a trail.

"Never mind all the busyness," Duifje waved it away in her happy-go-lucky way, but Edda felt even her sister tense at her side.

"When was the last time you were here, Duifje?" Edda asked before the Marchioness could sail in from behind one of the closed doors.

"Heavens, not since Elly was born. When am I ever invited here?" Duifje was still shrugging off the forebodings of change.

Ash said nothing, he stood perfectly still, as only a dancer can, no expressions on his handsome face but his lively eyes took in the opulent hall. Edda saw he noticed everything, including the cheerful cherubs who were involved in some pagan dance around the ceiling. She followed his eyes, suddenly remembering her conversation with them the night after she'd broken her ankle, now almost two years ago.

The first German officials had arrived then and stayed at Huis van

Leyden for a week or so. It had been unsettling to her, but her parents had entertained guests from all over Europe and sometimes even the United States as long as Edda could remember. So, she'd born it, not sensing anything out of the ordinary then.

A change of circumstance had clearly set in now. The increased number of staff and the almost exclusively German cars with their Swastikas lined up in the driveway. These Germans had obviously settled in permanently, spreading their wives and belongings across the bedrooms in the corridors where once the Jesuits and young schoolboys had slept.

The shock of this realisation made Edda literally stagger. Her ankle suddenly felt as fragile as the stem of a lily, like the day the cast had come off. Both Duifje and Ash gripped her tighter. Her sister and her boyfriend could hold her up physically, but they could not prevent the fragmentation of her heart and soul.

There were no two ways about it. Her family had in some form or other been involved in the invasion. Her parents had collaborated, facilitated the ease of the German takeover. Both her parents or perhaps only her father. It didn't matter. Not anymore. Though too hideous a thought to entertain, the stone-cold fact became clear to Edda as a tree is illuminated the moment before it is struck by lightning. At some point she would have to choose sides too, and the knowledge tore her apart as if earth and heaven diverging.

"Are you alright, Lientje?"

She couldn't even answer. She was sick and weak and wanted to flee as fast as her feeble self would let her. But the door opened, and her mother entered, dressed in a dark blue taffeta dress, her dyed hair done up nicely. *Mama!* The Marchioness's face broke into a sunny smile, the dark eyes, so like Edda's, lit up at the sight of her children.

It was blow after blow for Edda. Her mother, though thoroughly powdered and pomaded, had become almost half her original voluminous size. The blue dress sagged at her bosom, and she moved with difficulty. But the embrace was warm and perfumed. Edda suppressed a sob, wanting to stay in that embrace forever, guilty at having neglected her mama for her career.

"Eddaline, how good of you to come." Peeling herself free from her daughter's desperate embrace, the Marchioness shook Ash's hand and welcomed him with curt politeness.

"Mr Hoffmann, so glad to make your acquaintance. As you spend so much time with my daughter both on and off stage, as I've heard, my husband and I deemed it time to meet you."

"Thank you for the invitation, Marchioness Van der Valk. Very kind of you." Using her nobiliary name was a brilliant manoeuvre on Ash's part. Edda saw the immediate thawing in her mother's face. Mother liked a bit of a charmer. And by the sight of it, she could do with a bit of pep.

"We brought you some flowers, Marchioness," Ash continued, offering her the large bouquet of roses and carnations he and Edda had bought at a stall on the Singel, which had been Amsterdam's flower canal street since 1862.

"How kind of you, children." She took the beautifully arranged bunch and Edda, still struggling to compose herself, held her breath. Carnations were fast becoming a sign of resistance, as they were the flower Prince Bernhard, spouse to Crown Princess Juliana, always wore in his buttonhole. The Dutch secretly adopted the lovely white flower to support the royal family-in-exile in London. Her mother didn't flinch, and Edda wasn't sure whether her mother knew or not. But Edda had chosen them with care.

"Do come in, children," the Marchioness said in a much warmer tone, after a quick cool welcome to Duifje. She handed the bouquet to a fast-approaching, curtseying maid who got exact instructions of which vase to use and to place them on the small table in the Marchioness's boudoir.

Edda relaxed a little, still holding on to Duifje but letting Ash go. They followed her mother to the formal dining room. Her mother walked unevenly, as if one hip was too stiff to work with her normal stride.

The first thing that struck Edda, as her mother ushered them into

Huis van Leyden's most formal room, was the thick layer of smoke hanging over the large table and the brawl of German voices. It was more like entering a salon or a gentlemen's club than a dinner party.

A group of six women in evening dresses stood talking in a corner of the room, smoking and drinking champagne. An equal number of men, most in German uniform, were seated at the table with the Marquis Johannes Van der Valk in his lion's head seat at the far end. Edda saw no familiar faces of her parents' Dutch friends, and again wanted to balk as if they'd just walked into a trap.

Her father rose as they shuffled into the room. Edda saw his demeanor change immediately upon spotting Ash, and at that moment she was certain her mother hadn't spoken the truth. Her father knew nothing about their arrival. Whether it was supposed to be a surprise or a deliberately kept secret she would never know.

The Marquis excused himself from his German guests and came their way. He worked hard to give his face a neutral expression. There was no smile, no exterior gladness at the sight of his daughters and the new guest. Edda scanned his clothes, a civilian suit, black as usual with the NSB pin firmly on his lapel. No uniform, thank God.

"Duifje, Eddaline, what is the occasion? And who is this gentleman?"

Her mother jumped in, "Oh Johannes, it was supposed to be a surprise. Tonight is our silver anniversary. That's why I invited the children."

"You could have warned me, Olga, that we would have family mixing in," he grumbled, as he let Duifje and Edda kiss his cheek and he shook Ash's hand. Ash looked uneasy and Edda felt furious but kept quiet. Let her mother do the explaining.

"Who's the gentleman?" her father repeated.

"I'm Asher Hoffmann, Marquis Van der Valk." The use of the nobiliary name didn't have the positive effect on the mayor as it had had on his wife. He looked as if stung by a bee on hearing Ash's last name. Edda felt her intestines shrink, but her father made another effort to compose himself.

"And why do I have the honor of receiving you in my house, Mr Hoffmann?"

Now you'll get it, Edda thought. *The fat's in the fire this time.* But her mother swiftly intervened.

"He's an acquaintance of Edda's, husband. Now let us get to dinner and enjoy the evening."

Her father didn't budge but turned to his eldest daughter.

"And where's that husband of yours?"

"Home, Father, with the children."

"What an odd thing to do. To go gallivanting as a mother and leave your husband in care of the children."

"Oh, Papa!" Duifje exclaimed in an outburst of joviality and unfazed by his grumpiness. "You're in a foul mood tonight. Can't you be merry, we're here for your celebration?" She even put her arm through his and escorted him back to his chair.

The mayor said no more, gave Edda and Ash a curt nod, and sat down.

Her mother steered Edda and Ash to the other side of the table, where they were placed next to two of the German ladies who'd followed the development of the odd family gathering from where they had been standing and now took their seats at the table. Duifje skipped to their side and sat in between Edda and Ash.

"So much for our goodwill," she growled. "Does the man have no manners?" And putting a hand on Ash's sleeve she added, "don't pay any attention to him. He can be like this at times, but he'll turn around, don't worry."

Edda was less certain Duifje's optimism was justified. She'd seen how her father reacted to a Jew at his table. One half-Jewish son-in-law was quite enough for his Van der Valk genealogical chart. She regretted with every inch of her being that she'd brought Ash to her parents' house, into this rat trap. Well, it would never happen again.

The atmosphere at the smoky dinner table remained awkward, agitated, and artificial. The official language was German of course, which was also Ash's first language. No rude remarks or personal attacks were made at him. In fact, the three newcomers were ignored completely by their table companions, who'd settled in as the new in-crowd at Huis van Leyden and felt no need to include the family in their circle. If some of the mayor's children had happened to be at the same dinner as they were, it was none of their business.

Edda had always found Germans weren't particularly curious folk. They were mainly interested in their own culture and direct surroundings. And her mother made no further mention of the silver anniversary. Edda didn't mind the cold-shoulder. *Get through the darn meal and disappear at breakneck speed,* was all she could think.

She could never have fathomed the twist the party would eventually take. And that it wasn't Nazi against Jew, or even ridiculing of a male ballet dancer stumbling into an NSB meal.

The meal started normally enough. Soup was served and then hors d'oeuvres, all the best from the best, though most Dutch were already feeling how the Germans pinched their best meat, collected their wheat and corn by the armfuls, and then ordered the Dutch to grow their own vegetables.

There wasn't a shortage of anything yet, but most of Holland certainly wasn't enjoying the opulence that was laden onto Johannes Van der Valk's dinner table. Brought in by skittish maids in formal attire and carelessly consumed by a smoking and drinking Nazi crowd. An entire roasted pig, asparagus, tender green beans, three types of potatoes, and sauce so rich in cream the spoon stood upright in it.

Edda could hardly swallow two bites. Duifje didn't seem interested in the food, but drank copious amounts of Veuve Cliquot and smoked all the time. Ash plodded on heroically, but Edda was constantly aware of his tightness. Ash was never tight. Ash normally relaxed his formidable muscles at will, but he was on high alert now. *And not without reason*, Edda thought grimly. *What a dreadful charade.* But she didn't dare to say anything about it to him for fear of making him even more miserable.

So, she did what she'd never done before. She grabbed Duifje's package of Marlboros and lit one. Nobody but Ash seemed to find this a strange act. Edda coughed once; her eyes pricked, but there was comfort in the burning in her windpipe. More comfort than in the pain in her heart.

One of the skittish maids rushed in and went to the Marchioness's seat next to her husband. She whispered something in her ear. The Marchioness nodded, folded her serviette, and rose unsteadily. She followed the maid from the room. Nobody thought anything of it. Only Edda seemed to notice. Corks popped, smoke rose, voices grew louder.

Returning to the dining room a little later, the Marchioness was ashen-white and even more unsteady on her feet. She said something to her husband, who first raised his eyebrows in surprise and then waved his wife's obvious concern away with his hand. The conversations went on, rowdier and rowdier, until one of the Germans shouted, "Musik! Wir wollen deutsche Musik hören!"

After returning from what clearly had alarmed her, the Marchioness did not touch her food, nor say another word. She sat very still and white, with her hands folded in her lap, as if in a trance. When one of the German guests put a Schlager album on the record player, she simply stood up and left the room. Edda followed her immediately, with Ash and Duifje on her heels. The three of them had moved as one all evening.

They found the Marchioness in the back living room, her lace handkerchief pressed against her mouth, tears in her eyes. Edda raced to her mother and sank at her feet.

"Mama, what's wrong?"

"It's...it's Ludovicus."

"Ludovicus Van Limburg Stirum?" Edda and Duifje asked at the same time. *Is he dead?* She didn't ask aloud but couldn't understand what news about the Count could be so upsetting to her mother than that the lawyer had suddenly passed.

"He's been taken," the Marchioness yammered.

"Taken? Where?" Edda and Duifje continued to speak in synchronized syllables.

"Taken by the Gestapo," she wailed.

"The Gestapo?" Edda's admiration for her elderly suitor, who'd never actually been her suitor, rose with leaps. Ludovicus, a resistance fighter? The world wasn't devoid of miracles yet. But why had this news upset her mother so much? After all, the Count was related to the Van der Valks, not to the Scherzingers. But before Edda had time to ask the origin of her mother's distress, the Marchioness said in a very soft voice,

"something is so, so wrong in this country. That was Ludovicus's brother who called me. The Count and fourteen others have been arrested yesterday and are being kept as hostages, simply to threaten the Dutch. Ludo's been taken to St Michielsgestel in Brabant. They've rounded up over one hundred notables, judges, bankers, landowners, and such, and locked them up in what they call a Herrengefängnis, a 'gentlemen's prison." Should the Dutch pull an act of resistance on the German occupiers, they will randomly kill a number of these hostages. Oh, isn't it awful?!"

Her mother moaned again, and Edda felt the hair on the back of her neck stand up. She struggled to her feet to grab Duifje's hand for support. Her mother kept dabbing her watery eyes. Ash's eyes had grown big in horror. Without being aware of it, the Marchioness had resorted to her native tongue, so he'd understood every word. And the worst was yet to come.

"They took Ludo because he's acquainted with us. They'll put more pressure on Johannes and me to follow the Nazi rule. Any sign of resistance within this family and Ludo will be shot without mercy."

"Did they say that?" Edda fumed, "what kind of blackmail is that?"

The Marchioness suddenly seemed to get a grip on herself, "*Ach, mein Kind*, you don't know is the half of it, how terribly bad it all is."

She rose from the armchair where she'd been sitting, shivering and weak but with some of the old Olga Scherzinger vigor.

"You must go home now, children. Let this be a warning to us all. Keep your heads down and dance. And you, Duifje, raise your kids and pray this madness is over soon."

She kissed them and ushered them out of the door much like she'd ushered them in two hours earlier.

There was no Klaas to drive them back.

"Let's get a taxi and go to my house," Duifje suggested who for once seemed utterly sober.

18

A DIVIDED COUNTRY

Three months later

Amsterdam, 9 February 1941

The situation in Amsterdam is becoming unbearable. I fear with all my heart for Ash and his family. Today again there was heavy fighting on the Rembrandtplein, not far from the Amsterdam Jewish Center. The WA, the paramilitary arm of the NSB, provoked young Jews into a fight.

I was passing on my bicycle and watched from a safe distance. Klaas Bollema is also part of that sinister group. I saw him beating up a young Jewish boy. There was blood everywhere.

How can you condone this, Herr Hitler and Meneer Mussert? You must stop inciting hate. Now! Before it

*gets out of hand. My words are probably in vain, but
I need to write them down anyway.*

Edda raised the pen from her diary and stared out the window. The trees in the Vondelpark were bare. The sky was leaden. The supply of food in her store cupboard became more and more sparse by the day. And fuel for heating was hard to come by.

Mevrouw Meulenbelt still batted her doormat in the morning, but the *Geuzenbericht* pamphlet no longer dropped into Edda's letter-box. Hendrik IJzerdraat and his comrades had been betrayed and interned at Hotel Oranje in Scheveningen almost at the same time as Count Van Limburg Stirum had been taken hostage in Brabant. The men's fate, whether actively opposing the occupiers or just going about their own business, hung in the balance. And the harassment and restricting of Jews increased every day.

Edda had sensed the war would take this course from the beginning. Now with her own eyes she saw how life in her city was spiraling down into dejection and despair. Not by bombs or cannons, not even so much by German hands yet, but by vengeful Dutch hands. The hands of the likes of Klaas Bollema.

In 1941, NSB membership was growing like a festering wound. Three quarters of a million active members out of a population of nine million, and many more who condoned or outright supported the aggressive National Socialist ideology. These collaborators were like angry hounds, stopping at nothing to betray resisters and stir up Jew-hate.

Though she'd known this was where Holland was heading, Edda still found it hard to believe how easily led and morally wrong people were. All the while, the German occupiers laughed into their Swastika-adorned sleeves. The Dutch did their own dirty laundry.

The feeling that she could do nothing to change it but write it all down gnawed on her. Snapping the diary shut, Edda locked it and hid it in its usual place under her mattress.

Today would probably be an ordinary day at the dance studio, if there was such a thing as ordinary these days. She grabbed her bag and meagre lunch of two cheese sandwiches and half a pint of milk and pedaled through the icy morning to the ballet school, now located in an empty primary school in Amsterdam Zuid.

With fewer performances, and dancers leaving the country or getting other occupations, Miss Sterling had informed them she could no longer afford the rent on the A-location on the Museumplein, next to the Stadsschouwburg. None of the remaining Amsterdam Ballet Theater dancers had complained.

In the new premises, they only heated what had been the school's gymnastics hall and adjoining changing rooms. During breaks, they huddled together in the room that had been the staff's canteen. Edda hadn't even seen the rest of the building.

Miss Sterling regularly instructed her dancers to save their energy. They still trained every day with the intention of bringing Swan Lake to the stage in the summer, but the spirits were low.

Monsieur Sergeyev had left first for Paris and now lived in Nice, where the Italian fascists still didn't cooperate with the Germans in persecuting Jews. He'd written that he'd been relatively safe there, though he missed Amsterdam. That's all Miss Sterling had shared about her absent lover, but Edda could see she missed him terribly.

Her honey eyes were dull and the colorful shawls that used to wrap her blonde curls had disappeared. She not only missed her prop-and-stay, she feared for his safety every day. Even if he didn't.

Why has everything become so drab and complicated? Edda thought sadly as she locked her bike and took in the old brick school building with its small windows. The paint was peeling off the windowsills and doors. The place looked as forlorn as she felt.

Yet, dance was the only escape, the only way she could forget herself for a moment. And it was the rare occasion she could see Ash and feel his comforting embrace. His father's shop had been forced to close, but he and his father still worked long hours in their small workshop at home, doing all they could to earn an income for the Hoffmann family.

Edda lived for the breadcrumbs of dance, Ash, and her friends in the ballet company. Contact with her family had been rare after that failed anniversary dinner in November.

She'd phoned her mother several times but there was no news about Van Limburg Stirum and her mother seemed to have resigned herself to being the NSB Mayor's wife and hostess to the Germans. Whether she did it to save the Count's life or of her own free will, Edda was sure her mother would no longer tell her. Everybody was afraid these days. And with reason. Treason lay around every corner.

Miss Sterling was waiting for her as she came in the door. It struck Edda how tired and old her mentor had become in the past year. There was little left of the sprightly Marlene Sterling, though she was nimble on her feet as always and still applied her red lipstick every day. That was about the only thing colorful about the ballet mistress now. She'd even given up dying the blonde curls, which had taken an ash-gray turn like their owner.

Edda's heart felt heavy on her mentor's behalf. Miss Sterling had always been so attentive to her in the four years she had been dancing with the Amsterdam Ballet Theater. But she could think of nothing to ease the ballet mistress's burden except for doing her very best every day and never complaining.

Edda was used to coming in at the same time as Miss Sterling so she could help her start the ancient boiler to get the first chill out of the practice hall.

"Come into my office for a moment, Edda, before the others arrive."

"Of course."

No more bad news, please God, Edda prayed as she followed her mentor down the freezing cold corridor. "Everything alright?" she blurted out immediately. Miss Sterling's honey eyes looked amused for a second before taking on their serious glance again.

"Yes, yes. I just wanted a chat with you. Let the others start that darn boiler for once. See, I've made us some hot tea to get us by."

She handed Edda a steaming cup and it smelled like Darjeeling. Edda could hardly stop herself from inhaling the precious scent.

"A rare parcel that arrived in my hands from London," the ballet mistress explained. "Even managed to get proper milk. Enjoy!"

"Thank you!"

Little treats like this made one grin and bear the day.

"I haven't seen Ash and you together much." The mentor cut straight to the chase.

Edda turned the cup in her hands. It warmed her cold fingers in their half mittens.

"Ash is busy," she said apologetically.

"So, it's not because your parents don't want you to be involved with a Jewish boy?"

"Heavens, no! I'm not a Nazi," Edda spat. "And even if they'd objected, I wouldn't give a tinker's curse." Edda was catapulted back to that horrid dinner event in November, but didn't dare to tell Miss Sterling it had frozen the relationship between Edda and her parents.

"Aha, it's not a matter of your parents . I just wondered where the cool-off stemmed from. Is it Ash then, do you think?"

Edda didn't answer immediately.

"It's neither. It's just this wretched war," she sighed. "Nobody feels alright. I worry about Ash, but I don't dare to show it much. He worries about his family and to be honest I think he might be afraid for me being seen with a Jew. And then my family's involvement with the NSB and the Germans isn't much help either, is it? Ash surely doesn't want to be the wedge between me and my parents. Oh, how can I explain all this to him?" As in the old days, Edda confided in her mentor, who observed her with care.

"Talk with him, Edda. Spill the beans. That's what having a relationship is all about." And then with a wry smile the ballet mistress added, "though I'm not much of an example myself at the moment. You're right, this wretched war makes us way too cautious, even with our loved ones."

Edda nodded, wondering if she should ask about Monsieur Sergeyev but it didn't seem her place to pry.

"So how are you dealing with your parents' political stance?

Gosh, your life is complicated, dear girl." The chance to turn the conversation away from her family was gone.

"I worry about my mother," Edda admitted. "Her health is frail, though she seems to be in remission. But she gives the impression of being squashed between the Germans and my father's work. I'm not so sure she's that pro-Hitler anymore. But she has to remain loyal to my father, of course. Honestly, Miss Sterling, I find it so complicated that I keep the contact with them as short and infrequent as possible, hoping the war will be over soon. It doesn't feel good but what else can I do?" Edda sipped her hot tea, once again feeling cold and low-spirited.

"Are you not worried about your father? He's the one in the lime-light, from what I understand. You know what they say here in Holland, 'tall trees catch all the wind.' What will happen to him if the tide turns, and the Germans lose their footing here?"

Edda shrugged, "I don't think much about my father's fate right now. He's got to lie in the bed he's made."

"That's harsh, Edda."

"I know." Her voice was small, remembering that last meeting with her father in his office. The will he'd told her about. Edda shivered, sought her mentor's kind gaze. It was kind of her to recognize all the complications in Edda's life. And it was a comfort to share her conundrums with someone. They slipped in the mentor-pupil role as in a well-fitted glove.

"Oh Edda!" Miss Sterling patted her hand, "try and talk to Ash. You won't regret it."

They heard the others arrive through the front door, but the ballet mistress didn't seem in a hurry to greet them.

"I don't know." Edda hunched her shoulders.

"Oh, I just wish the lad would sail for New York with his family!" Miss Sterling exclaimed. "For sure, the long arm of the Nazi party can't reach as far as the Statue of Liberty."

"I wish that for them, too," Edda said in a small voice. "Though my heart would break seeing Ash leave."

"You could go with them..." Miss Sterling offered.

"They will never leave," Edda said. "Mr Hoffmann is adamant the family is safe here in Holland. It's a blind spot in him, I'm afraid."

"Same with my Pyotr in France, my dear. He keeps telling me the war will blow over soon, and the darling man wants to stay on the same continent I am."

Finally able to give some advice herself, Edda suggested. "Why don't you both go to London, Miss Sterling? The Germans lost the Battle of Britain. Nobody thinks Hitler in his right mind will try to conquer Great Britain again. You'd both be safe there."

The ballet mistress shook her head. "And leave you lot alone? You all need me here. And frankly, I need the money from your tuition fees and the performances for my own upkeep. Pyotr and I had intended to marry before this madness began. We already bought a house in Cornwall for our retirement. Most of my money is tied up in the property but there's no way to sell it now, even should I want to. And Pyotr's money is tied up in the Soviet Union. It's unlikely he'll ever see anything of his family money ever again. Ah well, why burden you with my botherations? You have plenty to worry about, navigating between your NSB family and your Jewish boyfriend."

Edda welcomed the insight into her mentor's life and how she, too, struggled to make ends meet.

"Thank you for telling me about Mr Sergeyev. I wondered how he was doing. We all miss him so. At least he's in Vichy France and if push comes to shove, he can probably still sail for the States. We're in much trickier waters here. How can we escape?" Not wanting to spoil the day with her sad tales, Edda put forth, "hopefully Mr Hoffmann is right, and the Germans will leave the Dutch Jews alone. They're more harassed by the NSB than by the SA."

"True," Miss Sterling agreed. "Though what's going on is very, very wrong. Yesterday I saw the windows of Leibermann's Gold being smashed in by an angry mob. That's right next door to where the Hoffmann's shop used to be, isn't it?"

Edda nodded, her face contorting with sadness and anger. It was no use to remain optimistic. "I fear the WA work together with the

SA. The Germans are just slowly turning up the heat through their Dutch counterparts."

Rising from her chair, the ballet mistress said, "Let's have this talk regularly. Just the two of us." Edda got up as well.

"Pity we can't talk longer. I do need it so." Her head was so full and her thoughts so somber.

Seeing Edda's sad face, her arms hanging limply by her sides, Miss Sterling stepped towards her. "Come here, let me give you a hug. You look like you need it."

The embrace felt bony but welcome. She whispered in Edda's ear, "I want you and Ash to take the day off, spend some time together. Maybe invite him to your flat?"

It sounded tempting but Edda replied, "We need to practice, right? You always say, 'a day without practice is a day not lived'."

Miss Sterling released Edda from her arms. "That was before all this nonsense happened, my dear. Now my motto would be: a day without love is a day not lived."

Edda was sceptical. "What if Ash doesn't want a day off?"

Miss Sterling broke into her first carefree laugh that day. How Edda had missed that tinkling, merry sound.

"You silly girl! That boy will carry a torch for you to the ends of the Earth. Scoot, scoot! I'll see you both tomorrow."

19

THE GIFT

"Would you like a cup of coffee? I was able to get some *real* coffee beans in the Albert Cuyp Market. I felt like a queen purchasing them."

Edda turned around in her small kitchen to face Ash. He'd been silent on the way to her flat and she didn't exactly know in what mood he was. Not that Asher Hoffmann was moody or changeable, but he had been very silent in the past weeks. Edda had no idea how to break through that barrier, and sometimes it felt like they were almost strangers, at best acquaintances, but not a couple in love.

Unless they danced. All was well when they danced. But it was not enough for Edda to only feel connected to Ash where others were constantly present. Miss Sterling in her infinite wisdom must have seen their struggle and wanted to help them.

The morning light filtered through her lace curtains and created an aura of light around Ash's dark blond locks. As if even the light danced around him. He was so magnificent, so regal. Edda thought her heart would break seeing him sitting on her kitchen stool. Not that he hadn't been sitting in that exact place before, but it seemed so much more precious now, yet fragile and flighty.

He didn't answer her question about the coffee, but he didn't take his eyes off her either. They were the color of the midday Mediterranean Sea—blue, clear, loving. Edda suppressed a gasp. She wanted to raise the roof, shouting. "I love you so! I love you so!" but she kept quiet too.

Then she heard the second person on that bleak February morning bid her closer. "Come here, my gritty girl, let me give you a hug."

She was instantly in his arms. The stool almost toppled over with Ash on it, but Edda didn't care. She didn't need his words. She wanted his kisses. She wanted to feel him, feel him, feel him. As she was feeling him now.

For a suspended moment, all Edda's worries were gone. He loved her and she loved him and there was nothing that could come between them, nobody could tear them apart. Not war, not Hitler, not the Klaas Bollemas of this world.

Edda was thinking of what Duifje had said. That she was ridiculous for not consummating their love, but she still felt neither she nor Ash were ready for that. They didn't want to rush, and Edda wanted it all—the white lace gown with the enormous veil, the gigantic wedding with all their friends and family merrily together, the faraway, romantic honeymoon where they'd probably stay in bed most of the time. When she and Ash got married, there was no war, and she could freely convert to his religion.

"Where's your head at, Edda-mine?" He kissed her nose and both her cheeks then her forehead with butterfly kisses.

"I was dreaming of ... the end of war and how we would be then." She wasn't going to say *when we're married*. Old-fashioned as she was, she believed Ash had to propose to her and he hadn't even alluded to that yet.

"Aha," he chuckled, "I was thinking of exactly the same thing. I hope the guys who started this war will hurry up to get to the finish so I can be with my girl for good."

"Oh Ash." Edda kissed him with all her passion until he finally wriggled free and spoke hoarsely.

"Will you be mine after the war, Edda Van der Valk?"

"Yes, yes, yes, Asher Hoffmann, a thousand times yes."

"Okay!" The blue eyes danced over her face. "I've got something for you but before you jump for joy, it isn't a ring." He laughed and pulled her to him again. "That's why I'm not going down on one knee yet, but I will, heart of my heart. In due time. And I promise I will make you the most beautiful wedding ring you've ever seen."

Edda didn't know what she desired most in the immediate present, stay in his strong arms and be kissed forever, or receive her present. Edda adored presents and they'd been way too sparse since the war. Duifje's leather bound diary, now tied to that same war, and her pearl earrings with matching necklace, from her parents for her twenty-first birthday, seemed ages ago.

"I want my present." She felt like a little girl as she uttered it.

"Alright, Edda-mine, close your eyes." He cradled her in his lap as if she was indeed a little girl. It felt heavenly.

"Stop," she cried. "Let this last a little longer. Don't give it to me yet." She squeezed her eyelids shut and let herself sink against him —as she'd done so often in their *pas-de-deux*—really sink into his body, until they were one. Soon she would fly away on her own again like his feather-light butterfly but for now she was at their homebase.

Ash also seemed to realize the preciousness of the moment. More precious than all the gold and silver of the world, more precious than their own individual breaths, more precious than the day they lived for. It was their eternity, and it would last throughout everything. Everything!

"Open your eyes or I won't give it to you because you won't take it," he teased her, as he nudged her ribs.

"No! I want it. Give it, give it to me!"

She felt how he pressed a box in her hands and then wrapped her fingers around it. The box felt velvety, smooth but it was quite big.

"Now!" he commanded, and Edda stared down at a square burgundy red box with a ribbon around in soft pink. The box itself was already an adornment. In small golden lettering, it read Samuel Hoffmann & Sohn, Vienna. The words made Edda swallow. They'd brought the jewelry boxes with them, never even being able to change it to Amsterdam before their shop was closed again.

"Did you make it?" she asked in a hushed tone, still having difficulty breathing. The tips of her fingers caressed the box. Edda's sixth sense throbbed. This was both a gift made of love and pain. If she opened the box, she would knew what would win. And yet, Ash waited for her to break the spell, untie the ribbon, lay bare their future.

The two most powerful Warriors are Patience and Time – Leo Tolstoy. The note Doctor Geuze had given her.

If she believed in Patience and Time, would she dare to face their future? She had to. There was no other option. So, Edda opened the box.

On the black velvet cushion lay a crystal butterfly brooch, both sturdy and fragile. Before Edda had even time to take in what it meant, Ash already began to explain the particulars.

"I've used platinum for the structure and laid it in with the best rock crystals from Brazil. I toyed with the idea of making it only of rock crystal because you are my gritty girl, but I decided on a bed of platinum for two reasons. You're a real platinum girl but I was also afraid that crystal alone would make the brooch too breakable. And..." he held the butterfly against the light.

"Can you see how the crystals reflect nicely against the solid white background? Their light slightly subdued because of the less reflective shimmer of the platinum, but I think it works well together. It was the first time I tried this technique, so I hope you..." He stopped in mid-sentence and did something Edda had never seen him do before. Ash blushed, deeply then hid his face against her shoulder and mumbled, "I'm sorry. I hope you like it. It was made with love."

How could she find the right words? How could she tell him how eternally grateful she was to him for giving her all these technical particulars? By keeping them with two feet on the ground explaining his workmanship, he'd lifted her over the abyss. It was a brooch. A beautifully, handmade brooch, given to her by her beloved. A present, nothing else. And it was stunning—the most exquisite piece of jewelry she'd ever laid eyes on. And there were some amazing heirlooms in both the Van der Valk and Scherzinger families.

Edda knew she had to do something drastic, so she closed the box momentarily and lifted Ash's head from her shoulder.

"Sorry," he mumbled again. "I got carried away. I should have just let you look at it with your own eyes."

Gazing deep into his eyes, she kissed him with all the tenderness and gratitude of her heart. "Hush," she said and kissed him again, more passionately, more urgent. "Asher Hoffmann, I will never ever part with this brooch. Not one day. I am and will forever be your crystal butterfly. Now please pin it on my ballet top."

"So, you didn't mind my rambling?" He smiled again as he carefully opened the pin and stuck it through the fabric of Edda's top.

"On the contrary. I can't wait to see you at work in your workshop. May I some day?"

"Of course!"

Edda jumped out of his lap and took Ash's hand. She pulled him to her bedroom where she positioned herself in front of the mirror in first position. The butterfly glimmered and shone on her breast.

"I am complete."

It was a humble expression, but it was how she felt.

Ash came to stand behind her and wrapped her in his arms. They stood body to body. And they were both crying silent tears.

20

THE FEBRUARY STRIKE

Two weeks later

Amsterdam, 27 February 1941

We've had two extraordinary days! But also very sad ones. I never thought it possible, but the Dutch actually stood up to the Germans in a two-day national strike. It started here in Amsterdam, but it also spread to other parts of Holland. I fear it will back-fire on us but at least it gave those who hate the Nazis a boost. I also now know for sure my neighbor Mevrouw Meulenbelt is anti-German, as we finally talked.

But let me tell you first what happened. I wrote before about the fights on the 9th of February. The strikes are related to those incidents. Apparently on the 11th of February one of Klaas Bollema's closest friends, a man called Hendrik Koot, was mortally wounded in the fights and later died. Of course, more fights broke out because the NSB was furious Koot had died.

But then the Germans got involved. A patrol of the Ordnungspolizei was ambushed in what we know as Ice-Cream Parlor Koco and one of the Germans got injured. The genie was out of the bottle and the highest Nazis here in Holland, Reichskommissar Seys-Inquart and Hanns Rauter, head of the SS, went complaining to their boss, Heinrich Himmler.

The result was awful. Hundreds of Jewish men were arrested in a razzia and taken away. We don't know where. I'm glad the Hoffmanns and Larry weren't involved.

But now comes the extraordinary part. Two days ago, tens of thousands of Amsterdamers simply stopped working and took to the streets to demonstrate against the German occupiers. The protest is both against the Jew-hunt and the forced labor in Germany. It was organized by the Communist Party but also many non-communists took part. I only went to have a look at the strikers. And that's when I saw my neighbor and she told me all this. Mevrouw Meulenbelt is apparently very well informed, but I haven't asked who her sources are, of course.

The strike was immediately knocked down by the Germans and I fear harsh repercussions. I truly hope they won't take it out on poor Van Limburg Stirum and the other hostages!

However, the spree of freedom was exhilarating. I just wish I had the courage to really show which side I'm on. Well, I don't. But I can tell you, Herr Hitler and your mouthpiece, Meneer Mussert, we won't lay down without another fight. So be prepared.

When Edda arrived at the old school building in Amsterdam-Zuid the next morning, she saw she wasn't the first. A group of people huddled near the doorway, small valises in their hands.

What's going on? she thought and had an eerie feeling the people didn't come to enjoy Miss Sterling's ballet instructions. They looked more like an extended family than a group of dancers. The ballet mistress hadn't arrived yet, which was strange as well. Edda locked her bike and slinging her bag over her shoulder made for the door. Recently Miss Sterling had given her a key, so she could open the school as well.

"Can I help you?" she addressed the man closest to her. When she realized they were a Jewish family, her dismay grew. *What on earth?*

"We're looking for Miss Marlene Sterling. We were told to come here."

"Oh, I see." Edda assumed her mentor was going to help these people get to England. So, she invited them in.

"Miss Sterling will be here any minute."

The man extended his hand, "I'm Isaac de Jonge, Leron's father, and this is my wife, Elsa. My daughters, Rosa and Judith. And my father-in-law, Daniel."

"Leron?" Edda looked puzzled. "Do you mean Larry?"

"Oh yes, of course. I always forget the boy wants to be called Larry. He finds that much more international."

"I'm sorry it's awfully cold in here," Edda babbled as she marshalled them into their canteen. The mother and daughters said nothing but looked stricken. The father-in-law was leaning on his cane. Edda wrestled with her thoughts and didn't know how to keep the conversation going. A tacit understanding hung in the air that she wouldn't ask what they were doing at the ballet school.

"Hello! Sorry I'm late!" Miss Sterling hurried in with a topped-up shopping bag in her arms. "Oh, I see you've already arrived, family de Jonge. Thank you for letting them in, Edda. I've done some grocery shopping for you."

That's a lot of food to take on a journey, Edda pondered inside. Feeling the aura of secrecy around the family's presence that wasn't hers to probe, she announced, "I'll get the boiler going, Miss Sterling."

"You do that, my dear, and start practising *tout de suite* while I sort out my affairs here."

Edda asked no more but had come to her own conclusions. De Jonge family weren't sailing for Britain; they were going to hide in the derelict school building in a remote area of Amsterdam. They were going to hide until this last wave of violence from the NSB and the Nazis died down.

Feeling immensely proud of her mentor, Edda sent smiles to the family and turned turned away to give them some privacy. Her lips were sealed. No mention would be made of the De Jonge family if she could help it. She let the boiler blast at top volume for once so that the whole building would become warm. That was the least she could do for a family who'd left their home and all their possessions.

What would become of the Hoffmanns? Was the same fate awaiting them? Edda shook the worry from her mind and concentrated on *un-deux-trois*. She put Tchaikovsky's Danses des Cygnes on the record player and blasted the volume. She wanted to only hear the music and dance, dance, dance.

Ash caught her in his arms and Edda cried with big sobs against his chest. Relieved he was there but anxious for his future. *Cry-baby!* He never called her that, but she seemed to be doing a lot of crying these days.

He danced her to the record player and turned down the volume.

"What's going on, Edda-mine?"

"Nothing!" She smiled through her tears, "I just wanted to hear the music."

"Are you sure?

"Yes."

Patience and Time. Those were her Warriors, and her Brooch was her Compass.

FROM THAT DAY FORWARD, Edda didn't see the De Jonge family anymore, but Miss Sterling regularly arrived laden with shopping bags and Larry sometimes lingered in the canteen after they were finished for the day. Something he'd never done before.

Edda turned to her diary for comfort and release, but a new idea was forming in the back of her mind. She realized that the trying times they were living in weren't just ordinary trying times. With her fine-tuned intuition, she diligently started to note down reality as it was.

> *1 March 1941*
>
> *One day this war will be over, and it will be a day of reckoning. I want to remember all that happened. If Ash and I are ever blessed with children, I want them to know what we had to go through together. This cannot ever be forgotten, so that it can never happen again.*

Before there could be a ration on paper, she bought herself four more diaries, exactly the same, black with a golden lock. And she stored them away. No one could ever know she kept a record of what was going on. Not until it was safe to let her diaries out of their hiding places. Like the Jewish families who were going underground.

21

MORE BAD NEWS AND SOME GOOD

Two weeks later

> *Amsterdam, 13 March 1941*
>
> *Hendrik Sijzerdraat is dead. Murdered by the iron-fisted Germans. Together with fifteen other Geuzen and three men involved in the February Strike. The eighteen men were taken from the Oranje Hotel to the Waasdorpervlakte and shot point-blank in the dunes.*
>
> *Why? For Heaven's sake, why?*
>
> *What did these young men—some with families, some students— do other than forewarn us against the Nazi occupation? They told the Dutch to mistrust Hitler's ideology and paid for that warning with their lives. It is blatantly clear what the Germans want. Every Dutch inhabitant must dance to their tune or get a bullet.*

The Geuzen never even touched so much as the sleeve of one German. Oh, the Dutch are enraged! But the pressure is on. The Germans must have believed the Dutch to be much more pliable. Well, we aren't. But, oh dear God, I fear for what's next. Neither side will go down without a fight and the Germans have the weapons, the power, and the infrastructure to squash us completely. And they're getting anxious. The war in North Africa doesn't seem to be going well for them.

I will just write down what I can glean from the papers and my illegal radio. It makes me feel more like a correspondent than a resistance fighter. I would never have the guts to openly resist. And with my family rubbing elbows with Hitler and Mussert, it would be idiocy on my part to do anything more overt.

But still! Herr Hitler and Meneer Mussert, I'll do my part. I swear to my Queen and Country that I will not lie down and give in to you if I can help it.

De 'Joodsche Raad' or Jewish Council was established in Amsterdam in late February. Nobody knew whether it meant a good thing or a bad thing. Its founding was ordered by the occupiers, it wasn't happening of free will, but Jewish notables like Mr Asscher and Mr Cohen stepped forward to take chairing positions. The new entity led to much speculation in Miss Sterling's canteen.

Ash, for the first time ever, showed some combativeness. "The Council is just a cover-up for collecting data on Jews. Read my lips," he brooded.

"I don't think so, Ash," Larry chimed in, despite his family being among the first to hide from the Germans. "It serves the Nazis no benefit when the Dutch continue to sabotage their law and order. They need us on their side."

Edda didn't take part in the discussion. Sitting close to Ash and breathing in his warmth, for once she was of two minds what this new council meant. Her intuition didn't give her a clear answer to why this Jewish Council was established now. It was 'by Jews, for Jews,' which seemed to imply to some autonomy. No Germans were on the board. But who could trust the Germans to not be pulling some strings behind the scenes these days?

Miss Sterling had abolished the *'no politics'* rule in her orbit. After she'd felt compelled to offer Larry's family shelter in her school, she allowed free reign for any who wanted to discuss the war. It would have been silly to forbid it anyway. Everything around them was tainted by the war. The shortage of new ballet shoes, to the lack of opportunities to perform, to Larry having difficulty finding materials for repairs like faulty floorboards and broken lamp bulbs.

"You're wrong there, Larry," Ash argued. "Just see what they've done to the Geuzen resisters. None of those men had done so much as raise a fist to the occupiers. If stencilling some protest pamphlets can get you killed in cold blood and without a proper trial, I tell you the Germans are taking revenge on the Dutch refusal to surrender. They're tightening the screws and it's the Jews and the resisters that will get the full brunt of their unbridled anger."

Edda sat straighter. She didn't even know Ash was following the news in Holland, but he was clearly well-informed on the atrocious Geuzen murders. She sat closer to him, and he put his arm around her, although his stance didn't mellow. Well, neither did hers. No longer able to keep quiet, she blurted out,

"I think the Germans miscalculated the Dutch freedom-loving spirit. They thought we were more like them. As if we, with a lot of pressure and by using scapegoats, would budge and accept their rule. But that's their own spirit. Follow the orders to the letter, or you'll be out. We're not like that. It's going to be the same with the hostages they took."

"What hostages?" Ash asked.

"A friend of our family, Count Van Limburg Stirum, was taken hostage in November." Edda blushed at mentioning his name though there was no reason for it. Just the memory of what could have been, had her parents had their say.

"Apparently, the Count, who's a respected attorney in The Hague, is being held hostage in a former seminary in Brabant with hundreds of other noteworthy individuals—professors, surgeons, artists, mayors, writers, judges, nobles. The most brilliant minds of Dutch society. Not because these men have ever been part of the resistance but purely as leverage. They're captives but they don't live in a real jail. They get proper food and can do all sorts of sports and education. However, on any ill-omened day any of these high-class men can be randomly chosen by the Sicherheitsdienst to be shot, should the Dutch decide to commit an act of resistance against the Germans. It's already been dubbed *Hitler's Herrengefängnis,* his gentlemen prison."

"What?!" Larry and Ash cried at the same time. Larry added, "why didn't I hear about this?"

"You will soon enough," Edda said glumly. "The Dutch were rather meek until now, but with the February Strikes and the Geuzen murders, the country will start to revolt. I fear the first Herren victims will be chosen soon."

"Will it crush the resistance?" Ash's question was rhetorical as none could answer it.

"I wish you and your family would leave," Edda said under her breath. "I fear the Jewish people are going to pay the highest price. Hitler is whipping the Germans into a frenzy with his Jew-hate. Will your father still not consider a safer place, Ash?" Her dark eyes looked at him pleadingly. The words burned on her tongue as she never wanted to go a day without seeing his beloved face but when his life was in danger, she could part with him. Ash shook his head.

"Father wants to give it another couple of months. He still believes the Germans and the Dutch will live in relative peace, side-by-side. And it's not like tickets to Britain or the United States are easy to get, and they cost a lot of money. We haven't got much of our resources left. I think it's the same with your family, Larry?"

The floor manager nodded. "But, I am considering leaving Holland. My parents aren't against me leaving on my own. I'm young and I can earn money. More than we can earn here now with all the restrictions on Jews. When I've made enough, I can ship my parents out. I haven't gone yet because I don't have the heart to forsake Miss Sterling. You both know how good she's been to all of us and she'd be in quite a big pickle herself now because of her generosity."

EDDA FINALLY DARED to ask how Larry's family was faring, now that they were living in the primitive circumstances of the old school.

"They cope," Larry shrugged. "That's one of the things that irritates me about my parents. They are so docile. It must be a generational thing. They just accept their circumstances and let their heads hang low. My sisters are going to different schools now than before. Mother pretends they're not Jewish, so they go to ordinary schools. Rosa is at secondary school and little Judith's still in sixth form. I don't think they're very happy in their new situation, but they don't complain either. My mother always says, *What's the use of complaining, you only make everyone miserable.* And then she will be looking at me as if I'm the cause of all their troubles." Larry sounded miserable indeed.

"You know what?" Edda suggested. "Why not come over to my place for the evening? I can make you some potato snacks and sausage rolls." She'd never before asked the lanky floor manager with his long, heron legs to her flat, but she'd never forgotten his genuine delight at her first performance as Clara.

"Will you come too, Ash?" She fingered the butterfly brooch as she pleaded with him.

"I'd love to, but I've promised to be home before six." He kissed her cheek. "And I will talk with my father about New York, Edda. I think we can all three agree we're in dire straits here. Is Miss Sterling out again getting more food? I haven't seen her all afternoon."

Edda listened. The rest of the building was empty. Fewer and fewer dancers came for practice. She feared the day Ash wouldn't show up again either. Everything was such a drag these days.

"I think she's gone. Why didn't she say goodbye? It's not like her."

"I think she's depressed, too," Larry remarked. "She could do with some of your potato snacks and sausage rolls."

"And I've got some beer left! So, you *should come*, Ash," Edda brightened, knowing he liked the occasional beer. For some reason she felt like a party after all the misery, though she hardly ever drank alcohol herself. It was not part of her regimen.

"Who's talking of beer and sausage rolls?" Miss Sterling stood in the door, looking tired and thin, but smiling broadly at her reduced group.

"Are you coming, Miss Sterling? I've invited everyone. Only Ash still needs to be cajoled."

"Alright, alright!" He threw his hands in the air, "everything for our star dancer!" Edda jumped in his arms. Now she really felt like a party.

HER THREE GUESTS were sitting in Edda's tiny sitting room while she handed around steaming plates and full glasses. With her hair in a polka dot shawl and a red checked apron over her ballet outfit, she looked like an exotic movie star. The mysterious beauty of Vivien Leigh with the bony strength of Katherine Hepburn.

She felt Ash follow her with his eyes everywhere she moved. He was brooding while sipping his beer. Was he truly going to leave her for America? Possibly Larry's idea of departing on his own had planted a seed in Ash Hoffmann? If he went, she'd go with him. Edda looked around her flat and knew it would be that way. She had enough money of her own and, as she was twenty-one, her parents had no say over her anymore.

Suddenly the idea of escaping Holland became paramount in her mind. Whether they would go to England or America, she didn't care. As long as it was far away from the long arms of the Nazis, German or Dutch. But then Edda's gaze rested on Miss Sterling, sitting cross-legged and relaxed on the blue settee, laughing and joking with Larry.

She couldn't leave her mentor. Not after all she'd done for her. But what if the four of them left together? She, Edda, could pay for all their tickets.

"Let's make a plan to get out of here," she blurted out.

Three pairs of eyes stared at her. Silence in the room.

"Where do you want to go? A movie or a café?" Miss Sterling asked surprised. "I thought we were having a great time here?"

"No, I mean, leave the country. The four of us. Dance somewhere else and Larry can help us settle. London or New York?"

"Edda what's gotten into you?" It was her mentor who spoke first.

"Never mind," Edda said, tears in her eyes. "I just... I just want us to be safe."

"But, honey, you are safe here. There's no one going to hurt *you*?" The ballet mistress skipped off the couch, taking the glass out of Edda's hand, placed it on the sideboard and hugged her. Edda cried; she was exhausted, she was afraid. Not for herself but for her Jewish friends and her mentor who was hiding Jews.

Something terrible was awaiting them and she couldn't stop it. No matter how she tried. If only they could all escape. But she knew they wouldn't.

Ash had risen as well and took Edda into his arms from her mentor. She felt like a little girl, a silly little girl who needed extra care when she wasn't the one who was in danger.

"Ash," she sobbed against his chest, that she actually wanted to hammer in anger. *Wake up, Ash, wake up!*

"Do you want me to stay with you tonight, Edda-mine?" he whispered in her ear.

"You can't," she sniffled, "your parents will be dying with worry."

"I can ask Larry to pass by my house and tell them you needed me here." He was talking very softly to her. Miss Sterling and Larry left them alone and resumed their conversation, seeing she needed Ash's comforting.

"Yes,' she whispered back. "If you can, yes please."

"Everything for my star dancer, for my gritty Edda-girl."

22

PREPARATIONS FOR A BALLET

Five weeks later

Amsterdam, 22 June 1941

I think Hitler's gone mad, but perhaps it's to our advantage. He's attacking his 'friend,' the Soviet Union. That will shake up things for the Communists! Some say Hitler's never been the soundest of minds and I'm thinking back to when I met him briefly in 1935 with my parents.

You may wonder why I spend time thinking about a man I loathe as much as Satan himself, but I think the soundness—or unsoundness—of his judgment is of importance to us. And to the rest of Europe that he's holding in his iron fist. With hindsight, I think I discerned traces of instability and fickleness under that *polite, diplomatic veneer. Because it was exactly that, a veneer. A coating by a house painter.*

Any sane person knows one shouldn't attack Russia. Don't go East! Napoleon would tell you so and Kaiser Wilhelm, as well.

But no, Hitler is going to show his teeth in what he, in his grandiose brainbox, has dubbed Operation Barbarossa. Well good luck to you, Sir! And Stalin, another man as Janus-faced as the devil, now wants to switch sides and join the Allies. Somehow, this is a good day for me. Not only will Hitler's new adventure take the pressure of us for a bit. He'll probably exhaust himself quicker.

So, Herr Hitler for once in this diary I congratulate you! Go east and go chase your own tail!

In Amsterdam, summer had just started. The finches and blackbirds were making a spectacle in the treetops of the Vondelpark. Sunshine was streaming in abundance into Edda's tiny kitchen, where she was packing a lunch for two. It promised to be a beautiful Sunday afternoon in the park in the sweet company of her Ash.

Her butterfly, as always, sparkled on her breast, but this time not on her ballet top but on a black, front-buttoned, calf-length dress sprinkled with sprightly daisies. Edda felt pretty and relaxed, humming along with Tchaikovsky's Song of the Swans. Miss Sterling still had the intention of bringing Swan Lake to the stage in early July and they were finalizing the last rehearsals. She tapped her foot lightly to the beats, internalizing the steps habitually.

It would be a *tour de force*, Edda thought, as she washed ripe tomatoes and tender leaves of lettuce. But if anyone could pull it off, it was Miss Sterling, even without her Pyotr.

Swan Lake needed a smaller cast of major dancers than the Nutcracker. All the swans would be young girls from Natasja's ballet studio in Amsterdam. Vivacious, petite, and speaking as rapidly as her tiny feet moved, this Amsterdam girl had been Miss Sterling's first pupil before Edda's time. But Natasja had never pursued a stage career herself, possibly because she was so short, and ballerinas needed to be at least 5-foot-4.

Natasja's Ballet School, as her dance studio was simply called, had been a thriving beehive of girls in tutus and some boys in tights before the war but like Miss Sterling, this younger ballet mistress also suffered from the war, and she now only had a trickling of girls who still came for her lessons. The two women had joined forces and Nastasja had been a frequent co-teacher in their school building in Amsterdam-Zuid.

Edda liked Natasja. She was fun to be around with her typical hard-nosed, Amsterdam humor. Stubbornly referring to her native city as 'Mokum', the young ballet mistress made no qualms on which side she was.

"In Yiddish, 'Mokum' means city. In the eighteenth century, the Jews started calling Amsterdam, 'Mokum Alef', using the first letter of the city's name to the root word. That's how long our friends have been here. Today Alef is dropped and only Mokum remains."

"I love it!" Edda had exclaimed. "I'm going to use it, too."

"Yes," Natasja had smiled. "It might become a Geuzen name now, though. The fact the Amsterdamers kept the nickname Mokum shows the Jews were more accepted here than in other European cities."

"So Mokum is only used in Amsterdam?"

"As far as I know, yes!" Natasja had replied. "I'm from a working-class family and over the years we've adopted so many Jewish expressions and words the Yiddish blended with Dutch in Amsterdam has almost become its own language."

Edda listened for the bell while wrapping the sandwiches in oiled paper and putting them in her wicker basket. She was happy. The steady and heavy rehearsal schedule, and the prospect of staging a new series of shows in two weeks, lifted her mood like it hadn't been lifted in months. It was also the lovely weather and Hitler pointing his greedy eyes and generals east. A breath of fresh air and freedom.

And there was more good news. Vincent van Rijn, who'd given up ballet when the war started to help in his father's construction company, would make a comeback as the evil Baron von Rothbart. It had been so good to see her former 'stage love' from the Nutcracker and she could tell Vince's ballet heart was beating firmly in his formidable chest again. If only he'd stay after the shows.

Edda, who was to dance both Odette and Odile, was fully prepared for another *pas-de-deux* with Ash as Prince Siegfried. Because in the original version Swan Lake ends badly, they'd decided to discuss over lunch which changes Miss Sterling had made in her choreography. And how they could fit the more positive spin into their dramatic performance.

When the bell rang, she hastened to the front door and, to her surprise, saw a letter sticking out of the letterbox.

"That can wait until later," she mumbled, as she opened the door. As always, she was struck by Ash's buoyant beauty, as if she was seeing him for the first time. A shining, god-like man. How he managed to look so poised and unshakeable under his less-than-fancy-free life was a constant marvel to Edda.

Ash produced a small bouquet of carnations from behind his back and presented them to her.

"For my girl who never speaks much with her mouth but always with her eyes."

"Oh Ash," she protested. "I do speak my mind. But we've made a promise. And if you weren't such a genuine person, I'd call you a charmer. Thank you for the revolutionary flowers! Come in so I can kiss you properly without my neighbors following our every move."

"Oh no, we can't have that."

Ash was in an excellent mood, and his kisses were sweet and

balmy, and as gentle as the subtle scents of the carnations. She could kiss him forever and wished they would never stop.

But eventually they went to the park, Ash carrying the picnic basket and Edda the tablecloth on which they would sit. As it was such a fine Sunday afternoon, the park was busy, but the atmosphere wasn't as exuberant and at ease as it had been in the summers before the war. People mostly sat alone or in pairs. But even the whole families or groups of friends kept conversations subdued, and quick glances were cast on the patrolling Germans in their *feldgrau* uniforms with their rifles slung over their shoulders.

A man dressed in black with his black hat upside down in front of him played melancholic tunes on his harmonica. People passed him by, but few had a coin to spare. The Germans left him alone. The sounds floated eerily into the air, beautiful and heart-breaking at the same time.

Edda and Ash found a secluded spot next to the big fountain and sat down in the shade. For a while they didn't speak but looked around them. Motorcycles and cars roared by outside the park, the birds hummed in the trees and the humans murmured on the ground. A distant Messerschmidt split the high summer sky.

The Hoffmanns wouldn't leave. Ash had told her as much. There seemed to be a lull in the war. Both the Germans and the Dutch had found some form of equilibrium to live side-by-side. Sure, there was still a lot of harassment of Jewish people. And small cells of resisters executed minor deeds of resistance, but it was as if the war was also taking a summer break. Perhaps the lull would last, now that a new war had erupted on the eastern front.

Edda and Ash never talked much about the war, as they had promised each other, and today would be about Swan Lake, not the German invasion of the Soviet Union. Ash didn't even know she kept a diary and followed the news as closely as she could. Not talking about what went on around them and in the wider world was a form of survival that worked for them both.

"Do you think we're ready for Miss Sterling's version of Swan Lake?" Edda asked, biting into a juicy bacon sandwich.

"I think it's a great idea. We've trained so hard. I just worry about you dancing both Odette and Odile. It will be such a strain on you."

"You know I like to work hard." she shrugged. "And it's not as if Prince Siegfried has it easy. You also have to dance *with* both Odette and Odile."

"In the supporting role, Edda-mine. You do all the heavy lifting."

She giggled at his expression. "I hope you will lift *me* and not the other way around."

He smiled too, "it was a pun. You know what I mean."

"Miss Sterling says I can do it. And honestly with everything that's going on, I'm just happy we can dance, and we can entertain people. There's enough misery going around."

"What sort of audience do you think will come to the Stadsschouwburg?" Ash mused. "People are so careful with their money these days. What if the theatre hall is half empty?"

Edda looked pensive, "I've been thinking about that as well. I really hope we'll not just get Germans. It would be great if Amsterdamers took the opportunity to enjoy an evening out. Will your parents come?"

Ash pulled a face. "I doubt it. Though Miss Sterling said they'd get free tickets."

"Oh, you must invite them, Ash! They must love to see you dance."

He avoided answering by redirecting the conversation at her "What about your family?"

"They'll be there. They always come. Usually the first night. I'm just not sure I'll have the opportunity afterwards to spend some time with them." A deep sigh escaped her chest. "I really need to go visit them soon. Should stop postponing it. We've just been so busy with the ballet." The white envelope in her letterbox leapt to mind but she pushed it aside.

"Do you miss them?" Ash pulled her into his embrace. At least let her feel *his* warmth. Edda considered her answer.

"I guess I miss how we were before the war. We've always been a bit of a malfunctioning family, but it somehow worked. We love each other dearly, but are all very different individuals. Putting all the Van der Valks together in a room is not always a great success. You were witness to that yourself during that awful dinner party."

As often had been the case, it lay on the tip of Edda's tongue to tell her boyfriend about her parents' politics. The real ins-and-outs of it. And why she wrote her diaries, but she kept quiet. Knowing everything would only burden Ash further and she assumed he already gleaned what the NSB mayor of Leiden stood for.

"Oh, I can't wait to dance a great show again," Edda said, steering the subject away from the vulnerable topic of her family. "It's been so long since Romeo and Juliet. Even if we can only do a couple of shows, I'm sure we'll all feel heavenly." Ash perked up on her good cheer.

"Yes, it will be marvelous!" He kissed her and made their arms dance in the air as they sat on the blanket. "Aren't we special when we dance together, my gritty girl? I can't wait either."

"Do you worry about the sadness of the ballet, though?" She looked up at him.

"I think it's a good idea Miss Sterling changed the end. Prince Siegfried losing his beloved and committing suicide wouldn't be a good thing for the audience right now. It's been done before, though —Swan Lake with a happy ending. In Russia, even, before it was the Soviet Union."

"What do you mean?" Edda asked.

"An adaptation in which Prince Siegfried manages to break the spell after all and gets his happily-ever-after with Odette." Ash explained.

"Oh, I didn't know that. I wonder why these ballets often have these dramatic sad endings," Edda mused. "Swan Lake is the gloomiest of all, I think. With Odette remaining a swan and Prince Siegfried being lured into believing the evil Odile is his beloved." Edda shook a weary head.

"That's 19th-century, high Romanticism for you, Edda-mine. It doesn't work in the 20th-century. All that *Sturm und Drang* and Goethe-like stuff."

"And we keep dancing those old-fashioned ballets," Edda laughed.

"Do you ever consider dancing modern? Taking lessons with Martha Graham?" Ash asked.

"Do you?" The classically-trained ballerina in Edda didn't dare to consider the freedom of modern dance.

"I would," Ash said self-assured. "I'm still very grateful for my classical training and it will always be my basis, but I'd love to free-wheel a bit, if you know what I mean."

"Then, I'd try to experiment as well." Edda's face shone. "I've thought about taking modern dance lessons many times, but I already had a hard time getting my parents to accept classical ballet as a profession. They still won't let me call it a 'career.' But modern? I think they'd really believe I'd run off with the circus."

"We are going to dance modern when we get the opportunity, Edda-mine!" The smile Ash gave her dispersed all the clouds in her mind and they said it at the same time.

"In New York!"

23

THE LETTER

St Michielsgestel, 5 June 1941

Dear Eddaline,

You will be surprised to get this letter from me, and I apologize for that in advance. As my days are numbered, I want to bring my affairs in order. That concerns not just material affairs, but also 'loose ends' with people.

Before you read any further—yes, I did ask your father if there would be an opportunity to marry you when you came of age— and of course— never without your consent.

Though the matter of our relationship was never openly discussed and I'm just a dry-as-dust lawyer with little experience with women, I could sense you were not at all interested in me. So, I dropped the matter completely and we only had very superficial contact, mainly in the presence of one or both of your parents. Though I'm related to your father, it was actually your mother with whom I discussed this at length and she too agreed that we would not be a good match. So please, Edda do not think your mother still harbors a wish to pair you with me in matrimony.

You've always fascinated me since you were a young girl. I know no one who is as bright and as strong as you. You carved out a career in dance coming from a family where that is frowned upon, and yet you did it with that stubborn and disciplined attitude of yours. I will never forget seeing you on stage in the Nutcracker and last year in Romeo and Juliet. I could see how happy you were. So perhaps I'm not completely dry-as-dust. Sparks flew between you and Asher Hoffmann, and though I fear for his future as he is a Jew, I wish you all the happiness of the world and hope all your dreams together will come true.

As I have a lot of time to think and reflect, let me take the liberty to tell you a little about me. Somehow, it is still important to me that you bear me no ill will when I'm gone. And I also know that you are the only one of your family to whom I can confess this. Yes, it's putting a heavy weight on your tender shoulders, Edda-line, but I know you can bear it better than any other Van Der Valk.

Here's an instruction, though. This letter has been smuggled out of the camp to avoid the censors and you must promise to destroy it, down to the last scrap, after you've read it. It is too dangerous for you to keep this letter. Please, do as I tell you, Eddaline, not for mine but for your own safety.

I'm in a so-called bail hostage camp in Brabant with hundreds of other men. Prominent men from all over Holland are kept here by the Nazis for the sole reason that we can be shot when an act of resistance against the Germans takes place somewhere. So far nobody has been selected and shot, but I'm on the first list. For some bizarre reason the Germans think that people of blue blood are all thick as thieves with the royal family. Maybe that's the case in Germany, but here in Holland nobility acts very independently from the Queen. I'm really not chummy with Wilhelmina, maybe met her twice but that's all. It's no use telling our captors this as the German guards hear only understand one sentence, "Befehl ist Befehl." Orders are orders or, in other words, somebody else made the rules.

You will wonder why I'm telling you all this. Somebody has to know what's going on here or we'll be a forgotten group. The censoring of our letters is vicious so, though we get enough food and are kept relatively in normal circumstances, these are ridiculous circumstances of course and everyone is tense and edgy under the jokes and witticisms that fly around our ears here. We also have many meetings and even organize courses in astronomy, debating, civil rights, journalism and such.

I'm not afraid to die. I just find it excruciatingly

unfair that I've never even had the chance to resist these fascists. I was locked up because of my title and my position as a criminal defense attorney, not because I wrung the neck of one of these schmucks. I wish I had. I wish I had done everything to prevent this war. I would have shouted it from the rooftops but now my silent grave will be the witness to my silent fight.

So, you, Eddaline, with your grit and intelligence, please fight my fight for me. Make my death not a random, useless murder. Avenge me if you can. I know I'm asking everything of you, with a father deeply invested in National Socialism, but your mother's faith in that ugly system is wavering. She wrote to me several times in the past months, and she regrets the course this war has taken. Her hands are tied, but her belief in Herr Hitler has waned.

I know my request is odd and I'm putting you in danger in many different ways. Still, I feel we're connected without really ever having been connected.

Don't write back. It's no use. I won't be here anymore. I didn't want to say it at the beginning of this letter, but a friend of mine will keep this until after I've been before the firing squad.

Finally, please forgive me, Eddaline, for burdening you with this. I always loved you, truly and fully in my imperfect way. I hope this letter will make you understand I wasn't just an annoying, middle-aged suitor passing by in your life.

It's been a privilege knowing you, and may your life be rich and abundant in love.

Your Ludo.

I t was dark outside. An owl hooted once from the sycamore tree in the park. Then was silent. Somewhere a clock struck eleven. Edda was frozen. She couldn't move. Even her eyelashes wouldn't blink. A wad as thick as a ball stuck in her throat. Her breathing was shallow.

His face came before her. The string of dark auburn hair carefully arranged over the balding spot on his head, the high forehead slightly freckled, slate-colored intelligent eyes, normal nose, normal mouth, no facial hair. A friendly energy but nothing that had drawn her attention, drawn her to him. And now they were bound forever. His letter had bound her to him. Dead. Ludovicus Van Limburg Stirum had swung from the periphery of her life where she'd kept him with force, right into center stage.

Edda could finally swallow. She needed to drink a glass of water, but her body wouldn't obey. As if she was partly dead too. Her thoughts were incoherent, but his image was as clear as if he was standing right before her.

"I will never forget you, Ludovicus Van Limburg Stirum," she spoke into the black night. "And I promise I will avenge your death. You came to the right address. You've given me the push I needed."

A push. She'd been nine, maybe ten. It was summer, like now. Early evening. She was idly sitting on the swing, waiting for Duifje to return from her date with her first boyfriend. Someone had pushed her on the swing. She'd been surprised, had looked around who it was. It was him. She'd smiled at him while shouting. "Higher! Push me higher."

And now Ludo had pushed her up the highest ladder. Fight the fascist schmucks. But how?

How do I do that, Ludo?

The owl hooted again, and Edda shivered. She was so upset she ran out of the door in her nightdress and banged on Mevrouw Meulenbelt's door.

"*Doe de deur open*! Open the door, please!"

24

THE ALLY

Mevrouw Meulenbelt opened the door to Edda with an alarmed look in her eyes. Her hair, in rollers with a silk scarf around it, and dressed in her nightclothes with a dressing gown quickly thrown over. She exclaimed. "Kindje, what on Earth is the matter? Have you seen a ghost?"

The familiar address of 'child' immediately calmed some of Edda's overwrought senses, but the ghost set her off again. She'd seen exactly that. A ghost. The ghost of Ludovicus Van Limburg Stirum who'd come to her with a message and a mission.

"I know it's terribly late, Mevrouw Meulenbelt, and I'm awfully sorry but I didn't know where else to go." Edda waved the letter in her hand, very much against the express wishes of its author, but she felt she had no other choice. She also felt if there was one person in the world she could trust with its contents, it was Mevrouw Meulenbelt.

"Yes, of course, you can come in. I was already in bed, but I can make us a cup of tea. However, by the looks of it, you'd better be served by a brandy."

"Yes. No. Please. Thank you." Confused she followed the elderly, Dutch lady through a hall identical to her own. Her neighbor's sitting room was very different from Edda's, though. It was bigger but so crammed with dark, bulky furniture that it looked smaller than hers.

"Sit and I'll get you that drink before you spill the beans." Mevrouw Meulenbelt navigated in between the tables and chairs to her cabinet, where she brought out two lemonade glasses. She poured them to the rim with an amber liquor from a bottle with a stopper, then placed them side-by-side on a tray.

Edda tried to calm her breath the way Miss Sterling had taught her, while scanning the room. It looked innocent enough, typically furnished as a neat working-class Dutch house would be, though not as practical as most because of the way the pieces were distributed through the room. Nothing alluded to the possibility the place could be a hotbed of resistance, though Edda had not expected to find any outward signs of disobedience in her neighbor's house.

"So, kindje, you drink that and see if that makes you feel better." Mevrouw Meulenbelt placed the lemonade glass on a coaster in front of Edda. Edda looked at the glass, trying not to burst into laughter.

"Is that alcohol, Mevrouw Meulenbelt?"

"Firstly, it's Tante Riet. That's what everybody calls me. My mother was Mevrouw Meulenbelt. I never married, you see. What's the point? And secondly, yes, that's home-brewed brandy. You'd better not gulp it down. My brother Jan makes sure it kills all the germs. Kind of poison, you could say." Tante Riet laughed heartily and took a firm guzzle. Then said "Aah" and placed her glass on the coaster and her bare feet on the coffee table.

Edda was so perplexed by the unorthodox behavior of her neighbor that she almost forgot her distress. But Tante Riet didn't.

"Firstly, you drink that as I can't put it back in the bottle, and secondly tell me why you're here." Edda hadn't touched Jan's poison yet. Now she took a polite sip and coughed the contents over her own nightdress. This made Tante Riet holler in amusement.

"Kindje, you're not accustomed to Dutch courage, are you? Heavens, of course not, you're that ballerina who weighs her sandwiches and only drinks tea without sugar."

"I don't," Edda protested and courageously took a firmer sip. It went down. Tante Riet was already on the bottom half of her own glass. The wise, crystal eyes fixed on Edda.

"All fun aside, what's going on?"

Edda hesitated but Jan's brandy gave her the aplomb to go ahead.

"Did you put the Geuzen pamphlets in my letter box, Tante Riet?"

Her neighbor's face went deadpan, and Edda saw her error and immediately excused herself. "I mean, I read them front to back— read them over and over. I'm against the Nazis, despite what you may think, because of my father." Her cheeks went red.

"Firstly, I have no clue who your father is and secondly yes, that was me." Tante Riet clearly spoke her sentences in firstly's and secondly's.

It was a liberating feeling to realize her neighbor didn't know Edda was Johannes Van der Valk's daughter. She'd clearly not linked them together yet. And now Edda had ascertained Tante Riet was with the resistance, the next step was easier.

"I got this letter today, and I don't know what to do with it."

"What's the letter about?"

"Here, please read it and give me advice what to do."

"Heavens, kindje, I left my reading glasses next to my bed. Can you not read it to me?" Tante Riet made another gesture to Edda's glass. "If it upsets you so, take a stiff drink first."

Edda did just that and managed to read the letter to Tante Riet. She choked a couple of times, but the liquor helped her to finish without falling apart. It was silent in the crammed room. For a long time. Then Tante Riet whistled, pulled her legs from the coffee table, navigated back to her sideboard and took a second glass of her brother's brandy.

When she was seated again, she said.

"I've heard of Hitler's Herrengefängnis but I had no idea they were killing the hostages yet. It will be all over the papers soon. Shit will hit the fan any day. As your friend says, now the resistance will ramp up. Horrible, kindje, just horrible."

"Should I really destroy the letter or keep it hidden as proof. You know, in case we win the war?" Then Edda told Tante Riet about her diaries. The first time confiding her secret to an ally felt like a relief, natural and sane.

Tante Riet whistled again. "Firstly, I think you should keep that letter as proof. Secondly, yes, we will win the war. Keep recording everything, *mijn ballerina kindje*. Oranje boven." With that last sentence Tante Riet pledged her loyalty to Queen and Country. Edda meanwhile warmed a little more to the strong brandy, and got a little bolder in her mind.

"Are you a resistance fighter, Tante Riet?"

"Heavens no, kindje, I just hate the Nazis."

"But how did those Geuzen pamphlets come in your possession? You distributed them. That's an act of resistance according to the Germans, isn't it?"

Edda wasn't prepared for the change in her neighbor's face. All the good-natured jest disappeared. The elderly woman with her hair in curlers and her smooth skin and clear blue eyes, turned pale and her breath became raspy. The hand that held her drink shook. Edda wasn't sure if she was very angry or very sad. Perhaps both.

"Sorry, I shouldn't have…"

Tante Riet interrupted her. "As you've been honest with me, I'll tell you my story. I never intended to get involved in this stinker of a war, but my nephew, Jan's son, Sjaak Meulenberg, is…*was* one of the Geuzen. As he was led before the firing squad in the Waasdorper- vlakte, he was singing Psalm 43:4 together with the eighteen other Geuzen."

And then Tante Riet sang loudly:

> *"Dan zal ik gaan naar het altaar van God,*
> *God mijn buitengewone vreugde;*
> *En op de harp zal ik U loven,*
> *O God, mijn God."*

"Can you imagine, *mijn ballerina kindje*, the bravery these men had!"

Tante Riet shook her head, wiped her nose with the sleeve of her dressing gown and sang again as loud as her voice would carry her.

"Then I will go to the altar of God,
To God my exceeding joy;
And on the harp I will praise You,
O God, my God."

Edda thought her neighbor rather peculiar, but somehow very touching.

"But..." Edda started but Tante Riet waved with her glass, spilling the amber contents. She was getting tipsy. Edda felt she shouldn't have woken the old lady, but it was a comfort to be with her after the horrible letter.

"Hush, I know what you want to say, mijn ballerina kindje. I was distributing the pamphlets before the swines killed our Sjaak. That's correct. He asked me to. Both Jan and Sjaak had been involved with Hendrik IJzerdraat's movement since he started it. Hendrik stood for freedom and democracy. He always said, 'We don't need Mussert nor Moscow. Just two extreme regimes.' I'm afraid that movement is dead with its leader now. Sad, sad thing. I've never been one for official politics, kindje, but Jan and Sjaak are my kin. I read those pamphlets and they made sense to me."

Tante Riet took another guzzle and Edda followed suit. The fuzzy warmness in her stomach was already addictive. Edda sat back on the sturdy couch and listened to that wonderful rapid Amsterdam accent. So liberating and simple after all the poshness of her high-class Dutch upbringing and the ballet vocabulary that was her daily bread.

Tante Riet had no trouble talking, even if Edda remained silent. "We Dutch love our freedom. We shouldn't be forced into any tight box, whether communist or fascist. That's not for the likes of us. So, when those Jerries wormed their way in, I was knocked for six. Said it loud and clear to anyone. I'm not one to keep my big mouth shut, but Jan said to me, 'Sister, you be careful. These Germans aren't just swines, they're also very cunning. So shut your big trap and keep your eyes open.' That's when I spotted the potential of my little mouse next door. Yes, you!"

Tante Riet pointed to Edda with her glass and roared with laughter. More liquor was spilled and her cheeks were getting blotchy and red.

"I thought to myself that's just the kind of girl we need. Strong body, but sheepish."

"Sheepish? I'm not sheepish!" Edda protested.

"Well, it's not like any Nazi would suspect *you*, kindje!" Tante Riet hollered, making Edda fear all the Germans of Amsterdam were hearing her being branded a resister at a late Sunday night in the summer of 1941. She really needed to get to bed. What was she thinking? She had Swan Lake to dance in two weeks' time. But Edda remained where she was, too afraid to go home alone with the letter.

"It was a risk." The crystal blue eyes rested on Edda. All drunkenness gone, "Because I do know who you are, kindje, and you're in a greater pickle than most of us. When the time comes, I've got a place for the Hoffmans. So don't fret about that, mijn ballerina kindje. But you make sure your name is clear when all this madness is over. Traitors' heads will roll. Make sure yours is not among them."

This was almost too much to take in. Edda realized how sandwiched she was between NSB parents and a Jewish boyfriend. It had never been put into clearer words before her. Her eyes were wide in surprise. More waving with the glass followed from Tante Riet's side.

"It's my job to find these things out, kindje. But don't worry. You've come to the right place. Now go home. Leave that letter here with me so it won't haunt you tonight. I'll keep it in a safe place, behind lock and key. And come back any time you want."

"I don't know." Edda suddenly felt protective of Ludo's letter. It was so personal, and it was for her alone. Tante Riet howled in her particular loud laughter, then suddenly was sober and serious again.

"That's what I wanted to see coming out of you, kindje. From under that sheepish exterior. You keep that letter close to you. It will change your life. Now you go home and dream your dance dreams. Tante Riet will always be here for you. No need to jump on the barricades right now. Off with you." She came to her feet with difficulty, swayed from left to right and laughed again.

"We're quite a pair, aren't we? The daughter of a dockworker and a marchioness. But we'll kick some tail together until we see the backsides of these Nazi devils marching back home to Germany."

"How do you know so much about me?" Edda couldn't help asking. It felt weird and welcome at the same time.

"Now that question will be answered when we're rested and clear-headed, Edda. Off to bed with you! And next time you come make it a more Christian time. You scared the living daylights out of me."

"Sorry, Tante Riet. I will. And thank you. Jan's 'poison' and this talk has helped me tremendously."

"That's the spirit," Tante Riet hollered and almost literally pushed Edda out of the door. She stood in the balmy night, slightly drunk and bewildered. Behind the closed door she could hear the disappearing voice singing Psalm 43:4. Full-loud and off-tune.

> *"Dan zal ik gaan naar het altaar van God,*
> *God mijn buitengewone vreugde;*
> *En op de harp zal ik U loven,*
> *O God, mijn God."*

A warm wave of relief washed over Edda. She had an ally. She wasn't crazy. Tante Riet thought what she thought. And what was even better, she would be able to discuss all her pent-up thoughts and emotions about the war with this loud-mouthed, lovely lady—an eccentric, unpretentious lady.

And she was Edda's ally now. An ally for the war.

THE TRUTH STILL HURTS

Several days later – Amsterdam, June 1941

Edda didn't storm the barricades together with Tante Riet as the latter had predicted. Her practices for Swan Lake took up all her time but when the initial sharp emotions of the letter had softened, she'd picked up the phone for that long-overdue conversation with her mother.

"Eddaline, my dear, I was just thinking of you," her mother said in an even voice, but Edda could hear the finer feelings raging behind them.

"Mother, I'm so sorry. I just read it in the news," Edda lied.

"Yes, isn't it an outrage? That poor Ludovicus. The man wouldn't even so much as kill a fly. Why! Dear God, why? What's the point of it all?"

"I don't know, Mama, but I'm appalled as well. I know he was a dear friend of yours and Papa's."

"Ludo was a good man, Eddaline, whatever mockery you and Duifje made of him." Edda let her head hang in shame and was glad her mother couldn't see it.

"I know, Mama." Her voice was thick. *Don't cry now! She will think you've gone soft in the head!*

"Are you planning to visit his grave, Mama, because if you do, I'd love to come with you."

"His grave?" Her mother spat out the words. "That's the worst of it! They shot five men in a secret location and those Germans won't say where the place is. Your father insisted his second cousin deserved a proper grave, but we have no clue where they left him, Eddaline. He's just lying there somewhere in the bushes. Maybe even in Belgium."

Edda stuffed her fist in her mouth not to cry out. She managed to bring out in a thick voice, "I'm so sorry, Mama. It's simply too awful for words. I'll come home soon. I promise I'll try."

"I think we'll see you first in Amsterdam, won't we, dear? Father and I are planning to come to the Stadsschouwburg to see you dance Swan Lake on the 3rd of July. Duifje will join us, and hopefully Teppo this time as well."

Edda could no longer hold back her tears, thankful her mother couldn't fathom their cause. "Thank you, Mama," she blubbered, "and I'll come home to visit as soon as the performances are done. I've missed you and home."

Home. What a strange thing, to suddenly call Huis van Leyden home. Home was the Valkena Estate in Leeuwarden.

"I miss you too, Eddaline. These are such trying times. Families must stick together, no matter what."

"Yes, Mama."

She hung up, feeling glum and depleted. But Ludo had been right. It was a nuance, but the way her mother had said *those Germans* held a detachment, even a condemnation.

"Edda, can you come into my office for a moment?" Miss Sterling, the invariable pastel cardigan over her shoulders, red-lipsticked, but pale and thin, called Edda away from the barre.

"Sure, coming."

Drying her face and neck on her towel Edda followed her mentor wondering what was going on. They were two days away from the first Swan Lake performance and the old injury in her left ankle was playing up again. Gritting her teeth against the pain, she hoped for the best. If Miss Sterling was going to cancel the whole thing because of her injury she'd protest it with everything she had. The show must go on.

"Anything the matter?" Better ask straight out and not draw out a possible disappointment.

"No, no! Not really. Well perhaps." Miss Sterling's honey eyes looked uncertain.

"I can do this, Miss Sterling, really I can."

"You can and you will. There's just one thing I want to tell you first."

Edda braced herself. These days this type of announcement seldom meant good news.

She waited, shifting her weight from her good foot to her bad one.

"Maria is back."

"Maria Petrova?" Edda's eyebrows went up.

"Yes, Mademoiselle Petrova."

"What's she doing back in Amsterdam?"

"The boyfriend, remember? Apparently it's serious now. But anyway, Edda, how would you feel if Maria danced Odile's part? It would take some of the burden off you, but I wanted to discuss it with you first."

Oh no! Edda thought, *Maria is not going to dance with Ash. Over my dead body.* But she kept quiet. The pain in her ankle throbbed. Maybe her common sense should win.

"Would ... um... would she even want to? Have you spoken with her?" Edda said with hesitance.

"No, I haven't suggested anything of the sort to her. Maria came to me asking if she could dance with us again. That's when I put two and two together. Your ankle and her availability. I know what dancing Swan Lake with Ash means to you, so we'll call it off if you don't want to, but I'm worried about that ankle. As I know you are."

Edda's thoughts raced. She wouldn't have to be on stage at the same time as Maria. Odette and Odile switched places. No threat there. And Maria would be the evil swan. Served her right.

"Can I talk with her first?" Edda asked.

"Wise plan. I'll call Maria into my office tomorrow. And you keep that ankle swaddled and cooled, my dear, or you won't even be able to dance Odette."

"I know. It'll be okay when we're done rehearsing. It's just the long hours now that my ankle doesn't like."

MARIA HAD CHANGED. Subtle but visibly. It wasn't so much the copper hair that had grown shoulder length, hanging wispy and wavy around her face, or the weight she'd put on. Something in her bearing, though still regal and brassy, was less overbearing. *She's been begging Miss Sterling to take her back*, flitted through Edda's mind as she shook the Russian's cool hand.

"*Enchanté*." They said at the same time, resorting to French, as in former days.

"How are you?" Maria asked, the gray eyes searching Edda's face.

"*Comme ci comme ça*. Could be better."

"Yeah, it can't be much fun here in Amsterdam at the moment." Maria dug up two digestive biscuits from her pocket and offered one to Edda. For some reason that reminded Edda of her mother and her secret emergency cookie supply.

"Thank you, Maria. Then why did you come back to Amsterdam? You must have been a lot safer in London?"

"I left London during the Blitz. Went back to Moscow. Until all hell broke loose there, as well. I might as well stay with Daniel here in Amsterdam."

"Oh," was all Edda could think of to say. She'd not given Maria

Petrova a second thought after she'd left the Amsterdam Ballet Theater in 1937.

"It must be rotten for you seeing me show up here again." Irony laced Maria's voice. Edda shrugged, but didn't reply. What was there to say?

"Listen, Edda Van der Valk, can we be clear about that broken ankle situation once and for good?" It was almost said with an angry undertone. Edda braced herself, feeling her own anger flare. How dare this women address her like that? For a moment they stood as two cocks in a ring. Gray eyes locked with dark brown ones. Maria made one of her dismissive movements with an elegant swoosh of her arm that Edda suddenly remembered.

"It wasn't me." Maria snapped.

As if the wind was sucked out of her lungs, Edda gasped for air. If Maria Petrova knew it wasn't her, then she'd seen something. Why had she not told the truth straight away?

"Then who was it?"

"It was Claire."

"One of the chorus girls? Why are you snitching on a girl who isn't here anymore?"

"Because I'm speaking the truth, Edda."

"So, you saw what happened, but you didn't tell Miss Sterling? Or me? Left us all guessing and wondering?"

"No. Yes. That's what I did and I'm not proud of it. I didn't say anything because I was involved in it."

"Darn, Maria. You come clean now, or I'm going to tell Miss Sterling you're not dancing with us ever again." Edda had seldom been this angry in her life. It seemed to impress the proud Russian, as the arms went up in defense.

"It was an accident, Edda. An accident. Do you hear me? No one, not Claire, not I, not Miss Sterling or you would have benefited from knowing what happened. Not then, but now, yes."

"Stop your riddles and speak, Maria."

"I had my career to think of. That was most important to me at the time. Now it's different. I'd be happy if I can do any dancing, but at the time I wanted to belong to the top. The absolute top. And a similar thing had happened to me in St Petersburg when I was with Bolshoi. I was afraid that would resurface when this happened."

"Just tell me what you did!" Edda was ready to shake Maria with both hands.

"Alright, easy, I'm getting there. It was the dark part in the forest. You know, where all the lights temporarily dim, and we had to quickly go to the other side of the podium before the lights go on again. I bumped into Claire, and I accidentally pushed her. She was in front of you, stepped out of line and landed on your foot. I bribed her not to say anything."

The arms went in the air again. "There! Now you know, and you can go whining in Marlene Sterling's office that you don't want that horrible Petrova dancing here ever again."

Edda was too baffled for words. She couldn't comprehend the entire contents of what Maria had just said. She also couldn't decide if Maria was still guilty, or not. She was just very tired and sank on a chair. That once-broken ankle giving her worries all over.

"I'm sorry, Edda. I'm really sorry. It's the reason I'm here. To tell you this. I didn't want to live with that dark event on my mind anymore. I can return to London if you don't want me here. Daniel can go with me. You don't have to believe me, but I came here for you. I wanted to see the dancer you'd become. Of course, I saw you and Ash in Romeo and Juliet in the Royal Albert Hall two years ago. You were phenomenal and I was so relieved to see your ankle wasn't giving you any trouble."

Edda slowly raised her eyes to Maria's face. She was weary.

"Please just shut up, Maria. Tell Miss Sterling I said you can dance Odile. I just want to be alone now."

"Are you alright?" There seemed genuine concern in the gray eyes.

"Yes, I'm alright. Please go."

26

SWAN LAKE

A few days later – Amsterdam, 3 July 1941

Larry was on his ladder, hanging the latest stage decorations for what had to look like a festive room. He was whistling the theme of Lake of the Swans as he decorated the pillars along the back of the podium. His display had to look like it was a worthy birthday party for Prince Siegfried, but Larry had had a hard time getting material for the décor pieces. There was a shortage of everything. Board, paint, paper, and glue but he'd done his best.

"Let's hope for the best," he murmured as he checked his watch. He had to be off stage pronto or the audience would think they'd come for a slapstick instead of a dramatic ballet.

"Psst, Larry!" Edda came onto the stage already in her snow-white swan's costume. "Do you have a second?"

"Of course. What's up?"

"I know you're always watching from the wings."

"In case of a calamity, Larry De Jonge must do his own 'pas-the-une' and get you dancers out of collapsed towers or entangled ribbons," he joked. It was good to see Larry light-hearted again. He'd grown morose and mopey over the past months. Edda realized the floor manager took as much pride and enjoyment out of performance night as the dancers did.

She blushed. What she was going to ask Larry suddenly seemed childish.

"Will you keep an eye on Maria for me when I'm in my dressing room between scenes?"

Larry laughed out loud. "You're not saying you think she'll put a spell on your Ash, because I can tell you beforehand it won't work?"

How could she explain to him what she meant without giving herself away? Of course, she was jealous. It was a new sensation and not a very pleasant one.

"I won't leave her out of my sight, Edda. I promise. But I don't think you have to fear anything from her. That one has changed. I don't know what happened to her or what she ran into, but the hoity-toity Petrova is no more. I actually think her quite a good sport these days."

"You're right," Edda admitted. Maria had been trying to be a good team-player. Their collective performance had improved with her fresh zeal and encouragement. Even Miss Sterling had a little color in her cheeks again. Still, it was a relief to share her silly worries with Larry, on whom she'd bet her last florin.

"Edda, Larry!" Miss Sterling clapped her hands, "what are you two doing loitering here? We're ready to go!"

"Sorry Miss Sterling," they said in unison.

⁓

FOR ONE NIGHT ONLY, Heaven was back on Earth.

EDDA SPUN across the stage like a force of nature, her limbs seeming to defy gravity as she flew up into the night sky. Her face was a perfect portrait of strength and beauty, her dark eyes radiating determination, her body framed in swiftness and light. Edda had become Odette, an angel of white with a halo of silver, her arms and legs reaching out to touch the moon as she pirouetted in front of the audience.

As she darted away from her pursuer's grasp, she could feel all eyes admiring her finesse and poise, from the loose strands of her curly hair to the graceful tips of her toes. Even scent was present. The rich scents of roses and lilacs, strawberries and jasmine wafting up around her. Her pointe shoes pulsed with energy, made from sumptuous leather and glimmering satin, now firmly planted in the fragrant earth, rather than floating away towards the ethereal sky above.

Her body transformed into a concerto of music, her limbs the strings and drums, her soul the maestro. Her hands felt cool to the touch, her fingertips like rose petals drifting down in the night air, her skin supple and silk-smooth, waiting for Ash's touch, like fine linen cool from the line caressing the waiting body.

As dusk cast its long shadows, she became the soundless vibration of nightfall. Her figure was nothing more than a song that lifted everyone in attendance and spirited them away on a mysterious journey. Edda felt as if every cell of every living being was touched by something greater than themselves.

THIS WAS LIFE. *This was what life was meant to be!*

AND THE BEST was yet to come. Ash as Prince Siegfried was going to make his entrance. In the next scene, Edda was met by opulent decorations of flowers, flags, and towering pillars as a greeting place for the hunting party. Bathed in sunlight, the lake behind them, and swans fluttering around them, making their way across the lake, Ash danced towards her with big sweeping steps, the gems on his costume glittering like his pale blue eyes. His hand pressed against hers, his eyes locked with her.

Edda smelled fresh flowers and perfume—orange blossom mixed with honeysuckle. They were surrounded by flowers and grasses, greenery and trees, the lake, and its fringes. It felt real, not staged, and happiness swept through Edda like a surge of sunlight. The feeling of his touch on her, his warm breath on her neck, the flicker of firelight on cheeks, on lips. All was touch, smooth beneath his fingers, against his thigh, in his arms. She was a queen of a different time and place, and he was hers forever.

THEY DANCED through time and space, in an abandoned apartment, a squat by the river, amidst aging walls of barracks painted black, windows broken and boarded up. The floor was bare stone stained by soot and blood, and still they danced. Two dancers' arms reaching for the skies, their legs bent, their feet stretched, fingers extended, their bodies yearning for the heavens. He lifted her and she twirled, her dress like butterfly wings, floating upward, farther and farther away from him.

WHEN EDDA FELL BACK to Earth, she was confused, shaken. She searched Ash's eyes and saw he'd seen it too. She hadn't made it up. It had been like a sign from the Heavens. Whatever would happen between them, they would dance in eternity. It was a sobering, solemn thought.

Edda stood shivering with awe and alarm as she and Ash, solid hand-in-hand, received a standing ovation from the audience. Had they *not* seen it? Had they only been mesmerized by their Swan Lake dance?

"Hold me,' she whispered to Ash, "or I'll break."

And he did just that. He held her as they bowed and bowed.

"Eternity!" he whispered back but it didn't comfort Edda.

"Hold me and never let me go. I'm so afraid."

"I know, my gritty girl, I know."

27

THE YELLOW STAR

Nine months later

Amsterdam 29 April 1942

The Nazis will never stop. A new humiliation has been announced today and I fear it will break my proud Ash. As of the 3rd of May, all Jews must wear a six-pointed yellow Star of David with the word 'Jood' on it.

It's a preposterous measure. Why would we want to label our fellow citizens on the street as Jews? It will only make them feel further isolated from non-Jewish Dutch. And if they don't wear the star, they can be sent to a concentration camp!

There will be much confusion, I fear. I haven't spoken Ash about it yet, but it is the "Joodsche Raad"

who must distribute the stars among the Jews in
Holland. Three days they've been given to hand them out.
And the Jews have to pay for these wretched stars
themselves. Four stars per person for four cents each.
Children as young as 6 years old have to wear them.
Apparently, a total of 569,355 Stars of David have to
be distributed.

I'm appalled! Herr Hitler, you are mad!

"Tante Riet, *doe de deur open*!" Edda rung her neigbor's bell with the newspaper still in her hand.

"Kindje, what's the matter? Firstly, your hair is loose in a most endearing way and secondly you sound like the devil's on your heels. I'm peeling potatoes as thinly as I can so I can't hurry to the door that quickly. Has a fire broken out?"

"This, Tante Riet!" Edda pointed to the article, "this is preposterous!"

"That," Tante Riet growled as she directed her peeler to the newspaper as if wanting to skin it. "That's the devil's work for sure, but I've got a solution. Come in, I'll show you."

Edda was glad to be invited into the overstuffed, homely kitchen. Minoes, Tante Riet's black cat, immediately jumped from the windowsill and came curling around Edda's legs. The kitchen smelled of grease and vinegar, but she loved the smell. Somehow it reminded her of the big kitchen at Valkena Estate when, as a little girl, she would slip inside to see their cook, Mevrouw Miedema, kneading dough or plucking a chicken.

"Hello Minoes, have you been catching mice lately?"

"Oh, she has caught many, that little starlet of mine," Tante Riet said proudly. "Thank God, Minoes brings them to me as presents. I'm saving them in old newspapers. My friends use mice and rats to fill up with explosives. Gives a nice bang when a Nazi steps on them and puff, he's gone. Minnie isn't an all-black cat for nothing."

Tante Riet howled her particular laughter and Edda exclaimed a shocked, "Tante Riet, for sure, you're telling tales!"

"No, I'm not. Not by a long shot. I've never loved mice and rats more in my life." Another holler with laughter. Edda investigated her neighbor's face, but the twinkling blue eyes held a perfectly innocent expression. One could never tell with Tante Riet.

That's why she makes such a formidable resister, Edda thought. The elderly Mevrouw Meulenbelt with her smooth skin, naïve gaze and cut-and-dry Amsterdam brogue would never be suspected of harboring dark thoughts of killing Nazis with ammunition-filled mice.

"So what is it you wanted to show me?" Edda's curiosity always got the better of her when she was with Tante Riet. Next to dancing with Ash, spending time with her neighbor was what got her through the war.

"Oh yes, I'd already forgotten why you came. Not that you have to have a reason for visiting me. My mind's like this sifter these days. Which gives me a better chance at survival as I tend to forget one murderous plan by the next." Tante Riet winked and brought out her sewing basket. She took out small pieces of red and blue cloth cut in five-pointed stars. The red had the word "Katholiek" embroidered on it and the blue "Protestant".

"Why Catholic and Protestant?" Edda asked.

"Oh, you ding-a-ling of a girl, don't you understand? I thought you were supposed to be the bright button here. If we wear those, firstly it will show those Jerries how half-baked they are telling Jews they are Jews. Secondly, I tell you putting a Star of David on your breast is as off-the-wall as stating you're white or brown, man or woman, cat or dog. I actually think I'm going to make one that says "Ape" and send it to Herr Hitler himself." The salvo of laughter that followed made Edda chortle, as well.

When she was sufficiently calmed down, Tante Riet continued, "We're going to wear these in solidarity with the Jews. If they get labelled, so will we. You're getting a Protestant star and I'm wearing my red one. How about it, compatriot?"

"Alright," Edda agreed, "I'll wear my badge with pride." But while Tante Riet pinned the blue star on her, she imagined Ash thoroughly disliking the idea of walking around with a yellow star on his breast. He never referred to his Judaism. It didn't seem a big part of his life though his parents were quite orthodox, as far as Edda understood.

"Off you go, child. I've got them potatoes to peel, and you've got a diary to write in." Edda gave Minoes a last caress and skipped out of the door into the sunlight fingering her blue star as a child might. But what her eyes caught on when she blinked in the sunlight was a sad and sorrowful sight. Two small Jewish girls, who didn't look Jewish at all with their dark-blond pigtails and pleated skirts, walked past with heads down, their small hands trying to cover-up the stars.

"I'm so sorry what my country is doing to you." Edda wanted to say but her voice had no volume, no power.

IN THE EARLY afternoon Edda took the train from Amsterdam-Central to Leiden to make the obligatory visit to her parents. Duifje had promised to be there with Benny and Elly, which had convinced Edda to make the trip.

Her blue star attracted many covert glances from fellow passengers, but nobody remarked on it. Nobody openly remarked on anything these days. *Keep your head down and pretend you have seen nothing. A policy the Dutch are good at, including me*, Edda thought wryly.

Then a patroling German stopped by her seat in the first-class carriage and asked for her papers.

"Van der Valk?" the young man in his *feldgrau* uniform with the oversized cap and hefty rifle stared from her identity card to the blue star on her chest with a mixture of distrust and bewilderment. "Are you...?"

"Yes, I'm Herr Van der Valk's daughter," Edda cut him short,

snatching her card from his fingers and getting up. Rising to her full
height she saw she was taller than him. She also realized it was her
first ever eye-to-eye with the enemy, though this specimen wasn't
much more than a boy—a milksop with his wispy white eyelashes
and eyes that hardly had any color. There was nothing to be afraid of
here. His presence just irritated her.

"Good day to you, *Fraulein* Van der Valk," she heard him call after
her in a deferential tone and she waved her hand, taking a seat in a
carriage he'd already inspected.

Despite her vow to Tante Riet that she would wear her star with
pride, Edda unpinned the piece of cloth and stuffed it in her handbag. The attention it drew made her uncomfortable, an obvious
target for Germans like that young officer. *Maybe if more people started
wearing random stars, I'll pin it up again. Until then I'll stick with my
brooch*, she'd thought rather cowardly and felt her own kind of milksop. How would it feel to be unable to take off that star? That the very
act of *that* defiance could mean being sent to a concentration camp?
Oh, the whole situation made her so depressed.

HER MOTHER WAS WAITING for her at the station, a thin smile on her
waiting face. Her summer coat three sizes too big. It seemed as if the
once formidable Marchioness Olga Van der Valk-Scherzinger shrunk
more every time Edda saw her. She'd spotted her mother first,
standing amidst the other waiting people on the platform, which
gave Edda a couple of seconds to take in her mother's changed
features. Whatever was going on in Mama's life, it was taking a toll on
her health and Edda felt a surge of panic. *No Mama, this wretched war
is making enough victims, don't let it take you!*

Edda sped out of the train, in her hurry forgetting the flowers
she'd bought for Mama, straight into her mother's thin arms. Because
of her almost violent embrace, the Marchioness staggered, and Edda
had to keep her mother upright, greeting her and apologizing at the
same time.

"Eddaline, behave yourself. What's gone into you?" Her mother feebly protested by way of greeting, but Edda would have nothing of it. She held her mother in a tight embrace and kept saying, "Mama, Mama, I'm so glad to see you. It's been way too long. I'm sorry, I'm sorry."

"Have I not raised you to refrain from showing such ostentatious emotion in public, Eddaline?" Her mother grumbled but she let herself be held and Edda felt it took her mother considerable effort to stand on her own two feet.

"You needn't have bothered to come all the way here," Edda said, putting her arm through her mother's as they made their way to the exit. "Oh and Mama, I stupidly forgot the flowers I bought for you. Left them on the train."

"Oh Eddaline, you're so cl..."

"I'm not clumsy, Mama," Edda chuckled, "I was so happy to see you that I forgot them. So, is Klaas waiting for us?" Edda felt her mother's body tense on the mentioning of the chauffeur's name.

"No, we're walking. It's only a short distance and my doctor says I need to take more exercise."

"Oh, can we stop over for a coffee at Albert's Corner? Just for a mother-daughter chat? And their cakes are delicious." She hoped that telling her mother she would not think of her diet for once would cheer her up.

"Albert's Corner is closed and besides Duifje will be arriving with the children."

"Why's Albert's Corner closed? It used to be one of the busiest coffee houses in all Leiden?"

Her mother shrugged. "Something about pamphlets. Your father closed it." The Marchioness's voice sounded tired, so Edda didn't dare to ask further. Though she'd have loved to ask what these pamphlets were about. Albert had been a loud and outspoken person who was loved in all Leiden. He had been vocal when her father was appointed mayor instead of the popular Mr. Adriaan Van de Sande Bakhuyzen. And apparently his clear-voiced opinions had irked her father.

Heavens, she thought. *Albert's Corner had been in business long before Johannes Van der Valk was even born. Generations upon generations had run the coffeehouse on the corner of the Rapenburg.* It was so unfair and simply very wrong.

"Don't Eddaline!' her mother warned, sensing her daughter's indignation. "It's no use."

"Oh Mama!" was all she could bring out. Her mother made it sound as if her father was just a cog in the German machine, but he was a powerful man with connections in all the important places in Dutch society. Either he was a coward, or he was wrong himself. And Edda feared the latter was true. The German on the train with the wispy lashes came to mind. The awe he'd expressed at seeing her name. Bah!

How should she approach her father, whom she'd always loved, always respected? Listening to Tante Riet and seeing the hardening of conditions in Amsterdam, it was impossible for Edda to still defend the occupation. But her father did. Wholeheartedly. And he was dragging her mother with him into the morass. And soon she would be dragged into it as well.

Leiden had changed but not as much as Amsterdam, possibly because it didn't have such a large group of Jewish citizens. Leiden had become one of the NSB bulwarks. It seemed like a happy place for Dutch and German Nazis. They'd created a good life for themselves in the age-old city and kept the nastiness they'd created out of sight of their own eyes.

A new housekeeper opened the door for them, and Edda was not surprised to hear her speak German. German was now the official language at Huis Van Leyden.

"So, where's Duifje," Edda asked, longing to see her slightly off-kilter but amiable sister and her little nephew and niece.

"Let's see if they have arrived. And I need to sit down. My legs are killing me." The Marchioness handed her hat and coat to the woman she addressed as Hilde and went to the smaller sitting room that was only used for personal visits.

Blonde Hilde, docile and somewhat slow of understanding, scurried after her mistress.

"*Frau van Leeuwen hat angerufen, um zu sagen, dass sie nicht kommt.*"

Darn, Edda thought, *why is Duifje not coming?*

"*Schon gut,*" the Marchioness sighed with resignation. "Just bring us tea and sponge cake, Hilde."

The German woman made a curtsy, which was a rather odd sight. Then disappeared to the kitchen.

"Who's that?" Edda raised her eyebrows.

"Ach, she is the sister of one of your father's secretaries and she was looking for a job. I have a hard time getting good staff these days. She's not too bad, just doesn't speak a word of Dutch."

Her mother sat with difficulty on the sofa and kicked off her pumps. Her ankles were swollen. "Ah, it's good to sit down, my dear, but Doctor Van Dalen is going to be satisfied with me."

"How is your health, Mama? You seem fine." Edda had to lie.

"Stable, my dear. Stable but I'll never be my old self again and this..." she made a gesture with her hand indicating the house without saying so much. "...Isn't helping either."

"And how's Papa?"

"Busy as always. He'll join us for tea. He promised he'd take an hour off to see you."

As if his ears were burning, her father came into the room. He too had aged. He was even slightly bent, and his hair was now completely gray. There was an artificial cheerfulness about him that Edda had never seen before. And his cheeks and nose were too red. As if he drank too much but it wasn't giving him any relief. She tried to ignore the prominent NSB pin in his lapel as she rose from her seat to greet him, adamant to forget all politics for the afternoon.

"Eddaline, so good to see you. Give your old Papa a kiss. How's my ballerina?"

"I'm fine Papa, though not dancing as much as I would like. I'll grow stiff this way."

"Why's that?" He looked as if it actually interested him, as he sat down in his easy chair and lit a cigar.

"We train every day, but we can't stage another performance. It's just too expensive. Miss Sterling doesn't have the means anymore."

"Aha," her father sipped his tea, smoked, sat thinking. Her mother looked like a perched bird, longing to flutter away, out of the window into the blue sky. Edda tensed, her feelers sensing danger.

"You know of the new measure, Eddaline? That Jews have to wear the yellow star?"

"Yes father." Edda swallowed her longing to add 'preposterous!' and thought of the blue star in her bag. "What of it, father?"

"Asher Hoffmann will have to wear a star."

"Why are you telling me this?" Edda clenched her fists, anger shooting through her like a poisoned arrow. Her father remained calm. Her mother stared out of the window with that pining look.

"Why was I asked to come? And why is Duifje not here? Was it on purpose?" Edda was getting angry now as if summoned to an appointment instead of a family visit.

"Of course not, Eddaline. You know how your sister is. Blow hot, blow cold but that's beside the point," her father said in a weary voice.

"What *is* the point, Father?"

"Watch your tone, daughter!"

An icy silence followed. The Marchioness's face turned white. Her father puffed on his cigar. Edda's tea got cold and the sponge cake remained untouched.

"You say Miss Sterling needs money. We believe in pure art being proper entertainment for the people. The government is willing to invest money in organizations like the Amsterdam Ballet Theater but..." another puff on the cigar. "These organizations must be made Aryan." He said no more. Edda's mouth fell open. She was too baffled to talk. Was her father actually saying his daughter's boyfriend could no longer dance in Holland? Was that the future he wanted? A defiant look came into her dark eyes.

"Say it out loud, Father. Asher Hoffmann can no longer dance with us."

"That's correct, daughter. I didn't make the rules but Jews will no longer be allowed to mix with non-Jews."

Edda rose from her chair. She didn't dare to look in her mother's direction for fear she would break in two. This seemed like goodbye. Here their ways would part. If Mama said nothing…She stared down hard on her father.

"Say it, Father, and you will never see me again. Asher Hoffmann can no longer dance with me."

"I didn't make the rules, Eddaline," his voice was subdued but determined. "But that's what it comes down to, yes. Asher Hoffmann can no longer dance with you."

No reaction from her mother. None.

THE FRONT DOOR of Huis van Leyden clicked shut behind Edda. She felt dead in her shoes, dead to her family, and yet there was a new spark of life in her. This was reality. This was not a time not to make choices.

It was a new, broken Edda who slowly made her way through Leiden to the station. She didn't know where she walked or who she met. She moved in a trance, sure she would never see her parents again. It was the oddest, emptiest feeling a small human being could have. Ungraspable, unplaceable. Edda was in shock.

28

ALL ALONE

Ten weeks later

Amsterdam, 14 July 1942

The cruelty of the occupation can no longer be escaped. Today, the German police summoned some 4,000 Jews to report for what they call 'work expansion under police supervision'. As most Jews didn't trust the summon, they didn't respond to the call. What followed were the worst raids we've seen in Amsterdam so far, especially in Amsterdam-South where our ballet school is and in the Center. There's no denying it anymore. Herr Hitler's goal is to round up all Jews worldwide and kill them. If you listen to his rantings, he's all about Entlösung, aka the 'Final Solution' to the Jewish people.

Why didn't we see this coming? Why were we so

blind? It's been his plan right from the start, under the pretense of building up Germany economically and taking revenge for what his country suffered after the Great War. That delusional man with his silly moustache and pompous voice is stirring up everyone to kill every single Jew they can lay their hands on. And that nasty piece of work, his crony Heinrich Himmler, excels at doing his boss's dirty work. He's showing his muzzle here regularly in Holland to concoct his plans with Seys-Inquart.

I rage and I fear in equal doses. It's too late for the Hoffmans and the De Jonges to leave the country now. The borders are closed. They'll have to go underground. And I, Edda Van der Valk, who would love to have a different surname right now, will join forces with Tante Riet and start helping Jews escape from the claws of the Gestapo.

I will also have to save myself. On the surface I'll continue to dance for as long as I can. Thank God for my allowance. I won't need a job, though I feel Van der Valk money is blood money right now. Well, let me put it to good use then.

Herr Hitler, Meneer Mussert, Papa—why did you think it your right to change the cause of human history in such a drastic and dreadful way? Future generations will repudiate you for your horrific actions.

"Duifje, what am I to do?" Edda swirled the coiled cord of her telephone around her finger. She needed her sister more than ever. But Duifje sounded cold and distant.

"What do you mean *what am I to do*? You're not the only one having trouble in this world, Edda. Can't you for once think of others?" It sounded so unfair. She was doing just that, thinking of Ash and of Larry, when it suddenly dawned on her Teppo was half-Jewish as well.

"Oh, I'm so sorry, Duifje. I totally forgot about Teppo."

"What do you mean *forgot about Teppo*? You're talking in riddles, sister." Duifje sounded snappy. She was probably tired or having one of her migraines.

"I mean him being half-Jewish."

"I still have no clue what you're talking about. We've become members of the NSB, so we should be okay."

"You did what?!" Edda thought she'd drop the receiver. Her breath came with difficulty.

"Well, it's the only reasonable thing to do, Edda. You should consider it yourself. These Germans aren't going to be chased away by our broom sticks and frying pans."

Edda still didn't reply. She felt the last string to her family being cut loose and it hurt as if someone was cutting open her flesh in small bleeding strips.

She managed an, "Oh I see".

Then Duifje turned the knife in the open wounds by adding, "you're not going to like this, Edda, but they've asked Teppo to help find hidden Jews, as he knows so many of them. We have no choice. It's either him or someone else. And it's not like the shop is bringing in much income these days. One must survive."

"I see." Edda almost choked on her words.

"Got to run, Lientje! Talk to you later."

And as if she'd just discussed her shopping list with Edda, Duifje hung up. Edda stared in the receiver for a long time, hot tears streaming down her cheeks. For once the '*cry-baby*' was a real cry-baby but she didn't care. Nothing mattered in the world anymore. She'd just lost her last tie to her family.

Duifje—her erratic, eccentric, extroverted big sister—choosing the NSB in order to have a future for her husband. Somewhere deep down, somehow, Edda understood and forgave her. Maybe she would do the same to save her family. But her brother-in-law snitching on other Jews to save his own skin, that was wrong and that, somehow, fit Teppo van Leeuwen's bill.

Edda's first reaction was to run to Tante Riet for comfort, but she was too ashamed of her family. And something inside her told her she needed to stand on her own two feet from now on.

"I need to dance," she moaned. "All I want is dance until I die."

EDDA WAS ALONE in the dance school. Miss Sterling had most likely gone home and sent the others away as well. The school building was silent as a tomb. The late afternoon sun filtered through the tall windows, playing through the foliage of the majestic chestnut in the school yard. It was a beautiful summer day, but Edda's heart was cold as stone. She went over to the record player and tossed a random record on the machine. Anything would do in this mood.

When the first lyrical tones of Chopin's Nocturne C sharp minor filled the high-ceilinged room, Edda was grateful for the choice the Universe had made for her. The piano piece was feather-light yet fast, emotional yet serene, tragic yet longing.

The tender music drifted through the room like a lullaby, sung by angels from above. Edda's movements, now classical ballet, now modern dance, responded to the dancing fingers on piano keys as if she was a fine-strung instrument herself, playing a rhythm both lulling and urgent, like the beckoning of a siren.

Tears streamed down her cheeks, wetting the front of her shirt but she didn't care. Tears were part of her dance, part of her pain. As the piano chords both healed her and tore her apart, all Edda could do was dance. Her whole being was one with the music, one with the movement, beyond time and space. She could die like this, die this moment and be complete.

But the music faded away to the last high note and she wasn't done. She ran back to the record player and zipped the needle to the start, over and over until darkness fell and her tears finally dried.

Then out of the corners of her eyes she saw a shadow dancing alongside her, coming closer and closer.

ASH...

HER HEART CRIED "ASH" but there was no Ash. She danced to Chopin in the arms of Ash's shadow. Too broken for more tears. Edda danced until her feet bled and she fell to her knees. She crept to Miss Sterling's office and fell asleep on the bunk bed. A vague scent of Chanel No 5 in her nostrils.

∽

SHE WAS FIVE YEARS OLD, walking in the meadow behind their Frisian estate. The tall grass came to her waist. Duifje was hiding somewhere in the grass, and she wanted to find her. "Duifje, Duifje where are you?" No answer. She lost her left sandal but couldn't find it anywhere, so hobbled on with one foot bare.

"Duifje!"

Dark storm clouds were folding together over the waving grass and her pleas became more urgent. She needed to return home, but finding Duifje first was all she could think of.

Edda came to an open area in the grass. It had been knocked flat and in the middle of the open space lay Teppo with his arms and legs sprawled wide. His eyes were weird, she could only see the whites and a trickle of blood running from the corner of his mouth. A patch of blood the form of a star where his heart was.

. . .

EDDA SCREAMED. She woke, sat upright and had no idea where she was. The dream had been so vivid, but thank God it was a dream. She scrambled to her feet, cried "ouch" as she landed on her blistered soles. A friendly moon shone through the window and she discerned Miss Sterling's office.

By the light of the moon, she made herself a cup of tea and returned to the bunk bed and sat down. Why had she dreamed of Teppo? And why had she been a child? Edda's head was confused but she drank Miss Sterling's Darjeeling tea with little sips and it calmed her racing heart.

"I'm all alone," she said aloud in the office. "I don't know how but I'm going to make it. But Teppo won't."

29

TANTE RIET

Ten weeks later

Amsterdam, 2 October 1942

All the Jewish men that were employed in Dutch work camps have been deported. We don't know where, but they must have been taken east - where else? - so probably to Germany.

I'm so worried about Ash and his family. They weren't working in a camp because they managed to get a 'Sperre', a kind of exemption so they could stay with family in Amsterdam, but for how long? Jews are driven out of houses they've lived in for generations, as if they're cattle.

Most of them used to live in the 'Joodsche Wijk.' The Germans put up a sign there in 1941 with 'Juden Viertel' and marked the neighborhood with yellow signs. Since then, so many of these dwellers have disappeared completely. And I can tell you they didn't go voluntarily. I think it's time to ask Tante Riet about the safe house she had in mind for the Hoffmanns. Larry and his family believe they're still safe in the school.

Life is quickly becoming unbearable. Not just for Jews but for every Amsterdamer. The Nazis are becoming more violent by the day. Everyone says it's because they're losing the war in Africa and Germans are bad losers. There are also persistent rumors of an Allied invasion in the south of Spain or Italy, or even perhaps on the Atlantic coast. Maybe Norway or France.

But the rumors—though encouraging— aren't much help in our current dire situation. It's getting harder to buy groceries. Other ordinary articles like shampoo and socks are almost impossible to get. I'd never before bought anything on the black market but that's what every Amsterdamer does these days.

Still, I don't complain. I can dance most days, though we're not going to stage any more performances. Apart from being tight on money, since the introduction of the Kulturkammer last year there are very strict—Nazi rules—what one may produce in any form of art.

Miss Sterling calls it Kulturhammer, and that's very apt. It's all about German composers, German literature, German artists. Aryans of course, no Jew is considered able to produce proper art. Well, Miss Sterling will never take a stand against Jews, so the dirty NSB grants are *not for the Amsterdam Ballet Theater. As if we would want them!*

I wish I had more optimistic things to share. Well maybe I have. I still have dance. As long as I can dance, I can live.

No word from my family. But I have Tante Riet and her brother Ome Jan, and I have Miss Sterling and Larry, even Maria. And of course, still my Ash. Always my Ash.

Herr Hitler, Signor Mussolini and Meneer Mussert, can you please stop your silly boys' game fighting over your sandpits? We— the rest of humanity—are totally done with your squabbles..

And that ridiculous Tripartite pact with Japan! Drawing the Americans into the war in the Far East. It's a World War now, not just a European affair. What are you doing???

"Ome Jan, are you there?" Edda heard a male voice as she entered Tante Riet's house through the back door. They'd decided it was safer if Edda went through the garden instead of openly ring the front doorbell. No unwelcome eyes could see her comings and goings.

It wasn't Ome Jan, but an unknown gentleman in a worn black suit and a black hat who sat at Tante Riet's kitchen table. The elderly man had gray whiskers and a beard that reached to his chest, half hiding the prominent yellow star. A small valise that looked much travelled stood at his feet.

As Edda rushed into the kitchen, he made a movement as if wanting to scurry away. Tante Riet's voice called soothingly from the back room. "It's okay, Chaim, Edda is good people." The elderly lady hurried into the kitchen herself and threw a protective arm around Edda.

"Meet my niece, Lientje."

It was the first time Tante Riet called Edda her niece, and Edda startled further at her using Duifje's pet name. All this show for the gentleman called "Chaim" was clearly important and Edda went along. Lientje, after all was a logical abbreviation for her full name, Eddaline.

"Thank you, Tante. I was just dropping by to see if you needed anything. I'm on my way to the Albert Cuyp market. I so hope greengrocer Hoppe will have oranges today. You need to keep up your vitamin C, Tante Riet."

While babbling, Edda smiled at the gentleman who sank back on the kitchen stool again.

"I'm finding Mr. Berg a five-star hotel," Tante Riet joked.

Again, playing along, Edda said, "then you've come to the right address, Mr. Berg. My aunt is the best receptionist in all Amsterdam."

The elderly gentleman managed a thin smile. "I'm glad to hear it, Lientje."

And so it came that after delivering one single orange to Tante Riet, which they sisterly shared, Edda walked Mr. Berg with his small valise to an address in the 1ste Helmerstraat, close to where, years before, the ambulance had delivered her with an broken ankle to the Wilhelmina Gasthuis. It felt special and important to be in charge of escorting a Jewish, fellow citizen to a safe place.

When they arrived at the address Tante Riet had given her, she had express instructions to knock on the side door with three short raps of her knuckles. The code was '2000.' After giving it, the door opened, and Mr. Berg walked through. Edda didn't know if she'd ever see him again but before he completely disappeared in the dark of the house, he said to her, "the Talmud in Sanhedrin 37a states, *'Whoever saves a single life is considered by scripture to have saved the whole world.'* Thank you, Lientje."

Edda was pleased to have helped Mr. Berg, but there was really only one family she prayed she could help. The Hoffmanns.

She missed Ash as if a rib was missing from her body. Not having heard from him in two weeks, she was more worried than ever. This had never happened in the three years since they knew each other. Tante Riet had said to give it time. That the Hoffmanns were probably relocating on their own and Ash couldn't come out of hiding yet.

"But what if Ash can't come out of hiding until the war is over, which may take decades?! I'll be an old woman and we'll never have babies," Edda had cried out. Tante Riet's crystal eyes had rested on her pseudo-niece with warmth and a pinch of mockery.

"Firstly, Edda Van Der Valk, this war won't last for decades, and secondly if Ash is still in Amsterdam and his legs are able to carry him places, he'll come scratching at your door as my Minoes does on mine. Anyone with working eyes can see that boy is wack-a-doodle with you. Plenty of time to make a baker's dozen of babies."

Edda had to laugh despite herself. And Tante Riet's conviction Ash wouldn't be able to stay away from her, dispersed the depressing cobwebs.

"Let me tell you a secret, young lady." Tante Riet's face had a cheeky expression. "You're a pretty mammal but you keep that lad of yours hankering after your body while you feed him piecemeal parts of your soul. That's all very noble but a bit of a shame if you ask me." She hollered with that booming sound that made even Minoes jump off the windowsill with an indignant meow and disappear to a quiet place in the sitting room.

Edda stiffened, struck at how Tante Riet's innocent joke flung her back to Duifje's snickering at the protection of her virginity.

"Do you think..." she started with a doubtful look in her dark eyes.

"No, I don't think at all, kindje. I'm not paid to think," Tante Riet interrupted Edda. "Besides, what do I know of men? I've only had one suitor in my life, but he managed to kick up his heels before we could so much as pat each other."

"I'm so sorry, Tante Riet!" Edda had somehow never associated her neighbor with amorous feelings. Which was naturally a failing on her part.

"Never mind, kindje. It was decades ago, and I just never met another man that could hold a candle to my Freek. I was destined to be a spinster, I guess." She took Edda's face between her red, working hands and said with tenderness, "Don't pay attention to what anyone says. And certainly not a loudmouthed old spinster like me. It's your precious body, mijn ballerina kindje, and you guard it the way you want."

"But what if I can only see Ash one more time, Tante Riet?"

The crystal eyes fixed on her. A sadness appeared in them. "In that case, Edda, you'll probably end up like me." But then the sun broke over the smooth older face as the cloud dispersed. Tante Riet could never be somber for long. "We'll be two knock-them-dead spinsters, what do you say?"

Edda couldn't help smiling. Her neighbor's resilience was infectious. Being like Tante Riet, a single woman who stood her ground, was a way of life Edda could see for herself.

"Oh, I wish I could be like you. Be a good aunt to Benny and Elly. Like you are to Ome Jan's daughter. And you must have been to...your nephew Sjaak." Her smile faded. Edda hadn't been in touch with Duifje for months. The war had torn all the Van der Valks apart. At least Ome Jan was in the Dutch Resistance together with his sister. Tante Riet's sharp eyes saw Edda shrink.

"Yes, you can be a good aunt, kindje. Marie is a treasure I couldn't live without. Certainly not after Sjaak's gone. Though she's a grown woman herself now. The war won't last forever. You and your sister will find each other again, I'm sure of it."

"Thank you!" There was hope. The warm rough hands wrapped around Edda's pinched face for a second time.

"And if everything goes wrong, Edda Van der Valk, you have your Tante Riet. You've become like a daughter to me these past two years." The crystal eyes became moist, and Edda felt herself wrapped in a bear hug that dissolved all old pain but brought new pain in its place. The fear of also losing Tante Riet.

Edda cried in Tante Riet's arms, but she wasn't the only one in tears. The strong, defiant Amsterdam woman wept as well. Loud and deep like everything Tante Riet did.

30

THE NIGHTMARISH NIGHT

Two months later – Amsterdam, 5 December 1942

Towards the end of 1942 Amsterdam, the proud, ancient city built on stilts, had lost most of its grandeur. Children, skinny and dirty, played in the rubble and ruins the streets had become. Haggard fathers looked for work, while mothers, still in their pre-war fur coats, dug through the trash in search of food.

With the shops becoming empty and the winter wolf at the door, everything that was vaguely edible was considered food. Moldy bread, sour milk, and green cabbage until only the look of it turned the stomach. All that was burnable was considered firewood. Old cabinets, tree trunks, abandoned carts. The city reeked of smoldering, wet wood, boiled cabbage, stale canal water, and diesel.

The days were cold, the nights were freezing. Daylight broke in gray smears late in the morning and settled back to dusk at four. Life, once the heart of merry Mokum, was but a shadow of its former self. Even the typical Amsterdam sounds had changed. No longer dominant were the bells of the Westertoren clock or the tingling of approaching trams.

Instead, there was the constant drone of approaching bombers.

The German Junkels or Heinkels always in formation from the east, while a single or small group of British RAF Lancasters or Blenheims drifted in from the North Sea.

The Amsterdamers greeted neither bomber with cheer. Both sides just brought destruction in their wake, burning houses, a shattered windmill, even once a blitz bomber caught fire, still streaking across the Herengracht canal. A stench of burning oil and gunpowder and a black smoke hanging over the city at dawn.

The loudest sounds in the streets came from the Germans on the ground. The roar of their Kubelwagens and Zundapp motorcycles as they zipped over bridges and along the water side. And after the sound of engines died down, there was always the heavy thumping of soldiers' boots patroling the streets.

The Amsterdamers, generally not famed for their soft-toned voices or tongue-tied temperaments, had fallen silent. The spirit was out of the city they loved and had cared for. Their fellow Jews, usually more subdued and less querulous but very much part of the inner tapestry, were gone. The busy shops closed, the centuries of craftsmanship stifled, the gold and diamonds stolen, violins forever silent as the wind dies down after a storm.

Because a storm it had been. 100,000 Jews deported in a matter of months. All Mokum knew was they were driven together and packed up with unknown destination— 'east to work camps' most said with a shudder.

Thousands of others who'd been able to save themselves from the razzias were trapped inside the city like bears in a pit. Gone underground with the help of the *Landelijke Organisatie voor Hulp aan Onderduikers*. The LO stood for *National Organisation for Help to Hiders* and was run by simple Amsterdamers like Tante Riet and her brother.

Edda had given up dance, but not of free will. Miss Sterling had closed the school. She'd declared it was just too dangerous to move through the streets, even before curfew. If you weren't hit by a bomb, you'd get caught up in an ugly mob of NSB men arresting Jews or resistance fighters. But the lack of daily routine and exercise had crushed Edda's already fragile heart. After more than twenty years of constant dancing, her strong limbs had fallen silent, and she'd curled up inside herself like a caterpillar in its cocoon.

On a Friday morning, with the first snow falling from a leaden sky, she sat in the windowsill of her apartment behind the lace curtains, very much like Minoes the cat one door down. With her hands clasped around her lower legs and her chin resting on her knees, she stared at the bare trees of the Vondelpark with very little in her head.

Edda had never imagined a day could last so long when one did nothing. This lethargy didn't compare to when she'd broken her ankle and had a forced break from ballet for a couple of months. Then there had been Switzerland... and the presence of her family. *Mama. Papa. Duifje.* This time it was much worse. This was like death. Alone, imprisoned, her heart aching for Ash.

A woman in a faded blue raincoat scurried past her window, her head down, the face hidden under a cotton scarf. She was carrying a bag of bread with black mold growing on it. Edda shivered. It was as if she could smell the dank stench through the glass, upsetting her own empty stomach. And yet she knew that bread would be eaten. Probably by a whole family.

Depression hung over her city, over her soul, like a dense cloud. Wherever she went it followed her around, from bed to kitchen to sitting room and back. Her mood was as black as the blackout curtains she hung in front of her windows at night. Sometimes day and night didn't seem to make much of a difference. December 1942 was a hard, hard month.

"Ash," she whispered, though even mentioning his name hurt like a curse. Her heart beat in silence, in time and stillness, like the ticking of an old clock.

Edda jumped almost to the ceiling when the phone rang. It had been silent for months, and she didn't even know it still worked. As she reached for the black receiver, her heart racing, it kept ringing. There was no doubt someone was trying to get hold of her. Edda's hand trembled as she picked it up.

"Edda here," she said, her voice shaking. Leaving out her last name just in case. Nobody could be trusted these days.

"Edda-mine? It's me," came the voice on the other end. It sounded strained and distant.

"Oh Ash, is it really you? I've been so worried about you." Tears streamed down her face, and she wiped them away with her sleeve. "Are you alright?"

"We're alright for now," Ash replied. "I can't say where we are for security reasons. Who knows who listens in to our conversations, but I'll try to come and see you when I can. The Nazis are getting more aggressive in their searches, though, so we're not sure we can stay here for long. We might need to move on, but I'll try to send message to you."

Edda's heart sank. She knew the peril any Jew still living in Amsterdam now faced. The Hoffmanns were in grave danger, and there was nothing she could do to help them. Nothing.

"Please be careful, Ash." Edda's voice was thick with emotion. "I love you so much." Simple words but they were her whole world. The world she hung onto with all her might.

"I love you too, Edda-mine." She could hear the tremor in his voice. "I'll do everything I can to stay safe. But you have to promise me you'll take care of yourself, too. Promise me you will."

"I promise," Edda's voice was barely more than a whisper. "And please let me know if there's anything I can do for you and your family. Anything at all."

Ash sighed. "I have to go now, my gritty girl. It's not safe to be on the phone for too long."

"Okay," Edda choked, tears still streaming down her face. "Please, please be careful."

"I will," Ash said. "I love you."

The receiver came down on the hook with a clattering sound. Edda sank next to it on the ground and curled up in misery.

"No, no, no!" she cried. "Dear God, no!"

But she knew chances were slimmer than slim she'd ever see Ash again. She had no way of finding out the address they were staying because the Hoffmanns hadn't sought an underground address through Tante Riet's organization. And in any case, Jews' hiding places were secret. The fewer people that knew where they were, the better their chances of not being snitched on or found out.

After a long span of anguished crying, Edda got up from the floor. She went over to the wash basin to dab her blotched face with cold water. Her own mirror image frightened her. She'd lost too much weight and her muscled upper arms were becoming thin and slack. Under the flush of recent crying, her skin was ashen, while her eyes seemed to be enormous, dark pools staring back at her in horror.

"Pull yourself together, Edda Van der Valk," she told the mirror. "Ash is alive, and he loves you. He told you so twice. And he's a careful man. He'll do nothing wrong to alarm the NSB or the Nazis. If there's one Jew that has a chance of survival, it's Asher Hoffmann. He'll keep his family safe at all costs. And he wants to come back to me. To me."

After this little pep talk, Edda grabbed her duffel coat to go to Jansen's Bakkerij and Wim's grocery shop to exchange her last food coupons for a half loaf of stale rye bread and a pint of milk. Curfew would be in two hours and the lines for food were growing longer by the day.

Just like she'd seen the young woman pass her window an hour earlier, head down and scarf bound around her hair, her butterfly brooch shimmering in the fading light, Edda nervously walked down the Vondelstraat towards the Overtoom to get to the bakery on the corner. One didn't look the Germans in the eye these days and one didn't greet other Amsterdamers. Walking down the cobblestone streets was as lonely outside as life was indoors. Silence reigned, a sinister sad silence.

Edda felt her heart still racing from Ash's sudden call. Her anxiety and fear only increased as she got farther away from her flat. Every sound, every movement around her wore on her frayed nerves. She'd never felt lonelier in her whole life.

When she turned the corner of the Overtoom she stopped in her tracks. The first building was surrounded by Nazi soldiers in black uniforms. She crossed the street to stay away from the tumult though it meant having to cross later again to get to the bakery.

Under the cloak of darkness, an arrest was unfolding, but nobody stopped to look what was going on. A group of German officers, clad in dark uniforms and equipped with radios and batons, formed a human barrier around a building. Another gruesome arrest, no doubt. Possibly Resisters, of which many lived in the Overtoom area.

Edda walked on, wired like the rest to stick to herself until, from the corner of her eyes, she saw Gestapo officers dragging a dark-haired man by his collar out from among the group of policemen. He looked familiar. She had to stop, and realized in absolute horror it was Samuel Hoffmann, Ash's father, hanging more than walking between the grim-looking Germans. Her heart stood still as did her feet.

The scene was illuminated by the flickering glow of waiting cars, casting eerie shadows that danced over the human corridor and the three-storey building with its wide-open front door. Screams, laments, Yiddish prayers. The horrifying sounds mingled with the reverber-ating echoes of Gestapo footsteps and the distant rumble of airplanes. Amsterdam bemoaned its fate. Edda stood frozen to the pavement, unable to move, unable to think or act. She was vaguely aware of another Amsterdamer standing next to her, also shocked and petrified.

Chaos ensued as shouts of command mingled with the clamor of bewildered voices. There was no sight of Ash. Edda hoped with all that was in her that he wasn't in that house. But if he was? Then he'd been at just a stone's throw away from her.

He can't be, she told herself. *He mustn't be. Not Ash! Not Ash!*

Amidst the commotion, the shrill wail of police whistles pierced the air, signaling reinforcements racing to the scene. Additional offi-cers arrived, emerging from the darkness, with their clubs and rabid faces. Edda shuddered.

No sight of Ash.

Until now.

Dragged across the threshold by four SA officers, fighting like a wounded lion, Ash was pulled from the front door. He acted like a chained beast, wildly moving his powerful body and shouting profanities at his captors. He was a strong man, an incredibly strong man that four police officers couldn't hold. It was too gut-wrenching to watch.

Edda stuffed her hand in her mouth, but a wild moan escaped her. The person on the pavement next to her put a hand on her shoulder. "Be still, or they'll get you too." With all her might she tried to stifle her cries while her eyes filled with helpless tears.

A club was raised in the night air and came down on Ash's head with a dull thud. He went limp. The person next to Edda grabbed her arm but she struggled to get free, dashing across the road, her sight misted by tears and towering rage.

"Don't, girl!" he shouted after her, but Edda could no longer be stopped.

"Ash, no!" she cried, as she bumped into the cordon of police officers who barred her way. "Ash, no!" She was almost surprised by the Germans' determination not to let her through. They had no right to stop her. It was a matter of life and death. Throwing herself at them with all her force once more, she bounced back. One of the officers pushed her aside.

"*Aus dem Weg, Fraulein.*" Out of the way!

"You don't understand," she cried. "Let me pass. I'm with them."

"You're not!" The unperturbed Nazi replied. "Go away!"

At that moment the cordon of SA men opened and Ash, still fighting but not as hellishly as before, was pulled over the ground towards the waiting truck. Only the sight of his crying mother holding Ash's sister by the hand, stopped Edda from making a new attack at the Germans. Frau Adina Hoffmann, in her black wig and woolen coat looked so lamentable that it knocked the wind out of Edda's resistance. Martha, her daughter, looked vacant. The head of the family stood stoically next to the truck, already resigned to his fate. Four yellow stars, still bright and shining.

Edda stumbled back, a deadly doom in her heart. It was over. And she, Edda, had done nothing to save them. Nothing. Shame on her. Eternal shame on her.

Before he was hoisted onto the back of the truck, Ash lifted his head. She saw the blood run down one side of his chiselled face, the eyes black with intense hatred. Edda had seen many emotions in those beloved eyes but never naked hatred. The look went right through her, though he didn't see her. The hatred was for her, for the spectators, the survivors, the ones who called themselves superior to him. It couldn't be the last she'd ever see of him. This raw hate. She'd never recover from it.

"Ash," she begged.

His eyes, darker than the darkest storm cloud, turned to her sorrowful plea. He saw her, just before the Gestapo loaded him and his family onto a truck. Their eyes locked. Desperately Edda sought the love, but it wasn't there. She looked and looked and then for a tiny moment his face broke as a new dawn. The smile was full of pain, the eyes never light again, but he smiled, nonetheless.

Edda stood frozen in shock and disbelief, her hand touching her brooch. The flaps at the back of the truck closed. The engine roared, the SA men went to their separate vehicles, slowly and certainly the truck drove off. Edda stared at it until it turned the corner, unaware she was in the middle of the street until a car honked behind her and she limped to the pavement. The few people who had watched the deportation of yet another Jewish family in hiding, went on their way.

Guilt, hate, and despair washed over Edda. The man she loved, and his family were being taken away to God knows where. She looked again but the truck didn't come back around the corner. It would never come back.

Not caring any longer, Edda collapsed onto the pavement, sobbing uncontrollably. She knew that this day, this hour, marked her more than anything in her life ever had or would. The day the tables turned. She would never forget how she had had to watch the love of her life and his family being taken away by the Gestapo. His eyes, that hatred, so deep and passionate it had killed all the love. Almost. Even for her. *Please God turn Ash's heart to love again. Have mercy on us.*

But it was also the night Edda knew she'd found the strength to fight for him. The *cry-baby* was no longer. Drying her eyes for the last time, she swore she would turn her failure to protect the Hoffmanns in a fight to save every Jew she could.

"Never again!" she kept repeating under her breath the hour and a half she stood in line waiting for her turn at the bakery. "Never again. Over my dead body! I'll avenge the Hoffmanns every day this wretched war goes."

A white-faced but very determined Edda, clad in her black ballet outfit, strode into Tante Riet's kitchen after curfew.

"I'm joining the LO fulltime. Now."

31

THE RESISTANCE DANCER

Two months later

Amsterdam, 2 February 1943

The tide of the war is turning, and this is what gives me hope. The only thing that gives me hope. At the end of last year, the entire German Sixth Army was surrounded near Stalingrad. The Soviets, now firmly on the Allied side, have demanded the German surrender. And today it came. General Paul had no choice. His troops were out of supplies and starving. Hitler isn't happy with the surrender. The man is mad! And this is —strangely enough—what gives me even more hope. If he goes against his own generals, the end is near! The Red Army will be on the heels of the Germans from now on.

I'm feeling a lot better and not only because of the German debacle on the Russian front. It was obvious it would happen from the start. But I'm feeling better because I now have a goal in my life.

When I go out, I wear a special corset that gives the impression I'm pregnant. I have a new Identity Card that states I'm Mevrouw Hannie Kuipers. My husband is working in Germany and I'm pregnant with our first child. But the corset is filled with fake ration cards and travel permits. Ome Jan makes those on a special press in his garden house on his allotment garden in Duivendrecht.

My task is to distribute these coupons and permits to the organizers who know where Jewish families are hidden. I usually go by bike, as I'm not so easily stopped by the police that way. And they are more lenient with pregnant women anyway. But I'm not afraid. Not anymore.

Haven't heard from Ash or from my family. Tante Riet and Ome Jan are all the family I have now. But Tante Riet says I must dance again. For the Germans. Just to avoid all suspicion. Under my own name, of course, and without the corset. I loathe the idea, but I can see it would be a smart move. So today I'm going to see if I can find Miss Sterling and ask if she will organize some dance event. Hopefully she's still in Amsterdam but if not, I'll dance solo.

One more thing before I must go. Prime Minister Winston Churchill and the US President Franklin D. Roosevelt have been meeting in Casablanca. They agreed they want the 'unconditional surrender of the Axis *powers', meaning Germany and Italy. And they're going to bomb German cities to undermine the morale of the German population and to destroy as many German Luftwaffe fighter aircraft as possible.*

You have them coming for you, Herr Hitler, and Meneer Mussert, your days in power are numbered as well.

Edda as Edda, without Hannie's corset and ID, was cycling through the cold January morning on her way to the last address she had of her ballet mistress in Amsterdam-Oost. Not looking left or right, she pedaled forward. The possibility of seeing more Jews or Resistance fighters being manhandled by Dutch or German Nazis was too gruesome after the Hoffmann's deportation. She'd taught herself to cope by only seeing what she needed to see and shutting out all that would weaken her.

And Edda was strong again. Not only from all the cycling on an old bicycle that hardly had any tyres left. She was dancing again.

With the furniture in her tiny sitting room pushed to one side and the carpet rolled up, Ome Jan had created a makeshift dance floor for her. He'd even attached an iron barre along one wall so Edda could practice her plies. And practice she did, as many hours as she wasn't Hannie Kuipers.

Miss Sterling's house looked abandoned, and Edda lost hope. *Where had she gone?* Edda also felt shame. Her mentor had never recovered from Monsieur Sergeyev's escape to France. And when his letters from Nice stopped, the ballet mistress had languished. Tough and tireless as she'd been while her Russian lover was around to spur her on, the formidable ballet mistress had become tentative and tepid when on her own.

Edda rang the bell. She waited with her breath held. Nothing happened. She rang again. The dead branch of a tree tapped rhythmically against the blacked-out window. Miss Sterling had finally returned to London as she should have.

Not knowing whether to be relieved or sad, Edda turned to get back on her bike when she heard the door creak. It opened ajar. Mumbling a *sorry wrong door*, she unlocked her bike. Then she looked up again. The slim woman who peeked around the door slightly resembled Miss Sterling. But the bouncy curls had made way for strings of uncombed gray hair and the once honey eyes had faded to a shade of weak old tea. No sparkling smile, no red-painted lips, no colorful shawls.

"Miss... Miss Sterling?"

"Edda." The voice was toneless, uninterested.

"Can I come in for a moment? It's freezing outside."

"If you want." Miss Sterling turned her back on Edda but left the door open. Edda slipped inside and locked it behind her. At least Miss Sterling's spine was still as straight as a soldier's, but her feet had nothing of their former nimbleness. The *grande dame* of ballet now shuffled.

Edda followed her into a sitting room that clearly hadn't been aired for months and that was so cold frost flowers blossomed on the windows. The ballet mistress huddled under a blanket on her sagging couch and closed her eyes.

"Are you unwell, Miss Sterling? Can I get you something? Maybe a cup of tea?" Edda felt horrible seeing her mentor like this. She should have visited sooner.

No answer. Miss Sterling just sat there slowly rocking back and forth, hugging herself, her eyelids fluttering. Edda didn't wait for an answer, but went over to where she expected there to be a kitchen.

The kitchen was a mess, with trash erupting out of the garbage bin and dirty dishes piled up in the sink. But there was a dented kettle on the stove and the water tap worked. Small victories. Another small victory was a box of matchsticks. Edda got the cooker working and soon the kettle shrieked shrilly, as if piqued at being put to use finally.

Minutes later, Edda returned to the sitting room with two cups of tea. She hadn't been able to find any biscuits. The ballet mistress's position was unchanged, she was still rocking herself with her eyes closed.

Very much like I was a while ago, Edda thought. *This is what it looks like when life no longer makes sense to you.*

She put the cups on the table and took a seat opposite the swaying blanket. What should she say? Where to begin? Because it was clear to Edda she'd come at the right time and with the right message. A ballet mistress is a ballet mistress and that was just what Miss Sterling had to become once again. Strangely enough, this time with Edda's help. As if the tables were turned. Well, they had.

"Ash is gone." Edda's throat protested the words, but they came out nevertheless.

"I know." The blanket answered, "Larry's gone too."

"Oh no," Edda gulped. "I didn't know that. All his family?"

Miss Sterling nodded and opened her eyes.

"I was there. He'd asked for me but there was nothing I could do."

Edda swallowed, shivered. "Same with the Hoffmanns. I had to witness their arrest without being able to lift one finger. That's the worst part of it, isn't it? That these darn German rifles can stop us from saving the people we love."

The ballet mistress seemed to revive somewhat. "I'm so sorry, Edda. So, so sorry."

"What about Monsieur Sergeyev?" she ventured to ask.

The ballet mistress shrugged and closed her eyes again. "Nothing."

Edda didn't dare to probe further so decided to raise the reason she'd come. "I actually wanted to talk to you about ballet, Miss Sterling." She waited for a moment, but the eyes remained closed, so she continued. "I've been thinking about going back into ballet despite the war."

"Why would you want to do that, Edda?" Still with closed eyes the ballet mistress took a sip of the tea. How she managed to drink without spilling the hot liquid all over herself was a wonder.

"Can I be honest with you?" Edda asked.

"Try as you may, my dear." Another sip with closed eyes and Edda suddenly wondered if there was something wrong with Miss Sterling's eyes. She'd always said she was too proud to wear glasses and with vitamin deficiencies of rationed food people contracted the weirdest diseases.

"Is there... is there something wrong with your eyes, Miss Sterling?"

The eyes opened and to Edda's surprise they had some of their pre-war glimmer.

"No, I'm just tired. That's all. Tired of this world."

"That's why you have to go back into dance with me." Edda said with hope in her voice.

The ballet mistress chuckled. The merriness of the sound was a relief. Edda yearned for her mentor's old spirit to return. That spirit had done so much for her in her years of training, but since the war things had petered out and that was just plain wrong.

"You said you'd tell me the reason you want to show your legs to these Nazis, Edda Van der Valk." The contempt in the ballet mistress's voice was enough for Edda to blurt out.

"I'm with the Resistance now, Miss Sterling, and dancing for the Nazis might be my best cover. But it must look professional. That's why I came to you, you see. I need you."

The honey eyes widened like clean windows. There was clearly nothing wrong with the ballet mistress's eyesight. She slowly shook the head with the gray tresses.

"You with the Resistance. I should've known. Yes, it fits the bill."

"Well?" Edda asked, impatient for an answer. "I know you must also miss ballet as if your arms are empty. Please consider it. Even if you were just to train me. Your star pupil, as you used to say." Edda used all her persuasive power to break through her mentor's placidity. And it seemed to work.

"Where would we train, Edda? Where? This whole town is nothing but rubble and ravage."

And Edda told her of the small studio Ome Jan had created for her in her sitting room. The ballet mistress stretched as if flexing her muscles for action and Edda's hope rose further.

"It's true I've missed teaching dance. And dancing myself. The longing and the missing have turned me into a miserable misanthropic woman. *E un tale spreco!* What a waste!"

"So, you'd be interested?"

The ballet mistress didn't answer but there was no stopping Edda now. "Yes, you and I need ballet like oxygen, Miss Sterling. And even dancing for the Nazis will be a good cause. Sprinkling sand in their eyes."

"But do you want to do a variation, Edda? Which solo?"

"I haven't given it much thought yet, Miss Sterling. I've just been doing my exercises the past couple of weeks. I'm terribly out of form, of course."

The ballet mistress tilted her head, the eyes mischievous.

"You're going to dance La Sylphide, Edda. That will teach the Nazis a lesson."

Though she knew the story of the Scotsman with the Sylph, Edda had no idea what her mentor alluded to. The merry chuckle followed.

"That ballet is all about illusion, don't you see? It will end badly for the Germans who are trying to reach for the sky. Yes, it's a perfect ballet as a resistance piece." The ballet mistress clapped her hands and Edda knew she was back with her in the saddle.

"I'll have to adapt it of course as you will be the only one on the stage and I'll miss Larry so much to make the set pieces."

"I know." Edda thought of all the love Larry always poured into his creations. How he would race up and down the ladder on his long legs and never stop until everything was perfectly in place. Often having to be shoo'ed off the stage by Miss Sterling because the show was about to start.

"Oh Larry!" Edda couldn't help exclaiming.

"Oh Ash!" Miss Sterling followed.

"I'll dance for them," Edda said with conviction. "I'll dance for them in my heart and soul. Not for the Nazis who will be watching."

32

A DOUBLE LIFE

A month later – March 1943

"More spunk, Edda. Come on you can do this! Up, up, up!" Miss Sterling, complete with bright red polka dot shawl and even redder lipstick, clapped her hands. She was back in business.

Edda balanced on her left leg, winging her right leg to her ear, stretching out the toes to the ceiling, all with a smile plastered on her face. Her left ankle throbbed but she ignored the pain.

"Like this?"

"Yes, that's what I want to see. That's *Sylphide. Bellisima!*" Sprinkling her upper-class English with Italian superlatives was always a good sign with the ballet mistress.

Edda kept smiling her dapper smile, but she was exhausted. Her faced taut, she tried to meet her mentor's need for *bellissima spunk* but sensed she was failing the dream of glory they'd spun together. What was dance without Ash? An empty shell of skill and schedule. No soul, no spirit.

Her mentor picked up on her struggle. "Let's make it an early teatime today. And you tell me all about your gallivanting last night."

The light tone and coy smile were deliberate. Fully back in her mentor's role, she was very aware of the strain Edda's other life caused her.

"Thank you. Yes, I'm exhausted. And I'm sorry I'm falling short of the task." Edda rubbed her face and shoulders dry with a towel. Then sank on a stool. She was sweating despite the room being only heated by some simmering coals in the fireplace.

"Are you sure you're alright?" There was concern in her mentor's voice, just like in the old days.

"Yes. Don't worry about me. Tea and something sweet to eat will do the trick. I shouldn't complain, you know. As distributor of ration cards, I could take some extra for myself."

"But do you do that? You need to eat more, Edda." The tone was stern. Edda looked away.

"How can I do that, Miss Sterling, when others have even less than I have?"

"You can and you must because you're living two lives and you've got to give them both your very best."

"I'll try," Edda said meekly. Miss Sterling wagged the pink-tipped index finger at her.

"Now you listen to me, dear. If you don't start eating more, I'm not going to continue choreographing Sylphide with you. Is that clear? You're undernourished and working two jobs at the time. If you want to shine for those Nazis, you'd better be in top form. Is that understood?"

Edda nodded. How good it felt that Miss Sterling was taking control of her life again.

"Truly, I promise."

With gratefulness she accepted the steaming cup of Ceylon tea with a luxurious spoonful of sugar.

"Maybe I shouldn't be driving you so hard, but you asked for it, my dear. So, what were you up to last night." The honey eyes rested on Edda with a little more patience.

"Oh, the usual." Edda didn't feel like dishing up another dispiriting story.

"I think you need to get it off your chest, Edda. It's bogging you down. You can't dance the way you want when you're all stressed."

Edda groaned. The whole scene evolved before her eyes again as she gave an account of the gruesome affair Ome Jan and she had witnessed the day before.

"Ome Jan knocked on my back door at eight last night, so after curfew. Backdoor is either Tante Riet or Ome Jan. No one else uses it. He looked surly. Ome Jan is a big man, at least 6-foot-2 and always whistling a popular song and being chirpy even when things go wrong. Though he lost his only son early in the war at the hands of these wretched Nazis, Ome Jan doesn't do surly and he's never silent, so I instantly knew something was amiss.

I asked him straight out, alarmed by the change in his expression.

He explained. "Cell 10 has been betrayed by the darn Dutch blackshirts. The entire cell was arrested. At the Plantage Middenlaan. Twelve people in total. I need to go and see if I can rescue the pamphlets and ration cards we'd hidden in the cellar. The Gestapo will be back either tonight or tomorrow morning to search the darn place. I need you to be on the lookout when I go in. Are you coming?"

"Oh no, that's Anna's group, isn't it? Of course, I'll come. Let me get my coat," Edda had told Ome.

"Aren't you a daredevil," her mentor interrupted with admiration.

"I don't know about that," Edda dismissed the praise with a shrug. "I've been out after curfew many times but it's getting trickier. The Nazis have searchlights on all the important buildings, and they've ramped up patrols as well. It was a long walk to the city center, and we had to hide behind trees and brick walls as much as we could. With his height, Ome Jan stands out wherever he goes even if he's wearing his entirely black outfit, which he calls his Duke of Hells Habit. I kept at a safe distance, some twenty feet behind him but making sure I kept him in my vision. I knew where we were going as I had been to the house on the Plantage Middenlaan many times myself. It was the meeting place of one of the most active LO cells in Amsterdam. Some of their members, like Anna, which is a code name of course, did much more than help Jews. She could shoot like the best and was said to have killed quite a few Dutch and German Nazi officers."

"Oh Edda, the people you mingle with!" The ballet mistress pulled her merino cardigan closer around her shoulders.

"I'm getting shooting lessons myself." It came out almost without thinking. "We all do. Anyway, in a circumspect way, we arrived at the house after about an hour and it looked all dark and abandoned. I took up a position among the trees close to Artis Zoo. I could hardly make out Ome Jan inching towards the place and taking the alley that leads to the side door. My code for trouble was the Spider monkey call, as they're near the entrance of the Zoo and though they shriek in a disturbing way, I've learned to imitate them rather well." Edda smiled, though weakly. Ome Jan teaching her the monkey's high-pitched *E-eh-eh-eeehh* sound had been much fun.

"A patrol car came by. The headlights illuminating the façade of the house where I knew Ome Jan was inside but fortunately they went on. It was very cold and very dark, and I kept hoping he would come back quickly. It was getting late, and I knew you were going to be here early in the morning."

"You could have told me straightaway you needed to catch up on sleep." The ballet mistress said but Edda's dark eyes shot fire. "Sleep? I have no time for sleep. I will sleep when the war is over. Then I'll sleep to my heart's content."

"Alright, alright. Just tell me what happened. I won't interrupt you again." The hands with the pink nails went up in submission.

"Then I heard boots coming near so I shrank back farther into the shrubbery but was on high alert. This was much more dangerous than a patrolling car. The boots could only belong to Germans, of course. They were Wehrmacht soldiers as far as I could see, two of them. They stopped in front of the house, talking and smoking. I was too far away to hear what they were saying but I was very afraid Ome Jan might switch on his torch to find the compromising papers in the cellar and that the Germans would see the light flash even if it was dimmed. I didn't know whether to shriek or not and decided to wait and see what they would do. And then they went to the front door."

The ballet mistress gasped and tried to silence herself by clamping a hand over her mouth.

"There was a tense silence. They tried the door, but it was locked from the inside. The Germans obviously didn't have the key but the fact they were trying that door made me understand they knew of the earlier arrests. I yelled the Spider monkey's cry. I couldn't help myself. I was sure they would go around and try the side door that *was* open. Ome Jan had to have a chance to get out. But my cry had the opposite effect. The Germans came in my direction, possibly to see what animal had made that noise. I slinked even farther back, but could hear one say to the other 'We're going to kill that horrible ape. No animal in its right mind makes such an ear-splitting sound.'

"I was hoping to stay invisible. I stood as still as a stump of the tree next to me and decided I'd stay there all night if necessary. The Germans were trying to clamber over the walls of the Zoo only a few feet away from me. I could hear their heavy breathing and their cursing as one slid down. Then a branch cracked and fell on top of me. I...I yelped. I thought I would be dead the next moment when two muffled shots rang. Ome Jan grabbed my hand and pulled me from under the bushes. The Germans, face down, didn't stir. Ome Jan doesn't ever miss a shot. We ran. That's it."

Edda shivered. "Can I have another tea?" Her mentor's eyes were big, horrified.

"I know what you're thinking," Edda added in a small voice. "We sometimes have to kill in this job. War isn't pretty."

Handing her a second cup of tea, the ballet mistress said, "Did Ome Jan have the papers?"

"Oh yes, and the map of a refinery in IJmuiden that's soon going to be blown up. It's where the Germans get a lot of their petrol from. Steal, I should say."

The ballet mistress remained silent for a while as they sipped their tea.

"How did your Ome Jan muffle those shots?"

"He has a De Lisle carbine. It's a British spy weapon and it comes with an integrated suppressor. He got it from an English secret agent who was here for a while. I wish I had one myself. If you have to kill, you'd better not create a racket."

Edda saw Miss Sterling put up her mentor's face and realized she was rambling on about shocking things.

"Sorry," she mumbled, "you must think I'm a criminal now." To her surprise Miss Sterling didn't say anything for a while, she seemed to be choosing her words carefully.

"I'm not here to stop you as Hannie Kuipers, my dear. I think she's a marvelous character and an absolute heroine, but..."

Edda waited, rather red-faced.

"... Hannie is a surprise to me. Last you told me about her, she distributed rations cards sporting a fake belly. Now she's on her way to become a die-hard killer. Even in ballet we don't often see such a turn of character."

Edda pondered her mentor's words. They struck a cord. She hadn't given thought to the hard person she'd become. She'd sworn on the night of Ash's deportation that she would become an active LO member. All the cycling and distributing had been physical work, but easy. But not enough to get the Germans out. Not enough by far.

As the Nazis got more vengeful, so did the Resistance. Edda had slipped into Hannie quicker than expected but the mirror of Miss Sterling's judgement now showed her that the real, more sweet-tempered Edda hadn't quite kept up pace with Hannie's radicalization.

"Where are your thoughts, Edda?" Miss Sterling asked.

"You're right," Edda admitted. "I have changed. I don't know if I can unchange. The war just needs to stop. I can't take it anymore."

"I'm just worried for you," the ballet mistress observed. "These dead German patrollers will be investigated, if not avenged. And you're involved in it, even though you didn't pull the trigger."

"I would have," Edda said with fire. Then sat back. "But you're right. I'm in real danger now. Still, it was a case of us or them. Ome Jan couldn't be arrested with all the stuff on him. He could have let me get arrested and I could have played the innocent bystander but there was no good explanation why I was hiding under the bushes long after curfew near that house on the Plantage Middenlaan they had just raided. It was best not to have any suspicion in our direction." Edda looked devastated as she explained further.

"We've lost our very best cell; Cell 10 had so much information and such a huge network, all over Holland. Through them we could route Jews in danger here in Amsterdam to more rural parts of the country where they had more chance of survival. Fewer patrols and more food. That network is now lost and Tante Riet is devastated. I haven't seen her this dispirited since I met her."

"Would you have use for an old woman like me?" It was said in an almost offhand manner as the ballet mistress shoved her scarf a little higher in her curls. And with that coy smile she added, "Not that I'll bring much to the table with my stilted ballet jargon and Italian repartee."

Edda's eyes lit up. "Tante Riet would say, firstly you're not old, Miss Sterling, and secondly, older women are the top of the heap in the resistance movement. They're less conspicuous."

Miss Sterling giggled and with self-awareness added. "I think I would stand out in a crowd of one thousand, but I can try to tone down a bit."

"Let me introduce you to Tante Riet," Edda cried but her mentor's pink nailed wagged to and fro.

"Uh-uh! You had your break. It's Sylphide first and curfew-breaking next. Remember that when the war is over, it's ballet that will sustain you and not gun-toting."

33

OME JAN

E dda went to introduce Miss Sterling to Tante Riet after their
rehearsal in Edda's flat.

"And who might this bird of paradise be?" Tante Riet
asked in her hail-fellow-well-met way while her red hands kept
scrubbing potatoes at high speed and plopping them back in the pan
with water. But Edda saw her neighbor knew exactly who the lady
with the polka-dot scarf and red lipstick was.

She couldn't think of two women more different in style, background, and looks than these mighty mavens who were helping her
through the war, and whom she both loved dearly. They did share a
common, indispensable trait, though, woven into the fabric of their
souls: a fierce temperament. Edda felt special introducing her
mentors to each other and watch the dynamics develop between
them.

"Edda has told me so much about you, Mrs Meulenbelt," the
ballet mistress began in her upper-class accent, but Tante Riet cut her
short.

"No last names here or anywhere, dear lady. We've passed that
station. Strangers lurking everywhere. Maybe even put a microphone
on my poor Minoes."

At the mentioning of her name, the black cat came curling her pliable body around the newcomer's legs while meowing in indignation at being assigned a collaborator's status.

"Tante Riet," Edda intervened quickly, "Miss Sterling wants to come and join us."

"Now does she? With her last name still stuck on her?" Tante Riet cast another glance over the slim, straight-backed lady in front of her as if studying her credentials. Then nodded with approbation.

"You're a bird of paradise...'Vogeltje' will be your nickname, Madam. And pray tell me what it is you can do for the cause?"

"To be honest I have no clue," the the newly-dubbed Vogeltje replied with one of her sunshine smiles. "I'd hope you tell me how I can make myself useful, Madame... uh."

"Tante Riet, for you as for everyone." The white-haired resister interposed.

"Tante Riet, it is then. Quite an honor." The ballet mistress made an elegant curtsy and Tante Riet roared with laughter. "Well, like Edda, I'm strong. I'm disciplined, and I know Amsterdam quite well."

"Yes, Vogeltje, you will be kept inside the boundaries of the Amsterdam canals like a good little birdie, that's for sure. Firstly, your accent would betray you everywhere so we can't have you opening your mouth. Ever. Secondly, you'd stand out like a sore thumb in that attire if we sent you out in the wild."

The ballet mistress seemed a bit peeved by these observations but didn't protest. Tante Riet, still with her hands in the pan of potatoes, continued rubbing the dirt off them and said, "with Cell 10 blown to smithereens, we're in need of anyone willing to be trained. We need new contacts and networks in the provinces. Edda, you'll be starting on charming short tourist trips outside Amsterdam. Vogeltje can take over your distribution tasks in the city. I take it you can ride a bike, Birdie?"

"Of course. And my legs are in good shape as well."

Tante Riet lit the stove and put the potatoes to boil, she added a pinch of salt and some vinegar. "And how will this all fit in with the ballet performance you two are setting up? Edda told me it's for a coverup. I think it's sassy and smart, but I guess you can't have Edda staying away from Amsterdam for too long or the performance will fall flat on its face?" A wild chuckle followed as she dried her hands on her apron.

Edda's thoughts rushed in. She hadn't been outside Amsterdam for almost two years and had no idea how the rest of the country was faring under the Nazi yoke. But somehow, she looked forward to a change of scenery, speaking with other people, seeing if opposition to the occupiers was growing or not. But she also needed to dance. Sylphide was going so slowly, and she was struggling getting into the spirit of the ethereal ballet without Ash. But no thinking of him now. She'd balance her two jobs. One way or the other.

"We might need to postpone the first show until the Spring," the ballet mistress explained. "I'm also still seeking a good location. All the theatres are so run down these days, or used as assembly points for Jews, like the Holland Theater. It's a disgrace." She let out an annoyed sigh. "Sylphide is a difficult ballet for every choreographer but Edda's such a good sport."

"Sylphide sounds like a disease to me anyway," Tante Riet snorted. "But, of course, I'll come and see *mijn kindje* dance."

Miss Sterling carried on as if she hadn't heard the fun the older woman was poking at her high art. "Edda's a unique dancer and she really tries hard, but dancing Sylphide as a solo is almost impossible. If only I had one more dancer, it would make all the difference."

Tante Riet pricked a fork in the steaming potatoes. "Well, it's for sure not me. All I could do is a clog dance. Anyway, we have a meeting here at six. Just my brother and two other members. Could you both be here? See how we can fill the gaps that have been created."

"Isn't that dangerous after last night, Tante Riet?" Edda asked.

"Everything is dangerous, kindje. If we start down that road we might as well curl up and die. I have a feeling I'm still under the radar of the Nazis. Jan may not be so, so we're looking at a place for him to hide."

"I will be here, no worry," the ballet mistress declared.

"You'll have to stay at my place tonight because you can't go home after curfew," Edda said.

"If that's no trouble?"

"Not at all!" Edda actually liked the idea of not being alone in the flat after the events of the night before.

"And you both come here for dinner," Tante Riet announced. "I've got this pan full of potatoes and there's still a tiny bit of lard left we can dip them in. It will be a feast worthy of a king."

THE MEETING NEVER HAPPENED. A small boy of about ten with a whiff of blond hair and scared, marble-round eyes came pounding on Tante Riet's back door, shouting that Ome Jan had been arrested. It was little Lex, the son of Ome Jan's next-door neighbor.

"Holy Moses," and some more expletives erupted from Tante Riet's mouth. "Let me get my coat, Lex, and I'll come with you."

"Let *me* go, Tante Riet," Edda said firmly. Her own words surprised her, but they made sense. "You stay here while I find out what happened. Not being family is better. They'll have no idea who I am."

"I don't know." Tante Riet for once was speechless.

"I'll find out where they took him."

"Are Ome Jan's wife and daughter also taken?" Tante Riet asked the frightened boy when she found her voice again.

"I don't think so." Lex's teeth were clattering non-stop. Miss Sterling retrieved a mint from her cardigan pocket and handed it to the boy. He sucked on the sweet with gratitude.

"Let Edda do this, Tante Riet," the ballet mistress chimed in. "I'll stay here with you until she's back."

"Alright then, but you be careful, kindje. I don't want to lose you as well."

"I promise I will be careful. And fast."

The last thing Edda saw as she slipped out the back door with Lex was Tante Riet's shocked face. She suddenly seemed at least ten years older. Just to feel more certain Edda slipped her gun into the inside pocket of her coat.

They quickly covered the short distance to Ome Jan's house on the Kinkerstraat. Edda had been to his place a few times. The three-story house was in an apartment block in the working-class quarter of Amsterdam-Oud West. As it was still before curfew, Edda and Lex walked as if going on an errand but with their heads down and not talking to each other.

Ome Jan's wife, Christina, opened the door to Edda, while Lex disappeared next door without another word. Christina was clearly in shock, white-faced but dry-eyed. She explained what had happened.

"Two SS officers came to the door. They didn't even give Jan a chance to grab his coat. Off he went in his shirtsleeves in March. It's unheard of."

"Do you have any idea where they took him?" Edda asked.

"I think they said something about the new police station on the Elandsgracht," Christina said. "But I'm not sure. Marie and I didn't even get a chance to say a proper goodbye to him. They also didn't say what he was arrested for. Marie is crying her heart out in her room. I really must go back to her. Oh, it's all so awful. Especially after what happened to our Sjaak. And Jan knows so much, too. I really hope they won't interrogate him in those ugly ways of theirs. Oh, it's so awful," the poor woman kept repeating.

Edda thought fast. She knew Ome Jan often worked together with a medical student, code name Rick, who lived two streets down.

"Does Rick know Ome Jan has been taken?"

"No, I haven't had a chance to let anyone know except for his sister."

"I'll go and see Rick," Edda said, "then I'll come back here."

She raced down to Rick's mother's house and banged on the door with all her might. A very anxious mother opened the door. She didn't know Edda and Edda didn't know her but there was no time for explanations.

"Is Rick home? It's an emergency." As he was a final-year medical student, the mother would think there had been an accident. She immediately called up the stairs for her son.

Rick, his tuft of dark hair standing upright and his glasses halfway down the bridge of his nose, sped down the stairways in his stockinged feet.

"What's the matter, Mother?"

On seeing Edda, the clever student put two and two together, but he clearly wanted to keep his mother out of his affairs.

"I'll go with the young lady, mother. Don't worry, I'll be back as soon as possible." Rick dashed back up the stairs and was back down in two seconds with his medical kit.

As he grabbed his coat from the coat rack, his mother warned, "it's curfew in ten minutes, son, you have no business going outside now."

"A doctor always has a reason, Mother," Rick replied in his most chirpy voice while his green eyes searched Edda's face for answers.

"You're not a doctor yet, Rick," his mother protested but let him go.

Staying away from the street lamps that soon would go out, Edda and Rick walked down the Kinkerstraat towards the police station on the Elandsgracht. Edda told him in a subdued tone what had happened to her and Ome Jan the night before.

"We're in serious trouble," Rick observed, "first Cell 10 and now Ome Jan."

"We need to get him out before they start torturing him." Edda said it matter-of-factly, but she felt far from sane that moment.

"My same thought, but how?"

"I thought you knew the building." Edda said.

"I do, but what help is that now? I've been called inside a few times when they'd brought in a wounded arrestee, but what do you mean? I don't have the key, or anything." Rick replied.

"But do you know where they take the resisters?" Edda insisted.

"Yes, but they never stay there long. They usually interrogate them and then take them to the dunes to shoot them. Whether they have evidence against them or not."

Edda was relentless. "Do you have your weapon with you?"

"Of course, do you?"

"Yes. So, here's the plan," Edda announced. "We wait till they come out of the police station and then we hitch along on the back of the Kubelwagen out of sight of their rear mirror. When they arrive at their location, we kill the guards and free Ome Jan."

"That's crazy, Hannie. It will never work. We'll be dead ourselves or at least walking targets ever after." Rick only knew Edda's code name as she did his.

"Come on, Rick, what could be worth more? Ome Jan alive or Ome Jan dead?" Edda didn't know from where her audacity came, but saving Ome Jan was the single focus of all her attention and worth every deadly fear that riled through her.

"I think we have a one percent chance to pull off such a stunt." There was much doubt in Rick's voice.

"One percent is one percent."

"But are you ready to kill, Hannie?"

"For Ome Jan, yes. He's like family to me."

They'd meanwhile arrived at the police station that lay along one of the outer rings of Amsterdam's canals. The box-like, red brick building of three storeys with a watch tower on top of the flat roof had opened at the beginning of the war. Most of the building was still in use by the hog-tied Dutch police forces, but in the western part of the building, the Germans took captured resisters for a first 'interview' and usually issued their verdict soon after:being shot in the head.

The light was on in one of the offices on the third floor, where Amsterdamers knew rebellious arrestees were taken. In one way the light was a good thing. If it was Ome Jan being interrogated in that room, he was still there, but it was still only a guess. Edda winced at the idea of what was going on in that room, of which she could only see the hellish electric light from the ceiling. That Ome Jan wouldn't say a word was beyond doubt, no matter the measures the SS would employ. But would he come out alive? Would the Germans still need to drive him to the dunes?

Without a word or sound, Edda and Rick took up positions in the tall grass on the edge of the waterline facing the building and the garage exit. Curfew came. Loud sirens announced the start of night and curfew going into effect. Edda felt strangely empty while her stomach rumbled. After a long day of dance training, she'd only had her cups of afternoon tea and had missed out on Tante Riet's boiled potatoes. But the emptiness had the strange effect of making her mind crystal clear and her senses sharp.

There was no activity in or around the building for a long time. The light in the interrogation room was still on. She felt her heartbeat against the cold soil where she was lying on her stomach. Her feet and hands were freezing. All she could think of was what the SS might be doing to Ome Jan during those excruciating hours.

Edda was sure Rick was thinking the same thing, but they didn't talk. His breathing next to her was soft and regular. Now and then she could see a plume of his breath like white damp in the night's air. He was the right person for the job. Like her he wouldn't waver if push came to shove.

And push came to shove earlier than they expected. The light in the room of their focus went out. The whole west wing was dark now. Edda felt Rick move next to her, just slightly. She, too, was on high alert. Her Enfield no longer inside her pocket, instead now strapped to her thigh under the black coat.

Though Edda had had many shooting lessons in the dunes near Haarlem, she'd never actually aimed her gun on a human target. But she blocked the thought. All thoughts. Years of harsh ballet training made it possible to concentrate in a way few people could. She only directed her attention on what lay directly before her. One step at the time, one movement at the time, one turn at the time. And one thought at a time.

Minutes later, the Kubelwagen backed out of the police station's garage. When it passed them, Edda and Rick, without exchanging a word, jumped each on one side of the back of the van, squeezing themselves against the backdoor to become as small as possible. She had to believe Ome Jan was inside though she could hear nothing but the roar of the vehicle's engine.

The Kubelwagen drove at high speed out of town in the direction of the dunes, where Edda had learned to shoot. She knew then she'd been right: who the person lying in the back of the van was and where they were heading. She breathed a little easier. Now that they were away from the city, the chances of being discovered as hitch-hikers on a German van were less. All she could pray for was that there were only two Germans up front with just Ome Jan, in whatever state, but likely handcuffed and with a gag in his mouth in the back.

It was a long ride, and her hands were so stiff from the freezing air she was afraid she would let go of the iron railing she was hanging onto. But she didn't.

You're what I call a fighter-dancer. It may not come to you easily, but your grit and warrior spirit will bring you places. That's what her mentor had said in the break of the Nutcracker. *The two greatest Warriors are Patience and Time.* The note Doctor Geuze had given her. For mental strength Edda kept repeating these sentences in her head to make sure she wouldn't let go of the railing. She also prayed to her butterfly, as always pinned to her coat. She even forgot about Rick being in the same position. All she could do was pray. All she could think was survival. Surviving.

Suddenly the Kubelwagen veered off the road and drove through loose sand, then sputtered and slowed down. Edda and Rick let themselves fall off the back before the car had stopped and hid behind a nearby dune. The night was dark and moonless. The North Sea roared in the distance. Two men got out of the front, just as Edda had hoped, and walked around the van.

"*Mal sehen ob er noch lebt,*" One joked to the other. *Let's see if he's still alive.*

How dare they! Edda fumed to herself.

One lit a cigarette while the other opened the back door. Edda could only see dark shadows, but it was as if she had laser eyes. Then a soft moaning came from inside the car. It only further increased the adrenaline levels in her veins. She cocked her gun and heard Rick do the same.

"You take the left one, I'll take the right one," she whispered, and he whispered back, "got him in my vision."

It was over before Edda realized what she'd done. Aim, fire, aim again, fire again. Rick's gun went off at almost exactly the same time. The Germans fell to their knees and then toppled to their sides. One left, one right. With guns aimed and cocked again, Edda and Rick inched closer, stealthily taking stock. Edda's victim was still moving, so she aimed again. She didn't think of the German. Her only thoughts were for Ome Jan lying in that car, moaning behind his gag.

When they were sure the Germans were dead, Edda searched their pockets for the car keys and stuffed their guns in her belt, while Rick unbound Ome Jan's hands and peeled the gag from his mouth. He seemed unconscious but alive. From cold-blooded killer, Rick instantly switched to doctor, listening to Ome Jan's heart and feeling his pulse.

"We can't take him to Amsterdam in this condition," he said. "He needs proper care as soon as possible."

"I know a safe house in Haarlem not far from here. Edgar's place. Let's go fast," Edda suggested. They tried to make Ome Jan as comfortable as possible on top of Rick's coat. Rick stayed with him in the back, while Edda steered the strange heavy car back onto the road and slowly drove the five miles to Edgar's house, a journalist from Tante Riet's LO organization.

Leaving the Kubelwagen under the trees of a nearby park, they carried the heavy, unconscious victim to the safe house. Edda prayed to God for extra strength because with every step she became more frazzled and exhausted. As they deposited the tall shape that once was Ome Jan on the doorstep, she panted for breath.

Rick knocked on the side door, which opened within seconds. Edgar in his dressing gown and pipe asked no questions, just opened the door wider. They carried Ome Jan inside and lay him on the sofa in the back room. He was in a worse shape than they had been able to see in the dark, breathing in a wheezing way.

"Let me light an extra lamp," Edgar said in his posh, Dutch accent. While he busied himself with dragging a heavy floor lamp closer, Edda stared down at Ome Jan's formless shape.

The right side of his face was as good as gone. Where his eye had been was one gaping hole with the eyeball hanging out. The rest of his face was a pulpy mess, his nose was broken, his mouth blown up like a balloon, teeth missing. His right arm was also in a strange twist and blood oozed from a wound on his chest.

"Will he make it?" Edda sobbed, fervently wiping the tears from her cheeks. Rick had already taken his small medical kit from his backpack.

"I'll do the best I can, but I haven't got sufficient equipment with me for these kinds of wounds."

"Let me run and get Doctor Geuze. He lives right around the corner. He's a specialist at the hospital but he might be able to help here." Edgar was already slipping into his winter coat.

"Great," Rick answered without looking up. Edda gasped. Could it be her doctor from the Wilhelmina Gasthuis? It had to. Suddenly, she could relax. If Rick got assistance from Doctor Geuze, Ome Jan had a chance.

She sank in a chair and momentarily closed her weary eyes. Someone pushed a glass of water in her hand, and with difficulty she opened her eyes again. It was Edgar's wife, Elizabeth. All code names, of course. Edda drank greedily and with gratitude accepted a piece of bread that was also pushed into her clenched hands.

Edgar was back within minutes with the white-haired doctor on his heels. Edda didn't know whether to stay where she was or to slip to another room. What would he think? He who saved people's lives, while she had just killed a man in cold-blood to save another. But it was too late. Her body wouldn't get up and the doctor was already in the room. He took no notice of her, though, his medical training drawing his eyes immediately and exclusively to the heavily-wounded man on the couch.

"Hello, my assistant-doctor, meeting under different circumstances, heh?"

"Yes, Doctor Geuze. I'm sorry to involve you in this." So, Rick was Doctor Geuze's assistant at the Wilhelmina Gasthuis? Edda pieced the bits of information together. Hadn't doctor Geuze told her he abhorred the treatment of Jews even before the war? Was the old doctor himself involved in the Resistance? He had to be if Edgar could fetch him late at night like this...

"Let me see what I can do here." The elderly doctor sank on his knees and opened his medical bag. "By God, they have roughed this one up."

"I fear for his eye, Doctor. It's been out for a couple of hours." Rick said.

"No worries, assistant, we'll pop in back in. Hand me the tweezers, while I let the poor man sleep a little deeper."

"I'm so glad you're here, Doctor." Edda could hear the thankfulness in Rick's voice. She felt exactly the same.

"No worries, lad. I'm just glad to help. Just glad to help."

The two medics worked together like a well-oiled machine, but seemed to take a long time. Ome Jan was, meanwhile, so deeply sedated he didn't wince or moan anymore.

After what seemed like hours later, Doctor Geuze, seemingly still as fresh as dew, sat down in one of Edgar's armchairs with the light-blue eyes resting on Edda. As he drank the coffee Elizabeth had offered him, he first said nothing. But after emptying the cup, he said, "Come here, girl."

Edda didn't know what he meant but she went over to stand by his chair. "Get that stool and sit in front of me." Again she did as she was told. As she sat opposite him, eye to eye, he studied her and finally said, "How are you feeling, my dear?"

"Not well," she replied honestly, pressing back her tears. "I've done something I'd thought I'd never do, and the worst is I didn't feel anything at all."

"You did the right thing, my dear. And doing the right thing is not always easy. Believe me. But, I think you need a little extra help in order to get some sleep."

Edgar and Elizabeth had been listening in, while they gave Rick food and coffee.

"If you mean that these three are staying here tonight, there is no question about it. But how do we get word to Jan's sister that he's going to come around? Using the telephone will be too dangerous."

"And we have to deal with the Kubelwagen that Hannie parked a few streets down." Rick observed. Edda had completely forgotten about the stray German car.

"I know just the men to push it into the dark side of the canal. Give me the keys, Hannie and we'll take care of that too," Edgar offered.

The elderly doctor's eyes were still resting on Edda with that benign look in them.

"My shift starts at six. And being a doctor has its benefits, though I mainly cater to German patients these days. I still have my car. I'll drive past the house and drop a note in Tante Riet's mailbox."

"You know, Tante Riet?" Edda asked surprised.

"You'd be better off asking who I don't know," the doctor chuckled. "But now that a sleeping place is arranged for tonight, I'll give you and Rick a chance at some proper sleep with this." He held up a small white pill between his fingers. "On one condition."

"And that is?" Edda asked.

"That you two *and* Ome Jan stay away from Amsterdam for a while. The Germans will be toughening their grip on all the contacts Ome Jan had. You three must disappear to the provinces for a while."

"But I need to dance,' Edda protested.

"If you stay out of the claws of these maniacs that are capable of doing this kind of damage..." the doctor pointed to the sleeping man on the sofa, "you can do all the dancing you want for the rest of your life."

"Doctor Geuze is right, Hannie," Edgar chimed in, "We'll get you three out to a farm in Zeeland for a while, far from the 'maddening crowds,' as Thomas Hardy used to write."

"How do we get there?" Rick asked.

"We'll get you there. I'll arrange it," Edgar assured them. "But now, sleep."

"Will you let Tante Riet know and my ballet mistress aka Vogeltje I'll be gone for a while?" Edda asked.

"All will be arranged. For now, sleep."

34

ZEELAND

Ten months later

A small village in Zeeland, 16 January 1944

I don't want to betray my kind hosts, the farmer couple Nan and Geert (code names) here on the island of Zuid-Beveland by writing down exactly where I am. Having had to hide in a hurry, without being able to bring any personal belongings, made me aware I'm not only putting myself in danger with these diaries but also other people. I knew being with the Resistance meant danger but silly me never considered becoming an actual suspect to the Germans. Well, I've certainly woken up to that reality now! But it could be way worse.

I just read in The Parool (our illegal national newspaper) that a horrible drama involving (mostly) Resistance women took place in Konzentrationslager Herzogenbusch near Vught. Seventy-four female prisoners 'sanctioned' another prisoner by throwing water over her, cutting her braids, and taking her mattress. This woman, Agnes Jedzini, had snitched on fellow-prisoners to Camp Commander SS-Hauptsturmführer Adam Grünewald in exchange for an early release. Jedzini reported what the women had done to her to the prison leadership. Horrible retaliatory measures followed. Seventy-four women were locked up in a tiny cell called 'de Bunker.' Grünewald himself kicked the door shut. The cell was not even 10 feet by 10 feet, and it did not have any ventilation. After fourteen hours the cell was opened. Ten of the women had died.

I can't stop thinking about them. I could have been one of them. Instead, I'm relatively safe here, having a lot more food and fresh air than in Amsterdam and great company.

Nan gave me this old notebook to scribble in. It's an abandoned ledger but who cares? Ome Jan is recovering well - thank God - and has lost none of his old fighting spirit nor his humor. But he's permanently lost sight of his right eye and his broken arm is healed at an odd angle. "I'll be a king forever now, Hannie," he said to me, fixing me with his one good eye. I asked him what kind of king. Which made him roar with laughter very much like Tante Riet, though with more bass. "Because we're in the land of the blind, girl. These Krauts have no idea what they're doing so, I'm the one-eyed king!"

Despite all the joking and big talk, Ome Jan's still quite weak and very grateful to be alive. He tells everyone who wants to hear it Rick and I saved his life. I even heard him sing our praises to Nan and Geert's black and white splotched dairy cows. Well, I guess we did save his life. I haven't come to terms yet, with what Rick and I did that night. The whole thing—from us lying in the grass to me pulling the trigger and then the night in Haarlem and seeing Doctor Deuze—seems as if it all happened to someone else, not to me, like I'm looking into a story about someone else's life.

I try not to think too much about it, to not revisit the images when I can help it because they upset me so much. I find it easiest just to live for today and help at the farm and concentrate on trudging to the end of this darn war. Rick and I also don't talk about it. I think he feels the same, but I don't know.

What I do know is that I couldn't face living without Ome Jan. He's like a real uncle to me and I feel closer to him and Tante Riet now than to my own family. They ARE my family now.

So, we're at a dairy farm in the middle of nowhere. I help milking cows (a novelty!) and play checkers for hours with Ome Jan or listen to Radio Oranje. Everyone is against the Germans here, so we're free to speak our minds.

The war gets crazier by the day. We all hope and pray it will be over soon. The Germans and Italian *fascists are getting squashed on all fronts, so that's good news. The American 5th army has launched the Gustav offense in Italy. Can you imagine? Allied troops are actually on the European Continent and they are heading north. German cities are bombed constantly by the Brits and the Americans, and Soviet troops are at the pre-war Polish border.*

So, Herr Hitler, your friend Signor Mussolini is already dead and you and Meneer Mussert, and all your henchmen, will soon follow. Oranje Boven!

Edda closed her diary and stuffed it under her mattress. Then she took to staring out of the window of her small bedroom on the first floor of Nan and Geert's farmhouse. The flat land with its meadows and polders, ditches in between, resembled so much the landscape of her youth and Edda suddenly yearned for her early years in Friesland, for the stately Valkena Estate, itself a country house with cattle and farmland.

How good life had been at the time, how peaceful and tranquil, at least on the surface. Mama, Papa, Duifje, and Mevrouw Miedema wielding her rolling pin and soup spoon in the kitchen. Her first dance steps in Madame Tissé's Ballet School on the Franekerstraat in Leeuwarden, the lazy afternoons reading in the hammock in the garden. To Edda's war-weary eyes, that period now seemed like heaven.

Though the cracks had been there right along. Mama's coldish attitude to her stepdaughter, Duifje's loud scrimmages with Papa, Mama's idolizing of Herr Hitler's charm and rhetoric. Edda had witnessed the Van der Valk disarray around her, staying silent and withdrawn. A bookish girl unless she was sliding along the parquet floor at the ballet school. Only then the subdued colors of her butterfly wings came to life. A gritty girl. *Oh Ash! Oh Ash, where are you now?*

The dark-gray January sky hung low and damp over the stretched-out, empty meadows. With no Germans in sight, the only reminder of the war was the occasional plane roaring overhead, invisible beyond the blanket of clouds.

The sky held no answers for Edda. It was as opaque as the question of what had happened to the Hoffmanns. Over a year had passed since she'd witnessed their arrest, and all those months, nothing—no letter, no sign of life. And now she herself wasn't at home in case Ash returned and was looking for her.

It was a small comfort Tante Riet knew she was safely away from Amsterdam, but would Ash go to Tante Riet? Edda consoled herself with the thought he probably would. He knew she was close to her neighbor.

And then there was Miss Sterling. What had happened to her mentor now Edda wasn't training for Sylphide? Had she fallen back into her blue funk? It was another small comfort knowing her mentor wasn't alone in her dreary house in Amsterdam-Oost worrying about Monsieur Sergeyev.

'Volgetje' was staying in her Vondelstraat flat to give the impression Ballerina Van der Valk still lived there. And that way Miss Sterling could more easily slip over to Tante Riet's house and support the LO organization. Edda missed her mentors and her Amsterdam life with a sudden pang of loneliness.

Loneliness?

Without warning, her thoughts wandered off to her family in Leiden and The Hague. No word from them for more than a year as well. And now the tide of the war was possibly turning, would she ever see them again? Would they be able to bury the hatchet when Hitler finally lost? Could she forgive her parents and her sister and brother-in-law for the betrayal of their countrymen and women?

"I have to write them a letter. I really must," Edda thought aloud. "They may have changed their minds now they can see for themselves Mussolini was insane, and Hitler not far from being off-beam either. They must have come to their senses, seeing how all the Jews have been deported and Dutch people are being killed for no reason at all."

But Edda didn't grab her pen and writing pad. What could she write? That she was a murderess hiding on a farmstead in the south of Holland? Because that was the truth. And the truth would be the final blow to their fragile family relations.

"Hannie, are you there?" Nan's strong voice called from downstairs. It shook her from her wool-gathering.

"Coming."

Edda descended the narrow wooden staircase that had no covering and entered Nan's bright, spick-and-span kitchen. It was the only place properly heated in the large farm stead and the hub of the house. Here folk entered to eat, rest, chat and catch their breath and some warmth. On this rare occasion Nan was alone in the kitchen. Her light eyes looked up from salting pork.

"You're alright?" The always-busy farm wife was kind and cordial but in the months Edda had stayed under her roof, she had never asked anything about her Resistance background. Though everyone seemed to know she was a dancer. Ome Jan proudly told everyone. But that was about it. The less one knew about someone, the better protected everyone was. That was the unwritten rule of the Dutch Resistance.

Edda had naturally gravitated to Nan's warmth, as she'd done to Tante Riet and Miss Sterling. Warmth was something she'd not found in her own mother but had always needed from an early age. As she sat down at the table, she started shuffling the black and white checkers around on the board.

"Yes, thank you, Nan. I'm fine. It's nice and warm in here. What are you doing?"

"Geert slaughtered our last pig today so I'm salting the meat. That way it will last us the rest of winter. It's just a pity the Salomons don't eat pork." Nan referred to the Jewish family hidden in the barn. Edda followed Nan's busy hands. Her own hands were so empty.

"Do you miss dancing, Hannie?"

The question struck Edda as if someone had slapped her

forehead.

"Oh, that's it," she blurted out. "I just didn't realize. Yes, I miss dance very much."

How could she not have thought of it herself? Because she was Hannie, she was in her *other* life, her Resistance life, that had dominated Edda's life for so long now. But ballet was the core of Edda's being. And she *was* Edda. Hannie was only temporarily. Hannie had heroically plodded on, done what she could, basked in the friendship of strangers, but Edda missed what had been her own since she was four years old. Her own and no one else's.

"So, it's dance I miss," she repeated with pursed lips.

"Well, there you've got the answer as to why you're so out of sorts. If you've got to dance, you know what to do."

"You mean I should return to Amsterdam? Will it be safe?"

"It will not be safe. Nothing is safe these days. But you can live with that. As long as you keep your eyes and ears wide open. Geert and I will look after Ome Jan a little longer Would that help?"

"Yes, it would. And what about Rick?"

"He'll be going soon as well. He told me he wants to return to his job at the hospital as soon as possible."

And with that Edda, with a small bundle containing the clothes Nan had given her and a borrowed toothbrush and gifted ledger, hitched a ride back to Amsterdam in the back of a lorry belonging to one of Geert's friends.

She arrived in the Vondelstraat in the early evening in mid-January 1944. Just before curfew, she let herself into her flat. No mail piled up this time behind her door like it had done after her return with her broken ankle. Ash had not written to her.

But Miss Sterling stood smiling in the door to her sitting room.

35

THE VISITOR

The next day – Amsterdam, 17 January 1944

The next morning it was so cold in Edda's apartment, she didn't have the nerve to get out of bed. There was not a brick of coal in the house and the water pipes were frozen. There was also no food. She knew she needed to muster the courage to run down the garden path and knock on Tante Riet's door, but she felt too weak and feverish.

Miss Sterling had temporarily gone back to her own apartment now Edda was home.

"Just a few minutes more," she promised herself as her teeth clattered and her cheeks glowed. "Then I'll make the sprint."

She must have fallen asleep again because, when she next opened her eyes, the light peeked through the blackout curtains and her watch told her it was eleven in the morning. Her mouth was parched and a fever was raging. She couldn't keep her legs still, they wriggled and spasmed under the covers as clothes blowing around on a washing line. Panic set in, as she lacked the strength to call on her neighbor, who didn't even know she'd arrived back in Amsterdam.

"Just a little longer. Then I'll go."

But Edda's thoughts were incoherent, her head swimming like sunbeams through floating clouds. Somewhere in her fever she heard a rapping on her door.

"Mama?"

Her cracked lips formed the sounds so slowly. The longing to see her mother was so overwhelmingly urgent, Edda crawled out of bed and towards the front door. Her hot, fever-plagued limbs almost froze to the frigid hallway tiles but the single focus of her mother made Edda pull herself along. Mama had come. Mama would make it alright.

"Mama, are you there?"

"Edda?"

The voice wasn't her mother's, but Edda passed out and had no recollection of what happened next. When she came around, someone was pushing a cup against her lips. She drank greedily. The liquid tasted like metallic, like iron, like blood. Still, she smacked her lips and felt how it wetted her cork-dry palate and throat.

"Is that better?" The vaguely familiar voice next to her asked. The voice was not from around here. Her eyelids were too heavy to open. Who was the woman? The thought occupied Edda for a fleeting moment until she was asleep again.

The ritual repeated every time she woke. A cup held to her lips, the iron-tasting drink, the vaguely familiar voice asking if she was alright. Her eyes too weary to open. Was she alright? She had no idea. She had no idea where she was and who was with her. Until the voice said with pressing determination, "Edda, I need you to tell me how you are. You seem very ill."

"I don't know who you are," Edda tried to croak but her voice was gone and it barely came out in a whisper. The woman shook her arm, repeating the question with even more urgency.

"I want to get you a doctor, but I don't dare leave you alone. Is there anyone who can help you? Anyone?"

That's a trick question, Edda's befuddled mind thought. *I'm not going to answer that. Perhaps, it's a spy at my bedside.*

She didn't reply and slept again. When she woke next, she could open her eyes. The light from outside was gone. Her head was swimming a little less. She could focus. She was sure there was someone else in the room with her. The person was snoring lightly, so she was asleep.

It must be nighttime, Edda realized. But what day or hour was unclear. How long she'd slept was also beyond guessing. As the room was draped in blackness, she couldn't see who the other person was. But the idea there was someone with her was strangely comforting. Then she remembered thinking it was a spy who'd come to snitch on her because of what she'd done. Clearly it hadn't been a trap, or she would have long been arrested by the Germans.

Who was she? It wasn't Mama or Duifje. It also wasn't Tante Riet or Miss Sterling. Edda tried to recall who else she knew, but thinking was hard. Could it be Natasja from the ballet school? But Edda didn't think she knew Edda's address. The woman stirred in her sleep, then suddenly spoke.

"Are you awake, Edda?"

"Maria?"

"Yes, it's me."

"What are you doing here, Maria?"

"Oh, thank God, Edda, are you clearer now? I... I came to see you. I actually came to ask you a favor, but I found you more dead than alive, so I ended up looking after you in the past days."

"Oh," Edda smiled despite her weak state. "I must have been a horrible patient."

"No more demanding than on stage," Maria retorted. "But I'm glad you're back in the land of the living. I'd brought some food, luckily, but I couldn't get the fire or the stove going. There's no coal. It's freezing in here. I tried to keep you warm but you kept throwing off the blankets every time your fever went up."

"Maria," Edda repeated, confused, puzzled, but also elated. If her Russian rival hadn't shown up, would she have pulled through? Maybe she now owed her life to Maria Petrova. How strange life was. "I've been rather ill, haven't I?"

"Yes, you've had a bad bout of the flu, very bad. I wanted to get you a doctor but I had no clue how to go about that. So, I did what I could. Kept you hydrated and as warm as possible."

Maria switched on the bedside lamp. She came into Edda's view, huddled in a bedspread. "Are you hungry? I can get you some bread."

Edda stared up at her former rival. Maria looked different. Still tall, copper-haired, and willowy, but taut and skeletal, with dark shadows under the gray eyes. As if she hadn't been eating for a month, but was eaten away by worries.

"Perhaps in a minute. How did you get here, Maria? Are you alright yourself?"

"I am now, Edda. I'm just very glad I could look after you. I came to ask you if I could stay with you for a while. Of course, I've got my food coupons and I can pay for rent. I've been... I am... in a bit of trouble."

"Oh, I see." But before Edda could ask what sort of trouble Maria was in, her head started swimming again. "We'll talk later. Okay? I'm awfully tired."

"Wait, let me get you another cup of cold tea and some broth. It's the best I can do without a heater. Then you sleep."

"Thank you so much, Maria," Edda mumbled as she dozed off even before the arrival of the cold tea, wondering what sort of trouble *La* Petrova had found.

When Edda woke the next morning, her head felt a little better. Maria was already up and puttering around in the kitchen. She could hear her hum an unknown song in an unknown language. A little later she stood in the doorway, wearing at least two sweaters and a cardigan. The extra layers made her look like a Matryoshka—the traditional, Russian, wooden nesting dolls.

"How are you feeling?" she asked.

"I'm better, thank you."

"I found some wood in the back garden, so I managed to get the fire going," Maria said proudly. "And there was a kind neighbor out there. She asked who I was, so I told her I danced with you and that I was staying with you while you have been ill. She said she thought you were gone. Have you been away?"

"For a while,' Edda replied vaguely. "That's Tante Riet. She's awfully nice."

"She is. She gave me a basket with three eggs and half a loaf of bread. Told me not to use the basket for firewood but leave it on her doorstep. We're going to indulge like queens this morning—A hot stove *and* eggs!"

As the girls ate, Edda studied Maria. There had already been a change in her attitude when she returned to Amsterdam in June 1941, but the war years had not been favorable to former Bolshoi dancer. She seemed edgy and skittish, her eyes going to the door as if she expected an unwelcome visitor any minute.

"What is it, Maria?" Edda was half sitting, half lying back in the cushions, still sweaty and feverish, but needing to know what was going on with her lodger.

"You really want to know?"

"Yes, or I wouldn't have asked. You seem so on-edge."

"I feel my story is small potatoes compared to the suffering the Dutch have to endure under the Nazi regime, but I can tell you the Soviet Union isn't all sweet cream and pies either. Far from it." Maria stopped talking, her eyes flitting to the door another time.

"Nobody is coming here, Maria. Go on."

"Stalin's arms reach far, as well. I was declared a *persona non grata* in 1937 because my family spoke out against Stalin's regime. We're old Russian gentry, a class that's been under scrutiny since the so-called Russian Revolution in 1918. There's nothing revolutionary about the new system. Communism is even worse than what we had with the Tsars. People in the West don't seem to understand. Western intellectuals and artists flirt with Communism as if it's the new Paradise, but I tell you, the way it functions in the Soviet Union is dictatorial and far from equality for all."

Maria stopped talking for a moment, but she looked less nervous.

Unburdening herself seemed to ground her more. Edda focused on her face, trying to keep her eyes open. She was fascinated, wanted to stay awake and listen.

"Anyway, my father, a newspaper owner, has always been critical of the Communists despite the consequences he faced. In 1937 he wrote about the mass murders conducted by Stalin, and called it the 'Year of Terror' and the 'Great Purge.' He should have gone abroad, taken us to Paris. But he didn't. He wanted to stay. My father is a silly hero. Of course, he and my mother were arrested and disappeared." Maria sniffed. Softly she added, "that's why I tried to get back home just before the war. To see if I could get information about them."

"And did you?"

"No, nothing. They disappeared without a trace. Like millions of others. Murdered, no doubt. But I had fled just in time, you see, to prevent facing the same fate. I'm as against Communism as my father is...was...but I also want to live. And I want to dance. I had made a name for myself as first ballerina with Bolshoi Ballet so I was in the limelight and with my last name I knew I was in danger. Friends also warned me I was on the list. They helped me escape over the Polish border. That's how I ended up here, first in Berlin and then travelled on to Amsterdam in 1938. I knew Pyotr Sergeyev, of course. He, too, was known in the Russian ballet scene. At the time, I thought I was on my way to London."

Maria stopped talking. Edda had closed her eyes.

"Go on," she said with a tired voice. "I am listening."

"But you need to rest, Edda. I can tell you the rest later. And I know you've got worries of your own apart from this flu."

"Then there's two of us, *personae non grata*, Maria. Just continue."

"Alright. So, I fell in love with a Russian here in Amsterdam. Thought he loved me too. Turns out he's a secret agent for the Kremlin. Here to keep an eye on me. So, I'm on the run again."

"Oh no, and here was I thinking your boyfriend was German. You must leave Amsterdam, Maria! Perhaps even Holland." Edda was wider awake now.

"I guess so. I took enough precautions, so he doesn't know where I am. I left when he was asleep. Put something in his drink and you know how Russians like their vodka—they'll finish the whole bottle if they can. I made sure he finished his. Still, it was frightful."

"It won't be easy to go abroad with Russian papers. We will have to get you a false passport. Or you could hide, or disguise yourself? Dye your hair, wear a wig," Edda suggested.

"I wish I could stay," Maria sighed. "I'm tired of being on the run but I have no place anymore. I can't go back to my flat. He now knows I know."

"Maybe Miss Sterling can help," Edda mumbled half asleep. "For now you can stay here, Maria. It's no problem."

"Are you still seeing Miss Sterling?"

"I was before ... uh... something happened, and I had to hide for a while. We were busy preparing a dance performance, Sylphide. Oh, I wish you'd stay and we could dance it together. Miss Sterling had such a hard time choreographing it for one. What if you joined me? It's a camouflage act for me as well."

"So, it's true you are with the Resistance, Edda?"

"That's a question you should never ask and will never get an answer to. At least not as long as this war rages," Edda mumbled. "But please consider dancing Sylphide with me." Despite her sleepiness, she was aware how strange these words sounded. Dancing with her rival. Who'd have thought, she'd ever propose such a thing to Maria Petrova?

"Sylphide with you sounds great." Gratitude laced the Russian's voice. "Old hatchets buried, that kind of thing. But I fear it's out of the question, Edda. My dance style is too well known. The spies would know in seconds it's me dancing. My height and everything."

"That's true..." Edda dozed off wishing life was different than what it was.

～

THE NEXT THING SHE KNEW, both Tante Riet and Miss Sterling were sitting on either side of her bed. And sunlight was pouring through the open shutters.

"Are you returning to the living, Miss Van der Valk," her mentor asked with a smile. "What on earth happened to you? Did you fall off the surface of the earth?"

"Where's Maria?" Edda sat upright with a sudden jerk. Afraid she'd dreamed Maria was with her.

"I'm here! I'm making tea," Maria called from the kitchen. Edda relaxed. She'd dreamed of Russian men with very long arms and knives between their teeth. They'd been cutting up her mattress but hadn't found Maria. They'd discovered her diaries, though, and cut up those as well, grinning and drinking vodka. It was a relief to find it had only been a bad dream.

"So how are you feeling, kindje?" Tante Riet asked, pushing a plate with a freshly baked bun under Edda's nose. It smelled delicious. She took the plate and kept holding her nose over it. It was almost too sweet-smelling to bite into it. The flu must be on the way out.

"Oh, and before I forget, I've got great news," Tante Riet smirked. "Jan's sent me a coded note through a messenger. He's doing well."

Edda had in her illness completely forgotten about her escape time in Zeeland.

"I'm so glad." Her heart made a little jump. It hadn't been easy to leave Ome Jan behind.

"Thanks to you, Edda. He couldn't tell me everything, of course, for fear of the letter being intercepted but I can read between the lines. You're amazing, kindje."

"Our Edda certainly is," Miss Sterling joined in "I'm so happy Maria is here as well. We've already discussed continuing with Sylphide as soon as you're on your feet again, my dear."

"But... Maria is in danger...," Edda begun.

"Don't worry about me." Maria came into the room with the tea. "If you can face your challenges, I'll face mine. We, the Resistance Girls, are strong and defiant."

"That we are!" Tante Riet hooted. "And we're here to kick some tail."

Edda bit into her bun and for a brief spell the war was far away, and female friendship was warm and plentiful.

36

DUIFJE BREAKS

Two months later

Amsterdam, March 1944

The war drags on and on. The Soviets are making good progress in the East, defeating the Germans a little more every day. However, after what Maria told me about her country, I'm not sure we want the Communists on our doorstep either. We may backslide into just another tyranny.

On the Western Front (mainly in southern Europe) the Allied progress is much slower. And there's an awful lot of talk about a landing somewhere on the Atlantic Coast to free us, but nothing concrete so far.

The Allied forces ARE constantly dropping bombs on Germany, but accidents happen as well. We still reel from the late February RAF bombing of Nijmegen. As we now know, hundreds of citizens died in this 'accidental bombing'. The tragedy is almost as big as that of Rotterdam at the beginning of the war, but it's all a bit hush-hush. There's shame involved with the sadness and rage because it was 'the good guys' who failed by accident. Oh, the horrible collateral damage of war. It simply must stop!

What's also getting worse is that everyday Resistance fighters are rounded up and shot dead. There is no form of legal process at all anymore. And if the Resistance manages to bring damage to German positions or installations, the Nazis immediately retaliate. The papers will talk of a razzia here or a razzia there. A dozen innocent civilians killed, sometimes fifty, or even a hundred.

We haven't heard of more murders of the gentlemen held hostage in St. Michielsgestel after Ludo became a victim. He lost his life for no reason at all. These massacres of innocent people— not even in the Resistance! — infuriates me so; it makes me even more determined NEVER to give up!

My work is not heroic at all. Tante Riet still wants me to keep a low profile after committing one of the worst crimes against the Germans: killing two of them. I would love to do more, take part in the sabotages, etc. but I agree. The Germans are still on the hunt for the perpetrator of the Mysterious Haarlem Dune Killings as The Parool termed it. I couldn't face having people killed for what I did with my own hands. Because the strange thing is - as far as we know - there has not yet been any retaliation for what Rick and I did. Just a manhunt.

One day soon I'll step forward. All I do now is relocate Jews who are on the brink of being discovered. It is horrible to see how many Dutch people are willing to betray their countrymen and women for a little extra food or cigarettes.

Yesterday I moved a Jewish family—man, wife and two little daughters—from the Merwedestraat to Alkmaar. I hope they will survive the war but it's becoming more difficult to feed and clothe all our hiders and to keep them safe.

I truly hope all these snitchers will be heavily punished after the war. How ugly can one's soul become for a little bit of material wellbeing. I honestly don't believe there's much ideology behind it. Not anymore.

Still no word of Ash, nor of Larry. I fear the worst. We aren't sure, but there are more and more rumors that very, very bad things are happening to the Jews and Resistance fighters in the camps in Germany and Poland. Also, Gypsies and even handicapped people are deported. I hardly dare to believe it's true, but they say prisoners are not working in labor camps but are actually sent straight to gas chambers to be murdered there!

Other people say that that isn't true. The Joodsche Raad also doesn't want to believe the rumors. They claim all the Jews sent East are working and will eventually return or relocate to where they are now. I don't trust the happy-ending story at all, certainly not if I listen to the anti-Jew rhetoric spewing from the likes of Hitler and Goebbels.

No word from my family either. I hope Mama is well. I do miss her, as I miss Duifje. Papa...I'm not so sure. He was so ugly to me the last time we spoke. Not allowing me to be in touch with Ash. I can't easily forget that. Still, I wish Papa well and hope he'll see his grave error in judgement at some point.

It's back to dancing and doing my duty for my country again. Maria is a great sport. Who'd have thought! We're friends now and I love having her stay with me. She sleeps on my couch in the sitting room but doesn't complain. Maria's a magical cook, able to turn turnips and potatoes into some sort of a tasty mash night after night. If it wasn't for her, I'd probably lose even more weight. Well, let's hope this craziness is over in a couple of weeks and we have more to eat. Or at least more variation! It's horrible to be hungry all the time.

Herr Hitler and Meneer Mussert, I'm so done with you! Just move on, will you and give us peace. And to Mr Churchill and Mr Roosevelt I'd like to say, hurry up! Millions of people in Europe and the Far East are suffering enormously. I can't imagine how many people are being killed for no reason all over the world. It seems like a whole generation is wiped out because of this senseless war, through the bombings, at the hands of fascists, and through useless battles by young *soldiers whose only wish it is to return home to their families with their limbs intact and their hearts beating.*

The world has gone insane and all I can do is dance to feel a little better.

"I think we're ready to roll, ladies." Miss Sterling was sitting next to the record player and put the needle to La Grande Valse Brilliante, the last piece of music in Les Sylphides. Originally Chopin's waltz, but rearranged by Stravinsky for this ballet, it was already Edda's favorite piano piece of all time, but certainly now. It was an upbeat waltz and great fun to dance together with Maria.

They were both Sylphides in Miss Sterling's choreography, spirit beings whose sole purpose it was to put a spell on human males, much like the Sirens in the Odyssey.

Feigning they were just two innocent ballerinas giving high-ranking German officials a magical night out, but to secretly throw dust in the occupiers' eyes. Whether the magic spell worked, they'd find out the next day when they were to perform in a small theater off the Rembrandtplein, where German officers came to dine.

"I'd like to see that last scene one more time and then we call it a day. It'll be time for our other job," the ballet mistress announced. Edda and Maria took up their positions facing each other. This was the only rehearsal they got. Tomorrow night was showtime.

Maria and Edda danced as best as they could in Edda's cramped sitting room. Used as they both were to spacious stages, it was make-do, but they didn't complain. Despite it being a cover-up, the two professional ballerinas wanted to give the very best performance they were capable of.

"Alright, that will do, girls. I'm proud of you." The ballet mistress clapped her hands. The record player fell silent. Dusk was already falling. Drying the sweat from her neck and face, Edda felt strangely elated. The ballet had come to life since Maria had joined and though it was a first for both to dance without male partners, they both felt liberated, free from conventions, and in-tune with each other's energy: Maria strong and technically perfect, Edda lyrical and a firecracker. Their competencies balanced perfectly.

"Do you have any idea who's invited to our show, Miss Sterling?" Edda asked.

"Invitations have been sent to all the major players—Seyss-Inquart and his top men like Rauter have been invited, as well as the Meneer Mussert and his wife but it is said that this former civil engineer knows so little about ballet, he wouldn't know a *pirouette* from a *polonaise*."

Edda stiffened. *Would her father be there?* But she shook the thought from her. Gone were the days that Papa sat front and center in the plush chairs to cheer her on.

When Maria had gone out to stand in line at the grocery shop and Miss Sterling had gone home, Edda relished in an unusual alone moment. Tiredness was her constant companion these days, but it now amplified with worries about her parents possibly in the audience tomorrow. Mama and Papa were from a separate part of her life, on-hold until the end of the war. Seeing them now would be too upsetting, especially as the whole show was in a different light from her earlier ballets.

Completely cooped up in her musings, she almost jumped out of her skin when the doorbell rang. Long and shrill. Her nerves already strained, Edda considered not answering the door but it rang again. Longer. Brave-faced and watchful, she opened the front door ajar. A rained-out mail man in a dripping uniform stood holding a...

"Telegram for you, Miss." His voice was too cheery, and he shook himself like a dog emerging from a pool. Edda clenched her teeth, her heart missed at least three beats. Ash? Mama? Telegrams never brought good tidings. The mailman seemed unperturbed both by his delivery and by the bad weather. He was already turning his back on her, whistling like a bird in a tree.

"Thank you," she called after him as she banged the door shut with the flimsy, half soaked paper between her fingers. She put it on the sideboard, stared at it, considering opening it after dinner. But the calamity might be too big. She tore it open.

Teppo is dead. I am going to kill myself now. Duifje.

The words her eyes read couldn't make a connection in Edda's mind. The two sentences didn't seem to correlate. Teppo was dead. Her brother-in-law, Duifje's husband, the half-Jew who'd made it his job to betray other Jews in order to avoid being deported himself. That part was clear. That was awful. What had happened? How did he die? No mention of the circumstances in the telegram. But the second sentence was oh-so alarming, a desperate cry for help.

I'm going to kill myself now.

Was it real or drama-Duifje? Edda sank in a chair, trying to read the square letters dancing before her eyes once more. Trying to make sense of nonsense. *Duifje!* Her first impulse was to phone her sister, but the phone had been dead for a year. Writing back would take too long. Was Duifje already dead? Why was she dying too? Edda's befuddled mind refused to reach clarity on the disturbing matter. She tried to think but couldn't. The road ahead was blocked.

But Edda was Edda. A girl with an inner warrior spirit. She grabbed her coat and handbag, left a quick note for Maria assuring her she'd be back early the next morning, but an emergency had arisen at her sister's house in The Hague.

The train journey from Amsterdam Central to The Hague Bezuidenhout went by in a haze. It was already late in the afternoon, a watery sun dipping towards the horizon, mere hours before curfew. Edda risked it anyway, knowing she might arrive in front of a closed door, with no Duifje at home. Or a dead Duifje inside. She shuddered at the thought of what she'd find.

More panicking thoughts tumbled over each other. What if her sister had moved altogether? They hadn't spoken with each other for over a year. Anything could have happened in the meantime. And what about the children? Benny would be nine or ten now and Elly about four. Gosh, it was all so complicated and so maddening.

Sitting huddled in a corner of the slowly moving train, Edda was glad no German stopped her to check on her papers. She wouldn't have been able to cope with the oppressors right now. Family affairs were dominating her thoughts.

She hastened through The Hague's leafy suburbs to the Van Leeuwens' house. It looked deserted, the curtains closed, the garden gate still crooked, the garden unkept, with a wild bush of bright pink roses blooming baroquely against the south wall. No sight of Teppo's Renault Monaquatre.

Edda sped along the garden path and rang the bell with all her force. She even banged on the front door.

"Duifje are you there? Duifje, it's me Edda!"

Nothing. Could the maid have returned into service?

"Corrieeee!" Edda cried. Still nothing. Edda looked for a way to get around the semi-detached house and reach the backdoor, but the path was overgrown with bramble bushes. She listened for children's voices, crying in alarm at what their mother might have done to herself. Nothing. Should she try the neighbors? Edda now seriously doubted her impulsivity to travel all this way and find herself locked out in the dark after curfew. All she needed was to be careful herself and to sleep well before Sylphide the next evening.

Darn, Duifje, you always manage to create so much upheaval? Edda banged on the door again with both fists until they hurt. Almost crying and incredibly angry. Then, finally, she heard the faint sounds of a door being unbolted.

Her sister stood in the doorway, looking like she was a million years old. She was drunk, half-dressed in a stained negligée, her blonde hair glued in wet strings to one cheek, smoking her inevitable cigarette. At least Duifje wasn't dead. That was something. The sisters stood staring at each other without a word.

"Edda?" Duifje slurred at last. "What the heck are *you* doing here?"

"You sent me a telegram that you were going to kill yourself. Remember? That's why I am here." Edda's anger heightened at the stupor and disinterest her sister displayed at seeing her.

"Well, I'm still trying to kill myself, but it's a slow process, you see." Her sister leaned against the doorframe, a shaking hand going to her mouth with the burning cigarette. It landed against her chin.

She let the cigarette drop and extinguished it on the doormat with her slipper.

"What happened to Teppo? And for Heaven's sake, Duifje, let me inside."

"Do you want to come in?" Her sister's eyebrows went up. "Does holy Edda deem herself worthy to see her traitor sister? Why would you? What am I to you? Teppo is dead, dead you know."

Edda had enough of this drunken talk and half pushing her sister aside got inside and shut the door. The house reeked of stale smoke and alcohol.

"Where are Benny and Elly?" She strode into the disorderly sitting room and looked around her.

Duifje had staggered behind her. "They're with my in-laws. Teppo is dead, you know."

"Let me make you a strong cup of coffee and then tell me what happened."

"Oh sis, is it really you?" Duifje plunged towards her for an embrace but tripped over the loose sash of her dressing gown. She fell flat on the floor and giggled. Stayed face down on the carpet.

Edda rolled her sister over and tried to get her to her feet, but Duifje struggled to free herself, first laughing, then howling, finally crying hysterically.

"Teppo is dead!"

In the end Edda let her lie where she was and went to the kitchen to find the coffee pot. As she filled the kettle to boil the water, her hands were shaking violently. This time Duifje's tragedy was real but as usual, it was Edda, the younger one, who would have to cope with it. Her sister simply couldn't.

Edda wondered if she should phone their parents, demand them to take control of the situation, look after Duifje and her children. After all, she Edda, really needed to return to Amsterdam first thing in the morning. And what about Teppo's parents, who she'd only met at her sister's wedding. They would have their own grief to cope with besides looking after Benny and Elly.

While she made the coffee, a plan formed in her head. The least complicated approach seemed to be keeping it in the Van Leeuwen family. It might be cowardice, but Edda simply wasn't ready to face her own parents right now.

With the coffee and some slices of bread she'd found in a tin she went back to the sitting room. Duifje had dozed off, so she put the pot and bread on the table and shook her sister's shoulder.

"Wake up, Duifje, you need to sober up and tell me what happened."

Her sister grumbled something in her sleep and started vomiting. Edda raced to the kitchen for a washing-up bowl, but it was too late. Duifje retched and retched, spilling loads of little white pills amidst amber liquor. Edda gasped at the sight. Her sister had indeed tried to commit suicide. Then she panicked. Duifje needed a doctor. She raced to the phone on the sideboard, but it was dead. What now?

All of a sudden, a detached calm came over Edda. If the pills and the alcohol were out of Duifje's system, she would live. It would be a matter of keeping her warm and hydrated. Get her to bed. She quickly gulped down a cup of coffee herself as she really needed it. Then she lifted her sister from the ground. This time Edda didn't accept any struggle. She was not only emotionally stronger, she was physically the stronger one, too.

It was quite an undertaking to carry the limp and uncooperative Duifje up the stairs and put her in the shower. Duifje couldn't stand up, so Edda eased her onto hands and knees, got her out of the dressing gown and slip, and let the warm water pour over her. Manoeuvring in the small cubicle, Edda got half-wet herself, but she managed to wash most of the vomit out of her sister's hair, dried her with a not very clean towel and got her into a pair of Teppo's pyjamas —the only thing she could find.

Coffee and bread didn't seem what Duifje needed right now, so she fetched a glass of water and helped her swallow small sips. She was half-conscious now but at least no longer so intoxicated. When she was propped up against the pillows, Edda attempted to get some sense out of her, but Duifje had become even more incoherent.

"Okay, you sleep for a while. Then you tell me what happened before I must go home."

She let her sister sleep and as it seemed like she wouldn't wake up for a while, Edda decided to lie down next to her on what would have been Teppo's side and catch some sleep herself. The bed smelled of Eau de Cologne and cigarettes. And a vague smell Edda couldn't identify but was sickening. Probably unwashed sheets.

Sleep eluded her. As Duifje slept in fits and starts, Edda lay awake remembering a time they'd been children. On Sunday mornings she'd slip into Duifje's bed and the girls had lain together. Duifje had smelled heavenly then, a fresh girl's body and shampooed hair. How simple and sweet life had been then. Not a blur in the sky, where there were now only thunder clouds.

At some point Edda must have fallen asleep as well because she startled as she heard soft crying next to her. For a split second she had no idea where she was, then recognized her sister's voice and everything came back to her.

"Are you awake?"

"Edda?" Duifje sniffled, "is that you?"

"Had you forgotten I was here?"

"I think I had. Thank you for coming."

Edda reached for the bedside lamp. Then looked at her sister with concern. Duifje looked like a drowned cat but somehow also quite serene.

"How are you now? I'm so sorry for your loss." It sounded hollow, but what else was there to say?

"Oh Lientje, oh dear, dear, loyal Lientje. What would I do without you?"

"I had to come." Edda was almost crying herself now. "It was so horrible to get your telegram. Can you now tell me what happened?"

"I wish I knew." Duifje lit a cigarette and blew the smoke towards the ceiling. "I don't know what happened. We didn't even get the opportunity to say goodbye. One moment he was here in bed with me. Next moment he was dead. He was found in the shop on the Bierkade. Shot in the back of his head. In white letters they'd scrawled TRAITOR on the window. So, it's clear what the motive was."

"Oh Duifje, I'm so sorry."

"Are you really, Edda?" It sounded aggrieved. "I thought you didn't approve of what Teppo did? But he did it for us, you know. So, he could stay with me and the children and didn't have to work in a camp in Poland."

"I know, sister. It's terrible. So, when did it happen?"

"Two, maybe three days ago? I've lost track of time. I lost track of everything. The children were staying with Oma and Opa because of the holidays. They said Teppo's sister Ariane would look after them for a bit until I gathered myself again." Duifje inhaled, exhaled, drank some of the water, sniffed.

"I couldn't stop drinking. I couldn't stop myself. I went mad in this house. I had to do something terrible, but I kept running around in circles. I'm so sorry I upset you, Lientje."

"I'm glad you sent that telegram."

"The strange thing is I don't even remember going to the post office. But you saved my life, sis."

Duifje bent over and kissed Edda's cheek. She smelled sour and full of tears.

"Teppo is...was my everything. I know he wasn't always the easiest of husbands and a bit wild around the edges, but I loved him and he loved me. Oh, Edda! I really don't know how to live on. I'm not like you. I'm not strong. I depend on people."

"I know, sister. You've got me. I'm glad I came in time. Will you please, please promise me not to do stupid things like taking pills again? You also have Benny and Elly to think of, Duifje."

"I know. I'm a bad mother. I'm a bad everything."

"You're not."

~

TEPPO'S FUNERAL was a simple and quick affair with only immediate family and people from Van Leeuwen & Zoon IJzerwaren in attendance. Edda came down by train from Amsterdam dressed in the only black dress she still owned, a small pillbox black hat with voile on her dark curls, black stockings that had seen better days and her ordinary day shoes, brown, as that was the only pair she had left. It was a relief to see she wasn't the only one having had to scrape an outfit together. One lady was even wearing a beige cape.

The other family members present were Teppo's parents and his sister Ariane with her husband and young daughter. Edda's parents came in late. The back rows were filled with employees from the three Van Leeuwen ironware shops.

Frosty smiles were exchanged between Edda and her parents but no words. They took up their seats in the front row on either side of the softly crying Duifje, who was sitting in between her young son and daughter. Benny and Elly both sat very still in their white socks and identical black coats, big dry eyes and small pinched faces under curly fair hair.

Despite Duifje sniffling and blowing her nose in her handkerchief at regular intervals, she was more composed than when Edda had found her after her suicide attempt. Perhaps even more composed than she'd been in years.

Dressed in all black, her face a white sheet under a black veil, her blonde hair covered by spidery lace, she outwardly resembled just another young, war widow. Which, of course, she wasn't. The way her husband had died was uncommon and not a matter to be brought up in public. Teppo's choices were a stigma Duifje would have to carry for the rest of her life.

After the short ceremony held by a protestant priest and the internment at the Sint Barbara Begraafplaats, Edda kissed her sister goodbye and left the small, sad gathering with just one more brief nod in the direction of her parents. She did take a good look at her mother though, who seemed poised and healthy enough. Some part of Edda ached and another was stoical. She prayed that when this rigmarole was over, they would be a family once again. Maybe even better than they'd been before the war, but not now. Not under these circumstances.

The Marchioness did make a move as if coming in Edda's direction, but Edda's mind was made up. She waved a sad goodbye and slipped away from the cemetery. She walked in the early April sun back to the station and once more out of her family's life.

Not now, she kept repeating, *not now but later.*

37

THE SHADOW

Two months later

Amsterdam, 6 June 1944

The big day has come. The Allies are landing on the coast of Normandy today! Who'd have thought? All the rumors were about Norway or perhaps Calais, the north of France. It was a well-kept secret that apparently took the Germans by surprise. It is near Caen, where we once went for summer holidays. I remember it being pretty there, the coastline quite rough, here and there steep cliffs but also sandy beaches. Nothing pretty about it today, I can imagine. Glued to BBC radio all morning. Hope the Germans in Amsterdam are too busy listening to their own channels to go around rounding up our radios.

I find myself constantly praying that these young

soldiers and their commanders—Americans and Canadians and Scots and Englishmen—will all come on land safely, but I fear there will be many, many casualties. The Germans took great effort to build the Atlantic Wall all the way from the north of Norway right down to the Gulf of Biscay. They fortified the entire coastline in their possession so it's going to be a bloody battle. But how brave the Allies are!

Let's hope all goes to plan and they'll arrive in Holland soon. We can hold out another couple of months, certainly as summer is arriving, but not another year. I suppose they'll be heading for Paris first. American troops are also storming up through France from the south. It's a great tiding and it's giving us, in the Resistance, an enormous boost. Our numbers are growing every day and Tante Riet can hardly keep pace to organize IO but she's so good at it.

Tonight, I'm going to take part in my first arms drop north of Amsterdam. I won't disclose the location. Though it will be a risky undertaking, I'm quite excited about this trip. We must be very, very careful though. The Nazis are like injured hounds these days, more vicious than ever. Last week ten of our friends were arrested and never heard from again. I'm so cautious these days.

The ballet remains a great coverup. We're quite popular with the German officers and get all sorts of invitations to parties and soirees. Of course, Maria and

Miss Sterling and I don't accept them. We always say we have to get to bed early to be able to continue dancing.

The other benefit is that the Germans gift us all sorts of presents, mostly food in the form of fruits and candy. I'm so happy I can distribute those to Tante Riet to give it to those most in need.

Ome Jan is still not fully recovered, so he's keeping a low profile in the provinces. After a short return to Amsterdam, he's returned to Nan and Geert's farm in Zeeland, accompanied by his wife and daughter Marie. Tante Riet agreed, although she misses her brother dearly in her Amsterdam organization. He was too much at risk of being captured again because of his delicate health. Just don't think Ome Jan is resting on his laurels. On the contrary! He's preparing Zeeland for an early liberation, now with arms' supplies and giving shooting lessons. The search for the Mysterious Haarlem Dune Shooters (aka Rick and me) seems to have died.

Duifje is better than before, strangely enough. She's looking after Benny and Elly on her own. Her in-laws help her as well. I go down sometimes just to support her mentally. There's very little I can do for her, but she stays sober and feeds the children so that's good.

Herr Hitler and all your cronies, you're losing and we're winning! How's that for a change?

Edda dressed in her dark ballet outfit, put on a black raincoat for the nightly excursion. This time she unpinned Ash's brooch from the lapel of her coat. As always, she turned the butterfly longingly around between her fingers but decided to leave it in its box. The diamonds might flicker in the torchlights and betray them. With difficulty she put the brooch back on its black velvet cushion, gave it a light kiss and closed the box. Whenever she could, she wore it as a remembrance of their love and as a talisman to lure Ash back to her.

"Just not tonight, darling," she whispered.

As it was a windless, moonless Monday night and there was a no-show, Edda had been requested to take part in the drop. All the reserve volunteers had been arrested the week before. Both material-wise and in manpower, the LO was spread thin and this was Tante Riet's constant concern.

"I don't want you to be involved in this, kindje, but I seem to have no choice," she had sighed.

"Don't worry, Tante Riet, it's exactly what I want to do," Edda had replied. "Bringing around messages and distributing false ration coupons is essential work, but not very heroic."

"Aha, so it's heroism you're after, you little fighter?" Tante Riet had grinned. "There's a high price on heroism, so I wouldn't opt for it if I were you."

She hadn't explained her cryptic message and Edda hadn't asked, but it was in the back of her mind as she made her way to the corner of the Vondelpark where she was to be picked up by a 1939 black Tudor Ford standard. Maybe Tante Riet was right and she had a romantic vision of what a Resistance fighter looked like, colored by her stage life.

"I'll apologize when I come back and tell Tante Riet I'm happy and grateful for what she asks me to do," she mused as she waited for the stranger in the black Ford to come around the corner. They had to be in the vicinity of Alkmaar before dark.

Edda checked her watch. There was still time but standing still in the street was considered suspicious these days, so she started walking to and fro constantly on the watch for patroling Germans or NSB traitors. She thought she saw a shadow disappear around the bend but shook it off.

"Hey, you!" a familiar voice called out and Edda turned to see the window of the black Ford roll down and Rick's smiling face behind the steering wheel. She quickly walked around the car and dropped into the passenger's seat.

"What a surprise!" they said in chorus.

"Partners in crime," Rick grinned. Edda smiled warmly. The trip would get even better now. "I've thought so many times about you, Hannie," Rick added, "what a night we had back then, eeh?"

"Yes, the less we say about it the better, I suppose," Edda replied in the safety of the front seat as the car rambled across the Stadhouderskade to get to the city's outskirts and then onto the road north.

"So how have you been?" Rick was the first to speak again.

"As well as I can be. Many things going on, on all fronts, and just staying alive generally."

Vagueness was everything despite the fact she liked him, and they had a history.

"And you?"

"I finally finished my studies. So, I guess I'm a real doctor now."

"Oh yes, you were studying amid all this craziness. How's Doctor Geuze doing?"

"He's retiring now that I'm on board. And it's as well. Did you know he's in his seventies?"

"No way! I'd never have guessed." With fondness, Edda recalled the youthful, white-haired, and blue-eyed physician. "Do you know what he gave me before the war when I was recovering from a broken ankle? Gosh, that seems eons ago now, but I've always kept the slip of paper in my purse."

"Let me guess," Rick laughed. "The greatest Warriors are Patience and Time. Tolstoy?"

Edda nodded, amazed. "How did you know?"

"Not a secret. That is Doctor Geuze's favorite quote. He used it all the time in his lectures at university to teach us how to treat patients and approach medicine in general, I guess."

"I don't think I have much patience," Edda pondered. "But I sure hope I have time."

"Did you ever read Tolstoy?" Rick asked.

"Heavens no! His books are so thick. I don't have the patience to sit with a book anyway and certainly not one that is at least a thousand pages."

"Oh, that's a shame," Rick observed. "Tolstoy's a prime writer and a great philosopher. Did you know he became quite a revolutionary at the end of his life?"

Rick and Edda chatted amiably until the lights of Alkmaar came into sight and Rick steered the car in the direction of a lonesome farm with extensive outbuildings and barns. He parked the Ford close to the wall of one of the barns and they got out.

"Let's have some dinner," Rick announced, which Edda found a welcome treat she hadn't anticipated.

The dinner turned out to be a taciturn event, but a meal made for kings. It had been months since Edda tasted beef and carrots. She simply couldn't stop eating until the farmer's wife laughed, "Look at you. Spindly as you get them but eats like a wolf.'

"It's so good," Edda said, her cheeks coloring as everyone was now staring at her and her plate.

"As it can always be our last meal, we'd better eat heartily," the farmer observed with dry humor.

After dinner they played cards. Some smoked, some rested but few spoke. The group consisted of a dozen people, dressed in camouflage clothes to go out at midnight. Most seemed veterans at these drops, Edda gathered from the sparse talk. Even Rick.

"You stay close to me, and you'll be alright," he told her. Edda nodded. Now the hour came closer she was apprehensive. This wasn't just cycling around doing small forbidden errands. This was one of the jobs for which you were shot dead on the spot. Now the resistance against the occupiers grew, weapons were the only thing they really needed to defend themselves. And the day the Allies arrived at the border, the fighters in the country had to be prepared.

"Everyone follow me," an elderly man with a black cap and very protruding blue eyes announced just when everyone was starting to get sleepy. All sat up straight and ready as if wound up by the same key. The man with the protruding eyes extinguished his pipe, tapped it empty in the ashtray, pocketed it and got up. He was the leader, that much was clear.

"Everyone knows their task except for the young miss." The bulging eyes rested on Edda. A crooked finger pointed at her and Rick. "Teach her the torch-work, Rick.'

"I will, Sir."

"I'll just follow Rick," Edda assured him she'd understood the instructions.

"You'd better do that, missy. And you've only got one chance to do it right. You will lead the plane in. Get it wrong and the plane crashes and we're all done in." That didn't sound very encouraging.

"You'll be alright. It's not that difficult. It's just timing the flashes right. I guess you've learned everything about timing in dance?" Rick whispered to her.

Edda nodded but wisely kept her mouth shut. The man in charge eyed her as if he didn't have much confidence in her.

The walk from the farm, through the fields, and along a strip of woodland was long and chilly but they made good progress. The moon was new, invisible, and low-hanging clouds would keep the plane out of sight. A perfect night for an illegal drop, far away from prying German eyes and their anti-aircraft artillery.

"We're about there," Rick whispered next to Edda, as they waded through thick shrubbery to what looked like an open space in the woods. They moved like shadows, soundless and swift. Edda had no idea where the other fighters were. Everyone had dispersed and stayed on their own course.

Suddenly her heart skipped a few beats. She heard a swishing sound, and something brushed against her leg, then moved away. Frightened she grabbed Rick's hand.

"That was a fox. We've stepped on its den," Rick said softly while Edda sighed with relief. She was very tense indeed.

They waited for what seemed like hours. Edda strained her ears but didn't hear a plane coming. Then the shadow of one of the men came into view. He made a sign and they all rose.

"Come on," Rick announced. "Time to flash. You stay here. I'll move over there. When you see me flash, you also flash three times."

Rick ran to the other side of the open space. Only then Edda heard the faint rumbling of a plane coming closer. It was exciting and frightening at the same time. She had to do it right or they would all be dead.

She peered with all her might to where she expected to see Rick's flash and when it came, she pressed the button on her torch three times as expected. Seconds later the plane roared over and she heard the thud-thud-thud of crates falling out of the plane's belly.

Before she knew it, the aircraft skimmed over them, rose steeply, and disappeared over the treetops and was gone. Edda marvelled at the nosedive, it was almost as if the plane had performed a dance, how elegant and light.

Shadows emerged from the bushes and moved quickly to the place where the boxes had fallen. They were carried away without sound. The walk back to the farm was even faster than the journey out. Edda was holding on to the handle of a heavy crate on one side with Rick on the other side until they were back in the safety of a big barn, and they deposited their load.

Swift hands buried the crates under loose straw, and it was as if their night excursion had never taken place.

38

A DEADLY MISTAKE

Eleven weeks later – Amsterdam, 26 August 1944

"I think I told you, Tante Riet," Edda began, while they were having tea in her neighbor's kitchen overlooking the long, narrow garden, with the well-trodden path to Edda's backdoor. "I've been keeping a diary from the beginning of the war. I felt I was never going to be a target but after all the recent LO arrests, I'm doubting whether I'm putting myself and others in danger.'

"Did you mention names, locations, actions?" Tante Riet looked concerned.

"Sometimes I mentioned places or people. Never real names or exact places. Mostly I commented on current affairs. It was an outlet for my rage against the occupation, starting with the bombing of Rotterdam. But now I'm worried and I want to hide them in a safer place. Any idea where?" Edda stroked Minoes, who had no complaints about that and purred almost louder than the Messersmith that roared overhead.

"It's a wise thing to get them diaries out of your house just in case," her neighbor agreed.

"But where?" Edda asked. "All of Amsterdam seems unsafe."

"Why not at your sister's? The Germans aren't likely to search her house."

"Uh... Tante Riet, it's about a dozen diaries, a whole box full."

"Heavens, kindje, I never knew you were a scribbler as well as a hip-swinger."

"I'm not a writer by any means," Edda confessed with honesty. "There's no literary value to them. The entries have no value at all other than as a recollection for myself. At the time, when Ash and I started dating, I also hoped they would be a memory for our children, but that future seems very unlikely now." Edda gazed out of the window wistfully. Almost two years. Not a word. Not a message. It couldn't be a good sign.

But then she sat straighter. "I think it's actually a good idea to store the box of diaries with Duifje in The Hague. No suspicion around her. At least not from the Germans, nor the NSB."

"But can she be trusted?" Tante Riet asked. "I remember you said she was a bit higgledy-piggledy..."

"Oh, she is. But one thing Duifje isn't is nosey. She's too busy being occupied with herself. She won't want to know what's in an old valise I leave with her. I was always the nosey one."

"Then that's the diaries in the bag, right? Now about the arms drop tomorrow night. Are you still up for it?"

"Of course, after I return from The Hague, I'll be ready to roll once more."

EDDA RETURNED to Amsterdam at the end of the afternoon. As she had expected, Duifje asked no questions and didn't request the key to the valise. It was a strange emptiness to no longer possess the diaries that had kept her company throughout the long years of the war, but it also felt lighter and less dangerous. She would not write again until the Allies were in her city, and they were liberated. But she would memorize important happenings in the coming months so she could jot them down later.

The Americans and Canadians had just conquered Paris, so it was now a matter of weeks, months at the most! "Before the winter," everyone said with relief. "Before another long winter."

Edda was sleeping badly. She was worried. Her sixth sense was telling her that something was off, but nothing showed it was. The arms drops all went according to plan. Hardly any Jews were hiding within the city anymore. Those whose hiding places hadn't been betrayed were dispersed over the countryside where they had more to eat and less to fear.

Thin as a rail and careworn to the bone, dancing had become an ordeal for Edda but she continued to do shows five or six nights a week with the loyal Maria and Miss Sterling in her wake. Maria had found other accommodation but often returned to cook Edda her turnip mash.

Eating had become hazardous as well, because there was nothing available but also because she had difficulty digesting the little she ate. Eating was almost as hard as breathing. As living in general. At the end of her tethers, she didn't realize she was physically in danger of losing the battle.

What Edda did realize was that she was in some sort of outward danger but no matter how much she spied around her, checked her mail, retraced her steps, she couldn't figure out where exactly the danger lurked. But there was the occasional shadow from across the street, the back of a man's coat that she started to recognize. She was tired, she was exhausted, she was terrified to make a mistake.

And then it came.

A loud bang on her front door in the middle of the night like someone was kicking the entire façade with a battering ram. Edda shot out of bed and escaped in her nightie through the backdoor to Tante Riet. Carefully locking the back door behind her so it seemed as if she wasn't home. She picked up the key from underneath Tante Riet's doormat and let herself into her neighbor's kitchen. Tante Riet obviously had heard the noise next door and came curlers and all in her nightdress downstairs.

"What was that?" she asked.

"I don't know. I think someone is breaking into my house," Edda's eyes were enormous, and she was shaking all over.

"Sounds like it," Tante Riet said unimpassioned. "Get into my bed. There's nothing else we can do."

The situation developed as if in slow motion, though Edda was clearer in her head than she'd been for years. A loud crash downstairs and boots on the staircase. A flashlight in her eyes. Tante Riet who tried to cover her up with the blanket and then that voice.

"Edda van Der Valk, *het spel is over.*" Game's up!

I should have known it was him, was all Edda could think. *I should have known.* As Klaas Bollema grabbed her by the armpits and dragged her out of Tante Riet's bed. But the next moment a shot rang, and he toppled over her, squashing her with his weight. Edda gasped for breath, fought to get from underneath the heavy man when another shot rang. Tante Riet stood wide-legged, in her dressing gown with a smoking gun in her hands, as Edda crawled out from under the dead man. A second NSB man stood, still propped up against the doorpost, but doubled over and fell to his knees.

"We have to get out of here. And quick," Tante Riet ordered. "Go home, grab the first things you can find, and we'll run."

Edda was so stupefied she obeyed without knowing what she was doing or where she was going. She dressed way too warmly for an August morning, packed random things into a small suitcase, pinned Ash's brooch on her coat and with clattering teeth waited for Tante Riet on the doorstep. She felt like she was seeing her Vondelstraat flat for the very last time. When Tante Riet emerged from her own door, the early sunlight caught her face and Edda could see her neighbor was more shaken than she'd ever been before.

"Where to?" Edda asked with clattering teeth.

"We'll take the train to the Achterhoek, God permitting. Away from this city," Tante Riet said, as they walked side by side in the direction of the station.

They'd only walked a few hundred meters when they were stopped by the Gestapo. Edda, in the confusion, had taken her own passport instead of her false identity papers.

"*Komm mit!*" was the order and she knew then that she'd made a mistake. A horrible mistake that might also cost Tante Riet her life. Perhaps even that of her parents. Though Klaas Bollema could no longer talk, he'd no doubt left his whole file about her on her father's desk.

Bollema's long shadow had finally caught up with her. It knocked all the wind out of Edda's lungs. She wished she could die on the spot.

39

ARRESTED

In a Mercedes 170V, Edda and Tante Riet were driven at high speed to the police station at the Elandsgracht, where Ome Jan had also been taken. Edda feared the worst, thinking back to how Rick and she had found Ome Jan and the injuries endured in his interrogations. She exchanged silent looks with Tante Riet. The older woman squeezed her hand as if saying 'you'll do fine' but Edda felt far from heroic now.

Fingering the butterfly brooch on her coat, she prayed to Ash for support rather than to God. Somehow, now caught by the Germans herself, she felt closer to him.

The two women were separated at the police station. Given no time to say goodbye, Edda waved a limp hand, wondering if she'd ever see her wonderful neighbor again. But she had little time to think about either their future or any strategy of how to go into the interrogations.

She was led straight to a tiny office on the second floor. It was so small it looked more like a cubicle than a room, with a rectangular table that took up most of the space, two wooden chairs, and a bright-burning light bulb in an old gray lampshade above. An overflowing ashtray graced the middle of the table as if a dead flower arrangement. A window with bars in front, no bigger than a child's valise, high up on one wall was the only source of natural light. As the most gut-churning room Edda had ever laid eyes on, it didn't bode well.

"*Hinsetzen!*" the officer who'd driven the Mercedes pushed her inside, then closed the door that screeched on its hinges. Edda was alone and thought she'd better do as she was told. She took the chair nearest to her, unable from their similarity to figure out if there was a hierarchy between the two seats.

Seconds later the door opened and a Waffen SS officer in his *feldgrau* uniform with the double S on his collar and the swastika around his upper sleeve, clanged in on his heavy boots. The man was rather short and stooped, and he looked bored and bland. Edda guessed he was somewhere in his fifties, with grayish hair in need of a trim and eyes as desolate as the bare walls around them.

The uniformed man nodded to her without a word, took the other chair without a remark and started reading the file he'd brought with him. Edda tried glancing over the top as he held it up but couldn't see its contents. The brown file had no name or number on the cover, but she was sure the inside was about her. How much did they know about her? What if... everything? Certain death awaited her then. She'd better prepare herself for the ultimate verdict, but how does one prepare for immediate death? Edda felt like crying but stifled her upcoming sob.

"Fräulein Van der Valk," the elderly SS officer sounded as if he couldn't believe what he was reading.

"Yes?" It was no use denying who she was.

"Wer ist diese Frau?" Who is this woman?

He showed her a picture of her standing outside the theater hugging Maria goodbye. Edda hesitated. So, the shadow had been taking pictures of her for weeks? Anger at herself now replaced the fear. How could she have missed— or rather dismissed—the shadow she'd known was hovering around her? What a lousy resister she'd proved to be. A danger to everyone.

"That's my dance partner." She snapped.

"Name?"

Edda hesitated again, while the bland officer repeated with more stress, "Name?"

"Maria Petrova."

At least that wasn't her cover name.

"Aha, a Russian? An enemy of the Third Reich."

"Miss Petrova just does ballet, Sir. She's not into politics." Edda lied.

"Hauptsturmführer Schmidt for you, Fräulein Van der Valk." The officer snapped back at her.

"Sorry," she mumbled. Politeness might get her somewhere. Hauptsturmführer Schmidt didn't look like an ogre, more like a weary, old businessman, but appearances could be deceptive.

"And who's this?"

A picture of Edda and Miss Sterling walking in the park. The same dilemma struck her, but she felt she wouldn't betray her mentor by giving her dance credentials.

"My ballet teacher and choreographer."

"So, you are a dancer?"

"Yes, Si... Hauptsturmführer Schmidt, I am."

"And who's this?"

Edda wasn't prepared for this one. He showed her a picture of Ash in his Swan Lake outfit holding her in an embrace while she performed the Arabesque Attitude. Ash looked straight into the camera. His eyes were bluer than blue. Edda swallowed hard, took in all the details while she remembered that moment as if it was yesterday. Memories and emotions tumbling through her at high speed.

It was a large photo, signed in a lower corner with his signature. Asher Hoffmann. Had he wanted to give it to her? Or had it been for the papers? What was it doing in her file?

"How did you acquire this photo?" Her teeth were clattering but her voice was strong.

"I ask the questions." The German's tone wasn't threatening, just weary. It gave Edda the nerve to push a little further.

"I'll tell you who he is, though I think you already know, if you tell me who gave the photo to you, Hauptsturmführer Schmidt. It would mean a great deal to me if you would share that information with me."

"You're truly your father's daughter, aren't you? Always wanting to know the backstory."

This was a new shock to Edda—his knowledge of her background —but, of course, she should have known. It would be all in that file. As long as the murders weren't. That was her greatest fear.

Schmidt raised his eyes from the page and looked straight at her. There was a glimmer of admiration in his eyes, but he immediately returned to his bland, impassive self.

"The source was Heerbanleider Klaas Bollema. I don't know how he got it."

"Of course," Edda said bitterly. "Who else." She thought, with some satisfaction, that at least her father's chauffeur was done doing his acts of cruelty. "It's Asher Hoffmann, also a dancer."

"And where is this Asher Hoffmann now?"

"I don't know, Hauptsturmführer Schmidt. I wish I did."

"Aha." He put the photo back in her file and started reading again. Edda was close to tears. The photo of Ash struck her to the core, shook her off balance, exactly as had been the plan. But Schmidt didn't say much for a while.

Then he looked up again and said in a rather fatherly voice. "Westerbork for you. They'll deal with you there."

Westerbork? Edda thought. Of course she'd heard of the transit camp in the East of Holland, run by Groningen, but for sure that was only for Jews. *Why was she being sent there? Could Ash be there?* This time she didn't dare to ask. As long as Tante Riet would be with her, they could go looking for Jews they'd known and helped. It might not be so bad, and the interrogation seemed over already.

"Any final questions?" Schmidt looked at her again and Edda had the distinct feeling he wanted her to bring up her family, plea with him but this she couldn't bear to do.

"No, Haupfsturmführer, or yes, perhaps I do have a question. Will I be sent to a work camp in Germany?"

The weary man rose from his chair.

"I have no idea, Fräulein Van der Valk. You're not staying here. That's all I know. Good day."

What a morose man, Edda thought. But at least she hadn't been tortured. Not yet anyway. Thinking of Ome Jan's dangling eyeball, she deftly felt hers. It was still there. As was the small valise at her feet and the brooch on her winter coat. The only belongings she now had in the world.

EDDA WAS OVERJOYED to see Tante Riet sitting in the same car, the Mercedes that had brought them to the police station with the same officer at the wheel.

"I'm taking you to the train station," he announced. At that moment two guards got in as well, young SS officers with long rifles and tight faces. One slid in the passenger seat and lit a Sturm Zigarette. The sharp smoke filled the cabin. The other prodded Edda with his rifle and she moved to the middle seat close to Tante Riet. He placed his rifle between his black boots and snarled, "Fahren." Drive.

Edda looked out of the window as they passed the familiar sights she wasn't sure she'd ever see again. Amsterdam was quiet at this hour on a Saturday morning. Germans were the regular visitors, as were the pigeons. Amsterdamers had nothing to look for outside these days, the shops were empty and their guards violent.

They passed the Leidseplein where she'd frequented Café Americain so often with her family after premiere night; the Leidsestraat with its tingling trams; then the Singel where Ash and she had bought her mother flowers for her twenty-fifth anniversary, that horrible dinner that had gone wrong; the Damrak where Ash's father for a short while had had his dream jeweler's shop; Dam square with more pigeons and more Germans loitering in front of the Queen's Palace. And finally, the Rokin, broad and stately, on their way to Central Station and away to Westerbork and then who knew where.

· · ·

GOODBYE AMSTERDAM. Goodbye most beautiful and most difficult years of my life. Bye Ash.

40

CAMP WESTERBORK

The two German officers who had joined Edda and Tante Riet at the police station, escorted them aboard the train at Amsterdam Central Station. They ushered the women into an empty 3rd class compartment that reeked of urine and wet newspapers. Closing the sliding doors behind Edda, the men took up their positions on either side of the carriage door.

Left to themselves, the two women sat opposite each other silent and shocked, their valises at their feet. Edda had no idea how far the journey to Westerbork was. She'd never been to that part of Holland. Groningen yes, as it was adjacent to Friesland but the province of Drenthe had never had any attraction for the Van der Valk family. It was the one province in Holland where people didn't go for tourist trips. Only when one had business there.

That could be why they set up the Jewish refugee camp in that forlorn place, Edda thought bitterly. After Hitler's 1933 rise to power, Jews with foresight of their fate had come thronging into Holland from Germany and Austria. It had been all over the papers that the camp for the quickly growing Jewish refugees would be built on the Veluwe but Queen Wilhelmina had protested. She didn't want a refugee camp in her backyard.

Ash had told Edda how he and his parents had passed through the desolate camp in 1938. It had been a couple of barracks in the middle of the wilderness, built with money the Jews had brought themselves, as the Dutch government wasn't particularly welcoming to the stream of desperate Jews looking for safety. Not one Dutch guilder had been spent on temporary housing or aid.

The Hoffmanns had been fortunate that they knew people in Amsterdam with whom they could stay and had only passed through Westerbork. Would Ash have travelled through the camp this time as well? Could he still be there? Edda didn't dare to get her hopes up but decided she'd ask around for the Hoffmanns as soon as she could.

The long hot train journey through the Dutch countryside in her winter coat made Edda's head spin—her armpits and back streaming with perspiration. Yet she didn't dare to take off the duffel coat for fear she would lose sight of her precious brooch. In her haste she'd forgotten to pack the gold-embossed case, which she now regretted with all her heart.

"Here," Tante Riet offered her a Wilhelmina peppermint. "That will help against the thirst."

Edda sucked on the peppery mint with a grateful sigh, wondering how Queen Wilhelmina slipped into her mind twice within seconds. Once negatively, once positively. Their Queen was safely tucked away with her government in London, leaving the Dutch to fend for themselves. Sure, she tried to lift their spirits with her radio broadcasts, and they all knew she needed to stay safe so she could reign again after the war. But still.

"What is it, kindje?" Tante Riet's warm hand reached across the aisle and rested on Edda's gloveless hand. Gloves. Another item forgotten in her haste. "You look like a cat come in from the rain."

"Oh Tante Riet, what about Minoes?" Edda was suddenly snapped out of her own misery thinking of her neighbor's poor cat.

"Oh no worries, Marie will take care of him. I've long discussed that with her in case of this..." Tante Riet gestured with her hand not mentioning the word 'arrest.' Edda peeked at the two stolid guards outside the compartment, wondering if they could talk freely in hushed whispers.

"You haven't answered my question, kindje. And for Heaven's sake take off that thick coat."

"But..."

"No buts. That million-guilder winged animal isn't going to fly out of these windows. Take it off, fold it so you can see it all the time and then put the darn coat on again when we arrive."

Edda did as she was told, glad Tante Riet hadn't lost her common sense and was still steering her through this new ordeal.

"Do you think we can escape from the camp?" Edda said in her softest voice.

"Oh, is that what you've been beating your brains out about?" Tante Riet hollered, and Edda glanced at the doors with fear. The soldiers looked back, annoyed but didn't come in. "I don't think that's our main concern right now. Survival I'd say."

Edda kept quiet, feeling put in her place.

"What will it be like?" she asked.

"From what I heard, it's not a palace but it isn't the worst place either. As I said, survival is the most important for the likes of us non-Jews, Resisters."

"Will we be sent to the labor camps in Germany, you think?"

"Again, as I said, if we get as far. If we survive the first days. That's my main concern."

Edda was silent, contemplating this. Tante Riet was telling her in no uncertain terms that they were facing the firing squad. But why hadn't they taken them to the dunes like they had Ome Jan? Why this hassle to take them far away from Amsterdam? She didn't want to ask any more questions that Tante Riet couldn't answer, though she was sure her neighbor knew much more than she was likely to share with her.

Edda's thoughts rumbled on just like the train wheels beneath them. They were quiet for a long while, both absorbed in their own thoughts. One of the two guards was dozing, his profile showing his sandy moustache covering most of his upper lip, light lashes over red-veined eyelids. The other, rather plump and hairy, with his belt tightened around his rotund belly, looked bored but alert.

There were no other visible passengers on the train. The journey was terribly slow. Weesp, Hilversum, Amersfoort, Zwolle, Meppel, Hoogeveen. Then finally, while the afternoon sun had hidden behind fly-by clouds, the train came to a halt and their guards prodded them out of the carriage. Edda quickly slid into her heavy coat, grabbed her suitcase, and gave her last semi-free space a second look to see if she'd forgotten anything.

Assen Station. Their escorts led them to a local train waiting on the other side of the platform. It was a short train, no more than three compartments and it looked old and forlorn, the window shades closed. More German guards paced the platform from the locomotive to the last carriage, and back again.

Thunder cracked right above their heads and a deluge poured down on them like a sudden tropical monsoon. Edda lifted her face to the opaque sky in a temperature still hot as a stove and let her face be drenched in the cool stream of water. The rain felt strangely good, suiting the atmosphere of despair, like a last welcome shower, a cleansing gift.

"Move on." One of the guards prodded his rifle in her back and Edda moved with the stream of passengers, still flooding from other parts of the first train. Most had yellow stars on their coats, all looked dishevelled and tentative, clutching their last earthly belongings. How had everyone's life suddenly become Destination Unknown?

Edda and Tante Riet were pushed to the front carriage by their two escorts. The compartment was filling fast with silent, drenched-to-the-skin people whose clothes gave off a damp smell, with hair and hats like floppy baskets.

More and more people were ushered into the carriage until no more seats were available. Edda shuffled to her feet to make space for an elderly Jewish woman carrying a small infant on one arm and a suitcase in her other hand.

She wriggled through the crowds until she was near Tante Riet, afraid of losing sight of her neighbor while she squeezed the handle of her valise between her fingers.

Surrounded by so many Jews, people who must have been arrested while in hiding, Edda felt both similar and different. She may be wearing a brooch instead of a yellow star. This brooch, Ash's brooch, was Edda's star. *When she'd marry Ash, she'd be as Jewish as these people. If, not when,* she corrected herself.

The heavily loaded train started with a jolt and a jump, throwing people against each other and belongings slipping out of hands. Soft moans sounded instead of shrieks. Nobody dared to cry out. As quickly as possible everyone scrambled back to their belongings and seats, while the train started running on a more regular track.

It was stifling hot inside. The summer storm that was still pelting the flat country outside, brought no fresh air in the closed-off compartment that had become a hothouse of damp clothes and sweating bodies.

They couldn't see where they were taken because of the closed shades but the journey held no anticipation or excitement, only resignation. Edda tried to think, tried to come up with a plan but no thought took shape and she swayed forwards like her fellow passengers, no more than a flock of timid sheep.

It was a short ride with no stops in between. Soon after departing, the train came to a screeching halt, the doors were unbolted and people almost fell out, packed as sardines as they'd been. Children started crying, women wailed, coarse German commands were shouted. One woman lost consciousness and was dragged out of the wagon by her arm and laid in the grass. A helpful man put her valise next to her but was poked in the back to move on.

Edda fought to get nearer to Tante Riet, but they only seemed to get pushed farther apart by the desperate people that crowded around them.

"Tante Riet," she cried out and heard a muffled, "I'm here, kindje." Edda couldn't see her but walked in the direction of the voice.

Finally, Edda was outside in a field with barracks that seemed to have no end. Barrack after barrack after barrack. All the same rectangular shape made of sturdy brown wood. It looked like a village of the forlorn.

"Tante Riet?" she cried again, louder now but there was no reply. Edda was pushed forward with the stream of people, unable to step aside and look for her Tante as guards accompanied the group on either side.

"Forward to the Registration Barrack." Was all she heard, keeping up her hopes she'd find her neighbor there. So, she marched with the group until she suddenly stopped and the people behind her bumped into her. Horror filled her soul. Her brooch was gone. Ripped off her coat where there was now only a tear. She turned around, fighting to get back to the train, tears streaming down her cheeks.

"No! No! No!"

A guard grabbed her arm roughly.

"*Diese Seite, Fräulein.* No going back." He grinned as he said it. Edda's whole body went limp, and she let herself fall in the grass. Wanting to die right there and then.

"Tante Riet," she sobbed. "Tante Riet, where are you? I've lost my brooch." But there was no Tante Riet, only the rough officer who pulled her up and dragged her along.

"*Laufen!*" he snarled, and Edda had no choice. She'd go back and look for her brooch as soon as she could. For her brooch and for Tante Riet. But what if she'd lost it on the train? The train had already whistled and left again.

More dead than alive, Edda was ferried into one of the many barracks that held three long lines with two people at each table. Edda was taken to the middle row.

"Name?"

"Edda Van der Valk."

"Profession?"

"Ballerina."

"Ah interesting! We have cultural performances here in the camp. I'll put you on the list." Edda was too weary to look at the man and woman asking her questions. She only thought of her brooch and of finding Tante Riet.

"Age?"

"Twenty-five."

"Last address?" She didn't answer. Couldn't care less.

"Last address?" A kind woman's voice asked, and Edda glanced at her through her eyelashes. She was a young Jewess with a fine face and thick dark hair.

"Vondelstraat 56, Amsterdam," Edda answered and quickly added, "I'm here with my neighbor but I don't see her anymore."

"You'll surely find her later, after we've given you your barrack number," the female voice replied.

"I also lost something of great importance to me when I got out of the train. Can I go back and look for it?"

"After we've taken you to your barrack, Miss." The voice was calm, soothing and Edda tried to relax. She realized she was shivering all over and needed to lie down.

"I'm not well," she managed to say before everything turned black in front of her eyes.

41

STAY ALIVE

A few weeks later – Camp Westerbork, September 1944

When Edda awoke, she had no idea where she was. It was noisy all around her and it smelled of camphor and antisceptics. Sounds resonated and smells hung half-way in the air. Ahh...there was Tchaikovsky's March. In her mind she was counting the beats—one hundred and eighty—before dashing onto the stage as Clara. Larry was standing in the wings cheering her on. She flew more than she danced and then everything went white as if she had ascended to Heaven.

The noise and the strong smell were still there. Waltz of the Flowers died down until there was only a single violin still playing. Edda strained her ears. It was so unearthly beautiful that she wished it would go on and on and she could dance to it forever and ever.

"Are you awake, Miss?" A voice next to her asked. A woman.

"Hush! I'm dancing."

"You're not, Miss. You're lying in a bed in the sick barrack. Open your eyes."

"Sick barrack? What do you mean?" Edda decided it didn't sound good and somewhere inside her she knew something, or someone was helping her not to arrive at the truth. But the voice was insistent.

"Open your eyes, Miss. I brought you a bit of soup."

The violin stopped playing. Soup? Did she want soup? Edda shook her head. She wanted Heaven, that was where ambrosia was served. Not soup.

The voice disappeared but the violin didn't play anymore. Another voice. Male this time.

"I'm Doctor Samuels, Miss Van der Valk. Will you open your eyes for me?"

"I know no Doctor Samuels, sorry," Edda replied, hoping she sounded friendly but resolute. All her being was stretched with wanting to dance, for the music to return. She was aware it was different from other times she'd danced; this was a dance for God, not for people, but she needed the music.

"Please put Tchaikovsky on again, Doctor Samuels," she pleaded, "that would greatly help. Thank you."

"I will see what I can do." The male voice retreated.

The music played again and Edda was in Heaven. Life was good, whole and simple. Life was dance.

It took three weeks before Edda could sit up and eat the soup instead of holding out for the ambrosia of her hallucinations. Doctor Samuels appeared to be an elderly, child psychiatrist, one of the very few Jewish physicians still in Camp Westerbork. Abraham Samuels, an Austrian-trained psychiatrist from the Jung School, saved Edda's life with his old gramophone record of the Nutcracker Suite and with his patience. Edda was undernourished, overstrained, and traumatized. He recognized all the symptoms and treated her accordingly.

She sat up in the barrack in the hospital unit and looked around her. There were only a few patients in the ward. A nurse was nodding at the entrance, her chin resting on her white apron. Slowly but certainly, the truth did sink in, and Edda's fighting spirit came back.

She needed to find her brooch. She needed to find Tante Riet. And then she needed to find Ash. There was so much she needed to find but she didn't know if she had the strength for finding. They all seemed unfindable.

Gray and bent, but with extraordinary vitality, she saw Doctor Samuels enter through the swinging doors. She'd come to depend on his stability these weeks. He was very different from Doctor Geuze, much more introverted and silent, sad almost, but he was always kind to her and truly seemed to care for her wellbeing.

"Ach, I see you're sitting up. Are you feeling better?"

"Yes, Doctor Samuels. You've been absolutely good to me."

"I'm glad to hear it, Edda. It looks like you were my last patient here so I'm glad I made a success of that."

"What do you mean, Doctor Samuels?"

"Ach, I'm leaving on the last train to the East. They say they have a better job for me in a camp in Germany." The elderly psychiatrist sighed soundlessly.

"Who's they?" Edda asked with some of her former vehemence.

"The Camp Commander Hauptsturmführer Gemmeker."

"I wouldn't take that job if I were you," Edda said. "I don't think it's safe to go East now. The Nazis will soon lose the war and then the Allies will think you were collaborating."

"Hush, Edda. The walls have ears here." He looked stricken for a moment but then the calm returned to his face. That resignation Edda had seen so often in other Jewish people. A wise, serene acceptance of their fate with a degree of stoicism she'd never achieve.

"Will I see you again?" It sounded almost like a plea.

"Ach, I don't know, Edda, but I sure hope so. You're well enough to go to an ordinary barrack now and maybe you can find the lady you were calling for in your delirium. Tante Riet?"

Edda's eyes filled with tears. "Have you looked for her, Doctor Samuels? I'm so afraid for her."

"I did, but they won't tell me anything, but I can tell you one thing, Edda, and I want you to understand what it means. I'm purely talking as a psychiatrist now, so I'm talking about your mind and soul, not so much about your physical self, do you understand?"

"Yes, pray tell me Doctor."

"They – I mean the Germans – want to keep you alive. They told me so in no uncertain words. Keep her alive. I don't know what it means but I want you to use that power to get through this ordeal and to get through it alive. It will be mentally and spiritually hard for you not to lose hope, simply to survive and nothing else. And if you survive, Edda, of which you now have a good chance, make sure you take time to heal your soul after the war is over. Give your soul time, pray to your God often and seek a qualified healer to help you. But for now, just remember that even they want you to stay alive. Use that power, *Mein Kind*, and you'll come out triumphant. I want that for you. I want Edda Van der Valk to live to an old age. Do you hear me? Never give up. Keep fighting. Will you promise me to survive and keep fighting?"

Edda had no idea what the old doctor meant but it sounded really solemn and important to him, so she nodded. "I promise you, Doctor Samuels, and I hope you will survive as well, and we will meet up after the war."

"Let us do that!"

And with those words the bent figure left the barrack, out of her sight. Another person disappearing out of her life.

EDDA WAS TAKEN to Barrack 62. After the quiet of the hospital, she suddenly found herself living amid other people, although there were many empty beds in the large space with the bare floorboards, wooden walls, wooden roof. The building had different compartments. In the middle was a small entrance that functioned as a kitchen area. To the left and right of this entrance area were large dormitory halls of some 100 feet by 30 feet, filled with three-storey bunk beds, a few tables and chairs, and some potbelly stoves. Washrooms with zinc gutters were located at both ends of the dormitory areas, where some twenty-five prisoners could wash at the same time. In one corner of each dormitory stood a lonely toilet bowl.

It was primitive, to say the least, but relatively clean and quiet. Most of the inhabitants seemed to have gone, which was surprising considering the crowds that had been on the train with her on arrival. Had they all been sent to other camps so quickly?

Nobody came to tell Edda where she should install herself, so she took the furthest corner, close to one of the washrooms. She chose the top bed as advised by Doctor Samuels. It offered some ventilation through the slits in the roof on hot fall days, and more space and safety for her valise. She also had a small table and chair. It wasn't much, but it was something.

Placing the brown leather suitcase, with its reinforced metal corners, on top of the table. Still somewhat weak yet with her legs feeling surprisingly strong, Edda gazed outside, trying to come to terms with her captivity, her aloneness, the mission Doctor Samuels had given her. Stay alive. Why had this never seemed a mission before? One breathed in and out, one lived, but getting orders to stay alive, seemed odd, unnatural. And yet there had been an urgency in the old psychiatrist's voice, as if commissioned by God to deliver this message to her. Stay alive!

Edda gasped. She suddenly understood. The epiphany made her sink down on the chair, open-eyed, horrified. She was the witness of a secret, inconceivable, inhumane act of barbarity. Far worse than the occupation, far worse than bombs and casualties of war. Her sixth sense had tried to tell her every day but she hadn't listened, couldn't listen. Hitler was massacring all the Jews he could get his hands on. They were not coming back from the East. Not coming back. Ash would not come back. Not come back.

And she? She had to stay alive to bear witness to the times her people were living through. She would testify to the rest of the world what the anti-Semites had done in Holland during the war. Find evidence, bring to justice those who'd systematically extinguished the Jewish race—innocent people, families, husbands, wives, siblings, children, babies, and grandparents.

"Miss Van der Valk?" A German-laced voice said behind her. Edda turned gracefully, as a ballerina would, tears in her eyes but her heart full of confidence in her mission. Before her stood an attractive German high official, whom she immediately recognized as the Camp Commander, Albert Gemmeker, who was better known by his nickname, the 'Gentleman Crook'.

She'd heard the talk he lived with Frau Hassel, who apparently doubled as his mistress and his secretary in the big green villa over-looking the camp. Opulence starkly contrasting with the hand-to-mouth existence in the barracks.

He stretched out his hand, well-manicured but ringless. Edda hesitated. It was against her principles to shake hands with Nazis, but Doctor Samuel seemed to whisper in her ear, '*Stay alive!*' so she snapped to attention without words of greeting but with a curt nod.

"I heard you've been quite ill, Miss Van der Valk. Was the treatment in our hospital satisfactory?" The tall German with his open face and polite manners looked at her frankly with what seemed a genuine smile of interest on his lips.

You're an enigma, shot through Edda's mind, *but you're not who you pretend to be.*

"Quite satisfactory, Sir. Doctor Samuels is an excellent doctor."

"He is," Gemmeker replied with a sigh. "The great doctor will be sorely missed here but his expertise was needed elsewhere."

Then why did you let him go? Edda wanted to shout but bit her tongue.

"Anyway, Miss Van der Valk, I came here to personally invite you to dinner with my secretary and me tonight. My housekeeper, Frau Asch, is an excellent cook and Doctor Samuels advised me you had not been eating well before you came here."

Edda was aware other prisoners were straining to hear what she and the Camp Commander were discussing, and her dilemma was real. She could not afford to reject the invitation but she would surely be treated with disdain by the rest of the camp if she went. Gemmeker, intelligent and shrewd, was no doubt aware he was placing her in an impossible situation. He undoubtedly knew everything about her and enjoyed this cat and mouse game.

The two greatest Warriors are Patience and Time.

"I'd gladly accept your invitation, Sir, but I had promised Ruth to discuss the organization of a dance evening on Friday night."

"You mean Ruth Birkenbach?" The polite veneer was back on the handsome German face. "Don't worry about her. You can discuss the program any time. I don't want you to exert yourself too early or you might have a relapse. Doctor Samuels told me so much. So, is it agreed? Tell the guards to open the gate for you at six thirty. I promise you won't be bored. I'll let you hear my own collection of favorite ballet compositions. Oh, I so adored you in Swan Lake, Miss Van der Valk. It's been...one of the highlights for me in these past years."

Edda felt like she'd been knocked in the chest and almost lost her balance. He'd seen her dance? Dance with Ash?! She started trembling all over her body, a tremor she was unable to hide or stop. Only all the years of physical discipline kept her on her legs. This man was evil to the bone. He knew how to break a person with mere words. He didn't need a gun or whip.

She swallowed hard. With her ears ringing, she managed to face the double-edged Nazi front-on, but it took every bit of strength from her. It would be hard to stay alive. But she would. She darn well would.

"In that case, I accept your kind invitation, Sir, but could you tell me in which barrack I could find my neighbor, Mevrouw Rita Meulenbelt? We traveled here together from Amsterdam, but I lost sight of her when we got off the train and then I was ill for several weeks."

A shadow of doubt—or was it guilt?— slid over the freshly shaven cheeks but Gemmeker collected himself within seconds. With that generous, gentlemanly smile he said, "Yes, of course, now I remember. Frau Meulenbelt is no longer here. She was taken to another place in Zwolle, but don't worry. I'll make inquiries and see if she can be relocated here again."

This made Edda smile for the first time and utter a grateful, "Thank you!"

Gemmeker clacked his boots, nodded in an overly friendly manner to the few other people inside the barrack and made for the door.

Oh, I wish I still had my Enfield, Edda thought with flaring anger. *I'd shoot the man. Right here, right now.* But Albert Gemmeker strode away unescorted, head up and smiling left and right as if the king of Camp Westerbork. Nobody would dare to touch one well-combed hair on the Hauptsturmführer's head. Mostly, Edda had been told, because Frau Hassel was the real hellhound behind her boss. She made sure any inconvenient person was put on the Tuesday transportation list *tout de suite.*

Conflict and anger fought in Edda's whole being. If Gemmeker did bring Tante Riet back, maybe he wasn't that bad. Her sixth sense screamed that everything was ambiguous these days and Gemmeker would make sure nobody would ever know the entire truth.

As soon as the Camp Commander was well out of sight, Edda set out across the terrain towards the train depot. It was an overcast, mild October day. A blackbird was singing a lonely song in one of the tree-tops. As if answering the bird's call, a woman's voice broke out in singing too. Edda stopped to listen, overcome by emotion.

"Then I will go to the altar of God,
To God my exceeding joy;
And on the harp I will praise You
O God, my God."

OH TANTE RIET! Do come back to me.

Leaves whirled around her and covered the grass and gravel pathways. A lone Spitfire roared overhead going east. Fall had come so fast in 1944. Edda walked carefully after her long convalesce. Why was she so fragile? It was as if her limbs were falling apart, her heart breaking, and her mind disoriented. The tireless ballerina was no more, and it was doubtful whether she'd ever reappear from the ashes again.

It's my brooch, she realized in horror. *Ash's brooch gave me the strength to carry on and that strength is now gone. Oh, how am I to survive without my butterfly? I simply must find it.*

She walked around aimlessly, eyes examining every inch of grass and gravel in front of her but she found nothing. It was already close to dusk when she knew she had to give up. The brooch was gone. She would have to find her strength from another source. Only what her mentors had said to her, Miss Sterling, Tante Riet, Doctor Geuze and now, finally, Doctor Samuels.

Stay Alive. Repeating the two words over and over as a mantra, Edda made her way back to her barrack, realizing it was time to go to the dreaded dinner at the green villa.

42

A PACT WITH THE DEVIL

Edda stood in front of the wooden, green-washed villa outside the barbed-wire fence weighing up her chances of escape when the front door swung open before she had a plan. A dark-haired man, middle-aged and slimly built, with a Star of David on his jacket opened the door. This took Edda by surprise.

"Come in, Miss van der Valk. Herr Gemmeker and Frau Hassel are waiting for you with the cocktails." *Cocktails? No way she'd drink alcohol in the company of these people.* The Jewish man opened the door wider for her to step inside. With one last glimpse over her shoulder, the vast terrain with the brown barracks and barbed wire fences disappeared from Edda's view.

The villa's private opulence was the next thing that hit her in the face. Hard. After weeks in spartan conditions and years of seeing her furniture and her clothes fray while having to scramble for every day's food, the splendor was like a stain on humanity.

Already, the hallway was adorned with a fine collection of old paintings in gilded frames, while artistic bric-a-brac stood on well-dusted hallway tables. An array of fur coats and silk stoles—most likely Frau Hassel's—hung like soldiers at attention on the coat rack. For Edda the confrontation was doubly hard, as it felt like stepping back in time—into her parents' equally opulent world, a world she'd sworn off to follow Ash and his people.

"Do come on in, Miss Van der Valk," he said on a friendly tone, without introducing himself. Edda was ushered into a large room with tall windows overlooking the scene she'd just left. She averted her eyes from the outside view as it only sparked a longing to bolt out of this room, and run far, far away. Where, she didn't know, but away from this barbed wire prison and even farther away from this green villa.

"Wait here for a moment, will you? Herr Gemmeker and Frau Hassel will be with you in a moment."

This was confusing. He'd said they were waiting for her. Was it a trap after all? The unnamed Jewish man must have seen her mistrust, as he quickly added. "Just make yourself comfortable, please. They'll be here in a minute. I promise."

Edda calmed her breath while taking in the lavish room. Recently polished mahogany furniture gave off a lemon scent that was supposed to be fresh but made her nauseous. The rooms were shut tight. The air was oppressive. Was it to keep out all sounds from the camp?

Her eyes scanned the room to ascertain where the windows and doors were. Just in case. Oh, how she longed for her Enfield. It would have made her feel so much safer. All the armchairs and sofas had crisp blue and green upholstery and looked comfortable and soft. The walls were wallpapered with speckles of tiny red flowers, as if spatters of blood. Thick, wall-to-wall, brown carpeting absorbed all sounds.

She sniffed. There was another, much more nauseating smell. The smell of rich food—sausages, greens, gravies, aromatic puddings. In the space behind the closed sliding panel a high-pitched voice was singing Wagner's Rienzi Opera. Her eyes wandered to the ceiling, finding what she was looking for. *Motion detectors. Oh yes, they were there!* She spotted two small black boxes with blinking glass eyes in two corners of the ceiling.

Knowing they were watching her from another room, she

perched on one bulky armchair, pretending to be listening to the screeching opera voice. Most of Edda's attention was focused on not shivering, not crying, not leaping up and breaking down the door with her bare hands to get out of this godforsaken place.

The door opened and her hosts appeared, all bustle and smiles. The Camp Commander, straight and elegant in his eagle-crested uniform, smiled benignly as he strode towards her with an outstretched hand. Frau Hassel, close to his side, was another kettle of fish. Young and beautiful, expensively dressed in a tight-fitting, navy lady's suit and white blouse, she was the perfect fit as the Gentleman Crook's mistress. But Edda saw Elizabeth Hassel was as hard as her long, lacquered nails, just as the camp people had warned her. The hand that shook Edda's was cold and hard, her rings pressed into Edda's flesh.

"Fräulein Van der Valk," she purred, "how lovely to make your acquaintance. I only met with your dear Father last week. How you resemble your Mother!"

Edda stood bravely, anchoring her ballet feet on the thick carpet, and nodded as if she discussed her traitorous Papa everyday with this conniving woman.

"Thank you for inviting me." She hoped it was sufficiently polite.

"Do sit down, Fräulein Van der Valk," Gemmeker invited. "Franz will bring the drinks in a minute. I take it you like a freshly made cocktail? We specifically bought the Apfelwein during Oktoberfest in Munich, where we celebrated with the Führer."

"I'm afraid I don't drink alcohol. It doesn't go well with my ballet career." Edda was determined not to be drunk near this couple.

"Ah, but Fräulein, apple cider is not alcohol. It's just juice with fizz." He waved elegant hands and turning to his mistress, asked. "Maybe 4% alcohol, *Mein Liebchen*?"

Frau Hassel stared at him with triumph painted on her lips.

"Didn't I tell you, Albie?" she sneered. "She is like an athlete. These people are so aware of what they allow themselves to eat and drink. How I admire you, Miss Van der Valk. I wish I wouldn't have such a weak will when it comes to sipping champagne and eating fois gras. I simply can't resist them. And Franz prepares these delicacies so well."

The Jewish man, whom Frau Hassel addressed as Franz, walked in holding a tray laden with three enormous glasses and a plateau of artistic-looking snacks. As soon as he placed the tray on the coffee table, Gemmeker and Hassel took turns questioning him how he could make a cocktail without the Apfelwein and the Schnapps. Edda thought it odd how both her hosts nosed into what the exact non-alcoholic contents should be. For a moment the idea arose again that they might want to poison her.

In the back of her mind was also the topic of her parents, which would certainly surface again when the cocktail dispute was settled. She needed to prepare herself for questions about her estranged relationship with her father. "*Stay alive,*" Doctor Samuels whispered in her ear, so she decided she would lie. She'd act the dutiful daughter who visited her parents often. That the Van der Valks were, and always had been, one big happy family. The risk was they knew the last time she'd caught a glance of her parents was at Teppo's funeral over six months ago. The lie was a risk worth taking.

Franz disappeared again with clear instructions and a warning to make haste.

Frau Hassel looked rather longingly at her glass. "We'll have to wait with the toast until you have yours. May I say Edda? I find all this Frau and Herr so annoying?"

"Sure," Edda answered, intending to avoid the use of their Christian names if she could.

"We're Albert and Elizabeth," the Mistress cooed. Edda nodded with a wan smile. She felt ill, tired of constantly being on tenterhooks, and was missing Tante Riet at her side in this difficult hour.

"Now let's relax and have a chat." Frau Hassel pointed red-varnished nails in the direction of the comfy sofa and chairs. It was clear she directed the show, at least inside the green villa, but from what Edda had heard, Elizabeth Hassel, a simple girl from quarry town Winterswijk, had the Hauptsturmführer firmly under her thumb. Also, where the camp decisions were concerned. Who went on the Tuesday deportation list and who was spared another week. If Edda wanted to stay alive, she would have to stay on Frau Hassel's good side. Not a very pleasant endeavor, Edda was sure. But she must be spared.

THE NEXT DAY Edda was put in charge of the cultural events in Camp Westerbork. Ruth Birkenbach had disappeared, and she didn't dare ask where. Tante Riet didn't come back, and a long cold winter awaited the very few people left in the barracks. For some mysterious reason the Tuesday trains no longer ran and increasing reports even filtered through to the prisoners that the Allies were on their way. That the south of Holland was already free. So, Edda kept hope it would all be over soon, and she would be able to take stock of what her life had become.

It wasn't fun to be a regular guest at the green Villa and to organize a solo dance for herself on the small podium in the performance barrack accompanied by Herr Gemmeker's own gramophone.

The days were short, the nights were long, one gray day latched onto the next. Snow fell and an icy Northern wind blew day and night. There wasn't enough firewood, there wasn't enough wood and Edda's heart and soul were completely empty. She feared many times she would just give up and die. But always when the lowest point came, Doctor Samuels whispered *'Stay Alive'* in her head.

"It's easier said than done," she grumbled back. "What have I got left? What can I do when this hell is over. To whom can I turn?"

Edda crawled underneath her thin blankets while her teeth chattered and her feet were frozen. Sleep was the only oblivion she still cherished but it came in fits and starts.

It would be the longest and darkest winter of her life.

43

THE DAY THAT WOULD NEVER COME

Six months later, Camp Westerbork, April 1945

Westerbork, 13 April 1945, 8:00 pm

I am so happy I think I'll burst and at the same time I'm way too ill to stand on my feet for longer than 5 minutes. What a contrast. We're free! We're liberated! The Germans are gone, gone, gone!!!! We couldn't believe our eyes but yesterday, 12 April 1945, the First Canadian Army liberated us. We saw them coming.

But let me first tell you how Gemmeker and Frau Hassel were made to eat humble pie. All the rumors were so loud that liberation was imminent. We only saw Allied planes fly over and they dropped us food! Real food! I mean flour, margarine, coffee, milk powder, cheese, chocolate. Things we haven't tasted for years. I was so hungry, but I remembered Miss Sterling saying we need to eat small portions, so I ate a little bite every hour. Honestly, I feel my strength already returning but that must also be the mental boost that it's really, really over.

See, I can't even return to the topic of that Gentleman Crook, but I need to. This notebook, by the way, was given to me by one of the sweet Tommys. I was talking with him last night, his name is Sergeant Stuart Gildersleeve (his last name sounds like a character from a ballet!!!) and he told me he'd been keeping notes ever since landing on the beaches in Normandy, which was over 10 months ago!!! The diary kept him sane, and I told him about my little notebooks hidden at my sister's.

"I've got a spare one, now that I hope to head back to Vancouver soon," he grinned. So now I have a Canadian notebook, a simple thin cahier with a brown cover but I'll cherish it all my life. It's my liberation gift, almost more important than the chocolate that melts on my tongue.

Alright, I promised you Gemmeker and Mistress Hassel. Well, there isn't a grand finale there. They just left. Like that. Each had a small suitcase and they walked away. I hope by God they'll be arrested before they walk hand-in-hand into Germany, but they kept their heads high. You know what Frau Hassel said to me on my last visit to them, which was months ago as they

didn't like my company anymore. I know I am a bore,
but I was a deliberate bore with them as I hated every
minute in the green villa. Anyway, back on track. She
said to me: "My Albert is the Jesus Christ of Westerbork." Can you imagine? I almost choked on the coffee
I was drinking and spit it out on that striped sofa. The
Jesus Christ of Westerbork. The woman is insane. I
won't be surprised he'll be convicted of sending all these
Jews and Sintis and Romas east with little chance of
survival.

Though I'm writing horrible things, you can't imagine
what joy it is to write freely again. Oh, how I missed
my own thoughts on paper. I simply love the act of my
pen going over the page. Maybe I've got a bit of a
writer in me? Who knows! But for now, it's Heaven on
Earth. Food in my stomach, the sun on my table, and me
with my diary.

The Canadians have ordered us to stay here until
Amsterdam is liberated but Stu told me it's a mere
matter of days now. I'll be going home. But I almost
dread the idea. What will I find at home? Will my
flat still be there? And what about Tante Riet? No
word of her all these months. Gemmeker kept promising
me he'd find out if she was still in Zwolle but he
said he couldn't find her. I fear the worst. My
instinct tells me something's wrong there. But no sad
thoughts today. There will be plenty of decisions to be
made over the coming weeks but for now I'm going

outside again and enjoy the company of the Canadians!
They're such fun.

Forty hours earlier

An eery silence reigned over the camp. It had never been a loud place since Edda had arrived there in September, but nothing like this silent anticipation had enveloped the remaining 800 prisoners huddled together in a few barracks. Nobody knew what to expect, good or bad. The return of the Germans or the arrival of the Allies. They were in No Man's Land in between two fighting armies, their fate in the hands of the victors.

The German guards had left. With Hauptsturmführer and Frau Hassel up front. In the evening, the last Germans of the Grenzschütz had also left their positions and hastened in their commander's footsteps.

Edda had wondered if she should just walk out of the gate as well, but the people were hesitant. What would they find out there? Was it safe or would they be killed in the last fights? "Let's wait for the liberators," was the general consensus.

It was a bright April morning with fresh green leaves sprinkled on the trees and songbirds warming up their vocal cords. About the only sound came from the birds. Nobody spoke but everyone was straining their ears.

"I hope we'll see the Canadians arrive soon," a sprightly woman called Rachel whispered. "Can you imagine? Canadians. One would expect the Brits, or perhaps Americans. Not Canadians."

Edda nodded. It was all so strange in every way. The spring morning, no guards, the rat-tat-tat of machine guns in the near distance, eating chocolate and sipping surrogate coffee.

Aad Van Beesd, a tall bald Dutch man with a goatee and intense blue eyes, came into the barrack where Edda was sitting at the window. He looked around. On the request of the other prisoners, he'd taken over leadership as soon as the SS had left. He was a calm man who'd first been head of distribution in the camp and was later employed by the municipality of Westerbork and knew most of the inmates.

"The rumors are correct," he said with a broad smile which made his goatee jump up. "It looks like our ordeal will soon be over. The Canadians are on their way. Please all gather in the main hall, and I'll send an envoy to greet the army. Otto Ziel, would you do the honor of standing at the gate waving the Dutch flag? I've brought them in illegally from the town hall."

A thin and worn-out Jewish man of about sixty sprang to his feet. "Of course." His fallen-in cheeks glowed with pride and his dark eyes gleamed.

The rest of the people, including Edda, made their way to the main hall. Edda could feel her heartbeat in her throat, she was so nervous it was almost impossible to keep her hands still, but she walked with the other people across the terrain when they heard a loud cheer.

"The Tommys are here! The Tommys are here!"

Hearing this, nobody continued to the hall, but all rushed out to see the convoy of trucks and rows of infantry soldiers sporting the Canadian Red Ensign Flag come their way.

The crowd broke out in a spontaneous singing of the national anthem.

"Wilhelmus van Nassouwe
ben ik, van Duitsen bloed,
den vaderland getrouwe
blijf ik tot in den dood.
Een Prinse van Oranje
ben ik, vrij, onverveerd,
den Koning van Hispanje
heb ik altijd geëerd."

It sounded tentative at first but as they saw the grinning faces of the Canadians, looking almost as battle-weary and tired as they were, the singing became louder, caps flew in the air, and Dutch flags suddenly appeared from everywhere.

Edda thronged with the others towards the gates to meet the long row of vehicles and foot soldiers. It was almost like a scene from the Iliad, a theater production she'd once seen with Duifje in 1937. Two banner-waving groups, the Greeks and the Trojans heading towards each other, only this time it was not to fight but to welcome each other. Also, for the Canadians, this must be another happy victory they rejoiced in, Edda realized.

With hungry eyes she took in their heroes, men some middle-aged, some still beardless and her heart almost burst out of her chest with gratitude for Westerbork and compassion for Canada.

The infantry men and the men on the jeeps waved, threw cigarettes and candy into the hands of the eager prisoners, who chanted their national anthem with ever more zest. More Dutch flags were raised on poles, miraculously appearing in the air.

As the convoy passed the barbed-wired gates, Edda could see a profound emotional response on the sweaty, smeared faces as well. What had these men already encountered on their long trek, possibly even from Normandy? More camps like this, starving people, people who'd almost lost hope, broken-hearted people? Thousands and thousands of people like Edda Van der Valk.

Edda couldn't help herself any longer. She needed her answers, and she needed them fast, before the moment had passed. Springing forward from the crowd, she pulled the sleeve from one of the soldiers passing her.

"Excuse me, sir, have you by any chance seen a lady called Rita Meulenbelt, a white-haired Amsterdamer, or perhaps a family called the Hoffmanns?

The eyes with dark lashes and a steely-gray glint took her in from under his helmet. He kept marching in formation with the others. Edda rang alongside the convoy to get her answers.

"Sorry, Ma'am, I don't remember. But rest assured we'll do everything we can to liberate all the Dutch and reunite families."

And on he went, deeper into the camp, where the infantry finally came to a halt near the main hall. Aad Van Beesd shook hands with the Canadian commander. The vehicles that had been part of the convoy parked at one side of the wired fence. Soldiers from within the tanks opened their turret hatchets and the Canadian flags were raised. More cheers erupted from the crowds.

Immediately after, a group of Canadians Edda supposed were guards with pointed rifles dispersed over the terrain for an extensive search of the camp. This time not for Jews, not for Resisters, but for stray Germans who might have hidden there.

Edda stood, turning slowly on her heels to take in a 360 degree of this magnificent moment. Canadians. She'd never met a Canadian in her life and now she was surrounded by them on all sides. How wickedly safe it felt and how beautiful it was that all the people present were instant friends. Almost no need for introduction.

As the all-clear was given and the commander had disappeared into the registration hall with Aad von Beesd, probably to go through the lists of people still in the camp, Edda saw one straight-backed soldier march back to the Green Villa and plant the Canadian Red Ensign flag brotherly next to the Dutch tricolor. A cheer so loud it reached the heavens sounded from every throat.

The Canadians flopped down on the grass, clearly allowed to have a much-needed rest and recuperation after their morning march. Tentatively, the former prisoners sat down among the soldiers, being offered more chocolate, more cigarettes and more smiles.

Edda heard a "hey Miss!" It came from the soldier whose sleeve she'd pulled. On gingerly legs, she walked towards him. To her surprise she saw he was using his rucksack as a small table and, while he drank from his thermos, and smoked a cigarette, he was scribbling at high pace in a thin brown cahier. He looked up from writing feverishly when she was next to him.

"Would you like to sit with me?" he asked in a deep and pleasant voice. "I'm 2nd Lieutenant Stuart Gildersleeve, 3rd Canadian Infantry Division, but originally from Vancouver. Everyone calls me Stew. I do stew a lot over things, so it's fine." He smiled, showing teeth that looked remarkably white in his dust-smeared face. Small laugh wrinkles also appeared at the sides of his clear eyes.

Edda smiled too, and still on high alert on her *qui vive*, sat down on the grass at some distance from him, pulling her skirt over her pointed knees. She eyed him and his notebook from under her eyelashes. Stew was obviously easy-going and kind, but also very foreign to her.

"Do you have a name, Miss?" Again, that white-toothed smile, while he fished a cigarette from his Philip Morris packet and threw it her way.

"I'm Edda Van der Valk," she said, "Thank you so much Stew, you and all the others, for liberating us." She felt tears welling but pushed them back, turning the white paper of the cigarette between her fingers.

"It's our honor, Miss Edda. We came here to fight for freedom, and seeing the people's smiles and gratitude makes this whole bloody war worthwhile." The steely eyes studied her, which made Edda uncomfortable and wondering if she should excuse herself and get up. So, she wasn't prepared for his next words.

"I hope you're not related to a certain Marquess Johannes Van der Valk, Miss Edda. We have strict instructions to arrest him at any time and in any form. But you look nothing like him. We were all shown his picture."

Edda drew in a deep breath. Here it was. What she had feared for years. The stain that would now follow her family name till eternity. Mustering all her ballerina discipline, she looked the Canadian liberator straight in the face and said in an off-hand manner, "no, not related." Her heart sank and she felt horrible. It wasn't the first time she'd have to deny her blood ties and it certainly wasn't going to be the last.

Stew let his gaze drop and looked back at the words he'd written in his cahier, thus giving Edda a moment to recover. Though Van der Valk was now a cursed name in Holland, wearing it up until now had probably kept her alive throughout the last year of the war. Oh, it was all so controversial, so crushing, but Edda pushed the thought away with force. Today was about celebration, not about complicated family ties. That whole package would come soon enough.

Stew fired a new question her way. "But you're not Jewish. What are you doing in a Jewish camp?"

"I'm a Resister. I was arrested in Amsterdam in September last year and brought here. I don't know why I wasn't killed before a firing squad or put on a transport east like most of the others."

"A Resister? You with the Resistance, Miss Edda? Holy Moly, I'd doff my cap to you if only I had a cap instead of a helmet." He tapped the metal casing next to him. Then saluted her.

"It's not that we made much difference, did we? All those Jews that were deported and so many Resisters killed," Edda said bitterly.

"No difference? Are you kidding me?" Stew brushed his fingers through his long blonde mane that had been flattened under his helmet. "Let me tell you that the Resisters in France, in Belgium, and in Holland paved the way for us. Without you lot we wouldn't even have scrambled up Juno beach at all. You made all the difference, and you'd better believe it. Maps, directions, sabotaging and destroying vital German infrastructure and depots, sharing all sorts of intelligence."

There was sheer admiration in his eyes, and he drew closer to her flipping open his lighter. He held the small flame before her.

"Accept my humble light, as you've given me yours. For years," he said with deep reverence in his voice. Edda picked up the cigarette from the grass, studied it for a moment, and put it to her lips that were trembling. The only other time she could remember smoking a cigarette was at that darn dinner party at her parent's house with Ash.

She inhaled, didn't cough but didn't like it either. Smoking was not for her, so she extinguished the cigarette carefully and handed it back to Stew. "Thank you. You keep it. It's more precious to you."

The small scene had relaxed Edda and she flopped without

thinking into a Buddha position while draping her skirt over her flattened knees.

"Some flexible body there," Stew observed.

"I'm a professional ballerina. At least I was, for years..." Edda's voice trailed off.

"No? Really?"

She seemed to grow in impressiveness in Stew's eyes by the minute and though the admiration was wonderful, it was also slightly disconcerting.

"What about you, Stew?" Better place the ball in his court. She saw him hesitate, wanting to know more about her but realizing this had to be a fair exchange.

"Oh, I had to give up my dream as well," he shrugged.

"What dream?"

"Being a playwright. I'd just finished the first year at the Canadian Film Institute in Ottawa when I was called to arms. That's why I'm writing everything down, you see. I'm a playwright, not a soldier."

He pointed to his notebook, then sighed and looked saddened. "I've lost so many comrades on the way. Even yesterday, my best friend from 1st grade, Harry Welburn, died in Hoogeveen before my eyes. Shot in the head by a German gun. Instantly dead. Joking and smoking one minute, dead the next. It makes no sense. No sense at all. Harry was only 24 and engaged to be married." Stew stopped talking, rubbed his dusty face. Then with more vigor, continued. "That's why I have to write it all down, Edda. In the memory of those that fell. I intend to make my first documentary about the Canadian forces liberating the Continent." He fell silent, staring down at the words on his page.

"That's...that's awesome," Edda's own voice was thick, "I've also been writing, but a diary," she confessed. "They're hidden at my sister's place because, you know, I've been writing compromising things about the German occupation of Holland." The clear eyes flicked to hers and Edda saw tears in Stew eyes.

"That's more than amazing," he said. "Do you intend to publish your diaries?"

Edda thought about this. "I've never even considered it. It was...it was more a record for when I had children but that doesn't seem to be happening anymore."

"What nonsense! What do you mean? No children?" Stew looked puzzled. So, Edda told him of Ash, of her brooch, of the big hole in her soul. Her story made Stew silent for a long time. He lit another cigarette, closed his notebook, and stuffed it in his backpack.

"You'll love again," he said with conviction. "You'll come across another good man, Edda Van der Valk. Mark my words." But Edda shook her head. "Some people can only love once," she said sadly and thought of Tante Riet and her Freek.

"There is one thing I can do for you, and that is give you a spare notebook so you can at least start writing again. Would you like that?" Stew was already retrieving an exact copy of his own slim brown notebook from his backpack and offered it to Edda. "But please seriously consider publishing your first-hand notes on the war, Edda. The last has not been said about this ordeal, but I can tell you this with certainty. For many years people will live on as if it didn't happen, because it was that bad. Then children and grandchildren are going to ask questions about the war, wanting to understand. Then you and I will be the ones who can give them first-hand accounts of what we lived through. Do you see?"

Edda nodded, feeling like she was listening to wise words. She accepted the notebook graciously.

"I'll cherish this gift all my life, Stew," she said, caressing its simple brown front. "This is more important than all the food, all the cigarettes. This is my liberation gift. Thank you so much." And their eyes met once more, in which Edda saw a flicker of something, of yearning, but also of deep understanding and friendship.

"You're a beautiful woman inside and outside," Stew said, raising himself to his full length. "I need to go and set up camp with the others now. We'll stay here for the night but is there any way we can stay in touch with each other after all this?" He made a sweeping gesture around the desolate camp that today was in sheer and utter celebration.

"I'd love that," Edda said, springing to her feet as well and looking the Canadian straight in the face.

"Scribble your address in my notebook and I'll write mine in yours," he suggested and thus they exchanged addresses and a promise. A promise to stay in touch.

"I hope to see you before we leave and I'll keep an eye open for your relatives," Stew offered and stretched out his hand. Edda crossed the short distance between them, stood on tiptoe and kissed his cheek. Then he kissed hers.

"Thank you," he said and turned his back on her. Edda looked until he was lost in a group of his comrades with all the same uniforms.

A FRIEND, a Canadian friend who'd given her a precious gift.

44

BROKEN BUT STILL ALIVE

Two weeks later

Westerbork, 30 April 1945

I'm still in the camp, as we have to wait until Amsterdam is liberated. Most of the Canadians - including Stuart Gildersleeve - have moved further to the North of Holland to liberate Groningen and Friesland.

Only a handful of them are still here looking after injured comrades (we still have the hospital, although it's primitive), but for the rest of us, we're a self-catering group of former prisoners now. We have enough to eat and without the Germans we feel really free and happy. The weather is gorgeous, and we can walk outside the camp if we want. We make music in the evenings, and I dance for them if I feel like it. My limbs are quite rusty though and I long for Miss Sterling's instructions.

Still, I can't wait to be able to go back to Amsterdam, to my own flat. On the other hand, I also dread the return. What will I find there? Who will I find there and how to solve the rift with my family? I try to think about all that as little as possible.

Just turned on the radio and heard the most amazing news! Hitler is dead. He killed himself in his bunker in Berlin together with his mistress, who he apparently married a couple of hours before they both did themselves in. I told you the guy is insane. Who does such a thing? Is even love a mockery to him? Clearly!

Anyway, I'm enraged by this news as well. What a coward, what a terrible coward not to face justice as he should but to slay himself. What will all his victims feel? He got away with everything and never had to face a tribunal for the millions he sent to an early grave. Grrrr!

Edda listened to the camp life around her. She was alone in the barrack at that moment, sitting at her small window facing the south side, not the part where the hated green villa stood. Two children were throwing a ball and counting, a woman was singing a Yiddish song Edda couldn't understand. A truck, most likely Canadian, rumbled by on the other side. A songbird twittered in the treetops.

It sounded like a leisurely, easy morning in which all the care

Edda had was to wash the few garments she still possessed, sweep the main hall, and chat with other camp dwellers.

But she used the time alone to take stock. Having invested years and years of her life into her physical and mental strength, she was gauging both and found them both lacking.

Pondering what Doctor Samuels had said to her about seeking help, psychological help, when the war was over, Edda shook her head. Yes, she would need to work through all she'd endured, to be able to dance at the top again. And that was all she yearned for in the few years she had left to still be a first ballerina before she was too old. Dance. Feel the ultimate thrill in tutu and tights and *on pointe* on a world stage. To dance until she shattered herself.

But Edda was Edda. Edda didn't choose mentors. They found her. Actively seeking a psychiatrist seemed artificial. Yet her problems were real. Her heart and soul eroded by years of hardship and horror and heartbreak. A serious hindrance to dancing freely and flawless.

"Maybe I can deal with it myself," she mused. "This has been the longest time I've gone without a mentor and I survived. And who knows, with a bit of luck, Miss Sterling will still be in Amsterdam. She knows me through and through."

Edda closed her notebook and got up from her chair. As the weather was so fine, she decided on a walk through the park. In her only dress—gray, cotton, knee-length and with a simple white collar —her shoes with holes in the bottom, Edda walked into the April sunlight, squinting against the light. Her skin was so pale, almost translucent and she was cold despite the sun.

I'm too thin to dance, she thought and despair set in. Eating was such a struggle at times. She took in the other people, going about their business and the next fearful thought gripped her. I haven't made any friends here, not even acquaintances. I constantly keep to myself. I'm not normal. But she corrected herself. Losing Tante Riet had made her a complete introvert, or rather, so afraid to attach herself to new people that she remained distant.

I have problems. Real problems.

But as she walked farther away from the barracks and found

herself among the trees and the flowers, where just the birds chirped and the air was thick with the scent of hawthorn, Edda revived. Inhaling the flowery scent, opening her ears to the melody above her and Chopin came to mind. Chopin's Nocturne C sharp minor, to which she had danced in that former school in Amsterdam-Zuid until her feet bled.

Her feet moved tentatively over the flowerbeds, hesitant at first, then wilder and wilder among the bushes, the birds, and the butterflies. Then Edda let herself go. And go and go. Until something pricked through the hole in her sole and she cried out, "ouch!"

She bent to see what the sharp object was and stood stunned. It was the wing of her butterfly brooch, filled with earth and broken off, just one crystal remaining. Edda rubbed it clean with her fingers, tears dripping down her cheeks.

Carefully putting the one wing in her dress pocket, she started a wild search for the rest of her brooch. She searched and searched but found nothing. With restless fingers she dug through the earth, uprooted plants and tussocks, wondering how the one wing could have landed here. Then she remembered that she was near the track, now overgrown as it hadn't been used for almost ten months, where she had descended the train upon arriving at Camp Westerbork. The wild search continued. She didn't think of food or drink. The afternoon sun was already low, and her knees were bleeding from crawling over the ground.

Suddenly she saw something glitter in the low-sinking sunlight and dashed forward. A second wing. This one still had two crystals. The wind was picking up in the poplars above her. Edda was tired, exhausted, thrilled, and yet pained at the same time. She lay down on the soft soil for a moment looking up at the treetops. Closed her eyes for a moment.

This is it, my gritty girl. Take your wings and fly. They are all you need.

Wide-eyed Edda jolted to a sitting position, looked around her. Was she going mad? She'd clearly heard Ash's voice as if he was right by her side.

"Ash!" she cried. "Are you there?"

There was no answer. She waited, not daring to call again. She stared down at the two broken wings in the palm of her hand. Then she understood the message. Right there and then, Edda understood everything. The right and wrong, the good and evil, God and Satan. Slowly she rose to her feet and stood upright under the trees.

If she couldn't be Edda Hoffmann, she would be Edda Valkena. Never again Eddaline Van der Valk.

HERE IN CAMP WESTERBORK on 8 May 1945 stood first ballerina, Edda Valkena, with two broken wings that would make her fly.

I WILL FLY, Ash. For you I will fly. Till the end of time.

45

THE SISTERS

One week later

Amsterdam, 8 May 1945

We are finally, finally FREE! Herr Hitler died a
week ago, Meneer Mussert has been arrested, and we're
dancing in the streets. Oh, how good life is! I'm writing
in my Canadian notebook, thinking of the past five years
and it's so much. So incredibly much has happened it
feels like it was at least ten years of my life.

I arrived in Amsterdam yesterday. I had to stay
in Westerbork until Amsterdam was liberated. Before I
got on the train to Amsterdam, I tried to get to Zwolle
to see if I could find Tante Riet but was told it was
still too difficult. So, today I'm going to see if I can
visit Ome Jan and hopefully he will tell me more about
his sister.

The arrival at Amsterdam Station was incredible. Everyone was singing and hugging the liberators, flags were waving, and people were openly drunk in the streets. Amsterdamers, and Canadian, Scottish, American soldiers mixing with each other. Young women and children being hoisted onto tanks and trucks. What a sight! What a festive sight!

While I'm writing this at my own flat at Vondelstraat 56, something much more impressive is taking place in Berlin. The signing of the official complete surrender of the German army. Those signatures from Britain, United States, the Soviet Union, France and Germany will be the official end of the war.

I was sure all along that this horrific Third Reich would crumble into nothing, but it took much longer than expected. And it turned out to be much, much more gruesome than anyone in their right mind could have concocted.

Every day the papers disclose more of what really happened in the camps in Germany and Poland. Estimates now are that not thousands, but millions of people have been murdered in those so-called labor camps that were actually extermination camps. People were killed in gas chambers right after arriving there! A place called Auschwitz was the worst of all.

The Nazis killed mostly Jews, but also Romas and Sintis and other minorities. And, of course, so many Resistance fighters from all the occupied countries. I can't wrap my mind around the horrors, and I can't look anymore at the pictures of skeleton-thin people in

striped pyjamas and heaps of shoes or bones. The
photographs make me sick to the stomach. And
desperate!

When I think of the Hoffmans and Larry's family,
Monsieur Sergeyev and all the Jewish families I helped
here in Amsterdam whose hiding places were discovered.
It's now practically guaranteed that hardly any of those
people will ever return.

I cannot think of that now or I'll go insane.
Yours truly, Edda Valkena

Edda looked up from her writing and felt her cheeks had become red
with anger. She jumped up and started pacing in her sitting room
that still had the furniture pushed to one side and the ballet barre
Ome Jan had installed for her pliés.

The flat was almost in order again, but it had been in complete
chaos when she entered the day before. All the drawers and
cupboards had been emptied onto the floors and the bed.

Her flat had been searched thoroughly after she and Tante Riet
had tried to flee to the Achterhoek and had been arrested by the
Gestapo on the way. Nothing seemed to be missing, and Edda had
grinned widely that they hadn't found the radio she'd hidden under a
couple of loose floorboards. Thank God for the diaries being with
Duifje!

Duifje!

Edda stopped her pacing. She needed her sister, dearly, dread-
fully. Grabbing her coat, a threadbare Macintosh someone had left
behind in Westerbork, in her shoes with the holes, the two butterfly
wings safely stored in their gilded-lettering box and wrapped in
tissue paper inside her handbag, Edda set out for the station.

She had to navigate her way through groups of drunk and merry
people who regularly gripped her around the waist to make her

swivel in a wild polka with them, but Edda wrung herself free every time, determined as she was to get to The Hague now. *Tout de suite.*

"EDDA?" Duifje's blue eyes shot an angry fire at her, "Where the hell have you been? I've been searching for you everywhere! E-v-e-r-y-w-h-e-r-e!"

"Oh Duifje!" Edda couldn't hold back and threw herself in her elder sister's arms, clinging to her with all her might. "I've been in a prisoner camp since September. Didn't you know?"

Duifje clung as hard to her as Edda did to her. "How was I supposed to know? Do you think carrier pigeons came to tell me? You stupid girl, what did you do to end up in a camp?" Duifje peeled Edda off her and held her at a short distance, inspecting her intently as if she might be full of lice. Then pulled her close again, not caring they were making a display of affection at her front door. A display that would have sent their Marchioness mother huffing with horror.

"Silly, silly little Lientje. Oh, my darling, I'm so glad you're back. You could have died in that camp, don't you know?"

"I know," Edda sniffled with her face against her sister's neck, "I almost did. Oh Duifje, oh Duifje, is it really over?"

"Who is that?" A girl's voice asked from the hall.

"Go back inside, Elly. We'll be with you in a sec." Duifje sounded much more authoritative than Edda had ever heard her.

With a sigh the older sister said wisely, "Alas, darling. This war isn't over for us yet. Have you heard Father was arrested?"

Edda stepped back to look at her sister. Though she'd expected this to happen sooner or later, it was a blow, nonetheless.

"And Mother?" she inquired with fear in her voice.

"Too weak. Mother's been sickly for months." The concern in Duifje's blue gaze was new as well. "Anyway, I'll tell you all and you tell me all. Come in, Lientje. You look like you're on your last legs. I suppose they didn't feed you very well in that camp."

With her arm around her sister, Edda was propelled to the sitting room that also looked very different than she remembered. It was clean, it was spacious and there was new furniture. A blonde boy of about eleven was reading a comic book at the table. Eyes Edda remembered as Teppo's looked up at her. He raised himself from his chair.

"I'll go to my room, Mama."

"No Benny, stay. This is your Tante Edda. Don't you remember her?" The Teppo-like eyes took her in again, he frowned. Then walked over to Edda with his hand outstretched.

"I'm not sure I remember Mama, but hello Tante Edda."

What a well-behaved young boy, Edda thought rather perplexed. Had Duifje done this? Then her sister had certainly changed.

"Ask Elly to come and say hello as well, Benny. We'll all have tea together and then Tante Edda and I need to talk grown-up stuff."

Benny was already out of the door, calling "Elly, come meet Tante Edda."

A girl of about five came in rather diffidently and Edda stood nailed at the spot. The very straight little figure was wearing a tutu and pink tights, dark curls and dark eyes in a face that was almost a copy of herself.

"Elly," she stammered, "are you a ballerina?"

The little girl smiled shyly, "I want to be like you."

"Oh Elly!" Edda looked at her sister and saw the emotion in Duifje's eyes. "I did nothing to encourage her, Edda. Honestly, I didn't, because I know quite well the sacrifices you made as a child for your dance career. But this little minx as headstrong as you. Really, without me even telling her."

"That's not true, Mammie," Elly protested while she swiftly crossed the parquet floor on her ballet slippers towards her aunt. "I asked you who the beautiful ballerina in the picture in your bedroom was and you said 'that is your Tante Edda.' So," she turned victoriously with a *pirouette* to Edda and said, "see, I knew you before I had seen you."

When Edda sat down on her sister's new couch, she felt light-headed and strange. As if she was in a new house, in a new family, where there was order instead of chaos. There was so much chaos in her, she wasn't sure she could cope with the order in her sister's life yet.

"Are you alright, Lientje?" Duifje's voice seemed to come from very far away.

"I'm not, Duifje. I'm not well."

Her sister slipped next to her on the couch, again put an arm around her and pulled her to her. Then Edda realized something else. Duifje's scent. She smelled of soap and clean clothes. The cigarette smoke and unwashed hair was gone. Duifje smelled like Duifje again and Edda inhaled her with all her force.

Her teeth clattered as a glass of water was put to her lips.

"Listen, Lientje," Duifje said through a strange fog that enveloped Edda's head. "That talk can come later. I now understand you're in shock. I've been hoping this past year that I could pay you back in the way you've always been there for me. The guest-room has been ready for you since forever. I'm putting you in the bath, and then in the bed. Corrie will look after you while the children and I go clothing shopping for you. You look like a beggar, and you smell like one."

Edda had no power to resist even if she had wanted to.

An hour later she was lying clean and in one of Duifje's frilly nightdresses under a silken duvet with soft piano music coming from the record player in the corner. In another corner, Corrie, all grown up and sporting reading glasses sat flipping through a lady's magazine. She looked up when she saw Edda was still awake.

"What a change has happened in the Van Leeuwen's household, hasn't it, Miss Van der Valk?" the housekeeper said with a warm smile. "I couldn't have found a better address to work. And it's all thanks to you."

"Thanks to me?" Edda said in wonder.

"Yes, you saved Mevrouw Van Leeuwen's life. Then she chose to live. And a good life it is. The children are adorable."

"They are. I'm glad, so glad."

Something good had come out of this wretched war, after all. Edda fell into a deep, dreamless sleep for the first time in a very long time.

46

THE POST-WAR VAN DER VALKS

The next day – The Hague, 9 May 1945

When Edda came down to breakfast in Duifje's house the next morning, she only found Corrie dusting the sitting room. The house was silent, no children's voices nor Duifje's shrill, high voice uttering commands or quips.

"Mrs Van Leeuwen is out trying to find some more articles of clothing for you, Miss," the housekeeper said as she saw Edda standing in the doorway, looking surprised and uncomfortable in one of her sister's flowery, knee length dresses. The housekeeper, dressed in muted dark blue with a white apron had none of her former flusteredness and was going about her dusting in a calm and composed way.

"Do sit down. I'll bring you breakfast in a minute. We're really surprised there's nothing in the shops here." Corrie folded her dusting cloth and came over to the table. She opened a flowery tea cosy and poured Edda a cup. Edda still stood in the middle of the room as if recently washed ashore on an unknown island, unsure if she'll be safe there.

"Sit, Miss," Corrie said again. "I've done my best to prepare you a proper breakfast but it's easier said than done with no eggs and only a pinch of flour." Then Edda remembered the hunger winter that had struck the big cities in the west of Holland in the past months. How had Duifje and her children survived? And her parents? Probably fed by the Germans, Edda thought, but strangely without any anger. Despite being captives at Westerbork, at least they had enough food.

As if guessing her train of thought, Corrie said, "You're lucky you found us here, Miss Edda. We've only just returned here, you see. We were on Valkena Estate all winter. Took the sickly Marchioness with us. So, we've had plenty of eggs and milk. We haven't had any shortages. Mrs van Leeuwen is only back here with Mr Sipkema to sell the house. We're all moving to Friesland for good."

Edda was aware she gaped at the housekeeper and uttered not very coherently, "Valkena Estate? Mother? Friesland?" Sinking on the chair, she tried to make sense of it all. The Sipkema name rang a bell. Her father's solicitor. Papa had mentioned him as Edda's go-to, should she need to talk business. That last strained conversation she had had with her father. Talking about his will.

Edda shuddered at the thought and at the realization that now struck her. Duifje had said their father was arrested. She might need Mr Sipkema herself. Quite soon.

Corrie, not devoid of common-sense wisdom, saw Edda struggle and quickly added apologetically. "Oh Miss, I shouldn't have told you all this. Mrs Van Leeuwen should have," And with some of her former fluster, she added, "I started blabbing because I'm still getting used to the idea myself, Miss. I've been a Hagenees— an inhabitant of The Hague— since forever, but I like it in Friesland, and in case we get another war, I'd rather be in the countryside."

Edda nodded, sipping her tea that tasted like real Ceylon tea to her.

"We still have supplies we brought with us from Valkena," Corrie explained. "It's only here we're running short of everything. Let's hope the shops will fill up soon now there's peace."

After Corrie had left the room to prepare Edda's breakfast, her mind ran over everything the housekeeper had said, while her eyes ran over Duifje's refurbished sitting room. Duifje moving back to Friesland now that she was a widow made sense. Though the stigma of the Van der Valk and Van Leeuwen name would follow her sister around there as well.

"I need to talk to Mr Sipkema how to go about changing my last name," Edda wondered aloud, when she heard the front doorbell ring. Surely not her sister, she would have her key with her. In a moment of panic Edda sought a place to hide, war adrenaline rushing through her veins. Would the Dutch police come for her now too?

Still riling with nerves, she heard Corrie answer the door and exchange words with someone with a deep, bass voice. But before Edda had time to slip out of the sitting room and hide upstairs, a tall and taut man with short salt-and-pepper hair and similar mustache in a beige trench coat came into the room rubbing his slender hands.

"A coffee, yes, please, Corrie but let me not keep you from your work." Dark green eyes with small brown flecks, with a friendly expression in them, took Edda in, who'd risen from her chair. The man clearly was an acquaintance of the family. With two big strides he was at the table, smiling, shaking her hand firmly.

"My eyes can't believe it," he exclaimed in the clipped voice with the Friesland accent. "Marchioness Eddaline Van der Valk. I'm so happy you've made it through these hellish years."

Edda stood straight as a ballerina, her feet firmly on her sister's parquet floor, weak and strong at the same time.

"And you may be, Sir?"

"I'm awfully sorry. I thought Duifje would have told you. I'm Jan Sipkema, your sister's betrothed."

The last words made Edda sway on her legs until her iron will kept her upright once again. She saw first surprise, then disappointment in the green eyes.

"Oh, I'm so sorry. My mistake. I see I've talked out of turn." He swallowed, making his pronounced Adam's apple go up and down. Edda sank back on her chair. Duifje's surprises were still hitting her from wherever way they came.

The origin of both Edda's and Sipkema's embarrassment swished into the room with her arms full of parcels and a giddy smile on her red lips.

"Lientje, Jan, how wonderful! I see you've already met." Duifje waltzed over to the solicitor and planted a full kiss on his shaven cheek.

"Have you told my sis, you cheeky devil? I see you both looking like two forlorn kittens. There's no secrets in this house anymore, my dear ones. I'm happy to the moon and back. And so are the children."

Edda stared from one to the other, too bewildered to understand the full extent of the changes taking place around her. Half of her was still in a prisoners' camp, the other side mourning her lost friends, and here was Duifje gleaming with happiness.

"Jan, Corrie, will you please go for a moment? I need to talk with my sister." Duifje took control of the situation as Edda had never known her do. "Oh, and bring us coffee and something to eat, please Corrie." She shouted as the door was being softly closed.

Turning to Edda, Duifje said, "Come here, Lientje, let's sit on the sofa together. I can see it's too much for you to take in. I had wanted to have this talk with you yesterday, but you were too exhausted. I'm sorry you had to find out in a haphazard way and not through me but trust me it's all for the best. Also, for you."

With her arm around Edda and pulling her real close, Duifje told her story, the last year of her war.

"After Teppo was gone, I realized we'd lived in chaos since we met. Our love was grand and tumultuous but at times destructive. I found a kind of peace after he was gone that I had never known before. It was odd but real. Of course, I mourned him, but I also felt liberated. And of course," She gave Edda's arm a small squeeze, "I had made a promise to you not to do anything stupid anymore. I suppose it all happened of its own accord. I first stopped drinking as I knew I couldn't control that. The world looked really different when I was sober. And then there were the children and Mother..." Duifje stopped talking, took a sip of the coffee Corrie had noiselessly put on the coffee table in front of them.

"What about Mother?" Edda asked.

"I'll tell you when you first eat something, Lientje. I want to see proper food going inside that skeletal frame of yours. How are you ever going to dance again when you look more like a scarecrow than a Clara?"

Edda had to smile despite herself. Duifje was still Duifje, oscillating between light and dark like a pendulum clock. Only the hysteria seemed to be gone. Edda ate obediently and to her surprise it was rich fruitcake with a cream topping.

"Where did you get this?" she asked munching the last crumbs.

"Remember our childhood heroine, Mevrouw Miedema? She still wields the scepter in the Valkena Estate kitchen and she's the best cook in the world. Mind you, she's in her sixties now."

"It's delicious." Edda felt her body relax with the food in her stomach and the warm body of her sister next to her.

"Mama? You'd tell me about her?"

"Yes." But Duifje didn't continue talking, and Edda sought her sister's eyes in alarm.

"Tell me, Duif, whatever it is!" Edda insisted.

"She's not well." Duifje said in a hoarse voice, "we don't know if the cancer is back because she refuses to be examined. Honestly, sis, if you ask me—and I have none of your intuition— she just wants to die but she's probably waiting for you."

"I see." Edda took in this information more calmly than she'd expected. It would be just a matter of how fast she could travel to Leeuwarden. Then she'd see how the sight of her mother would affect her.

"She's under house arrest, of course, as a collaborator with the Nazis and a prominent NSB member," Duifje said in her matter-of-fact voice. "Too ill to be detained and she can't flee anyway in her state. There are guards at the door at all hours, though."

"How the switch has flipped in a matter of days." Edda's voice was level as well.

"It has. And I'm so glad you've come back to us so soon after the liberation, Edda, because all now depends on your decisions. We were legal lame ducks without you."

"What do you mean?" Edda sat up straighter, fearing the worst-case scenario her father had painted her in his office flanked by the portraits of Hitler and Mussert two years earlier.

"Towards the end of the war Father understood there would be no escape for him and mother, and not for me either, having all joined the NSB." She paused, "When it's hard like now, I could really do with a fag, but I don't allow myself anymore."

Duifje took in a breath, then exhaled as she had done as a heavy smoker. "Father knew he would be arrested, and he took it valiantly. Honestly, Edda, in the final year of the war it wasn't just Mother who had sincere doubts about National Socialism. I think he also understood the whole thing was far out of control, but you know Father. He'll lie in the bed he's made for himself. Stubborn, Frisian pride." Duifje fidgeted with the fringes of her scarf, clearly craving her former addiction.

"What will happen to him?" Edda asked anxiously, "have you even been able to visit him. Where is he?"

"Oh, Lientje. All your questions. They burn a hole in my heart, but it also feels so much better being able to share the Van der Valk burden with you. Or I should say Van der Valk stain, because that's what it is. For the time being Father is in Oranje Hotel Scheveningen. You know, where they used to lock up Resistance fighters."

Edda's thoughts went to the Geuzen, Hendrik IJzerdraat and Sjaak Meulenbelt and the early resisters. She shivered. The tables had truly turned.

"Will Papa be shot?" Edda hardly dared to speak the words.

Duifje said nothing. Then sighed deeply again. "Who knows?" Edda fell silent for a long time as well, sipping her coffee. Trying to make sense of her conflicting and racing emotions. Duifje went on in an almost toneless voice. "Father changed his will in November of last year. He left all his belongings and the estate to you, Edda. Jan has shown me the documents."

Edda nodded. She'd gleaned so much already.

"You're the only unblemished soul in our midst, Lientje. You'll probably even be decorated as a war hero soon. With you, Valkena Estate will be safe forever. I'm glad about Papa's foresight. It was a wise decision."

"What about Huis van Leyden?" Edda's voice had no tone.

"No worries about that. That was never owned by our family. It's been confiscated by Leiden's municipality and will no doubt get some neutral or philanthropic purpose in the future. It's only important you'll let Mother stay at Valkena Estate. She's too frail to be transported elsewhere."

"Of course!" Edda hadn't grasped the full extent of the change in her position yet. There was so much to think and so little time.

Duifje put a hand on Edda's sleeve. "Now about Jan and me. That had nothing to do with Father's will, if you would believe it. Jan's been my and the children's support since we relocated to the Estate at the beginning of last winter. He's much more than just Father's solicitor and his reputation is immaculate. He was never with the NSB, on the contrary, he and his wife hid Jews in their basement for two years."

"Wife?" Edda exclaimed.

"She passed last summer. Sudden heart attack. He's still not fully over it. So, we're both widowed and help each other through. He's the best that could have happened to me and the children, Edda. You must believe me. You may think him boring and strait-laced but he's actually a great amateur actor. Very funny and lovely when not in his business suit. I love him to pieces. And the children adore him."

Edda slipped closer to her sister. "I'm happy for you, Duif, really I am. You look radiant." Then she hesitated "And please, please help me navigate Papa's affairs. I have no clue where to begin."

"I will, darling. Jan and I will make it a piece of cake for you."

"Aren't you at all jealous Papa didn't make you his heiress? After all you're the eldest."

"Nope. You're our only hope in these dark days. I can't wait till I'm Mrs Sipkema and rid myself of the Van Leeuwen stain. The children will also take Jan's last name. I don't want them to be called 'collaborators' children' forever and ever."

"I'm changing mine to Edda Valkena. For the same reason."

"Wise decision, sissy. Oh, I love it. Edda Valkena. It has a lovely ballerina ring to it, with these two a's at the end. Come here Edda Valkena and let me give you a hug."

"Certainly Mrs Duifje Sipkema."

They hugged and laughed. It was a happy sister moment suspended in time.

47

ADIEU!

Two days later – Scheveningen, 11 May 1945

The black taxi with a very grumpy Dutchman at the wheel dropped Edda off at the gates of the Oranje Hotel in Scheveningen. Getting out of the old Volvo PV60, Edda pushed a few guilders into the man's hand, after which he dashed away as quickly as he could. Nobody wanted to have anything to do with the traitors now held inside the red brick walls with barbed wire on top. No matter many of them were hypocrites themselves and just changed sides when it was convenient.

Edda's own emotions where a whirlwind of ambivalence and affliction. What was her father to her now? Should she have done more to save her parents? But how? They wouldn't have listened to her. They had been as blind and biased as two innocent fools after Hitler had bewitched them in 1933.

And now?

A guard at the gate was eyeing her suspiciously. Edda contemplated turning around but then she would be a coward too. She had to make this one visit to her father. Just to see how he was.

If he still believes in National Socialism, it's the last time he'll see me,

Edda told herself as she reluctantly directed her shoes, a pair of new black pumps that Duifje had loaned her, towards the gate. It felt a luxury to walk on shoes without holes.

"I have an appointment to see Marquess Johannes Van der Valk," she announced with as steady a voice as she could muster.

"And you are?" the young man in an ill-fitting uniform and a bad skin asked on a haughty tone.

There was no choice. She showed him her papers.

"The daughter," he growled. "Would have thought so." And the look full of hatred he gave Edda, sent shivers up her spine. This was the new now. NSB members and their children would be outcasts from now on. She didn't know from where her courage came or the longing to clear her name, but she met his eye and said.

"Don't misunderstand me, Officer. I was with the Resistance and detained in Westerbork until the liberation. Also, in families there were schisms." Edda thought the young man's face broke open as the sun reappearing from behind a cloud.

"Miss Van der Valk," he hastened to say, "pardon my rudeness. I'm just so angry. My father was detained here in Oranje Hotel as one of the Geuzen and killed at the Waasdorpervlakte early in the war. I always hated this place where he was detained, but it's an honor to guard it now the real culprits are behind bars."

"I'm so sorry about your father," Edda replied. "I, too, lost many good people in this war."

"God Bless you, Miss." And he opened the door for her.

Edda was led through a maze of corridors with cell doors on either side by another guard. What struck her about the building was that there was a complete absence of noise. It was almost as if walking into Sleeping Beauty's castle, which was a strange analogy. No one talked, no sound of radios, no shuffling of feet or scraping of chairs. Absolute silence reigned in the prison, apart from the echo of her footsteps and those of the guard.

"Wait here." The officer stopped in his tracks and retrieved a heavy keyring from his jacket pocket. He opened a cell door that read 64 and went in.

"Prisoner Van der Valk, you have a visitor."

Edda heard more rattling of keys and seconds later her father, bent, in blue overalls and with his hands in handcuffs, shuffled out of the door. For a moment Edda wasn't sure this broken man was her proud, tall father. She blinked, looked again. Yes, it was really him. He stared at his shoes, old working shoes with scuffed shoe tips. He didn't meet her eyes. His hair was greasy and gray, uncombed, and hadn't been cut for a while. But he didn't look like he had been maltreated.

"To the visitor's room,' the guard ordered, and her father started walking mechanically in front of the guard. He hadn't greeted her, hadn't even acknowledged who'd come to visit him. Edda stood for a moment staring at the backs of the retreating men, then slowly followed, swallowing hard.

It didn't look like this was going to be an easy conversation. Not that she had expected that. But this?

She was the only visitor with her father in a large room with small tables each with two chairs. Guards stood at the two entrance doors, listening to every word they would exchange and ready to grab the prisoner by the arms should he so much as utter a favorable word about the NSB.

Edda fumbled with the button on her jacket, racking her brain what to say. Her father stared at the formica table. He sat very still, hunched and withdrawn into himself. Edda knew she would have to open the conversation.

"How are you, Father?"

"Good."

Better be honest. "You don't look like you're 'good', Father."

She saw him shift slightly in his chair.

"What do you expect me to say then, Eddaline?"

"You could perhaps start with asking me why I am here?" she said it as lightly as possible.

"There was no need to come. I left everything in your name." A toneless, dead voice.

"That's not what I mean, Father. I needn't have come here to find that out. Duifje and Jan Sipkema already told me."

Later Edda thought it must have been the mentioning of his solicitor that made the change. Her father looked up and Edda almost jumped back in her chair. His eyes, her father's eyes, once merry and blue like Duifje's, were colorless, lifeless, disinterested. His soul was dead. What had happened to her formidable Papa? And that was what she blurted out.

"Papa, what has happened to you?"

"What do you mean? I was arrested. As I should have been. So, all's well."

There was a long silence, in which Edda fought over her thoughts, wanting to tell him about her own life, about missing Ash, about Duifje being happy, about looking after Mama, about the liberation and how they could start with a clean slate, but the absolute silence returned to the building. Then a guard broke through it.

"If you don't have more to say to each other, we'll end the visit."

"Wait," her father held up a weak hand, "I have something to say to my daughter."

Edda waited as she saw the struggle in her father to formulate his words.

"I don't know what the verdict will be, Eddaline, whether I'll live and face a long sentence, or this will be it. Either way, I want you to know, the blame is all on me. Your mother wanted out much earlier in the war, but I wouldn't let her. I too understood we were heading in the wrong direction, not long after Ludo was murdered, but I was in it too deep. I wouldn't have minded being killed for my sins then, but your mother would have faced the same fate. We would both have been shot. I wanted to spare her, so I did the wrong thing. The totally wrong thing. But I'm not afraid to die for that, Eddaline. I've made peace with my God. I never killed or incited anyone to kill another human being. But I was very, very wrong otherwise." He paused, squinted. "I just don't want your mother to suffer more than she already does. Don't tell her my verdict. Never. Please promise that. Will you promise that?"

Edda swallowed and swallowed trying not to cry. She just nodded and managed to bring out.

"I promise, Papa. Duifje and I will look after her. And I will look after Valkena Estate. Can I just ask you one favor?"

"Of course, daughter. Anything."

"Will it be alright if I change my name to Edda Valkena. No Eddaline. No more Van der Valk."

Some of the light came back to her father's eyes. "You have such an excellent brain, Edda Valkena. What a perfect solution. For the rest do as Jan tells you. I trust him implicitly and he's not in any way been involved with the wrong side."

Edda was so glad to see her father revive before her eyes.

"Before you go, Edda. One more thing. Marry whom you want. Marry for love, Jew, Black or Orange. I should never have thwarted your happiness. That was my greatest sin. And the one I regret all my remaining days."

"It's alright, Papa." She touched his hand and he squeezed hers.

"Time's up," the guard announced.

Edda rose. "I'll be back."

"You don't have to." The toneless voice was back, the eyes downcast.

"I will be back, Papa, because I love you."

Tears streamed down her cheeks, and she saw his shoulders shake. Her big Papa was also crying.

"I love you too, Eddy. Blessed be your path. Get back into dance! Adieu."

THE DOOR of the prison closed behind Edda. She blinked in the shrill afternoon sun and knew with gut-wrenching certainty she would never see her Papa again. It was the worst—absolute worst—feeling a human could feel because the heartbreak was tinged with so much shame and regret.

48

MAMA

Three weeks later

Leeuwarden, 5 June 1945

I have no words and yet I have to put this on paper. Papa is dead.

An awfully long silence followed until I wrote the next words. But you cannot see that in this diary.

He hasn't even had a trial. I wasn't allowed to be present, should I have wanted to. An anonymous firing squad in the Orange Hotel courtyard killed Marquess Johannes Van der Valk, 59 years old.

Another long pause. My thoughts are so incoherent. Mother doesn't know. Not only did I promise Father, but if I told her, she'd probably not even understand it. She's dying as well. Duifje and I seem to be losing both our parents in the matter of weeks, right after the liberation. But Mama is still with us, hanging onto her physical form, though unconscious most of the time.

I still don't know what to say. I guess a lot of Dutch people are relieved when they read the news this morning that another high-ranking NSB member is no longer able to spew atrocities. But did Father ever? He seemed to have so much remorse when I visited him. And he was never a criminal or a crook. He said and believed the wrong things at the wrong time, and he made me very angry and upset but I think he didn't get a fair chance. He could have been someone who repented his sins and could have educated next generations not to do what he had done. But that door is closed.

All doors are closed for Papa, now. In some ways, I'm strangely relieved myself. He seemed to have come to terms with death when I visited him. I think he would have found it hard to live with the atrocities that have been carried out in his name. Oh, the complexity of it. And the utter, utter sadness of it all.

We are invited to the funeral service, Duifje and I, and I think we will go incognito. Someone has to bring Papa's ashes home. I think we will be the only people present.

I've been at Valkena Estate now for two weeks and it's been crazy. So much has to be organized. The name change request is with Queen Wilhelmina and Jan has been in touch with her secretary and was assured her signature will be under the legal document soon. Then, I

can get a new passport. Duifje and Jan are also
preparing their simple wedding and want to speed it up
so Mother can still be present.

Through it all I long to go back to Amsterdam and
find out about my friends. I've been so cooped up with
family affairs that I haven't even managed to let Ome
Jan know I'm still alive.

As soon as everything is done here, I'll return to
my own base. I've signed the papers for Jan and
Duifje to take care of the estate in my absence. I might
buy the entire premises on the Vondelstraat. Jan says I
have enough money to buy it and it's a good property in
an excellent part of Amsterdam. Jan is so good with
business. Papa was right. I only think about how happy
I have mostly been at my flat there and would love to
stay close to Tante Riet should she have returned.
Or Ash.

I even manage to smile a little as I write this. I
want to make my Papa proud as the new Marchioness of
Valkena Estate.

"Edda, are you coming?" Duifje's voice called from downstairs. Edda
quickly closed her diary, resisting the old urge to hide it under her
mattress. She left the new diary on her desk under the window that
faced the Valkena Estate meadows, where black and white cows
grazed and a pair of partridges flew over the hawthorn bushes
uttering their rapid, scratchy kut, kut, kut.

It was the same desk and the same view where Edda, as a
secondary school pupil of the Stedelijk Gymnasium Leeuwarden,
had toiled over her Greek and Latin homework. A time now so far in

her past, she could hardly recall being that slender, young girl with the big eyes and big feet, who danced better than she recited Ovid.

Edda smoothed her new black dress and checked herself once more in the oval mirror on the opposite wall. She was filling out a little. The dark shadows under her eyes seemed less but she still looked tired and the haunted look in her eyes stirred nightmares in sleep and dark thoughts when unchecked by discipline.

No thinking now, Edda. You have to be strong for them all.

"Edda!" Duifje was becoming impatient.

"I'm coming."

The light in the main sitting room of the Valkena Estate was shaded, with all the blinds closed, which gave the room that was large enough to fit in a Philharmonic orchestra, a dusky look.

Propped up in a plethora of cushions on a bed in the sitting room lay the Marchioness, under a rose-patterned duvet. A nurse was sitting next to her bed, knitting a blue cardigan. Edda tiptoed over to say goodbye, though her mother was usually asleep most of the day and night. Pressing a kiss on her mother's forehead, she didn't expect her to react, so Edda almost jumped when the eyelashes fluttered open and her mother's dark eyes fixed her.

"Edda?" It came out as a question in a faltering, croaky voice.

"Yes Mama, it's me. Duifje and I are going on a quick errand, but we'll be back soon. Nurse Wilma will look after you."

"Edda?" It was said with more urgency and the Marchioness even made an effort to sit up. The nurse was at the bedside immediately.

"Don't strain yourself, Marchioness. It's alright. We're all here."

But Edda saw her mother make a vague gesture with her hand as if to dismiss the nurse. To be sure Edda asked, "You want me to stay with you alone for a minute, Mama?"

A weak nod followed.

"It's alright, Nurse Wilma. Please just tell Duifje I'll be with her in a sec. I know we have to go, but Mother is important as well."

"I will," the nurse affirmed, leaving the room on soft squeaking soles. "I'll be around the corner, if you need me."

When Edda was alone with her mother, she slipped a hand under the duvet and took the thin hand between hers. Wide awake, but with fear in her eyes, her mother demanded with some of her former authority, "Is it true, Edda?"

"What Mama?" While Edda pondered if her mother had somehow divined she no longer wanted to be called 'Eddaline', she heard her mother ask in an almost clear voice.

"Is my Johannes dead?'

"Mama!" The shock was almost too big. And Edda's dilemma enormous.

Her mother sighed. "I thought so. I dreamed about him last night. Oh Edda, it was so romantic. It was exactly as when he proposed to me, here at Valkena, right in this room. He went on one knee and looked up at me so endearingly. I had said yes before he even spoke the words. I was so clumsy and in raptures." Her mother giggled, almost as a girl, then looked serious again. "Now I can go in peace as well. I needed to know, you know. Please make sure our ashes are mingled. I want that. I want that so very much."

"Mama, no!" Edda cried and her voice must have been heard outside the door because Duifje raced in like a summer storm.

"What is happening? Mother? Edda? What's going on?"

The Marchioness turned her face to her stepdaughter and a warm smile spread over her white face. "Duifje, dearest, you've taken such good care of me. You're a better mother than I ever was. I love you, darling."

"I love you too, Mama! Oh Mama!" Duifje sank on her knees on the other side of the bed and gripped their mother's other hand. Edda was too shocked to understand what was happening but Duifje calling her Mama made everything right.

"My dear, dear daughters." The voice was becoming very weak now. "You two are brighter than sunshine and you've made me so very happy. I couldn't be happier than this."

The Marchioness closed her eyes and a peaceful smile lit up her face. She took one more breath, a tiny squeeze of both young hands on either side of her. And then she was gone.

49

MOKUM

A month later – Amsterdam, July 1945

R aw and full of pain, Edda arrived back in Amsterdam four weeks later. She'd returned with one single thought in mind. To dance again. She felt only dance could rescue her soul, flatten her grief, pull her through. It had been too long since she'd spread her crushed wings. But where to start? For sure the Amsterdam Ballet Theater didn't exist anymore.

The house was silent. A layer of dust had crept over her furniture and her rooms smelled unaired and moldy. Edda opened all the windows and then tentatively the back door. The path to Tante Riet's house was overgrown with weeds and tall grasses.

The curtains of her backdoor were changed. Would she still live there? It seemed impertinent to just knock on the back door. Edda's curiosity got the better of her, so she walked out her front door and rang the bell next door, waiting breathlessly.

Nobody answered the door.

"It's time to go to Ome Jan," Edda said to herself aloud, "I can't postpone it any longer."

She stuffed the box with her brooch wings in the pocket of her dress and made the short distance to the Kinkerstraat on foot, squeezing her box and praying with all her might Jan Meulenbelt still lived at the old address with Christina and Marie.

"Edda? Is that you?"

Jan opened the door himself and scrutinized her with his one good eye, "Heavens girl, you give me a fright. I thought you were gone! You know, gone to God." The next moment Edda was in a bear hug from the former dockworker, an embrace so tight she could hardly breathe.

"Come in, come in!" he said. "Christina has gone to the market and Marie is married you know. To a Canadian soldier, can you believe it? Thank God, Edward has agreed to stay in Amsterdam, or we would have lost our last child as well." Ome Jan babbled on, overcome with emotion, while pushing her towards the sitting room.

"Sit girl, sit!" His one good eye took her in.

"Tante Riet?" Edda couldn't wait any longer. She saw Jan let his head hang and she knew enough.

"What happened?" Her voice was tiny as a mouse.

"Firing Squad. Zwolle, 28 August 1944."

"Oh Ome Jan, it's all my fault. It's all my fault." Edda couldn't stop crying. How was she ever going to survive all these deaths?

"What are you sobbing about, *kindje*? You had nothing to do with it."

"But the Gestapo came to my house first and I ran to Tante Riet, so I betrayed her. They were coming for me. Not for her!"

Jan steadied her with the good eye. "I never knew, kindje, but rest assured you are not to blame. They knew exactly who my sister was, and she had no chance. Still, I'm glad to know you were with her for a bit. That gives me much peace of mind. She loved you like the daughter she never had, you know. But oh, you must have had a horrible time yourself. I tried to find you, you know, after the war when we finally heard what had happened to Rita. But I had no idea you were arrested together. Sorry I'm talking incoherently now. I'm going to make us some coffee and then you tell me what happened."

"Where's Tante Riet's grave?"

Jan looked stricken. "They buried her in a mass grave in Zwolle but I'm working with the Amsterdam Municipality to bring her home. She's also going to be decorated posthumously for her Resistance bravery."

Edda stayed with Jan for a long time. At some point Christina came home and listened in, silent and white-faced. Edda told everything, in as much detail as she could but choked up when she told how she had lost sight of Tante Riet in Westerbork and how she had been singled out to stay alive.

"It makes all sense to me now," Jan said in a sad voice. "They wanted you to stay calm until they had you at Westerbork. I think my sister left that train and was immediately transported by car to Zwolle. That's how you lost her in the crowds. It was their plan all along, Edda, so please be comforted that you could have done nothing to change it."

"So, you're not angry with me?" She had to ask.

"Dear child," Christina chimed in, "you do not know what a Godsend it is that you are sitting here alive and that you meant so much to Rita. So incredibly much. You helped make her days through the war happier and I'm sure she sang these words when she was facing those guns:

> *"Then I will go to the altar of God,*
> *To God my exceeding joy;*
> *And on the harp I will praise You,*
> *O God, my God."*

"Like your Sjaak," Edda said and the Meulenbelts nodded.

"Come back here often, Edda, please," Jan said. "You saved my life, remember?"

"What about Rick?" Edda suddenly remembered the medical student, but bit her lip in fear.

"Rick's alive. Thank God. Though his real name is Maarten van Lanschot. He managed to escape all the razzias against Resisters, which is no mean feat itself. We see him from time to time. We'll invite you both to dinner soon. You've got some catching up to do as well." At this last remark Ome Jan grinned widely, which contorted the scar on the left side of his face.

With another bear hug from Ome Jan and a freshly baked cake from Christina, Edda slowly walked back to the Vondelstraat. Her heart was as empty as the wind without Tante Riet. Though Edda had known all along she was dead. That wretched Gemmeker! Of course, he'd known and lied to her.

"I'll dance for you too, Tante Riet," Edda told the trees in the Vondelpark, "I'll always be your *ballerina kindje.*"

2 months later – October 1945

The doorbell rang, long and loud. Edda wiped the perspiration from her face and shoulders, as she'd been practicing at the barre in her sitting room all morning. Her body was still so stiff and recalcitrant, she didn't dare to join a ballet group yet. With the white towel wrapped around her neck and in her ballet outfit, she opened the door expecting the post man.

"Miss Sterling? Monsieur Sergeyev?" Edda's mouth fell open and an immense surge of joy filled her heart.

"I see we're coming at the right time, my dear?" The red lips of the ballet mistress had already landed on Edda's cheeks. Monsieur Sergeyev stood shaking his head of distinguished, silver hair as if he wasn't believing his eyes, "Edda, Edda, Edda!"

"Are you going to invite us in?" the ballet mistress demanded with a coy smile.

"Oh yes, of course, I'm so sorry. I'm so pleased to see you, I'm totally forgetting my manners." Edda opened the door so wide the door handle clanged against the hall wall with a loud bang. She mumbled another "sorry."

It was as if she heard her mother's voice from above, kind and compassionate now, "Oh Eddy you're so clumsy."

"I am Mama!" Edda agreed wholeheartedly, at which Miss Sterling asked, "What's that?"

"Nothing," Edda giggled. "I'm just being daffy!"

She led her mentors into her sitting room, aware with sudden bashfulness that the magnificent Monsieur Sergeyev had never entered her humble abode. She saw him looking around at her pre-war, worn-out furniture and the strange arrangement of her belongings to make space for dance. Miss Sterling, however, was intimately acquainted with this setting, having coached Edda and then also Maria through La Sylphide in exactly this sitting room.

"Do sit down please. I'll put the kettle on."

"Wait Edda!" the ballet mistress waved a hand with pink lacquered fingertips "Don't you think that since this is such a festive occasion, we should celebrate with coffee and cake at Le Americain?

"And cognac!" Monsieur Sergeyev beamed.

"Bit early for that, Pyotr!" Miss Sterling giggled.

"Never too early for a good glass of Courvoisier!" Her partner protested.

SITTING in between her two mentors with a fine Wedgwood tea set in front of her and a view of the busy Leidseplein, bustling with tingling trams and shoppers, Edda felt a warmness washing through her, as she'd not felt in years.

There were no bombers, no patroling German soldiers, no black-clad NSB men harassing Jews. No Swastikas. But there were no Jews. Her Amsterdam was still not as it was before the war.

Edda swallowed and the fine-tuned Miss Sterling followed her gaze.

"Amsterdam has changed," she agreed, "but the city is resilient and robust. It will bounce back."

"Mokum," Edda said softly, "Natasja once told me that real Amsterdamers call the city Mokum. The name the Jews gave it when they came here centuries ago. I heard Tante Riet use it once as well. I think I'll call this city Mokum from now on. In my mind at least."

"Oh, dear Edda, you must tell me all that happened to you and

Tante Riet. I was so worried when I didn't find you at home. I tried every day for over a week. Then I was sure you were arrested but nobody knew where you were. I tried your Ome Jan but even he knew nothing about either of you. Maria was as mystified as I was." The ballet mistress stopped talking. Stared wistfully at her untouched glass of Courvoisier.

"Tell her, Marlene. It's okay!" Her lover touched her arm lightly.

"I even contacted your parents, Edda. I hope you don't mind. They were really kind to me when we met at the hospital, you know, when you had broken your ankle. So, I thought, why not? This has nothing to do with politics, but they had no clue where you were either. They were very worried. I spoke with your mother briefly and I got the impression she was not at all well herself."

The honey eyes sought Edda's face. "I hope you forgive me. I know your pathways had diverted after they didn't accept Ash."

Blow, after blow, after blow.

Edda stared hard at the window where small spatters of rain now blurred the view. She clenched her jaws. How to say it all? Did it need to be said all? Her mentors certainly didn't read Dutch newspapers so would be quite unaware of her parents' passing days after each other.

"So how did you know I was back here then?"

"We didn't," Monsieur Sergeyev said. "We were walking through the Vondelpark and I said to Marlene, 'Let's try one more time.' Et voila! Bingo this time. We're so, so delighted, *ma chérie*, you cannot imagine. Certainly, after we lost so many good people." The Russian took another deep sip from his cognac. It seemed to steady him.

"How did you escape?" Edda asked, suddenly aware it was a miracle he'd survived as a Jew.

"Easy-peasy, *ma chérie*. When the Germans took control of France in November 1942,Nice wasn't safe anymore. I directed my dance feet towards Casablanca, and that's where I sat out the war. Among Berbers and expats. It was actually quite fun but a little too much of this." He tapped the round-bellied glass, then said in his light-hearted way. "That's why Marlene urges me to get back into ballet. It always stops this rather persistent habit of mine to touch liquor. And now we've found you..."

"... and Maria!" Miss Sterling added with a wide smile.

"Maria is still here as well?" Edda asked surprised.

"Oh yes, the two of us stuck out the last winter of the war together. We ate tulip bulbs and once a cooked rat, but we survived." The tinkling laughter that followed was tinged with pain and horror.

"The Hunger Winter," Edda observed. "In one respect I was lucky to be at Westerbork, at least we had food. Not a lot, but more than the people in the cities."

"At Westerbork?" Her mentors exclaimed in horror.

"Yes." And Edda told them the whole story of Tante Riet's and her arrest. Then she couldn't stop herself and blurted out.

"Both my parents are dead and so is Tante Riet. And we know nothing of Ash and his family."

The ballet mistress pulled Edda towards her and hugging her, said in a tear-filled voice. "I know, my sweet. What the Nazis did to the Jews is too unbearable to think of. I fear we will not see any of them back. Also not Larry and the De Jonge's."

"Oh, Larry." Edda's thoughts went to the lively floor master with his love for perfection and his longing for America. There was another vicious stab at Edda's heart.

"Would you want to dance again, Edda?" her mentor asked giving her another hug, "From the likes of how we found you, you were practising."

"Oh yes! I want nothing else. I want to dance until I forget all we went through. All! We must bring back the light to Mokum."

50

FRIENDS

Ottawa, 20 November 1945

Dear Edda,

Thank you so much for your letter, which arrived the day before yesterday. The day before I was to show my documentary to my professors at the Canadian Film Institute here in Ottawa. So your letter was a very welcome pick-me-up.

But first, let me send you my deepest condolences for the loss of both your parents. When I read that part of your letter, it moved me so, I had to temporarily stop reading. Especially in your situation, you a Resistance fighter and your parents on the other side of the spectrum. Oh, that must have been so hard!

And then the loss of your Tante Riet, for whom you still had hopes when we met in Westerbork. I'm so sorry they lied to you, and she was dead all along. How cruel!

I truly hope you have people around you who support you and from what I understand you have! How wonderful to hear you're dancing again. That's what you were made for, Edda Valkena! Not to be the big mistress of a large estate, though you're that as well, if I understood correctly.

To me you'll always be that beautiful, thin girl in her frayed, gray dress with an eager face as we marched into that desolate camp— Camp Westerbork—and you pulled my sleeve asking after your relatives... As old as I may get, and I hope I will be granted old age and white hair, I'll never forget your face and both your pain and your elation. So much emotion in that one face.

I hope you do not mind but your question, "Have you seen my Tante Riet, or perhaps the Hoffmans," has become the basis of my documentary. As we tramped through France and Belgium up into Holland that was the question my battalion got over and over, the search for relatives, any little titbit of information on them. But you know what is so strange? We got those same questions when we finally arrived home in Vancouver on the 20th of July. "Were you in the division with my brother, my fiancé, my uncle, my cousin? What happened to him? Where is he buried?"

That's when I understood the extent of the human tragedy of war. So, I titled my documentary, "Have

You Seen My Brother?" Encapsulating all these searches into one word, "brother." I hope you think I've chosen the right approach.

I think I told you I wasn't so much interested in what battle took place where, and who defeated who or how fast or slow our trek was. I wanted to document the stories of the comrades we lost, the people we liberated - those two. And of the questions we got, over in Europe and here in Canada.

I know I'm rambling on about this documentary and I hope you don't mind. You see, it's all so fresh in my mind as I've worked on it without rest since I came home. Luckily the professors gave me access to the Film Institute's film studios during the summer. They want to help us catch up on the year we lost when we were overseas as soldiers.

Anyway, long story short Edda, I ended up getting a standing ovation for my documentary, my own words, my own photographs! It made me feel so great and so humble at the same time.

And you know what's best of all? I've got an invitation to show my documentary in different places in Holland next May when we celebrate 1 year of freedom from the Nazi yoke! I will be coming to Amsterdam! Can you imagine? 'Have You Seen My Brother?' on a film screen in your city! This must be fate. I do hope we will meet up and you'll be my guest of honor. Then I can explain to the audience it was you and your questions that spurred the whole idea. What do you think?

Well, enough about me. I'm hoping with all my heart you found your beloved Ash in the time it took our letters to get to one another. That he's one of the miracle Jews who survived! I truly, truly hope that because you deserve all the happiness in the world. If only I could meet a girl like you! I'd never let her go.

Anyway, dear Edda, I wish you a Merry Christmas and a very, very happy 1946, in which I hope we will meet again. Do write! I cherish your letters!

Never forget you changed my life. I hope I was a small cog in the liberation of your life too!

Your affectionate friend,
Stew Gildersleeve.

E dda sat with Stew's letter in her lap, her eyes misty. Dear, dear Stew. It had been such a brief meetup, but it had carried such a profound impact. She thought of his white-toothed grin in a dust-smeared face, the steely, gray gaze, the thick brown hair. The elation and the insecurity she'd felt in his presence. He had been an instant friend, showing his own vulnerability and strength. He had marched thousands of miles to liberate her, thousands of miles from his own home and his own passions. He was her hero. Until eternity.

"Oh Stew," she exclaimed, "Thank you for your documentary. Thank you for telling me all about it. I hope you will be happy. And yes. Let's write. And let's meet up next year. Let us be friends forever."

She kissed the airmail letter and folded it again. Then put it in the front of the brown notebook he'd given her.

THEY WERE REHEARSING for a Christmas edition of The Nutcracker. Eight years after their first edition. Miss Sterling and Monsieur Sergeyev had resurrected The Amsterdam Ballet Theater and were busy recruiting new ballet dancers. Edda had wanted Maria to dance Clara this time, but Maria had firmly said no.

"No way! I love dancing Sugarplum and you're such an endearing Clara. I won't have it otherwise."

The two ballerinas were sharing a large dressing room downstairs at the back of the Stadsschouwburg. They had become inseparable. Even when they were not dancing or rehearsing together, they could be found drinking tea or coffee in the many cafés that resurfaced in post-war Amsterdam or hanging out together in Edda's sitting room.

Jan Sipkema was still negotiating a good price for both Edda's house and the one next door where Tante Riet had rented the ground floor.

"When my brother-in-law gets this house business settled, you're coming to live next door to me, Maria. Do you hear?" Edda said over a steaming cup of tea, with her hands wrapped around the porcelain cup for warmth.

"If that's what you want, I'd not have it any other way," Maria smiled. Then looked straight at her friend with those slanted, gray eyes, "I thank God every day for how we managed to find each other because of the war. I think we would still be enemies if the war hadn't happened."

Edda pondered this, "You're right. We've come a long way, Maria. I wouldn't have it any other way, either."

"Then please call me Masha. Nobody calls me Masha here in Holland. It was the name my parents used for me."

Edda took her friend's hand and squeezed it. "On one condition, Masha, that you call me Eddy. My parents only called me Eddy when we were really close. Which we seldom were."

"Masha and Eddy. I like it," Maria said.

51

THE STAGE IS SET AGAIN

One month later - Amsterdam, 21 December 1945

On a grand stage of Royal Theater Carré, a glistening winter's embrace of enchantment and dreams was rolled out. White was the dominant color, with small details of gold and red and green. The yellow lamps shimmered through white cotton wool which increased the atmosphere of a fairy tale landscape.

Miss Sterling's new floor manager, a young Rotterdammer called Louis Brandsma, had weaved a tapestry of wonder that surely would bedazzle the spectators when the curtains opened, and The Nutcracker ballet begun.

Still standing in the middle of his magical winter wonderland, where snowflakes seemed to dance as they hung on strings from the ceiling, Louis checked the last details. Next, he did something he'd planned a long time in advance but had told nobody. He retrieved a golden, six-pointed star with the name Larry De Jonge on it from his pocket and hung it front and center on the huge Christmas tree. Then he made a bow to the star and with swift steps exited the stage through the back curtains.

The stage was silent, as if paying tribute to the former floor manager who would not return from Auschwitz. Never again would Larry – or Leron - create such an enchanting winter scene nor the gleaming Stalhbaum parlor with the blazing fireplace. Never again he would run up and down his ladder on his long, heron-like legs and be shooed off the stage at the last minute by Miss Sterling.

None of the De Jonges would ever return. Still, the gilded ornaments twinkled, casting a golden hue while the towering Christmas tree stood tall and true. Standing in remembrance of Larry for the entire dance troupe.

And there, amidst the wondrous set, the orchestra took its place in the pit. In a sea of elegance, each musician tuned their instrument. Their instruments poised, ready for the symphony to unfold— strings, woodwinds, and brass and the conductor with his baton ready in mid-air.

A silent cue and then like magic, the orchestra stirred, came to life, one instrument at a time. The violins wept, as if whispering ancient tales, the cellos and basses rumbled, with deep and resonating scales. The flutes and clarinets fluttered, like birds in the air, while trumpets and trombones heralded triumph with all their might. In the intermezzo, a gently plucked harp with a melody so sweet, followed by softly tapping percussion, like a rhythmic heartbeat.

Edda as 'Clara' whirled onto the stage in her white costume, featherlight and hand-in-hand with a new 'Fritz' by her side. She pushed aside all thoughts of Papa and Mama not being in the front row, as she knew Duifje was there with Jan,Benny, and Elly. Also in the front-row was Ome Jan with his family, 'Rick' aka Maarten van Lanschot with Doctor Geuze, and the resistance fighters who survived the war.

Secured to Edda's costume with tiny stitches were the two wings of her butterfly, and she danced for Ash above all. The scene of the Christmas party wasn't hard for Edda to dance, but she dreaded the dark night of Evil with the Mouse King. She wasn't afraid that another dancer would step on her, that seemed like a childish fear now, but the tug between good and evil was still so raw in her soul.

Yet she showed none of her trepidation. It was a dream! It wasn't real. So, in that wondrous realm where dreams take flight and in the enchantment of the Nutcracker's light, she moved in grace and poise, captivating her audience as in the early days, elegant and uniquely hers, each step a brushstroke, painting beauty with grace.

As the music swelled, she felt a flicker of mischief, as if her spirit awoke once again. Nimble fingers released the slipper and in a daring feat, her aim so precise it was like an arrow unleashed, the slipper soared through the air, spun, defied gravity's hold.

Then like a shimmering comet, a symbol of rebellion, it found its target. While the audience gasped, the Mouse King, with eyes wide with surprise, ducked but was too late. The spell was broken, the audience roared, and the lights went on. The Mouse King was defeated. The Era of Light and Peace would reign again.

Edda stood panting, with fiery eyes, bowing to the public as the curtains closed for the first Act. Her Nutcracker was Prince...

...ASH....

STILL REELING from her heroic action, Edda blinked in the light. Blinked and blinked. For sure she was dreaming. Ash, in the costume of the Prince, came walking towards her with big ballet strides.

Edda clamped her hands over her eyes, crying, "No! No! No! No! Go away!" as she was sure she was seeing a phantom, a very unwanted phantom. She sank on her knees, sobbing her heart out, while on the other side of the curtain the audience cried for an encore.

Seconds later Edda heard Miss Sterling's voice above her and someone's comforting hand on her shoulder. "It is not a dream, Edda darling. Ash is really here!"

Through her fingers Edda looked up, seeing the pillars of Miss

Sterling and Monsieur Sergeyev flanking her, while Ash— beautiful, regal, magnificent Ash with deep blue eyes—stood holding a white rose and bowing to her.

The next seconds were like a slow-motion series of photographs. She rose, she leapt, she was in his arms.

"Edda-mine! My gritty, beautiful Edda-mine."

"Ash, oh Ash!"

52

MY BUTTERFLY GIRL

There was no time to talk, not even time to kiss. Soon the curtains would reopen for the second act of The Nutcracker. Yet Edda had so many questions. Where had Ash come from? How could he be in such good shape? How long had Miss Sterling and Monsieur Sergeyev known Ash was back in Amsterdam?

All these questions burned on Edda's tongue but she was taken care of as a boxer in the break. Hydrate, rub neck and shoulder, put on pointe shoes, more hydration, eat some cake. All the while she kept looking over at Ash, who sat poised and speechless on Maria's stool, taking in the busyness around first ballerina Edda Valkena.

"Later, later," the ballet mistress kept saying. "Dance with Ash first, my dear, that will mean more than all the words in the world. Dance until you both shatter the past."

In the enchanted realm of the Nutcracker's Forest, Edda and Ash's mesmerizing *pas-de-deux* unfolded. It was as if they had never been apart, had danced all the years of the war and had never been separated by famine, imprisonment, torture, and time. They were and always would be just a masterpiece couple of grace and elegance, born to bewitch and enthral audiences across the world and their own hearts filled to the brim with love.

They danced on a tapestry of swirling snowflakes and majestic evergreens, while branches swayed gently around them like a celestial melody.

The stage was bathed in a soft, moonlit glow, casting a spellbinding aura over the scene. Frost-kissed tendrils of mist delicately floated in the air, as if carrying whispers of enchantment through the forest to everyone's heart.

From opposite ends of the stage, the chorus dancers emerged, embodying the core of the Nutcracker's timeless tale of dreams coming true. Ash, noble and commanding as the valiant Prince was resplendent in his regal attire, exuding an air of chivalry and strength. His every movement reflected the determination and courage required to conquer the forces of darkness. Which he personally had been victorious over.

Edda, on the other side, adorned in a flowing gown reminiscent of delicate snowflakes, personified the rapturous Clara, while the enchanting Sugar Plum Fairy danced in their midst. Edda's ethereal presence illuminated the stage, her graceful form was a testament to the elegance and resilience of her character. Every step she took exuded both gentleness and authority. She too had conquered it all.

Their bodies intertwined and separated as if of their own accord. Nothing has changed between us, Edda thought, as she floated in Ash's arms, and it made her wonder. How could it be? How could it be so easy, so effortless?

With every lift, every spin, they defied the gravity that had bound them to the heaviness of the earth, creating an illusion of weightlessness, as if the very laws of nature were now bowing before their mutual power. Their two bodies had become one instrument of unity and longing, a divine connection.

As the music swelled and Edda felt their *pas-de-deux* reaching its crescendo, the seamless gliding across the stage became sheer joy, absolute trust, and stability. She saw Ash smile, a soar of contentment. He felt it too.

With their eyes locked, their bodies and hearts as one, there was no pain, no past, no pressure. All was said and done in the symphony of their precision and passion. Miss Sterling had been right. All words afterwards would be balms on the wounds, as the wounds had already healed in the dance.

In the enchanted moment time stood still. The audience held its breath, captivated by the beauty, praying for their love.

Edda had found her Prince. And he was real. He was alive. He was here with her.

As THE FINAL notes of the grand *pas-de-deux* reverberated through the air, Edda found herself locked in Ash's embrace, their bodies entwined like branches of a majestic tree. The stage fell silent and in that suspended moment, while the beauty of the *pas-de-deux* lingered, Ash put Edda on her two feet and took off in a series of *cabriole* leaps that were not part of the choreography. But the audience loved it, clapping their hands rhythmically with his jumps.

Edda stood in the middle of the stage, a little forlorn, not knowing what to do, when Ash landed precisely in front of her feet, deftly on one knee. The audience had raised the roof to become silent, just as a raging storm can fall silent the next minute.

"Will you marry me, my butterfly girl?" He retrieved a small box from within his top and clicked it open. It held the most magnificent diamond-studded ring Edda had ever seen. For a moment she swayed on her legs, overcome by all the emotions of the past hour and the hundreds of pairs of eyes on her and Ash.

"Yes!" she said, wiping away a tear. "Yes, Asher Hoffmann, I will marry you. Forever and ever."

Ash slipped the ring around her finger, jumped to his feet, grabbed her hand, and waved goodbye to the audience.

"I hope you don't mind if I kiss my fiancée in the privacy of my dressing room?"

"Here! Here! Here!" Hundreds of voices chanted.

The next moment Edda was in Ash's embrace being kissed in a way that said, 'I missed you so.'

She kissed him back, over and over, oblivious to the roaring cheers around her.

EPILOGUE 1

Amsterdam, 22 December 1945

When Edda and Ash finally had time to talk after all the hugs, speeches, and congratulations from the other members of the Amsterdam Ballet Theater, they found themselves looking at each other in Edda's dressing room. Wonder for words danced around them, now their limbs no longer communicated. Maria had discretely taken her belongings out of the room and moved in with Miss Sterling for the night.

Edda agonized over how to bridge with words what their bodies had already done in dance. She needed to know, plainly and straightforwardly, where Ash had been, what he and his family had endured, how he'd risen as from the dead before her eyes. And she wanted to touch him, touch him, touch him.

Ash just stood there in his Prince Costume as as if skewered to the floor, drinking in her presence with ultramarine eyes that brimmed with hunger and passion. But Edda sensed more than she saw. She'd seen his eyes change the moment of his arrest. An anger had risen in Ash he'd not possessed before. A deep-seated hatred for the perpetrators of his people's horrific fate.

It was there, in his soul, crumpling his heart and blurring his vision. No matter how he tried to tape off hate with love, Edda felt it and she knew she'd have to help him unburden his heavy load. In a thin voice and unable to hold his strong, loving gaze, she stared down at her trembling hand adorned with the engagement ring.

"How did you...survive, Ash?"

He didn't answer at first, took a step in her direction as if coming over to embrace her but then stopped and stood still, clearing his throat as if something nasty stuck there.

"Do you really want to know now, Edda-mine? Most of it is far from pretty." His voice was thick as if the words refused to leave him.

"Unless the memory is too hard for you." Edda still had her eyes cast down. "I know we can't share everything that happened to us in the years apart, but I'd like to share your burden. For sure, it must have been so much heavier than mine."

"I doubt that, my love, I truly doubt that. I at least had a reason to stay alive. To fight with every ounce I had to come back to you. How could I let you live on with the uncertainty of my fate? But *you* could only survive for yourself, you had to live with the knowledge that with every passing day chances were getting slimmer you'd see me back. Thank God, I didn't know you were with the Resistance, Edda. I thought your family's ... uh... political views would keep your safe through the war. You could have died so easily too, my darling. Miss Sterling told me you were interned in a camp yourself."

Edda nodded, now fingering the broken wings on her costume while thoughts and memories whirl winded through her head.

"Were you also at Westerbork, Ash?"

He cleared his throat again, took another step towards her. "Here's the deal. I'll tell you what happened to me and my family when you come and sit in my lap, my sweet one. I want to feel you alive and breathing against me when we go into the depths of horror together. Hitler's Entlösung, his Final Solution."

Edda was only too happy to respond to Ash's request as she felt quite unsteady on her own feet. With his arms securely around her and his chin resting on the crown of her head, she braced herself for what was to come.

"Are you ready for this, my gritty girl?"

"I am, fiancé, now I know you're safe."

"Alright. I will never know who betrayed our hiding place on the Overtoom, but the SA broke down the front door so suddenly and so unexpectedly we had no time to flee. The cruelest thing is that the policemen gave us time to pack a few belongings so we were deceived into believing we could hold onto them.

My father, always the goldsmith and businessman, wrapped the gold and precious stones we still had in tissue paper. Also, all our finished jewelry pieces went into his suitcase." Ash breathed angrily. "It doesn't matter one way or the other now. If we'd left our last fortune behind, it would've been stolen as well. As for me, I was way too angry to pack anything but the ring that's now on your finger."

"Oh Ash." Edda leaned deeper against him.

"Yes, I was working on it at the time. Just in case peace would come swiftly, and we could marry."

"How did you manage to keep the ring safe?" Edda stared at the gleaming platinum and gold ring on her finger with its five delicate diamonds and two sapphires set in the solid gold, as twinkling stars plucked from the night sky.

"I hid it in different places on my body, or in the sole of my shoe. Sometimes I swallowed it."

Edda shivered. Her ring, her ring had traveled with Ash everywhere.

"I'll tell you how I finally managed to finish it after I was liberated, my darling, but let me first tell you about the camps. Of course, my dear mother, practical and with foresight, had our suitcases packed just in case so I, too, had the bare essentials thanks to her when we arrived in Westerbork."

Edda immediately pictured the rows and rows of brown wooden buildings in the wide terrain with barbed wire fences.

"Which barrack did you stay in?"

"Father and I were separated from the women. We were sent to barrack 62. My mother and Martha were next door in 64.

"What a coincidence. I was in 62," Edda interrupted.

"It wasn't too bad there, was it?" Ash observed. "My father and I got a job loading potatoes from the underground cellar in wheelbarrows and bringing them to the kitchen where the women were peeling them by the tons all day."

"How long did you stay there?"

Ash sighed. "Not long. They only kept Jews there who were useful to the camp like doctors and bookkeepers. They had no use for a goldsmith and a ballet dancer. We were put on the train east in early January. Can you imagine? Cattle trains, only a few square meters and at least 80 people in them with their luggage. Only one bucket of water that would freeze overnight and another bucket that functioned as a toilet in the other corner. The journey took us at least three days without stopping, no fresh air, no food. I didn't even know what time of day or night or what day it was. It was without doubt the longest and the worst experience of my entire life, but then we didn't know yet what was awaiting us, of course."

Edda wanted Ash to stop talking. She wasn't sure she wanted to hear the rest but there was no stopping him now. His voice had become monotone, metallic, morose and, went on and on.

"When we arrived in Auschwitz it was snowing. We shuffled out of the train onto that slippery platform, almost too drained and destitute to stand on our own feet and shivering all over with cold and fatigue. Though we were hungry too, food in our stomachs seemed from another planet.

All I could focus on was how worried we were about Father, who Mother and I had to keep upright between us. Martha had to carry his suitcase for him, so she had to haul two, one in each little hand.

Back in Vienna, Father had been treated for a heart condition and he was so frail, we feared he couldn't walk independently and would have to be taken to a hospital. Well, Edda, there were no hospitals for people like my father in Auschwitz."

Ash growled the last words. "There was an SA officer, wrapped in a thick winter coat pointing his white-gloved hands left and right. There were two different rows, a long one and short one. I was singled out, sent to the short row, while Father, Mother, and little Martha with the two suitcases were sent to the long row." Ash almost choked on his words and Edda sat up straighter, trying to turn around and look at him but he wouldn't let her. In a voice she almost didn't recognize, he choked out. "That was the last I saw of them."

There was a long, drawn-out lull in the conversation, in which angels wept and Edda hardly dared to breathe.

"What happened to them?"

"Gas chambers."

Edda felt Ash's tears drip down her neck and her own eyes spilled tears as well. They grieved together until Ash said in almost his normal voice.

"I often told myself that at least they didn't have to suffer long. I wouldn't have wanted them to go through the next two years and four months of my life. Not one minute of it."

"Did you ever see anything of Larry and his family? I heard they were sent to Auschwitz as well."

"No, I didn't. Miss Sterling asked me the same question. Auschwitz was a huge camp anyway, but I have no idea if he was there at the same time. I didn't stay long in that camp. I hated to be transferred to Theresienstadt, still thinking Father and Mother and Martha would be looking for me. You see, I didn't know they were dead. I thought they may be, but hope keeps you alive when all else is gone."

"Were you in Theresienstadt for the rest of the war?"

"No, I wasn't. But I survived that one through ballet, strangely enough. The Nazis used Theresienstadt as an elaborate hoax, staging social and cultural events for visiting dignitaries. At times we had to beautify the camp before such an important delegation arrived. Barracks were painted, and gardens planted, that sort of thing. One time they even invited the Red Cross to show nothing was wrong. Dignitaries in through the front door, thousands of Jews deported to other death camps through the back door."

Ash sounded disgusted. "Well, I survived that one to be sent to the last one. Dachau." He spat out the word again. "Dachau was summer 1944 and the worst summer of my life. I was weak from malnutrition and the strain of having had to perform while physically weaker and weaker. Then I contracted typhoid. I was sure I was going to die but there was an elderly doctor in my barrack who told me not to succumb to the fever. To stay awake. He kept talking to me, giving me intricate puzzles to solve, all night long. He kept whispering sums and riddles to me and when I nodded off, he shook my arm, saying he wanted the answer. He was lying next to me on my bunk bed and never gave up on me. That man saved my life. His name was Nathaniel Samuels."

"Noo!" Edda cried out, "Doctor Samuels also saved my life. In Westerbork." And she quickly told Ash the story of her recovery in the hospital ward.

"Doctor Samuels died a week later of dysentery. I had no tears left to weep, but I almost gave up wanting to live myself then." Ash said with great sadness.

Edda shuddered. The man who'd saved them both had died.

"The last thing Nathaniel Samuels said to me before he passed, was "Stay alive, boy.""

"He said exactly the same thing to me," Edda brought out "But he never knew about us?"

"No, we weren't given much time to talk. When he came in, I was ill and then when I got better, he fell ill. What also made Dachau wretched was that a couple of weeks later I had the joy of finding out my friend Carl Bernstein was also in Dachau. But that joy was short-lived."

"Carl? Esther's fiancé?"

"Yes."

"Oh Ash, what happened?"

"He died in my arms a couple of days later. Pure exhaustion," Ash sniffled, then continued. "At least Carl and I had some time together. I'll cherish that for the rest of my life. But it's getting late, Edda-mine, let me finish this story and then we go out and have a drink in free Amsterdam. I want to have this over and done with."

"I understand, dear Ash. All this makes my heart so heavy."

"Alright, I'll keep it short. I somehow survived working in a factory on minimal food, thin clothes and with more and more people dying around me. I kept repeating what Nathaniel had said to me and I added a sentence to it. "Stay alive, boy. Edda needs you."

"Somehow it worked, even though the winter of 1944-45 was terrible. We had no idea the Allies were coming but at some point, the Nazis and the Kapos became agitated, even crueler than before and spurring us on.

"Then we were driven out of the camp and started walking. It began to be springtime. We walked and walked and walked, with no shoes on our feet, too little food, and hardly any water. The people dropped like flies by the side of the road. And still the guards shot them, even if they were dead." Ash inhaled deeply, as if ready to rush to the end of his account.

"I had two things that helped me. Years of physical training had given me a strong body, and I understood we were almost free. Though the guards didn't say anything, I sensed we were fleeing, and it would be a matter of holding out until we would be liberated.

"We were walking south, and I knew we were heading for Austria which felt good. I recognized the eastern shore of the Starnberger See, then we went towards Eurasburg and headed in the direction of the *Tegernsee.*

"I didn't know the date, but they later told us it was the 2nd of May, 1945. We had passed through Bad Tölz and were nearing Waakirchen, some 37 miles south of Dachau and it was still snowing. An oddly cold start of May. Everywhere, dead people lay on open ground, their bodies covered in a thin layer of white snow.

"We were spotted by advance scouts of the U.S. Army's 522nd Field Artillery Battalion. The American troops did what they could to save us, those that were still alive. Of course, the Germans guards had run off and left us on our own. That's how I was saved and liberated."

"But it's December now, Ash? Where did you go from May until now?"

"Good question. The first weeks I have no recollection of at all. They are a complete blank. I start remembering things from late June, beginning of July. I was in a hospital in Bern, Switzerland. Switzerland has been amazing in helping surviving Jews from the camps recuperate. I knew I wasn't in a fit state to come back to you yet, and I wanted to know what had happened to my family.

"More and more records of murdered concentration camp prisoners were revealed and that's how I found out that Samuel Hoffman, Adina Hoffmann and Martha Hoffmann had been sent to the gas chambers the day we arrived in Auschwitz. It was such a blow that I decided to stay in Switzerland until I knew I wasn't just physically well again, but also mentally and emotionally. I took ballet lessons and found a goldsmith who let me work on your ring.

"Last week I felt well enough to make the trek north to you. So here I am. Wondering if you still want me? Battered, scarred and orphaned."

"That makes two of us, my Ash."

Now Edda wrung herself free to face him. She wrapped her arms around his neck. Kissed him tenderly and said, "Thank you for telling me all this, what must be so hard to do, my darling. I promise I will listen always and be very, very patient with you."

"Ah, my gritty girl. Thank God, we have each other. You've had a tremendous battle yourself. But we're together now and we'll never ever let each other go. Promise?

She had no time to answer him as his lips landed on hers and he kissed her with a force that told her they wouldn't part again. Finally, he let her go.

"You haven't even asked why I decided to come last week. And why I didn't rush to see you." He looked at her with lightness that dispersed all heaviness.

"Is there something you need to tell me, Asher Hoffmann?" Edda inquired.

At that moment there was a short rap on the door. Edda looked disturbed while Ash called a chirpy, "come in". About to protest the intrusion, after all it was *her* dressing room, the door swung open, and it was too late.

In the doorway stood a small ensemble with among them Miss Sterling, Monsieur Sergeyev, and Maria. But then Edda also saw Ome Jan and Rick and Edgar. Then Duifje slid inside, half hiding behind the others. There was also a man Edda didn't recognize.

"What's going on?" Edda looked from one to the other. The unknown man marched inside to hand Ash a small box. Now Edda was really puzzled. Was Ash going to marry her now? Was this an officer of the Civil Registry? Confusion fought with anticipation.

The unknown man, likely in his forties with carefully combed back black hair, a prominent-featured face, wearing a suit with a ribbon in the buttonhole, stepped forward.

"Marchioness Edda Valkena, it pleases Her Majesty Queen Wilhelmina to award you with het Verzetskruis, the Resistance Cross. Until now this high decoration has only been awarded to deceased resisters, so you are the first one to receive it in good health. Mr Asher Hoffmann, you as one of the mere 5000 Jewish Dutch citizens to survive the Nazi concentration camps and return to Holland, would you do the honor and pin the decoration on your fiancé?"

"What? No!" Edda exclaimed. "Ome Jan and Rick deserve this decoration as much as I do!"

The well-coiffed secretary to Queen Wilhelmina waved a hand with an impressive signet ring on his pinkie. "In due time, Marchioness, in due time! They didn't have to balance their act of defiance with a collaborating family. In fact, they had all the support of their family. You were quite alone in your fight."

True admiration colored the secretary's eyes as he added in a soft voice, "Please, Marchioness Valkena, it is Her Majesty's personal wish you accept this token."

Edda was still of two minds as she saw Ash open the box and take out a heavy-looking, bronze Latin cross hanging from a purple ribbon with two orange stripes. She was equally unprepared for the reverence in Ash's eyes as he pinned the cross on her chest next to the two broken butterfly wings.

"Marchioness Valkena, may I present you with the Resistance Cross in recognition of the special courage and policy you displayed in the Resistance against the Enemies of the Dutch cause and for the preservation of spiritual liberty." Completing his task with trembling fingers, Ash even bowed for her as he took a step back. Everyone clapped their hands.

"Thank you," Edda managed to bring out, for a moment feeling as forlorn and lonely as she'd felt in the years she'd actively been battling her enemies. "I'll cherish the Cross always. But you, my dear, dear people, you have become my family over the years. You are all that matter to me now. For you, I'd do it all over again. And also for Tante Riet and Larry, for Ludo, and for all the Hoffmanns of this world." She paused a moment to catch her breath, then looked defiant.

"Tolstoy wrote 'the Greatest Warriors are Patience and Time.' Well, I've conquered both and here we are. Free! Free! Free!"

She spun a pirouette and landed elegantly in Ash's arms.

"Tolstoy was wrong," she giggled. "The Greatest Warrior is Love. Love Eternal."

EPILOGUE 2

At the break of dawn on 10 June 1941 in a forest on the Belgium border, Ludovicus Van Limburg Stirum was assassinated with four other notables from the hostage place St. Michielsgestel. They were first forced to dig their own shallow graves before being shot. The Germans never disclosed the location of the graves, but a passing forester heard the shots and marked the place.

After the war he showed the Dutch authorities where the prisoners were buried. Edda and Duifje lobbied for a remembrance monument on the secluded spot in the forest to commemorate the Count's senseless death.

In 1937, the hard-working Jewish floor manager Leron de Jonge, who called himself 'Larry' and dreamed of creating perfect stage settings and a bohemian life in New York, was working at the Amsterdam Ballet Theater, not knowing he would never achieve his dream of New York.

None of Larry de Jonge's family survived the concentration camps. The family arrived in Westerbork in January 1943 and were put on the train to Auschwitz at the beginning of February 1943. Following in the footsteps of, but never meeting, the Hoffmann family.

Grandfather Daniel, father Isaac, and son Leron/Larry saw the De Jonge women for the last time on the Auschwitz train platform.

Daniel Rozenkrantz, a retired legal advisor to the Municipality of Amsterdam, was sent straight to the gas chambers and died on 15 February 1943. Isaac De Jonge, who had been a professor of Yiddish literature and a well-known novelist, and his son Larry were set to work digging tracks for a railway line, until Isaac collapsed and died of typhoid in his son's presence on 10 July 1944.

Mother Elsa and the girls Rosa and Judith didn't have a single chance. Hand-in-hand they entered the gas chambers in the women's quarters of Auschwitz and died on the same day as their father and grandfather on 15 February 1943.

Larry stayed alive until the Death March in January 1945. As Soviet troops approached Auschwitz, the SS shot most prisoners and evacuated the rest. Larry was forced to march westward with some 60,000 other prisoners. His group was trekking northwest to Gliwice in icy cold conditions, with hardly any food and inappropriate clothing and shoes. He is presumed dead as of 25 January, only three miles from Gliwice. He is remembered with other deceased members of the Death March on a monument in Gliwice, now in Poland.

The De Jonges share their fate with 107,000 Dutch Jews who died in concentration camps either of exhaustion, torture, or murder. Only 5000 of them survived. Almost all of them passed through transit camp Westerbork on their way to the extermination camps. Among the victims was seventy-one-year-old child psychiatrist, Doctor Nathaniel Samuels, who'd told Edda to 'stay alive.'

The Westerbork Camp Commander, Albert Gemmeker and his mistress/secretary Frau Elizabeth Hassel, were never sufficiently punished for sending 102,000 Jews, Sintis, Romas, and others to their death, and for facilitating the death of Dutch Resistance Fighters. Claiming they 'had no idea what went on in the east' they got off with short prison sentences and lived till old age in peace and abundance. Although not together.

When separated from Edda and transported to Zwolle, Mevrouw Rita Meulenbelt (Tante Riet) was severely interrogated by the SS. They had an extensive file on her and knew all about her Resistance organization, Cell 2000, from other Resistance fighters who had broken under torture. Brave as she was, she never gave up another name and certainly not of her brother Jan or her next-door neighbor Edda. Put in the back of a Kubelwagen, and without Rick and Edda to save her, she was shot dead with four other Resistance Fighters on the Witterveld near Assen.

Tante Riet was reburied at Begraafplaats "De Nieuwe Ooster" in Amsterdam in March 1946. A memorial plaque on the wall of the graveyard remembers her and other resistance fighters buried there. Rita Meulenbelt and her nephew Sjaak Meulenbelt were posthumously decorated with the bronze Verzetskruis 1940-1945 (Resistance Cross).

Ome Jan and his wife Christina and their daughter Marie continued to live in Amsterdam and remained friends with Edda and Ash all their lives.

Doctor Geuze lived to the remarkable old age of 96 and never talked of what he'd done in the war, although he was certainly a resistance fighter himself.

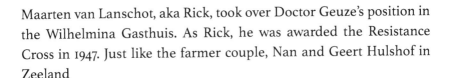

Maarten van Lanschot, aka Rick, took over Doctor Geuze's position in the Wilhelmina Gasthuis. As Rick, he was awarded the Resistance Cross in 1947. Just like the farmer couple, Nan and Geert Hulshof in Zeeland

Stuart Gildersleeve, Edda's Canadian liberator, toured France, Belgium and Holland with his documentary "Have you Seen My Brother?" and managed to coincide his visit to Amsterdam with attending Edda's and Ash's wedding. He eventually married the Canadian actress Bella Rich and had three daughters. Stew and Edda continued to correspond with each other all their lives.

Duifje married Jan Sipkema and lived permanently on Valkena Estate keeping it in order for Marchioness Edda Valkena-Hoffmann. It was a happy and stable marriage and Benny and Elly, who took their stepfather's last name, grew up to be wonderful adults. Benny took over the Van Leeuwen Ironware shops in the Hague, while Elly followed Edda as a promising ballerina in her own right.

Maria Petrova was never able to find her exiled parents in the Soviet Union. In 1947, she naturalized as a Dutch citizen. She continued to dance with The Amsterdam Ballet Theater until the age of forty. In 1948, she married the Dutch Resistance Fighter and painter Pierre Bosch van Rosenthal. Together they had one daughter, Anastasia. Masha and Edda remained life-long friends and often holidayed together at Valkena Estate near Leeuwarden or at the Bosch van Rosenthal's pied-à-terre on the Côte d'Azur.

Marlene Sterling eventually married her soulmate, Pyotr Sergeyev. They divided their time between their country house in Cornwall, Marlene's flat in London, and their canal house on the Keizersgracht in Amsterdam. They both remained connected as choreographers, dancers, and directors of The Amsterdam Ballet Theater until they were in their eighties. Edda and Ash became their closest friends.

Edda and Ash married in a mixed Protestant-liberal Jewish wedding on the 5th of May, 1946, the first anniversary of Liberation Day in Holland. Edda had her dream wedding including a 15-foot-long lace veil, her nephew and niece as page boy and bridesmaid and Duifje as her matron of honor. Monsieur Sergeyev was Ash's best man.

They held their wedding party at the beautifully decorated Valkena Estate near Leeuwarden and then boarded a passenger plane for New York. They stayed in New York, dancing and enjoying each other's presence, until Edda was pregnant with their first child. Before little Addey (short for Adina) was born, the couple returned to their house in the Vondelstraat. Edda took a break from dancing during and after three rapid pregnancies, girls Addey and Olisa (short for Olga) and son Ike (short for Isaac).

She used her maternity leave to sort through her war diaries and make them ready for publication. But post-war Holland was still licking its wounds, unable to look back at the war yet. So, it wasn't until the 1970's that Edda felt the time was right to share her WWII experiences with the rest of the world.

Ash, next to being a devoted lover, husband, and father, made quite a career for himself in the dance world as a modern dance choreographer. His most famous compositions, "Silent Shadows," "Through Broken Mirrors," and "Echoes of Yesterday" were all based on his experiences in concentration camps, though they spread much hope and light.

He and Edda danced till well into their forties and travelled extensively with their three children to make sure they would have a broad appreciation of other cultures and peoples.

Together they lived, loved, and spread joy on whichever stage they danced or whatever room they entered. Edda savored her bliss every single day and never grew tired of loving Ash with all her heart.

~

THANK YOU SO MUCH for reading **The Crystal Butterfly.** *This was already book 6 in the captivating world of* **The Resistance Girl Series.** *There is one more!*

I'm thrilled you've read the sixth installment. Your enjoyment of my stories about Resistance Women in WW2 means the world to me and I hope you'll continue to read all 7 books.

BUT WAIT, THERE'S MORE!

As a token of my appreciation, I invite you to join my exclusive newsletter community and read the EXCLUSIVE bonus chapter on Edda & Ash's wedding here.

By becoming a part of my inner circle, you'll gain access to exciting extras and promos.

Instead of the Bonus chapter you can also choose for a FREE novella - **The Partisan Fighter** *- an exclusive companion story to* **The Resistance Girl Series** *you won't want to miss.*

DON'T LET THIS OPPORTUNITY SLIP BY — immerse yourself in my WW2 world of resistance, courage, and passion by unlocking

The Partisan Fighter here.

Print: www.hannahbyron.com/newsletter

Warmest regards,

Hannah Byron

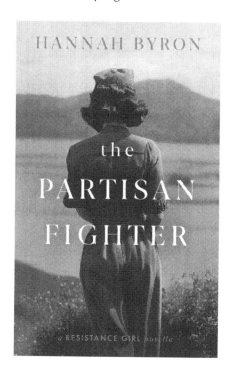

AUTHOR'S NOTE

I hope you enjoyed The Crystal Butterfly, though I realize the word 'enjoy' may not strike the right tone for this book, which certainly has many dark moments. I always try to keep my WW2 novels 'on the lighter side' as I'm a romance writer, not a thriller writer, but the horrors of World War 2 cannot be ignored. In every new Resistance Girl Novel, it's a fine line I hope I've managed to walk.

The largest part of this Author Note will touch on the important happenings in The Netherlands that appear in *The Crystal Butterfly* with links where you can read the blog posts on the research I did. In no way these topics cover the Dutch years under German Rule. I only focused on the historical aspects addressed in my book.

But before we delve into the research, I'll share with you where I deviated from the facts for fictional reasons.

The official name of this post-stamp size country bordering the North Sea on the west, Germany on the east and Belgium on the south, is The Netherlands or The Kingdom of The Netherlands. You may have noticed, though, that I use Holland throughout the book. I do this because The Netherlands sounded too heavy and official, whereas Holland sounds more in line with storytelling. Holland is, in fact, only the western part of the Netherlands. The Dutch call their country 'Nederland' and internationally often refer to it as 'Holland'.

Contrary to Great-Britain with The Royal Ballet established in 1931, The Netherlands had no organised ballet ensemble before or during the war. The first one, "Het Nederlands Ballet", was established in 1954.

I have repeated what I did in earlier books regarding names of resistance fighters. For the privacy of their descendants, I've taken the first name of one resister and the last name of another. That way more heroes and heroines are honored in my books.

I've taken the liberty to stage the Westerbork Camp commander Albert Gemmeker and his Dutch mistress/secretary Frau Elizabeth Hassel with their own names and in their real settings. Historical data showed me that would now be allowed. Both have long passed, and I don't fear reprisals from their descendants. The same refers to other Nazis like Adolf Hitler, Arthur Seys-Inquart, and others. Also the NSB leader Anton Mussert is mentioned by his real name. I generally only protect the privacy of victims and resisters.

The **real date** of the rounding up of hundreds of Dutch notables as hostages was 4 May 1942 and the five *Todeskandidaten* (death candidates), among whom Otto Ernst Gelder, count van Limburg-Stirum (so not Ludovicus), were executed on 15 August 1942 (see also blog post below). The real Count Van Limburg Stirum was Audrey Hepburn's uncle.

Strangely enough, het **Verzetskruis** (Resistance Cross) has never been awarded to living members of the Dutch Resistance. It was only posthumously awarded to Dutch citizens killed by the Nazis. Contrary to other countries, The Netherlands never had a separate award for resistance fighters who survived the war. Of course, they were decorated with other medals.

After the war the stigma for members of the NSB and their children was enormous. Especially innocent children of NSB-ers were punished for their parents' deeds for decades. See also the blog on the NSB.

For the rest, the largest part of the events mentioned in The Crystal Butterfly really took place at the time mentioned but the entire story is, of course, **fiction.**

Onto the research. Please note that some of the blogposts will be published in the weeks after the release. I've aloofly added the link to the first blogpost. The rest you'll find.

The Dutch NSB Party and Collaboration during World War 2 in Holland.

The rise of De Nationaal-Socialistische Beweging, the National Socialist Movement (NSB), in the Netherlands before and during World War 2 and its collaboration with Hitler's Germany. Read more https://www.hannahbyron.com/blog/musserts-wall-netherlands

Rotterdam: From Bombed-out to Best Travel City

Rotterdam was bombed by German bombers on 14 May 1940, and 711 people died. About 80,000 residents became homeless. The bombardment was the retaliation of the German invaders for the fights the Dutch troops put up, which had slowed down the German advance. The Netherlands surrendered to the Germans on 15 May 1940. Read more https://www.hannahbyron.com/blog/rotterdam-from-1940-to-today

First Dutch Resistance Movement: The Geuzen

After the surrender in May 1940, most Dutch citizens aimed to maintain their normal way of life amidst German control. This involved cooperating with the occupiers to prevent increased interference in the government and economy. While the authorities initially urged the population to obey and avoid resistance, some individuals immediately opposed the German occupiers. On 14 May 1940, the first Dutch resistance group, 'De Geuzen' (The Beggars) was established. Read more https://www.hannahbyron.com/blog/the-first-resis tance-the-geuzen

Het Oranjehotel: from Nazi prison to National monument

The Oranjehotel was the nickname for the Scheveningen prison during WW2. More than 25,000 people were imprisoned here between 1940 and 1945 for interrogation and trial. Arrested for actions that the German occupier saw as a violation. Resistance fighters, but also Jews, communists, Jehovah's Witnesses and black marketers. The prison was already called the 'Oranjehotel' during the war. An ode to the resistance fighters who were imprisoned here. Read more https://www.hannahbyron.com/blog/oranjehotel-from-nazi-prison-to-national-monument

The 1941 February Strike

The February strike was a strike on 25 and 26 February starting in Amsterdam and spread out over the Netherlands. It was the first large-scale resistance action against the German occupiers and an open protest against the persecution of the Jews in occupied Europe. Read more https://www.hannahbyron.com/blog/the-1941-february-strike

The Difficult position of The Jewish Council (De Joodsche Raad)

The Jewish Council was a Jewish organization set up on order of the German occupiers to govern the Jewish community. In essence, the body became a conduit for anti-Jewish measures. In September 1943, the leadership of the Jewish Council was deported to the Westerbork transit camp, and the council ceased to exist. Read more https://www.hannahbyron.com/blog/difficult-position-of-the-jewish-council

Notables as hostages: A Nazi attempt to prevent acts of resistance

Between May and July 1942, almost 1,000 Dutch MPs, judges, company owners, journalists, professors, scientists, etc were lifted from their beds by the Germans. There was no reason for taking them as prisoners of war as they were not with the resistance. They were imprisoned in Brabant in a former seminary, dubbed Herrengefängnis (Gentlemen prison) to serve as Todeskandidat (death candidate). Read more https://www.hannahbyron.com/blog/notables-as-nazi-hostages

The Bunker Drama in Concentration camp Vught

The bunker drama was a retaliatory measure on 15 January 1944 against 74 female prisoners in the Nazi concentration camp camp Vught in the Netherlands in which ten women died. Camp commander Adam Grünewald locked the women up in cell 115 in 'de Bunker'. The cell had an area of 9 square meters and did not have adequate ventilation. After 14 hours the cell was opened again. Read more https://www.hannahbyron.com/blog/the-bunker-drama-in-concentration-camp-vught

Camp Westerbork: 97,776 Jews deported to German and Polish concentration camps

Camp Westerbork was a Nazi transit camp in the province of Drenthe in the Northeastern Netherlands. Transport trains arrived at Westerbork every Tuesday from July 1942 to September 1944; an estimated 97,776 Jews were deported during the period. Anne Frank and her family arrived in Westerbork on 4 August 1944 and the family was put on a transport to Auschwitz on 3 September. Read more https://www.hannahbyron.com/blog/camp-westerbork-97776-jews-deported

The Hunger Winter

The Hunger Winter in the Netherlands was the winter at the end of WW2 from 1944 to 1945 with a great scarcity of food and fuel. It led to famine, especially in the cities of the western Netherlands. At least 20,000 people died of starvation and cold. Read more https://www.hannahbyron.com/blog/the-hunger-winter

Overview of the Dutch Resistance in WW2

The Dutch resistance in WW2 is the collective name for all persons and groups who resisted the German occupation between 1940 and 1945. Compared to other occupied countries, the resistance was characterized by relatively little armed and violent resistance and more focused on hiding Jews and people who feared arrest by the Germans. The largest resistance organization was the LO (National Organization for Help to People in Hiding). Some 350,000 Dutch people went into hiding (a record in occupied Europe), including more than 25,000 Jews. Read more https://www.hannahbyron.com/blog/overview-of-dutch-resistance-in-ww2

The Liberation of Netherlands took 7 months

The liberation of the Netherlands lasted from the fall of 1944 to the spring of 1945.

In the fall of 1944, the south was liberated by the allies: British, American, Canadian and Polish armies. The area north of the main rivers failed to be liberated, which resulted in the 'hunger winter'. In the spring of 1945, the Allies succeeded in crossing the rivers and break through the German defenses. On May 5, 1945, the German army surrendered and the whole country was free. Read more https://www.hannahbyron.com/blog/the-liberation-of-netherlands-took-7-months

Extra blogs:

In the footsteps of...

In the footsteps of Audrey Hepburn

Visiting the places where Audrey Hepburn lived during WW2: Arnhem and Velp. Read more https://www.hannahbyron.com/blog/in-the-footsteps-of-audrey-hepburn

In the footsteps of Anne Frank

Visiting the places where Anne Frank lived during WW2 in Amsterdam. Read more https://www.hannahbyron.com/blog/in-the-footsteps-of-anne-frank

ABOUT THE AUTHOR

Hannah Byron's crib stood near the Seine in Paris, but she was raised in the south of Holland by Anglo-Dutch parents. In her bestselling WW2 historical fiction series, *The Resistance Girl Series*, Hannah's heroines also traipse from one European country to the next, very much like their creator.

Now a retired university lecturer and translator, the European traveler and avid researcher still regularly crosses borders to learn about new vistas.

What started as curiosity about her family's connection to D-Day, evolved into an out-of-controlish study into WW2 history. To blame, or thank, must be Uncle Tom Naylor. If he'd not landed on the beaches of Normandy and helped liberate Holland, her British mother would never have met her Dutch Dad after the war.

Strong women are at the core of Byron's clean and wholesome romance novels. Every book is a tribute to the generation that started the women's lib movement, got dirty in overalls, flew planes, and did intelligence work. Today's girl bosses can but stand on the shoulders of these amazons.

Side-by-side with their male counterparts, Byron's heroines fight for freedom, equality and... love.

Under pen name Hannah Ivory she writes Historical Mysteries. *The Mrs Imogene Lynch Series* stars the kind but opinionated Victorian widow of Constable Thaddeus Lynch.

amazon.com/stores/Hannah-Byron/author/B08H88B7ZY

bookbub.com/profile/hannah-byron

facebook.com/authorhannahbyron

instagram.com/authorhannahbyron

x.com/HannahByron8

youtube.com/@hannahbyron2997

tiktok.com/@hannahbyronbooks

ALSO BY HANNAH BYRON

The Resistance Girl Series

In Picardy's Fields

The Diamond Courier

The Parisian Spy

The Norwegian Assassin

The Highland Raven

The Crystal Butterfly

The London Spymaker (preorder)

The Agnès Duet (spin-off)

Miss Agnes

Doctor Agnes

HANNAH IVORY

HISTORICAL MYSTERIES

The Mrs Imogene Lynch Series

The Unsolved Case of the Secret Christmas Baby

The Peculiar Vanishing Act of Mr Ralph Herriot (preorder)

THE LONDON SPYMAKER
CHAPTER 1: LIFE IN HANNOVER

October 1937

A bluish-pink halo of a rainbow settled over the *Neues Rathaus* on Trammplatz in Hannover, lighting up the green-copper dome like a large colorful hat. All day, it had rained long and hard and the cobble-stoned square shone with a treacherous wet gleam.

The sun, sparse since the beginning of the Lower Saxony fall, came out, first tentatively, then stronger as the late afternoon pushed towards evening. The dancing sea of umbrellas, dripping black circles moving unevenly across the square, came down and people, mostly men in suits, appeared from underneath them, rushing hither and thither to home and hearth.

A small boy, no more than ten, pulling a cart with one wheel on the brink of coming off and a dirty cloth over it, was begging along one side of the square.

"Some bread to spare? A pfennig, please?" His voice was small and shrill and persistent. The shop door of *Der Brotmeister* opened, followed by a waft of freshly baked pastries and the stout, blond bread master's wife appeared. Sturdy and broad-faced, with sleeves rolled up above her elbows showing fleshy arms, she stood squarely in the door opening, looking displeased.

"*Juden Raus! Auf Nach Palästina!*" She shouted, shooing the boy off with dismissive, flabby hands. Away with the Jews. Go to Palestine. The dark-haired boy startled, then scurried away, pulling his squeaking cart behind him. A little further down the square he started calling out again, "Some bread to spare? A pfennig, please?" Seemingly unperturbed.

Quite perturbed was Anna Grynszpan, passing by *Der Brotmeister*, the cotton satchel with her schoolbooks pressed against her chest. Half hidden under her Macintosh, still dripping with rain, she walked with swift steps as if the German baker's wife had scolded her. Anna sensed the hostile atmosphere more than she saw it, keeping her eyes fixed on her shoes, good black leather shoes and white socks that were clean and undarned.

She wasn't a beggar. She was Yeduha Grynszpan's daughter. Her family had money and repute. There was nothing to fear. Safely hidden under the hood of her raincoat, fearful eyes behind dark-framed glasses, with shoulders hunched, Anna slipped off the square and into the warmth of *Bücherladen im Herzen*. Her father's main bookshop was on the corner of Trammplatz and Friedrichswall he'd aptly called 'Scholar's Haven'. The familiar clacking sound of the mechanical types being hammered against the carriage told her her father was working on his other job, being a journalist.

The typing stopped the minute the doorbell rang. Shuffling feet and her father appeared from his office at the back of the shop.

"Anna? You're early?" Slim and wiry like his daughter and sporting dark-framed glasses of his own, clad in a black suit of good quality gabardine, Yeduha Grynszpan smoothed the worries from his forehead as he caught sight of his drenched eldest daughter. Rubbing his ink-stained hands and smiling, Anna didn't miss the worry in her father's eyes. The shop was quiet as dreaming trees. Customers were few and far between these days.

"Take off that wet coat and let me make you a cup of tea."

"I *am* early, Father," Anna replied with quiet stubbornness, still standing with her satchel clamped against her, dripping onto the doormat. "I wasn't allowed to take part in the gymnastics hour."

Again, that worry in her father's eyes, which he quickly camouflaged with another smile.

"What are you telling me, Anna? I pay for your tuition at the Friedrich Schiller Gymnasium, just like all the other parents. That includes your physical wellbeing."

Anna shrugged, took off her coat and hang it on the coat rack. "Never mind, Vati. I'll have that tea with extra sugar. I got caught in the rain."

She followed her father to his office, that also held a small cooker. Yehuda was already busying himself with kettle and teapot, every movement economic, as if he measured the space he had to move in. Anna sat down at the table that also functioned as her father's desk, finally letting go of her satchel, watching him. Even in locomotive they were similar. Not theatrical or grandiose like her mother, but reserved, regulated, almost reclusive.

Father and daughter didn't talk until the tea was ready. Anna thought of all the times she'd come in here after school. First when she was still at primary school, *Die Sonnenschein-Grundschule*, and then at age twelve when she'd transitioned to the Gymnasium.

It had always been her father with whom she'd shared her friendship perils and her academic questions. She'd often stayed with him in the bookshop until closing time. Six o'clock sharp. Reading books or doing her homework while her father wrote his articles or talked with customers.

Vati seemed to always have the proper answers to Anna's inquiring mind, whereas Mutti was often preoccupied, certainly after the birth of the twins, Sarah and Eva, two years earlier.

"Mutti's sweet and loving but her nerves sometimes get in the way," her father had explained to Anna when she'd fallen off her bike and instead of comforting her daughter, her mother had started screaming at the top of her lungs at seeing the blood oozing from Anna's knees. To the seven-year-old, this had been a lesson in caution and many more had followed where she'd been more concerned about her mother than seeking her help. Of course, Anna loved her mother as dearly as her father. The relationship was just different.

"What's happening to us, Vati? There seems to be one decree after another against Jews. We have to do something!" Anna looked up from blowing on her hot tea. The question was frank and open, as the discussion between them always was.

"I know, Anna. Hitler's dedication to corner the Jewish population keeps me awake at night. But for now, I have no solution. I have been here since 1911 and built up a good life for us. Once upon a time, being the chief editor of the '*Judische Rundschau*' was an esteemed position. The whole Jewish community in Germany depended on our newspaper. And I own two bookshops. That's a lot more than my father had in Warsaw."

"So, you don't think we should go back to Poland?" Anna took a tentative sip of her tea.

~

Preorder now here.

Or join my Newsletter here to stay in the loop.

Printed in Great Britain
by Amazon

57758323R00251